P9-AGF-070

"Tempest? Are you in there?"

As Jared stooped to enter the hut, he saw the flash of a blade across the low-burning fire. A blanket was twisted around her slim hips and the lunge she'd made for the knife had torn the bodice of her dress.

"Put down the knife, Tempest," he murmured. "I have a proposition to make that will be beneficial to both of us."

She grinned contemptuously, her eyes bright with shrewd intelligence. "Ah, now we be gettin' down to it?"

"Yes," he said crudely, "but you're still safe across the fire right now, aren't you?"

"Because of my knife, not your honor," she spat, flashing it again.

He smiled at her. "You don't look willing," he drawled softly, "and I never use force."

Not So Wild a Dream
by Francine Rivers
Romantic Times Award Winner

Other books by Francine Rivers

KATHLEEN
SYCAMORE HILL
REBEL IN HIS ARMS
THIS GOLDEN VALLEY
SARINA

Not So Wild A Dream

FRANCINE RIVERS

A JOVE BOOK

To Grandma Johnson,
the pretty Swedish girl who married Claus Janssen

To Grandma Wulff,
gone but not forgotten

To Grandma King,
*too soon lost,
but an integral part of me*

NOT SO WILD A DREAM

A Jove Book / published by arrangement with
the author

PRINTING HISTORY
Jove edition / April 1985

All rights reserved.
Copyright © 1985 by Francine Rivers
This book may not be reproduced in whole
or in part, by mimeograph or any other means,
without permission. For information address:
The Berkley Publishing Group,
200 Madison Avenue, New York, N.Y. 10016.

ISBN: 0-515-07982-0

Jove books are published by The Berkley Publishing Group,
200 Madison Avenue, New York, N.Y. 10016.
The words "A JOVE BOOK" and the "J" with sunburst
are trademarks belonging to Jove Publications, Inc.

PRINTED IN THE UNITED STATES OF AMERICA

PART ONE

A Daughter
of Absalom

Behold, this dreamer cometh.
—Genesis 37:19

Rocky Mountains, 1832

The place was perfect!

Set back into the rocky side of a mountain, almost hidden by the aspen and pine forest, yawned a great, dark cave. Before it lay a small, protected valley. Shelter, a downward sloping meadow from the top of which one could see an approaching enemy, a good stream, and plenty of game—this place offered everything to sustain life.

Beyond, jagged mountains rose like armed warriors safeguarding this peace against the raging world beyond—a world from which the buckskin-clad, black-bearded man had fled and of which he wanted no part.

Soon, the winter snows would shroud these mountains and make them impenetrable. Already gray clouds swirled overhead like angry, warring dragons waiting to breathe white death.

Time had run out.

The man and his woman, now heavy with child, could climb no more, search no longer. This was as close to Eden as God himself would let them come, for they had been cast out, and the gates were barred against them.

This is the place.

Yet first the man must make the kill, obliterate the serpent. He must bring his enemy out, for his woman would not stand the stench of blood and death in her home. The enemy must be drawn into the open and conquered.

The man looked toward the cave again and bared his white teeth in a savage smile. His heart drummed. His breathing quickened. Turning toward his woman, the trapper motioned sharply. "Stay here."

The woman's dark eyes widened. What was the man thinking to have that sparkle in his sky-colored eyes? Whenever the man had that look, trouble lay ahead and death would reap a bloody harvest. She put a detaining hand on his hard-muscled arm. "McClaren..."

He shook it off. "Dunna interfere, lass. I canna be killed. Ye ken that."

Her English was thickly accented as she whispered, "You are a madman, McClaren." She reached up to stroke his rough cheek.

McClaren gazed at her, the familiar surge coming in his blood, the rush of desire that had caught him unawares the first time he had seen her by a stream in the great, mist-shrouded mountains. Her Cherokee features were as fine as any European aristocrat's and she had the proud carriage of royalty. After all, her line was longer than the king of England's.

He had gone to her father's lodge to bargain. Winona was the fourth of five daughters, and the chief was willing to give her to McClaren in exchange for horses and seed and the Scot's departure from their territory. McClaren paid the price and agreed to the terms, and she was brought to him, dressed in her wedding finery. Her dark eyes were fathomless. Yet there had been something in her walk and the tilt of her head that had made him smile, and then laugh joyously. Here was a woman. No Highland lass of impeccable breeding could have walked more proudly or better hidden her fear. At her look, McClaren had fallen silent. Standing, he bowed before her like a court gentleman. She stared at him with wide, grave eyes. He looked at her openly then and knew she saw his craving, sensed the stirring of his man's blood. The wild pulse beat visibly in her slim throat.

"Come, woman," he commanded, and she had obeyed.

"You will be killed, McClaren," she said now, her fingers curling tightly into the sleeve of his buckskin shirt.

"Dunna begrudge me my fun." He came closer and ran his huge hand down over her swollen belly. "Ye never have before."

She stroked his cheek again like a mother soothing an agitated child. Her eyes pleaded. "McClaren..."

He turned away. "We canna have the bairn birthed in the snows." He raised his head to the sky like a wolf. "Time is gone. We are here. We will stay."

Turning back to her, his eyes colder than the threatening winter skies, he repeated, "Stay here."

His woman knew better than to argue.

With his Hawkins on his shoulder, McClaren leaped down from the ledge and strode across the meadow. He disappeared among the brush and trees near the great cave. Winona closed her eyes and put trembling fingertips to her lips.

Silence followed. A long, terrifying silence.

She waited.

A scream rent the cool mountain air and sent a shiver along her rigid spine. She had heard it before, but still she shuddered and felt her blood recede from every extremity. No scream of pain or fear or anger, this was one of impending death, of war, of blood lust. Again it came, and goose bumps rose on her flesh.

She remembered how a war party of Blackfoot had ridden on them. McClaren had jumped from his horse and rushed at them, uttering that scream of defiance and challenge. A vision of madness, wild hair, and buckskin fringe flying at twenty warriors, and she had seen their fear. She had watched as they spun and rode away. But McClaren hadn't stopped there. He had run on, shouting for them to fight. They had ridden faster. Then he had laughed and laughed, dancing around and kicking his legs in a strange dance of jubilation. Finally he strutted back and vaulted onto his horse again. He grinned at her and pounded his chest. "Madman. Very bad medicine." Then he had laughed again, loud and long, as they continued their journey westward.

Staring now at the black mouth of the cave, Winona heard the answer to McClaren's war cry. A roar of demonic fury issued from the cave and seemed to fill the high valley. She watched McClaren's swift retreat and the black horror that hurtled after him from the cave. They were lost to view in the thick forest. She could heard the swish and crackle of brush and branches as the wild escape and enraged pursuit continued. Another roar and she searched frantically, seeing nothing, hearing much.

Then McClaren appeared again, bursting from the brush and trees into the meadow. His long, leather-clad legs stretched out to eat up the ground beneath him. He was *laughing!* Head thrown back, long black hair and beard whipping wildly against his immense shoulders, he dared death. Right behind him was a huge black bear, snarling and determined to savage the intruder. Its roars echoed up to Winona on her high, safe ledge. She could see that the clumsy lope of the beast was deceiving, for it was catching up with McClaren.

She leaned forward, her lips parted in a strangled cry.

The bear was close, much too close, and the foolhardy man was still laughing! He slowed and turned back to face his pursuer. Winona watched in horror as McClaren threw his arms into the air, the Hawkins in one hand.

"Stand up, ye bloody bastard! Up I say! Up!"

And the bear obeyed. It rose higher and higher, its huge, clawed forepaws spread as it shuffled forward, its black glistening head wagging back and forth, mouth wide, teeth bared. Just when the monstrous beast seemed about to clasp the man in its fatal hug, there was the report of the Hawkins and the rise of powder-smoke. The sound echoed into the canyons beyond.

Too late!

McClaren was gone.

The woman couldn't see him. The bear was there where McClaren had been, wobbling on its hind legs, wounded, but not dying. Did it have McClaren? She couldn't see! He had had no time to reload the gun.

Then she heard his wild laughter again.

"Here, bear! Up again!"

She saw McClaren spring like a mountain cat, mounting the staggering bear from behind. His long knife glistened as it plunged in a swift, downward arc into the neck of the beast. The animal screamed and thrashed, trying to dislodge its attacker. McClaren held on and yanked the knife free, driving it in again and again, aiming for the inner ear and the throat, the vulnerable places not protected by thick winter fur and fat.

Finally, with a shudder, the bear fell forward and lay still.

Still astride, McClaren waited, one hand clutching the thick, black fur of the monster's back. He sat motionless for several seconds, head cocked, then bounded to his feet and raised his arms to the heavens, one bloodied hand still clutching the knife. His head tipped back and his hair shaking about, he shrieked and danced around the beast in primeval celebration.

Weakly the woman sank down once more on her safe pedestal above the valley. She released her breath slowly and stared down at the awesome sight. McClaren was a brave man, braver than any she had known—even her father, who had been a great chief. Yet more than that: McClaren was possessed by the Great Spirit.

The snows came four days later. A fire kept the cave as warm as the woman's full womb. McClaren lay naked beside her on the soft, thick beaver pelts she had sewn together. His hand moved slowly over her body as she smiled at him. He caressed the rounded belly, leaning down to put his ear against her taut, warm flesh. The child's heartbeat was fast and strong. The babe moved within her, restless beneath the pressure of McClaren's head. He raised up to grin down at his woman.

"The babe runs out of room."

She gazed up at him—his eyes, his mouth, his massive white shoulders and bulging arms, his hair-covered chest. The night McClaren had lifted her to his horse and taken her from her people, she had resigned herself to death. When they had camped, he sat staring at her, and fear had risen in her like a cold sickness as she had seen again the strange, blue fire in the Mad Scot's eyes. He would devour her like the silver-coated wolf feasting on a hapless fawn. Those huge, strong hands would tear her to pieces.

That first night, McClaren did not touch her. Nor had he the night after, or the night after that. He had only gazed at her and smiled.

Two full moons had passed before he had laid a hand on her, and then he had done as now. He had removed her doeskin and gazed at her body. He had stroked her gently, exploring her hills and valleys with the same reverence he showed to the land over which they traveled. Even after he had discarded his own clothing so that she could see everything he felt showing with immense boldness, he had not possessed her. Many more days and nights had passed before McClaren had come into her. When he had, he was welcomed. The fear of him had long since passed away, overridden by other emotions, newer needs.

Sometimes he spoke to her of sheer, stone cliffs, of green lands where the earth was cut and used for making fire, of mystical lakes where strange dragon creatures dwelt, of a place peopled with men as mad as he, but she could not conceive of it, nor did she care to. There was only him. There was only this tall, hard-muscled man with his wild dreams and gentle touch, and all she needed to know was in his pale eyes, the color of a hot, cloudless, summer sky. That was all that mattered. All else had passed and was unimportant.

McClaren nuzzled her neck. "Winona...sweet lass...I want ye..." Turning her slowly on her side to face him, he brought her close, taking her hand and moving it down over his flat abdomen. She smelled of earth and sun and woman. He breathed in her scent, renewing himself. Lowering his head, he sought the hardened tip of her full breast and sucked at it like a babe. Winona moaned softly. Her body grew warmer. Her hands quested. She lifted one slender leg and draped it over his hard hip, arching toward him. Closing her eyes, she took him into her body, luxuriating in the feel of being one with him again. It was natural, this timeless cleaving together, the mutual giving and taking that brought exquisite pain and pleasure, a blinding light in her head and new life within her.

It was good.

A blizzard came to the mountains. A fierce wind whistled through the towering pines and naked aspens and welled in the valley. Snow piled up, white mountains of it blanketing the dark earth and rock. Trees cracked and fell beneath the cold, dead weight. And still it raged on.

At the storm's height, the child strained for entry into the winter-bleak world.

The cave was quiet, except for a cracking fire. Flickering flames made grotesque shadows on the stone walls and illuminated the sweating face of the laboring woman.

McClaren watched.

Her silence frightened him. She did not scream as his mother had when she bore his younger brothers. Only Winona's dark-pooled eyes told him of her travail.

Since dawn and the first tightening of her womb, she had not uttered a sound. When he touched her, wanting to help, to comfort, to do something, *anything,* she did not look at him. It was as though she did not acknowledge his part in this creation, or even his existence. All that had passed between them in their journey together did not matter now. All there was for her was the child.

For a time, McClaren was darkly jealous of the life he had seeded in his woman. And he was deeply afraid. Would the special bond he shared with Winona die with the new life of his own babe? Or worse, would his child kill her as his youngest brother had killed his own mother?

My spawn may kill her!

The small glistening spot of bloody mucus that had begun the long siege was suddenly washed away in the flooding waters that burst from her body. McClaren's brave heart gave way. He cried out. He came down on his hands and knees next to her on the pallet, damning himself.

Winona turned her head and looked at him. He reached out to hold her, tears rushing to his blue eyes in abject remorse for his manly lust, but with surprising strength, she pushed him away. He tried again, but she hissed at him to go away, to leave her alone.

Stunned, he edged back, his face almost comical in its misery. He stared at the great, glistening mound of her abdomen with revulsion and loathing. In the firelight, he could see the contraction of her belly as his child was pressed downward from its dark, warm bed. Again and again, with less time between contractions, the firelit golden flesh strained. He tried one last time to touch his woman, but her look was so fierce that he drew back and made no further effort. He stood against the wall, useless, helpless, forgotten.

Watching her, he was filled with silent awe by the strength he saw in Winona's sweat-beaded face. The fine, smooth features twisted and hardened, shone wet. Her muscles quivered in a strange fit. Pushing herself up, she squatted. Cradling her hands beneath her, she bore down one last time, grinding her teeth and groaning deeply. She looked like a snarling animal ready to do battle. McClaren stood paralyzed as he saw his child slide free of his woman's body. Shaking, Winona went to her knees, crouching over the wet infant on the beaver-pelt mat.

She spoke softly in her own language and then hung her head, her shoulders heaving.

McClaren went down on his knees in front of her. The child between them whimpered, drawing in its first breath.

"What be wrong?" his hoarse voice pleaded. He looked from the grieving woman to the crying child, now beginning to flail its arms. A strong heartbeat was visible through the pale, mucus-covered skin.

"A girl-child," she whispered brokenly.

McClaren stared at her. "A girl?" Then he understood. He

began to laugh, relief and joy rippling through him, his jubilant voice filling the cavern. "Aye! A lass!"

It was over. His woman was alive. So was his child.

Winona stared at him, amazed. "It does not matter, McClaren?"

"Oh, aye, lass, it matters. She *lives!*" He leaned across the infant to press a hard, proud kiss on the woman's parted lips. Then he bent to clean the baby of the white womb coat.

Winona lay back as the afterbirth came. McClaren cut and tied the cord. Wrapping the babe well, he lifted her away from her mother. Winona's sleep-heavy eyes opened. When he carried their child toward the mouth of the cave and the snowstorm beyond, she cried out. He did not stop, but disappeared into the flurry. She had not the strength to follow.

The Mad Scot held his daughter close inside his coat as he bent into the hard, white wind. He walked some way through the night until he came to the stream. Breaking the ice with his boot, he bent and cupped water in his palm. Then, slowly, he trickled a few drops on the child's dark-haired head. She screamed, her tiny arms jerking, fisted hands spreading to the gray sky.

"I christen thee Tempest McClaren. A fitting name for a wee one born on the tail of such a storm." He stared down at the tiny, red, infuriated face of his daughter, thinking that his seed had created this. Then, smiling, he stood, cuddling the squalling babe against his own flesh inside his heavy coat. He started back toward the cave. After a moment, the child stopped crying, lulled by the warmth and movement of her father.

Winona had staggered to the mouth of the cave, her eyes wild, her face tear-streaked. Her trembling legs were washed in birth-blood.

"Go back," McClaren ordered and she returned to the pallet. He then deposited Tempest gently in her waiting arms. "Fool woman," he whispered. "She's mine, too. I wilna harm her."

Winona looked up at him in sorrow. He knelt and kissed her. Nestling the child to her breast, she sighed as the infant's mouth sought and found her breast, sucking strongly. There was no milk yet, but there would be plenty soon, enough to satisfy the little one's hunger and the man's curiosity.

McClaren took his bagpipes from his pack and went outside. Winona stared in terror toward the darkness as the screaming of the dead came at McClaren's beckoning. She crawled deep into the cave, clutching her child close, and huddled there wrapped in pelt blankets among the fire-shadows.

McClaren returned later, grinning broadly. Winona did not find it strange that the storm abated after he called his powers. The madman was of the Great Spirit, after all.

Lying on the pallet with the tiny girl-child sleeping in her arms, Winona slowly closed her eyes. The last thing she saw before she slept was the tall, leather-clad man with the black hair and beard sitting against the cave wall. His blue eyes burned as they watched her.

She smiled, unafraid.

Hades is relentless and unyielding.
—Homer,
The Iliad

Rocky Mountains, 1840

Tempest bounded from one slippery rock to another, finally crossing the wide, spring-gorged river where she saw her father bending over one of his traps. The pungent smell of pine filled her lungs. She looked up through the lacy green of embracing limbs along the riverbank and saw the whirls of white against blue. One particularly large cloud looked much like one of her da's loch dragons.

"Tempest!"

She left off gazing at her cloud-dragon and ran along the bank toward her father, her thin brown legs flying as she raced between the trees, her thick braids beating softly against her thin shoulders.

"Set it back, lass," he ordered, and she knelt to the task of replacing the trap. He stood, a stiff, glossy beaver carcass in his arms. He lifted it to his shoulder and carried it well up and away from the river.

Tempest followed. She watched him make several skilled cuts and pull the pelt free of the body in one piece. He left the stripped carcass for scavengers.

"Dunna ye worry that someday there be no more beaver or fox, Da?"

"When there be no more here, we will go west. But that will be a long time from now. This is a good place. It provides." He tied the bloody pelt on top of the pile already strapped on his packhorse. Later, Winona and Tempest would scrape the flesh away and rub alum in to draw the moisture.

"I'll be going downriver to the fort soon," her father said, looking at her. She looked away. "You and your mother stayed behind last time."

"As we will again, Da."

"I dunna like the bastards either, lass, but—"

"I'll not go back, now or ever." She swung onto her pony and rode swiftly ahead. She remembered only too well the last time she had gone downriver, and all the times before.

She had never liked the fort filled with people. She had never belonged there. She had not understood, but she had felt the insurmountable barriers between her and the others who lived and traded there.

Someone said she was a "half-breed brat," and she later asked her mother to explain. After that, she thought it was her parentage that set her apart. Unlike the others, she had a startling combination of raven-black hair, dark skin, and the palest blue eyes, which proclaimed her breeding to everyone who looked at her. She was not white. She was not Indian. She was something else—something apart from both, accepted by neither.

Yet there were others like her, and they were allowed to join in play with white or Indian children. Only Tempest was ostracized from all groups.

Inwardly, she cringed from the hostile looks, the wary glances and frightened avoidance. She ached to belong, to be just like all the others, or at least to be accepted for whatever she was.

But what was she that they should hate her so without even knowing her?

During her last visits to the fort, Tempest took to seeking out dark corners. She sat behind the flour barrel in the trading post, or in the shadows of the stable, or beneath the open window outside the room where the white women gathered to sew. She listened. She learned. And the child in Tempest McClaren died an early, unnatural death.

"Christ! The Mad Scot's got his bagpipes out again," a soldier muttered, drinking ale from a mug as he stood with a friend near the main gate in the evening shadows. Tempest stood near the wall behind a tall bush.

"I saw him down half a bottle of brandy an hour ago."

"Someone ought to shut him up."

The blond soldier laughed. "You want to try, John? The last man who did lost four teeth. He'll stop in an hour or so anyway, if you let him alone. He's harmless enough, just crazy as a loon."

"If it weren't for his pelts, Downing wouldn't tolerate him here."

"That's true enough."

"Where's his squaw?" the dark-haired man said, glancing back within the fort.

The blond man laughed softly. "You got a mind to dip your wick in her?"

There was a soft answering laugh in the darkness. "If it weren't for McClaren, I'd give her a good try. She's damn pretty for a squaw."

"Walks proud and doesn't talk to anyone but McClaren and that girl of hers. Wonder how she ended up with that Scot."

"She doesn't seem afraid of him. The only time I ever saw her smile was at him."

"Jealous? Maybe she likes a man dim in the head and hung like a horse."

Both men laughed softly. Tempest listened to her father play on in the darkness beyond the fort.

"Wonder where his girl is," the man named John muttered, wiping ale from his mouth with the back of his hand.

"She's a strange one. She's got his eyes, don't she? I don't want my girl near her. Missy says some foolish things sometimes and I don't know how little it'd take to set that heathen brat on her with a knife."

"Mary thinks she's pathetic. She looks half-starved."

"Who gives a goddamn? Would you want her playing with one of your young-uns?"

"No, but Mary's right, Carver. She's all eyes."

"And ears. I seen her sitting behind a water barrel listening to the children once. She doesn't talk much and when she does, all that comes out of that hellhole mouth of hers is McClaren's cuss words and that damn Scottish burr. Jesus, who ever heard of an Indian with a burr? But she sneaks around like a rat in the pantry, watching and listening. She's like McClaren, crazy as a loon."

So she knew. It was McClaren's madness they feared in her, not her mixed blood.

The women of the fort were worse, for they spoke about her in her presence, seeming to think she had not the intelligence to understand.

"You can't tell *what* that girl's thinking. She just stares at you with those horrid blue eyes of hers," whispered a yellow-haired woman in a faded gingham frock and bonnet.

"Sylvia, she's only a child. She can't be more than six or seven by the looks of her, and she's so skinny!" said the soldier's Mary. "I wonder if that dreadful father and mother of hers even feed her properly?"

"She probably eats raw meat. And do you think her size matters, Mary? Haven't you heard the stories about what these creatures do? They're vicious, murdering monsters weaned on the blood of good Christians!"

"Lower your voice, Sylvia, please," Mary murmured, her cheeks pink as she glanced across at Tempest standing near the flour barrel.

"She's right, Mary," said another woman.

"Oh, Amanda, don't you begin . . ."

"You said it yourself, Mary."

Sylvia began again. "When Carver told me he was being sent west, I thought he meant Illinois—not this godforsaken wilderness. There isn't a moment when I don't fear for my life, and that child—why, she's as mad as her father and she has her mother's murdering Indian blood. She's just waiting for her first chance to murder some poor, unsuspecting person in their bed some night. You've only to look at her to know that!"

"You're just overwrought because of that raid—"

"Butchered, Mary," Sylvia said, her voice cracking. "A man and his wife, and all four of their children. The youngest was just eight. And know what that little savage did when my son, my own Jonah, spoke to her. She almost ruined him for life! They should get rid of these little mongrels, just take them out in a tied sack and throw them in the river when they're born. Why, they—"

She broke off abruptly as Tempest began to walk slowly toward the three women, weaving her way between the barrels and mounded sacks. She held the yellow-haired woman's eyes, watching as they grew round and glazed. She could smell her sweat, see it bead on her pale forehead. Tempest came close and stopped, looking at each of the women in turn and then back at the one woman named Sylvia. Her mouth twisted and she spat full on the bodice of the woman's clean, faded, blue-flowered dress. The spittle dripped down one breast and soaked into the gingham. The woman's mouth fell open and her expression couldn't have been more stunned and frightened had Tempest stabbed a knife hilt-deep into that same breast.

Turning, Tempest walked out of the trading post. A shocked

silence hung behind her for several moments, succeeded by a tearful burst of squawking, like chickens being attacked by a fox.

Tempest refused to return. She would stay with her mother in the peace and the known dangers of the mountains. Let her da go back. Let him get drunk and disorderly. Let him play the bagpipes in the night. Let him make them fear him. Perhaps he was mad, but McClaren had never been cruel. He and her mother offered her the only gentleness and tenderness she knew.

With three horses loaded with pelts, McClaren set off. Standing beside her mother, Tempest watched him go with a sense of despair. It would be too long before he returned, before she heard his laugh again, felt him lift her and swing her around. She looked up at her mother and saw tears. If not for Tempest, she would have gone with him.

Feeling Tempest's gaze, Winona looked down and smiled. She put her arm around Tempest's shoulders and hugged her close, brushing her temple with a light kiss. "He'll come back with the next moon." She saw much in the child's upturned blue eyes, almost more than she felt she could bear. Being the daughter of a god held great cost, and only here in the high valley did Tempest laugh like any other child.

During McClaren's absence, Winona and Tempest idled and played. The traps remained hung in the cabin. Mother and daughter foraged for food, explored fields, streams and slopes, and rested. They had no fear. McClaren was gone, but they were well armed, well sheltered, and well fed, and they knew he would come back to them.

Few people ever came to the high valley and those who did never lingered. The Mad Scot was powerful medicine.

The new moon came, but McClaren did not return. Winona grew restless. Tempest watched and waited.

Five weeks after McClaren's departure, a band of Indians appeared from the trees, sitting tall on their horses. Each brave proudly wore feathers proclaiming past coups. Their faces were painted for war.

Tempest recognized the young chief. He had come several times before, approaching more closely with each visit. The last time he had dared to reach out and touch McClaren, and then leaped back on his horse when the Mad Scot had laughed.

Winona recognized him also.

Tempest heard her mother cry out a sharp warning. She looked back and saw that her mother had the Hawkins in her hands. Then Tempest heard the warbling war cries and turned toward the forest again, stunned to see the horsemen riding on her, lances raised, their horses' hooves thundering over the grassy ground. Tempest ran, her moccasined feet racing over the distance toward her mother and safety.

Winona screamed and Tempest tried to run faster. Her mother raised the gun and fired; seconds later a lance pierced her left breast and a spurt of blood streamed down the doeskin dress. The gun clattered to the ground.

Screaming, Tempest hurled herself toward her sagging mother. As Winona went to her knees, an arrow struck, entering her right eye and coming out the back of her skull, flinging her backward with her arms outstretched.

A hand caught Tempest from behind, lifting her and carrying her forward with great speed toward the rocks at the side of the hill. Her captor flung her brutally among the rocks as he rode by, and blackness engulfed her.

It was only a short time before Tempest opened her eyes, for she could hear the whoops of the marauding Indians. She could smell the acrid smoke as they torched the cabin, feel the vibration of hooves on the hard ground, taste the blood and dirt in her mouth. The rise of panic threatened to choke her, and her throat worked. *Mama! Mama!*

But instinct held her still and silent. One move and she would find herself speared. So Tempest followed the example of the opossum and remained as motionless as death, breathing so shallowly that it was imperceptible. One brave rode over, dismounted, and prodded her with his foot, then bent down. She felt him lift her braids. Her heart stopped. He grunted something in his own language and let them drop, then went away again.

Finally the Indians tired of their sport and rode off into the woods, leaving the smoldering cabin and the two bodies. Tempest forced her head up despite its throbbing and tried desperately to reach her mother. She crawled the distance from the rocks to the clearing, stopping a few feet from where her mother lay.

Winona lay on her back, her arms flung wide, her mouth ajar, and one sightless eye staring upward into the blazing afternoon sun. Blood had pooled on the ground around her head. Already flies were buzzing about the sickly, sweet-smelling, blackening mass, crawling over her damp doeskin dress and into her open mouth and eyes.

"Mama . . . Mama . . . ?" Tempest whispered, and fainted.

Sometime later, she awakened as a sharp pain jabbed through her shoulder. Thinking that the Indians had returned and found she had moved from her previous position and were now prodding her, she pretended to be dead again. Once more, something jabbed hard. She flinched. Claws dug into her back. She gasped, suddenly comprehending, then rolled over and heard a loud squawk and the flap of great wings as a carrion crow made a startled retreat.

Turning her aching head, Tempest saw that two were hard at work on her mother.

She hadn't the strength to fight off the ravagers, but she managed to throw a few stones. The birds fluttered off momentarily, perching in a nearby tree. They watched Tempest with patient, baleful eyes. Their time would come; they could wait.

Next the wolves will come, Tempest thought in full understanding of the law of the wild. She must hide. But where?

The cabin was rubble. The stone fireplace was all that remained and even it was partially crumbled from the heat of the destruction.

The cave where she had been born and where her parents now stored supplies was too far away. Tempest knew she could never reach it, being too weak, too dizzy, too frightened. Her shoulder hurt abominably and her head still throbbed. Gingerly, she explored with her fingers and found a big lump above her right eyebrow. Blood had dried on her face.

The wolves will come soon.

She needed a hole into which to crawl, a place to hide. She had no means of protecting herself. The gun and ammunition were gone, stolen by the Indians.

Tempest dragged herself into the burned-out cabin and crawled into the mouth of the fireplace. Struggling against her weakness, she piled the fallen stones before her so that she was closed inside its dark, soot-blackened belly. She coughed as she stacked charred sticks beside her, for use later as spears against any animal that tried to claw its way in to get her. Then she waited.

They will come soon.

She dozed.

Six wolves loped silently into the clearing, one after another, and circled Winona's cold, mangled body. They sniffed. Two began to feast on the still fresh meat. A fight broke out among the wolves.

One huge, shaggy, silver-eyed wolf nosed near the rocks. He began to follow Tempest's scent like a bloodhound. His nose to the ground, he loped along, approaching the dead woman, then circling and entering the burned-out cabin. He reached the fireplace and drew in the strong scent of his prey.

A low growl awakened Tempest. She could hear snuffling and smell the dank fur; she gasped, grabbing at a stick. The wolf pawed at the piled rocks. Her heart thundered. Sweat broke out all over her body as the beast began to tumble the wall she had worked so hard to build.

Then she saw his fierce, glittering eyes between the stones. He was twice as big as she.

She slid back as far as she could, bracing her back against the wall of the fireplace, gripping the thick charred stick. The wolf tumbled another rock and pressed its furred muzzle into the small opening. She saw her own reflection in the feral eyes and thrust the stick straight and true into one of them.

A high-pitched scream came from the animal as it yanked backward out of the hole. She held tight to the stick, but it snapped, the sharpened end still in the beast. The wolf continued to scream, rubbing its head in the dirt, clawing at its face, trying to rid itself of the torturing dagger in its eye. Tempest sobbed, cowering back and shaking violently.

The other wolves gathered.

Tempest once again went still and silent, hearing the growling and yapping, and then a low, moaning howl. She felt them all around her, trapping her in the dark, airless hole.

Four more times the wolves tried to reach her. The second time, she shoved her stick into a wolf's throat. The next one that tried caught the stick in its snarling teeth and wrestled it from her. She grabbed another stick and struck twice, gouging a chunk from the beast's tender snout and sending it jerking backward with a yowl.

For a while, there was silence.

Tempest sensed their malevolent presence. She was afraid to lean forward and peek out, sure that a wolf would tear her face away in its powerful jaws. She shook violently with fear and the growing chill. The temperature had dropped noticeably since the sun went down. It was dropping more rapidly now as the North Star shone high in the heavens. Tempest stared up through the tunnel of the chimney, her throat working, tears streaking her blackened face.

The wolves howled.

Tempest drew back her head as one came close and clawed at the stones again. "Da!" she screamed.

The beasts grew silent, and then they moved in again, digging earnestly at the barrier.

"*Da!*" she screamed again and again, cowering back, seeing the snarling snout of a wolf as it tried to get to her. She struck at them again and again. They retreated.

The walls of the fireplace seemed to close in around Tempest, pressing her into a tiny ball. Night deepened and the air grew more chill.

Near dawn, the wolves finally loped off in search of easier prey. Exhausted, Tempest slept fitfully through the day. Her stomach hurt from hunger and she was very thirsty, but she dared not leave her shelter. Later in the afternoon, the sky clouded over and the temperature dropped again. It rained near dusk, and, cupping her hands, Tempest gratefully drank the sooty water that ran down the inside of the chimney. Sleep overcame her again, though she was wet and shivering.

The wolves came again that night, but when they found her still strong enough to fight, they went off again looking for other prey. By morning, fever burned through Tempest. Her breathing was labored; her blue eyes were sunken and dull. She was beyond fear. She closed her eyes.

When they return tonight after the sun sets, they will kill me.

She awakened dimly to a loud cry and sobbing profanity. She tried to open her eyes, and her hand closed convulsively on the stick in her lap. Her body was numb, almost useless.

They are coming.

When she drew in a breath, her lungs rattled harshly. Her face contracted sharply in pain and she gripped her buckskin shirt over her chest. Light burned into her head, blinding her. She could hear the rocks being clawed away. More light poured into her safe, dark hole. The wall was down and she was backed into a trap with no escape. She could hear heavy breathing.

They are here.

Sound swelled in her head as the last stones clattered down. She thrust her blackened spear blindly, again and again. It was

caught and ripped from her hands. Then she was grabbed and
dragged out amid howling. She gave a gurgling cry and shuddered once before her eyes rolled back.

    Warmth.
    A fire crackled somewhere close by. Tempest could smell
smoke.
    The cabin...
    Mama!
    She forced her eyes open and saw the walls of the storage
cave. She couldn't move. Something was wrapped around her,
something heavy and warm and soft. She tried to cry out, but
the sound that came was low and harsh and tore at the inside
of her lungs.
    A hairy, haggard face with blazing blue eyes came down
close to hers. For an instant, she didn't recognize him.
    "*Da*..." she croaked, and tears of relief came in a rush so
strong it shook her body. His face glowed in the firelight as
he hunkered down beside her. He said nothing, but lifted her,
hugging her against him and moaning softly.
    "*Da*..."
    "Sleep, bairn. Ye be safe now. Sleep, lass." He started to
put her down again, and she whimpered, clutching frantically
at him. He held her until she slept.
    It was the last time he ever held her.
    It was more than one full moon before Tempest was well
enough to venture outside the cave where she had been born,
but she had long since seen the difference in her father. He
said nothing. He sat late into the night staring into the embers
of the fire, the muscles of his face working.
    Seeing that Tempest was finally regaining some of her lost
strength, McClaren brought seasoned deer stomachs full of
water and hung them in the cave. He indicated the dried beef
and fruit. She didn't understand until he barred her into the
cave and rode away.
    She screamed for hours, but he didn't come back. She clawed
and pounded at the planks until her hands were bruised and
bloody. Finally she gave up and huddled at the back of the
cave near the fire he had built for her.
    How many days passed, Tempest never knew. The fire went
out within a few days and the only light came through the
spaces between the thick pine planks of the door. The cave
became fetid.

After what seemed like months, McClaren returned. He threw the bar aside and banged the door open, and Tempest sat up, blinded by the sunlight streaming in. The shock of fresh mountain air, so different from that of her confines, almost made her faint.

Her father strode into the cave, a sack in one hand. He leaned the Hawkins against the earthen wall and dropped the sack near the long-cold remains of the fire.

"Get wood."

Tempest stumbled outside, confused but obeying.

McClaren's blue eyes held an odd gleam as he cut the meat into chunks and tossed it into the hot frying pan. His skin was stretched taut over his cheekbones. His hair and beard were dirty and wild. The meat sizzled and a rich smell filled the dank cave as he added water and herbs. Tempest sat down, her mouth watering.

Taking the pan from the fire, McClaren spooned a portion of the stew into a bowl and handed it to her and ordered, "Eat it. *Eat all of it!*" Then he sat back on his haunches with his own heaping bowl.

Tempest stared in confusion at the hard, cold, implacable face as she ate. He was so different, almost a stranger. She watched him closely, frightened by the dark glow in his eyes. The meat was tough and salty. She ate it all as he had commanded.

McClaren smiled. It was a small curve of his hard mouth, a smile that didn't reach the strangely burning eyes. He ate until there was nothing left in the pan. Tempest had never seen him eat so much. Then he leaned back and stared at her, his face slackening.

"The murdering heathen bastards wilna enter their happy hunting ground now," he said with chilling self-satisfaction.

Tempest didn't understand. Her eyes searched his face, and the line of his mouth curved again, a mere twitch in the darkly bearded face.

"They canna meet the Great Spirit unless they be whole men. We've eaten their bloody, murdering hearts and what little courage the bastards had is ours now. In here!" He patted his engorged stomach as Tempest stared at him in horrified comprehension.

Shaking violently, she looked down at her empty bowl. Tiny, quick gasps came as she tried to stand. A cold wave of nausea swelled up in her.

McClaren reached over and grabbed her. He gripped her by the throat and shook her. "Ye'll not be sick! Keep them in you. *Keep them in you! They murdered your mother!*" She saw only his crazed eyes as she fainted.

Tempest roused slowly. Green aspen leaves and blue sky came into focus above her. The cold ground was hard beneath her back. Sounds filtered dimly into her consciousness, and turning her head, she saw her da moving about his packhorses. He tightened the ropes on the last one carrying his gear. When he turned toward her, she saw his flooded eyes, the tears streaming silently down into his wet beard. The front of his dirty buckskin skirt was damp.

Her stomach churned as she remembered what he had said and realized what she had done. She squeezed her eyes shut and gritted her teeth. *Keep them in you! They murdered your mother!* Her throat worked spasmodically and burned as her gorge rose.

Her father came and lifted her, carried her to her horse, and set her on it. Her skin felt clammy. He handed her a blanket Winona had woven. Her small, frail body trembled as she wrapped it around herself tightly, watching her father.

He mounted his own horse. Glancing back, he said, "It be over now, lass. We're going west, away from this place and what happened. It be over." He turned away from her.

It would never be over for Tempest McClaren.

Who will bell the cat?
—Eustache Deschamps

New Helvetia, California, 1846

Early morning sunlight cut the chill air and shone over the high adobe brick walls of Johann August Sutter's New Helvetia. Slowly, warming rays traversed the earthen floor of the wide inner courtyard. A cocky rooster stood on a hitching post, stretching his scrawny neck as he crowed at the sun and called his harem forth. Already the clang of iron on anvil rang from the blacksmith's shop. Women's voices came from the weaver's quarters. A barefooted squaw in a bark dress cast handfuls of corn to the clucking hens. The barracks were rapidly emptying of Indian workers, and a white man on horseback shouted orders as they formed a human train and set off for the corn and wheat fields, where they would remain until dusk.

Sutter stood outside the compound watching the Indians and speaking to McClaren, while Tempest went back in through the gate on an errand for her father. He wanted another sack of alum and Sutter had agreed readily, knowing it would season the prize pelts he would later receive from the trapper. Before she went her father asked her for her knife, and, although surprised, she had handed it over. Unease filled her.

Glancing back, she frowned. Sutter had given her one of his broad grins as she left. She neither liked nor trusted the amiable, rotund landholder, who claimed he had been a guard in the Austrian king's army.

"He's a bloody brigand, Da," she had told her father earlier. Sutter had taken all their prime pelts in exchange for meager supplies, as much wild grape brandy as her father could drink in a week, and empty promises of gold. Sutter had never yet laid gold in her father's palm, though the promises had been voiced repeatedly.

23

"It doesna matter, lass," her da had said, swilling the strong brew from a jug. "I dunna care 'bout the gold."

"He's cheating you!"

"Aye, the mon's a freebooter, but he makes damn fine brandy. I care not for the other and 'tis none of yer damn concern." His voice held with cold finality. He tipped the jug and drank lustily, then wiped his mouth with the back of his hand and pointed. "It's an empire the mon wants. He sells the eastern fools dreams of a new land. Aye, he'll bring them out and bring the scourge on our heads. It takes fools, liars, and cheats to make a place civilized." He laughed loudly and drank again. Then he fell into one of his long, morose silences.

They were leaving the fort this morning, and Tempest was eager to be away. She loathed Sutter's Fort, loathed the putrid smell of human excrement, the confusion, the bold-eyed men and silent, acquiescent squaws who did their bidding. She hated the words that roused her father's vile, often violent temper. But even worse she hated the way they laughed at him when he fell and lay snoring in a deep, drunken stupor.

The wilderness and the mountains were kinder and safer than this place. Here she felt trapped and threatened. She felt the eyes watching her as they had before, saw the mouths whispering, saw the secret smiles.

Yet it was not the same. Instinct made her aware of the difference.

Carrying the ten-pound sack of alum on her thin shoulder, Tempest came back toward the open gate. Her head was down and she did not see the tall, broad-shouldered man step out in front of her until she collided with him. Startled, she stepped back sharply and almost lost hold of the sack. The man removed his wide-brimmed farmer's hat.

In a quick, all-encompassing glance, she took in the wavy chestnut hair, the clear hazel eyes beneath heavy brows, the long sideburns and mustache, the firm mouth and square jaw. He wore a homespun white shirt, clean but well-worn dungarees rather than buckskin, high boots, and a leather belt. He was unarmed. She had seen him before and knew him to be an eastern farmer who had arrived by wagon train some time before. His name was Abram Walker.

He smiled. "Good morning, Tempest."

Her mouth tightened. She dismissed him with a contemptuous look and started to step around him. He moved to block her way again. Her eyes widened and she glanced up sharply and saw his watchful, assessing look, his determination.

At fourteen, Tempest was still a child, not having bled yet, but she was no fool. She was aware of the men's growing interest in her.

She was growing up fast, and beneath the ragged leather garb and the dirt she had a promising ripeness. Tall and painfully slender, Tempest walked with supple grace and a proud bearing. Her thick, untidy black braids fell past her tiny waist. Her features were sharp from youth and lean living. She had her mother's high cheekbones, her father's fine-bridged nose and firm jawline. No blackened teeth or gaping holes showed when she spoke, as was true of so many of the other men and women at the fort. Her teeth were straight, white, and healthy, like McClaren's. She had the same savage, humorless smile.

Her coloring attracted attention, as it always had. That combination of blue eyes in a dark face drew a man in and held him captive. She was quick and cold, self-protective and distrustful. She could be vicious. It was that look combining animal wildness with innocent vulnerability that made her even more desirable.

But Tempest was unwilling; every advance met with hostility. In a place where women could be had for a few beads or a piece of shiny tin, Tempest's contempt became a potent stimulus. Every man wanted to be her first, but none would have complained about being her next.

Tempest was aware of the men. She saw their eyes, dark and glowing, following her. She heard them whisper as she passed. Several had tried to buy her willing participation. She had seen the squaws go off with the white men, had heard them late at night within the fort.

The first time she had seen Walker, he had been rutting on a squaw down by the river. She remembered the woman's writhing body and her twisted face just before she screamed. Later, Tempest had seen them together again, talking within the walls of the fort. The woman had seemed to *like* him. Walker, however, had lost all interest and even seemed embarrassed by the squaw clinging to his arm like a fly on horse dung. The stupid woman had smiled and rubbed his arm, murmuring something that had made Walker's face redden.

Had it been Tempest by the river, she would have put a knife between his ribs. If not then, later.

Now, Walker dared block *her* way.

A chill premonition spread through Tempest's young body

as she looked up at the big farmer standing before her, hat off.

Walker has no woman.

Tempest had heard that his wife had died on the way to California. She knew he was no longer interested in the squaw for she was now trailing after one of the other men in the fort. Last night, Tempest had been disturbed because Walker and her father had talked long and hard, and there had been no fight. That was a very bad sign.

Her body stiffened. "Move yer bloody arse out of my way, mon," she commanded in a low, fierce tone. She saw him wince at her language and was grimly satisfied. White men shocked easily. She had learned that early. Direct attack in any way earned quick freedom, and it was a lesson she often put to good use. She glanced beyond Walker and saw her father checking the pack animals in preparation for their departure.

Walker widened the distance between his planted feet so that he stood even more solidly between Tempest and her father, even blocking her view of him. "We need to talk."

Her heart pounded in sickening jolts. "I've no wish to talk to a white pig." She tried to step around him again, and he moved quickly. She almost came up against him again before she jerked back.

"I'm not moving, Tempest McClaren, and if you don't want to talk, then you'll listen. I've already come to terms with your father."

Her heart stopped and her throat went dry. "Get out of my way!"

He took a deep breath. "You're not going with your father. You're coming with me."

She stared at him, her mind working frantically. Then she used a well-practiced ploy. Throwing her head back, she laughed raucously in a purely masculine manner that was so much like her father at his wildest that it was alarming. Knowing it, she did it again with cunning deliberation. Most of the men at New Helvetia were convinced McClaren was mad, and indeed he was—now. Let them believe her to be mad as well, and then they would leave her alone, Tempest thought.

Walker had seen her use the tactic before and knew what she was doing. He stood firm, his eyes clear. Then he reached out for her.

The laugh choked to a stop. "Touch me and I'll gut you like a fish!" she warned, her blue eyes glowing fiercely.

He didn't try to touch her again, but he didn't move out of

her way either. "You can't ride with McClaren anymore. It's no fit way for a girl to live, Indian or not."

"Da!"

Men in the fort stopped what they were doing to stare.

"He won't come," Walker told her.

Dropping the sack, she twisted her body in a sharp movement and raised her moccasined foot for a swift, disabling kick. Walker just managed to dodge the blow aimed at his groin, but when he reached for her again, it was too late. Tempest ran.

"Da!"

McClaren didn't turn around. Tempest reached him and clung to his arm as he reached up for the saddlehorn in order to mount. "Da!" She glanced back over her shoulder and saw Walker coming toward her. There was no urgency or hesitation to his approach, only a calm determination. "Da, where's my horse?" she cried breathlessly.

McClaren had changed inside and out over the years since Winona's death. His long, matted black hair had wide streaks of white, and white showed also in his full, unkempt beard. He wore filthy fringed buckskins and a sagging, wide-brimmed Spanish hat. His eyes were dull and the skin beneath his eyes was discolored from heavy, incessant drinking.

He still didn't look at her. She jerked at his arm frantically. "Da! Where's my horse?"

"Walker has it." He tried to push her hand away, but she held on.

"I'm going with ye."

He shook his head slowly. "You're staying."

"No! I dunna want to stay with him! I dunna want to stay with anyone. I belong with you!"

"No. And it doesna matter what ye want," he said flatly. "A mon makes up his mind what he wants and a woman abides by it."

"No!"

"Been that way since God created Adam. Always will be. Walker wants ye. He con have ye."

"No!!"

He looked at her then, his eyes painfully cold. His hand closed on her wrist hard, yanking her fingers from his arm. "Yer mother dinna want me when I took her from her da. She hated me and she was afraid. But she learned to accept, and she learned to love me. Walker will teach ye like I taught her."

Tears flowed from Tempest's wild eyes as she tried madly to clutch at him. "I not be staying . . . I wilna stay!"

Her father caught hold of her shoulders and shook her viciously. "Ye're a McClaren," he said through his teeth. "Where's yer bloody pride? Stop squalling!" He released her abruptly and she stumbled back. He pointed at her. "Ye stay with the mon. Ye let him take ye. Ye give him fine, healthy bairns. Do it!" His brogue was thick, his voice hoarse. He turned away and started to mount his horse.

Tempest catapulted herself at him. "You wilna leave me, Da! Not again! By God, you wilna!"

He kept his back to her. "Let go," he said in a low, flat voice, his body rigid.

"I go where you go," she rasped.

"Walker gave me whiskey and five dollars in gold for ye. Ye belong to him."

It was a few seconds before she could speak. "Give the gold back," she pleaded.

"It's done, it is. Let go."

"I wilna!"

Her father turned on her; he pried her hands loose and shoved her roughly away from him. She sprang back. This time he yanked her loose and hit her hard with the back of his hand across the side of her head, knocking her flat. She lay there, stunned.

"For God's sake, McClaren, don't," Walker said weakly.

McClaren mounted his horse.

Tempest rolled to her knees and raised her head to see Walker bending toward her. She slapped at him with clawed hands and drew back her lips in a snarl like a wild beast. Then she came to her feet and ran to McClaren again. She curled her fingers into the fringe of his leggings and McClaren couldn't pry her loose. He swore violently and hit her again, but still she held on.

"Da . . ." Her eyes were crazed.

"Take her, mon! Or aren't ye mon enough?" McClaren roared at Walker, who stood frozen, watching them in appalled silence. Walker strode forward then and put his strong arms around Tempest, pulling her back and finally away. She screamed and fought. Twisting, she went for his eyes, but Walker caught her wrists. She kicked, thrashed, and bit, but he held on.

McClaren turned away and gave his mount a hard kick. He

rode off swiftly away from his daughter, his pack animals following on the string. The gear jingled and bounced as McClaren forced the horses to a gallop.

"Da!!"

Walker held Tempest hard against him, her arms pinned behind her back to keep her locked there. He took her kicks at his shins and her stream of profanity until McClaren was some distance away.

Her body shaking, her heart pounding, Tempest went still in the big farmer's arms. She could feel his great strength and knew she hadn't enough to fight him, so she pretended to relax, to accept. She could hear his heart beating fast and hard. More, she could still hear the faint sound of horses' hooves beating against the earth. She waited, slowing her agitated breathing.

Walker's arms eased slightly. Frowning, he looked down at her. He knew what he had to do; he knew what she was doing. McClaren was almost out of sight. She had to learn. She had to accept.

Walker let her go.

Tempest bolted. He started to reach for her instinctively and then clenched his hand and let it drop back to his side. He watched her for several minutes as she raced across the wild-wheat-covered slope after McClaren, crying out his name. Then he turned back toward New Helvetia.

Tears streaked Tempest's face as she ran, her head thrown back and her braids lashing her back. Rather than slowing, her father whipped the horses into a full gallop. Tempest ran harder.

Mile after mile, Tempest ran and walked and then ran again. Long after her father was gone from sight, she followed the wide trail he had left. Her breath rasped harshly in her lungs and the muscles of her legs began to ache and then cramp. Still she refused to give up.

Yet the distance between her and her father grew, for he did not slacken his pace and she couldn't continue hers. Sweat poured from her overheated body. The sun beat mercilessly on her back. Her throat was hot and dry, and her lungs burned.

Oh, Da, dunna go. Dunna leave me alone again!

But he had. Again.

Tempest ran after him until she could run no more, and then she crawled.

It was dusk when she finally collapsed near an outcropping of rocks and a grove of oak, pine, and madrone. She lay there semiconscious, her feet bleeding through the torn moccasins, scratches and bruises lacing her body. Everything felt heavy and dark around her. She was alone, completely alone. Like the last time. And night was coming again.

Da!

The whinny of a horse made her open her eyes. Again she heard it. Relief and hope gave her enough strength to lift her head, but it was Abram Walker who stood looking down at her—not McClaren. Several yards away, Walker's horse blew gustily and then lowered its great head to graze.

Tempest stared blankly at the big farmer. She pushed herself up and edged back away from him. The high rocks around her closed in like the blackened walls of an old fireplace, but instead of wolves wanting her life, it was a man. He moved steadily toward her, his hand outstretched. Tempest inched back until she was against the granite wall and could go no farther. Her eyes grew huge.

"I won't hurt you," Abram said softly. He stepped closer. She cowered back, her eyes closing tightly as her mouth dropped slightly open. "I won't hurt you, Tempest." She opened her eyes again as he hunkered down in front of her and held out his canteen. She didn't take it, but sat staring fixedly at him.

Abram didn't know what to do; he had never been up against anything like this before. Something in this girl had moved him from the first moment he had seen her, six months before, something beyond the physical promise she had. He knew somehow that it was vitally important to touch her. He moved even closer. She pressed herself back against the rock, cringing away from him, her body trembling violently like some beaten cur. Her breathing was fast, too fast, and he could see plainly the hard, racing pulse in the slim, dusty column of her throat. Did she expect another beating? Had McClaren often hit her that way, like she was a strong boy rather than a thin girl? Or was her fear more elemental? McClaren had had no woman either. Abram squelched the thought before it progressed further.

Reaching out, he put his fingertips against her cheek where McClaren's blow showed black and blue. Tempest's body went stiller than death. Abram caressed her cheek gently, watching the frozen terror in those enormous blue eyes.

"I've a farm started two days from Sutter's Fort. It's good land," he told her softly. "I've built a cabin. It's not much, but it's more than you've ever had. I'll take good care of you,

Tempest McClaren. Before God, I swear I will. I promise."

She said nothing.

Abram sat back on his heels, leaving the canteen in her lap. When she still didn't touch it, he stood slowly and went back to his horse. It was well trained and would not wander far, even unbridled and unsaddled. As the sun set, he gathered wood and built a fire. He noticed that Tempest was finally drinking the badly needed water. She looked hollow-eyed and emotionless.

Taking dried beef and fruit from his saddlebag, he set it before her like an offering. Before eating any himself, he clasped his hands and said a prayer. When he opened his eyes and raised his head, Tempest was staring at him as though he had tried to conjure a devil. He smiled at her and bit off a piece of dried beef. She turned her head away. Tears slipped down her cheeks, staining her dirty face.

"I had a wife once," he began as darkness gathered and the flames of the fire drew them closer. "She wasn't beautiful, but she was good and gentle. She had brown eyes and her hair was the color of ripe wheat." He stopped and looked away, falling silent for a long time. "She died of mountain fever a few days past the Great Divide. I buried her underneath a big pine overlooking a valley." His throat worked. "She would've liked that, I think."

He glanced at Tempest. She was staring into the darkness, her body rigid and her eyes wide. The tight muscles in her jaw stood out. Did she expect something to come lunging at them? There was no sound out there but a lonesome, soulful-sounding coyote and the chirping of a million crickets. Yet she was shaking, and he knew it wasn't just the growing coolness of the night.

"There's nothing to be afraid of, Tempest. I'm here. You're safe," he assured her gently, finding it strange that a girl who had lived as a trapper should be so afraid of the dark. "I brought an extra blanket," he told her, and placed it beside her. She looked at him sharply, wide-eyed, and then away to the darkness again, keeping her vigil.

The night with all its sounds closed in on her. She tried to beat off the old fears, but they returned again and again like the pack of wolves that had tried to devour her. In the end, it was her body that emerged triumphant over her will, for her eyes drooped in an exhaustion too deep to fight.

When her eyes finally closed and she sagged, Abram stood slowly and came around the fire to sit beside her. He drew her slight body close against his massive one; instinctively her muscles tautened in protest and she let out a faint, frightened whimper. "I won't hurt you," he whispered against her hair.

She smelled of dirt, sweat, and smoke. He stroked her, whispering soothingly of anything he could think of—coming to California, his hopes, his life in Pennsylvania, his faith in God's plan, until the slow calmness of his voice relaxed Tempest and she slept deeply. He released her long enough to spread the blanket on the cooling earth and then placed her gently on it. He lay down beside her and pulled the other blanket over them both.

Abram put his arms around Tempest, and his body tingled warmly to life. He had been too long without a woman, and the feel of her breasts and gently curving hips made him ache. He needed a woman to share his life again, to help him with his new farm, to give him strong, healthy sons to carry on his work in this wild, new land.

He needed Tempest McClaren.

This girl was not yet a woman, but she would soon become one. She had something in her that stirred him deeply. It would not be easy to tame her, or to win her trust. And love. Love would have to come later, much later.

Abram Walker had no idea what kind of life she had lived up to this moment. He could only guess by what he had seen: McClaren, a strangely brooding man who looked capable of anything, and this girl who had clung to him with mad desperation. Walker had followed her for miles and had begun to wonder if she would run until she dropped dead. Was it love that had driven her so wildly, mile after grueling mile? He could still hear her screams when he had torn her away from McClaren, the screams of a terrified animal. And McClaren—he had not looked back once after he started away. _Not once._

Yet just before the Mad Scot had turned his horse away, Abram had seen the agony carved into that hard, wild face. And there had been tears pouring from the old trapper's eyes.

Love so strong. Was it natural?

Tempest grew restless in her sleep. She moaned and thrashed her head back and forth. Her arms moved in sharp jerks. She jabbed and thrust. She whimpered and then cried out sharply for her da.

Afraid he might be holding her too closely, Abram eased

away, though he didn't let her go. He spoke softly, stroking her hair back from her temples. For a few minutes, she continued to fight. Then she relaxed again and slept quietly. Abram drew her closer. She nestled against him, drawn by his warmth, and he smiled. He lay behind her, curved around her. Her legs were drawn up tightly like those of a baby in a warm womb. Propping himself up on his elbow, Abram looked down at her; even in her sleep, the girl cried.

"Little one," he whispered against her hair, brushing his lips lightly against the smooth, musky skin of her temple. "I think you need me as much as I need you."

A dreamer of dreams.
—Deuteronomy 13:1

Abram awakened well before dawn. He eased himself out from under the blanket, added wood to the low-burning fire, then went to the stream to wash and shave. He combed his hair and mustache. When he came back, dawn was just firing the sky above the eastern hill. Tempest was still asleep, her face smooth, the hollows of her cheeks deep. She reminded him of a starved cat, all sleek flesh and protruding bone.

Staring down at her, his hands deep in his pockets, he frowned. She wasn't going to be easy. She'd fight him. She was wild and fierce and terrified. Her father had probably beaten her into obedience, but Abram had no intention of using that method with her. A wild animal could be subdued, but not tamed by brute force or cruelty. He'd learned that as a boy.

A shaft of sunlight crept over the rocks and struck Tempest's face. Her eyelids flinched. She started to roll away from it, and her lips parted in a sharp, indrawn breath.

Abram watched her open her eyes, the blue orbs clouded by sleep and pain. They focused, searched, and stopped on him. She frowned, uncomprehending.

"Good morning." He smiled. Sitting with one leg raised as he rested his forearm on his knee, he watched her. Her eyes fixed. She pushed the blanket off and sat up, grimacing and moving like a very old woman. When she began looking around again in frightened, frantic search, he understood.

He rose. "He's gone," he told her, his smile fading. "For good."

Her head snapped up.

"You're better off with me, Tempest."

She just stared at him, those blue eyes huge. Her back was rigid, one small, white-knuckled fist pressing against her stomach. Her jaw worked slowly.

"You're better off with me," he repeated more firmly, his eyes holding hers steadily.

"I want my da," she said in a low croak. The child in her

34

shone out from her moistening eyes, and Abram felt like he'd just been kicked.

"You have only me now."

Her lips parted slightly. "I dunna want you. I want Da."

"He doesn't want you back."

Her chin trembled before she clenched her jaw, the muscles standing out tautly.

His face softened. "I want you, Tempest. I'll take good care of you. We'll make a fine life together."

Tempest turned her head away, staring off toward the mountains.

Abram spooned thick oatmeal porridge onto a tin plate and came around the fire to set it down in front of her. She drew back from him as far as she could, watching him warily.

"We'll head back to the fort as soon as you're finished." He pushed his hands deeply into his dungaree pockets again. "Your horse it still there, and the supplies I bought for my farm."

When he leaned down to pour himself some coffee, Tempest jerked back. He pretended not to notice, and sat down a few feet away from her, cupping the mug in his hands. She sat very still.

He nodded toward the plate of food. "Eat something."

Slowly, still watching him, she picked up the plate. She scooped up some of the porridge in her fingers and put it in her mouth. She grimaced and quickly spat it out on the ground.

He smiled faintly. "You want some coffee to wash it down?"

"What is it?" she demanded contemptuously.

"Oatmeal and barley with a little dried fruit mixed in."

"It's crap."

"You'll eat it or go hungry."

She just looked at him and tossed the plate away, splattering oatmeal against the rocks.

The first test, he thought ruefully. "Suit yourself." He finished his own breakfast in silence. Then he poured himself more coffee. The dark-lashed, incredibly blue eyes glared straight at him with unnerving intensity. He stared back.

Stacking the tin plates and mugs, he headed for the creek. He clicked his tongue, making sure his horse was closer to him than to Tempest. Quickly rinsing the plates and mugs, he packed them in his saddlebag, then shifted things around so there would be room for Tempest to ride behind him. When he led the horse back to the little camp, Tempest was gone.

He looked around, angry with himself for having assumed she would stay put. He'd have to go after her.

The bushes rustled and he glanced around sharply. Tempest emerged, hitching up her buckskin pants and glaring at him. Abram cleared his throat, then chuckled at himself, shaking his head. He kicked out the fire, tamping the burned coals with his heavy-booted foot and then covering everything over with dirt. Not a spark could remain, for one small spark could start a range fire in this wild-wheat land that would race for a hundred miles.

Abram rolled the blanket and tied it to the cantle. Then he mounted and extended his big, brown, callused hand to Tempest, who still stood watching him grimly. She stared at it.

"I'll help you swing up behind me," he told her, wondering bleakly if his palm was sweating. She raised her head slowly, her gaze traveling up his powerful arm, across his strong chest and shoulders, and up to fix on his face. She limped closer, then reached up and took his looped rope from where it was secured to his saddle. She knotted one end around her neck and flung the coils at him.

Abram dismounted and calmly untied the rope, rewound it, secured it to the saddle again, and remounted.

"You're riding. Now, give me your hand," he said, and hoped there was enough command in his tone to make her obey. He didn't want to have to drag her up by force, but she was too physically spent to indulge in pride.

Slowly, she lifted her hand. Abram didn't move. He waited. He let her hand slide fully into his before closing his fingers in a firm clasp. This gave her the leverage she needed to swing up and land softly behind him on the horse.

"Put your arms around me. I don't want you falling off and hurting yourself." As soon as the words were out, he groaned inwardly. Tempest McClaren had been riding with the Mad Scot and covering the most rugged terrain, and here he was saying she might fall off the back of a horse. She must think him an utter fool!

Tempest's hands crept to his waist. He took her wrists and brought them around in spite of her stiffening muscles. She tried to pull free, but he held her. Then he uncurled her fingers and flattened them against his ribs. The horse moved restlessly.

Abram said nothing; neither did Tempest. Finally, her hands

relaxed and remained where they were. Abram pressed his heels
into his horse's sides.

The rhythmic movement of the animal rocked them together.
He felt her body brush his again and again. After a while, she
rested against him and her hands slid down and curled into his
belt. Her body sagged and her cheek rested against his warm
back. He knew she slept again. It was what she needed. Yet
when her hands slackened and slipped free of his belt and
bounced softly against his hard thighs, he became uncomfort-
ably aware of how long it had been since he'd known a woman.

Six months ago, he'd given a shiny tin looking glass to one
of the squaws at the fort so that he could lie with her by the
river. He'd needed the release; and she'd been more than willing. When he'd stood up and rebuttoned his pants, he'd looked
down at the woman in her filthy bark dress as she gazed into
the cheap tin reflection, and felt sick. He'd thought of his
beloved wife, Kathy, and guilt smote him painfully.

Now, he could feel Tempest's small young breasts burning
into his back. Warm trails of fire heated his flesh at each bounce
of her hands. Gradually that heat centralized and pulsed, finally
throbbing agonizingly.

"Sweet Jesus," he murmured and swallowed hard. He wanted
to take Tempest's hands and press them to that hard pain, rub
them there to ease it, but when he looked down, he saw the
soiled palms and the softly curled fingers, and his desire ebbed.

Tempest McClaren was little more now than a dirty, ignorant, neglected girl half his age. She'd had less choice in
this matter than that squaw who'd sold her favors for a cheap
metal trinket. How was he ever going to gain this girl's trust
and respect if he could not even control his baser instincts?
She needed time. He wanted to protect her, care for her, teach
her. He wanted to love her. He ached to go into her, too, but
when he did, he wanted her willing, giving, and, he hoped,
enjoying. Until she could do that, he would have to seek privacy
and the use of his own hand. Pray God would forgive him for
wasting himself, but what else could he do short of rape?

Abram cupped Tempest's hand in his own and lifted it.
Kathy's had been thick, capable, callused. Piercingly, he remembered how she had caressed his cheek and looked at him
with doe-soft eyes. How he missed that woman's tenderness,
how he longed for it.

Would Tempest ever be capable of learning it after the life

she'd led with McClaren? He stared at the small hand lying in his. It was dirty, callused, stained. Yet there was grace in the slender, tapered fingers, the square palm, the fragile-boned wrist. He turned the hand slowly and placed it palm-down on his thigh, then urged the slow-walking horse back into a faster pace.

It was dusk when they reached the gates of New Helvetia. Several men were standing outside Sutter's quarters as Abram rode in with Tempest behind him. They stared.

"So, you went after McClaren's brat?" one called with a laugh. Sutter appeared, his fleshy face affable and crinkled in a knowing grin. He looked the worse for wild grape brandy. His son, who had arrived only months before, looked at him with open disgust.

Abram dismounted and reached up for Tempest. Her jaw set as he lifted her down, and she looked through him, not at him. Turning away, he took the reins and led the horse toward the stable. Abram wondered what she was thinking as she followed him, but had no chance to dwell on it, for half a dozen men approached, boldly curious.

"I saw you talking to that Mad Scot night before last," one said, eyeing Tempest.

Abram's face was stiff. "I'm taking her back to my farm with me." His hard glance swept the men in open challenge.

Michael Nye, a medium-sized man of slender build with brown hair and eyes, laughed. His body drooped in a languid pose. "Then you'd better sleep with one eye open, Abram. She's as crazy as that father of hers. I tried to talk to her once— mind you, *only* talk. The girl has a tongue worse than a poxed sailor."

Tempest might not have been there as the men talked around and about her. Her face remained expressionless.

"If you wanted a woman, why didn't you take one of the squaws? There're several who'd do you well," Sutter slurred licentiously.

"What'd the little bitch cost you?" another asked, and Abram's head snapped toward the offensive man.

"She's my woman now—like unto my wife," he growled, and a silence dropped over the surrounding men. Nye's face paled.

"Then you're keeping her for good?"

"And worse," Abram stated firmly.

Nye looked at Tempest then and a bleak expression stole over his face. Sutter cleared his throat.

"Then we've some celebrating to do." He slapped Abram on the back amiably. "Come in for a drink."

Abram glanced at Tempest. Without looking at him or the others, she took the reins from his hand and led the horse away. He frowned heavily as he watched.

"She won't go anywhere," Sutter assured him, and nodded an order to one of his men. "Franklin will keep his eye on her to see she doesn't."

Abram was in no mood to drink, but Sutter was his host. He'd been helpful and friendly and to refuse would be an insult. Abram followed Sutter into his stale-smelling quarters.

The room held several straight-backed chairs, a pile of cowhides stacked against the back wall, and a long sideboard. The hearth was cold, Sutter's warmth coming from the jug on the table that was strewn with papers, ledgers, and dirty glasses. The place smelled of smoke, earth, sweat, and sour spirits.

Sutter picked up the jug and poured a glass of brandy. He handed it to Abram and poured another for himself.

"In the words of Julius Caesar, 'Women—you can't live with them and you can't live without them.'"

It had been Marshal, not Caesar, but Abram didn't correct him. The brew was strong and warmed his belly. He wanted to gulp it down and go back outside to Tempest, but Sutter was in a sipping mood. He looked at Abram thoughtfully as he licked brandy off his full lips.

"McClaren's daughter is a beauty, or will be. I've noticed her myself," he admitted without embarrassment or tact. "But Michael Nye is right."

"I'll take my chances."

"That is your choice," Sutter agreed, and sipped again. "You had a wife, didn't you?"

"She died."

"Mine hasn't," he said glumly. "She's on her way from Europe, or so my son has told me." He caught himself. "It is unfortunate that you lost your wife, but other wagon trains will come. Men die along the way and others bring their daughters. Or you might think about marrying one of the Californio women. Such a marriage would solidify your position in California."

"I have the woman I want," Abram said, his mouth tightening.

Sutter remained silent for a moment. Then he shrugged and

turned the conversation to crops and Abram's future trade with
the fort. Sutter would help him in any way he could, as he had
done already, and, of course, anything he grew would find a
ready market.

Outside, Tempest curried Abram's horse. She was aware
of the man leaning against the outer wall of the weaver's quarters, watching her. She was sure she could outrun him and
outride him as well, but she had no knife and no gun, and night
was coming.

Why did ye do this to me, Da? The question churned in her
mind. Her chest felt like it was squeezed into a hard knot and
the muscles of her face were locked stiffly.

Shouts beyond the walls of the fort announced that the Indian
workers were being brought back from the fields. Already
buckets of slop, food for the Indians, were being carried out to
the troughs to feed them. Tempest rested her forehead against
the smooth, warm coat of the horse. *If I disobey that damn
farmer, will that be my fate?* she wondered. *Will he turn me
over to Sutter or his men to either be used in the fields or
mounted for their own quick pleasure? I'll kill him first!*

A warm, strong hand covered hers where it lay clenched
against the horse. She froze.

"Old Dusty hasn't been better groomed in his life," Abram
said behind her. She could smell brandy on his breath and it
reminded her piercingly of her father. She closed her eyes
tightly.

Abram took the brush from her and tossed it aside. Then
he turned her around to face him, his hands firmly grasping
her shoulders. Her breath came swift and shallow. Warily she
lifted her head and looked at him.

"We'll leave early tomorrow," he told her. "Sutter's given
us a room for the night. He's sending supper over."

She kept her face still with an effort, only just bearing his
touch. He searched her face. It revealed nothing.

Abram's fingers spread apart, his thumbs gently rubbing
back and forth on her collarbones beneath the smooth buckskin.
"I'm never going to hurt you."

Her heart thumped faster.

He watched her face closely, frowning slightly. "I know
you're afraid of me, that you resent my taking you away from
your father."

Her lip curled. "I *hate* you," she snarled, her eyes glittering.
His thumbs never stopped their rhythmic caressing. Her hands

clenched tightly and a tremor of expectancy raced through her. He glanced down, then back up again. He smiled wryly.

"Are you planning to hit me?"

She didn't answer, holding her breath, preparing herself for a blow.

"You couldn't do me much damage, you know," he told her softly.

She met his eyes. "That would depend on where I hit ye."

His hazel eyes narrowed. "I wouldn't advise it."

She trembled slightly at that flat, cool tone. He lowered his head and she drew back sharply with a gasp. His hands tightened, keeping her close. "I want to take care of you, not harm you. I want to love you."

"I ken what ye want." She gave a laugh that was sheer bravado. "I'm no bloody fool, mon. I've eyes and ears in me head." She dropped her eyes to the button-fly of his dungarees. "Ye want to wield that, and that be the truth of it." She raised her eyes again and saw the deep color mounting in Abram Walker's face. She laughed maliciously.

"Come with me. We're going to talk straight."

She jerked free. "Go to bloody hell!" she hissed.

Abram caught her arm. She dug her heels in, but he gave a hard tug and then pulled her along until they reached the south corner of the inner court and the room Sutter had let them have for the night. It was next to the candlemaker's workroom and the smell of beeswax was heavy and cloying. Abram opened the big door and swung her in.

The room was small and filled with the stench of a brimming earthen chamber pot, which Abram picked up and set outside the door. Next he got rid of the filthy, rumpled blanket that had been left on the leather-slatted bed in the far corner. He lit the lantern and closed the door before saying anything.

"All right, you tell me exactly what you think I want of you," he commanded.

Her lip curled again. "Ye want to mount me like that stupid squaw ye had down by the river."

His mouth fell open, and his face went white, then bright, berry red. "How did you know about that?"

"I watched ye. What I canna understand is why the fool didn't slit yer throat or remove yer family jewels!"

"The way you'd have done had it been you."

"From the crotch up!"

Nye was right. Tempest McClaren had the tongue of a poxed sailor, and Abram knew he had better watch himself. He rubbed the back of his red-hot neck. "I paid her what she wanted, and she enjoyed herself." He felt hot to his very bone marrow. How many others had witnessed his lust?

"Enjoyed it? She screamed bloody hell!"

She looked at him as if he were some repulsive slug she'd found under a rock. He combed agitated fingers through his thick, wavy hair and rubbed his neck again.

When he'd made love to Kathy, she had moaned softly and gasped when she reached her crisis. Never once had she cried out. But that squaw! When she'd screamed and begun the hard, uncontrollable jerking, he'd gone off like a cannon, more from shock than anything else. Now this girl he wanted to make his wife was looking at him as though he'd beaten the easy woman. What in Hades was he supposed to say? Lord, why had he ever taken that woman down by the river anyway?

"Some women come off louder than others," he managed to say. Obviously that explanation wasn't enough, for Tempest gave a snort of derision.

"And ye thought my da was mad," she spat.

Abram squared his shoulders stoically. Surely she'd seen animals mating before; it was seldom silent or gentle. Maybe she just didn't understand that it was almost the same with people. "It's what a man and a woman do to make babies."

A malicious gleam lit her eyes. "Da called it rutting season in the wild. I've seen animals stuck together before."

She was baiting him, fully aware of his discomfort. He looked at her squarely, taking up the challenge. "It's what you and I'll be doing when it comes time to start our family."

Tempest's face went still and pale, the blue eyes widening. She was silent for a frozen moment. "If ye want bairns, mon, go buy the squaw. She'll come cheaper than five dollars in gold," she told him straight and slow.

"I don't want children from her," he said frankly.

She blanched. "Well, ye wilna get them from me!"

"In time."

Her hands clenched and unclenched as she watched him closely. He wondered if she thought he intended to jump her right now. "I gave my word about not hurting you," he assured her. It seemed to do no good. He sighed. "I've a few things to take care of. You can stay here." He waited, but she said nothing. Turning away, he opened the door and went out.

Tempest leaped toward it, but the handle lifted easily. He hadn't locked her in. She could get out. She relaxed against the door.

Damn you, Da...

Shoulders bent, she paced the room. She paused at the door again and balled her hands into hard fists, fighting back the tears that swelled hot and heavy in her chest.

"Damn ye, McClaren, ye bloody bastard..."

The door opened and she jumped back as Abram entered, loaded down with saddle, bridle, blankets, and pack in the corner and unslung the rifle to lean it against the wall. She wondered if it was loaded. He glanced at her, his mouth curving slightly.

"It's not."

Her eyes rounded. Could he read her thoughts?

"You'll get used to me, Tempest."

"And if I dunna?" she challenged, her heart racing. "Will ye sell me fast and cheap like my own da did, mon?"

He flinched inwardly, hearing more than the words. He studied the bleak, hard face that looked almost old. He put his hand out and approached her slowly. "Give me your hands, Tempest."

She backed away from him until she came up against the back wall. Abram stood squarely in front of her, big and powerful, but gentle-eyed. She swallowed hard. He reached toward her. She closed her eyes and drew in her breath sharply.

Her hands were icy in his. He felt the dampness in her palms. All that spirit and bravado, and he could feel her shaking violently.

"You're never going to be one of those miserable wretches out there, Tempest. No matter what you do, or say, or won't do, I swear that. I'm never going to sell you, or give you away. If you ever leave me, I'll follow until I find you. I'm never going to beat you. I'm never going to take anything from you or expect anything you can't give freely."

The tension slowly melted from her face. She opened her eyes and studied him, confused and clearly bewildered by his words.

God, help me find the words to make her understand, Abram prayed desperately.

"Something more," he murmured. "I vow before God Almighty that I'm going to keep you with me *always,* as my wife, not my concubine... in sickness and in health, for better or worse, for as long as we both shall live. I'm going to take care of you and protect you. I'm going to honor and love you, Tempest McClaren Walker. I swear."

His thumbs stroked the backs of her dirty, cold hands. He gave her a faint, apologetic smile. "There should be a man of God here saying the words first for us to repeat. But the nearest Methodist minister is at least a thousand miles away, so I'll have to do. Every word is as binding as any repeated in a church back East. God is my witness. He can strike me dead if I ever break a word of my vows."

Abram held her hands a moment longer and then raised them, kissing each one softly before allowing them to slide free.

Tempest studied him with a deep frown. He spoke so strangely. He was unlike anyone she had ever known. His hands and body were very strong—but was his mind weak?

Her eyes narrowed in speculation. That was something she would need to find out.

There is nothing more difficult to take in hand,
more perilous to conduct, or more uncertain in
its success, than to take the lead in the
introduction of a new order of things.
—Niccolo Machiavelli

Abram and Tempest left New Helvetia at dawn for
Fairfield Farm. Abram, being no fool, put a lead on Tempest's
horse and tied it securely to his own. He'd brought another
horse on which he loaded the supplies he'd procured. Beans,
dried beef, two woven Indian blankets, boxes of candles, seed
corn, and coffee beans had set him back plenty. On his next
trip to the fort, Abram hoped to barter fresh produce for a milk
cow and some chickens.

As they rode northwest, Tempest was silent, her face grim.
The face of an Indian, Abram thought to himself, glancing
back at her. He didn't try to make conversation, knowing he
would meet with frustration. She was bound to punish him and
silence was a powerful weapon in a lonely land with a lonely
man. Glancing back again, he wondered. Her blue eyes seemed
so distant, turned inward. He turned away.

A wry smile curved his mouth as he thought of their wedding
night just past. Ten years before, with Kathy, he'd found a
woman warm and willing, though very nervous. He'd been as
nervous as his bride, afraid she'd guess that he had almost as
little experience as she. Two rolls with the town whore hardly
qualified him as an adept lover. He had been so worried that
his clumsiness would alarm her or, worse, repulse her. Yet
everything had gone well. After the first time, they had relaxed
and learned what pleased each other. For Kathy, it had been
a gentle kneading of her breasts.

Now there was Tempest.

Abram hadn't expected to bed her or even touch her that
first night, but he had hoped they would at least talk. She'd

been silent after his vows to her—silent and watchful.

Sutter had provided their supper as promised, but it had been delivered by the squaw Abram had lain with by the river— a cruel joke. He had wanted to crawl into the earthen floor when Tempest looked at the woman, and then at him, with grave consideration. No word passed the squaw's lips, but she had looked boldly at Abram while pointedly ignoring Tempest. He showed her the door.

While he bowed his head to say the blessing, Tempest plunged in, stuffing pieces of hot venison into her mouth with her hands, chewing with her mouth open. She lifted her bowl and slurped down the remaining juices, then wiped her mouth with the back of her smelly buckskin sleeve. Her knife, fork, and spoon lay unnoticed on the table. She was finished before he had raised his head or lifted his fork.

"What're ye staring at?" Her eyes glinted, and her mouth curled into a challenging sneer.

He shook his head ruefully. "I'm going to have to teach you how to eat like a civilized human being, instead of an animal."

Her hand went to her knife, turning it over and over. Abram looked straight at her, one brow raised, and slowly her hand moved away. She stood up and went to the corner, snatching up the blanket they'd shared the night before. Wrapping herself in it, she sat in the corner with her back to the wall and glared at him venomously while he ate his meal alone.

"Am I allowed to go without ye watching, mon?" she asked contemptuously.

Embarrassed, though trying not to show it, Abram nodded and left the room. He stood in the courtyard for several minutes, his hands shoved deeply into his pockets. Michael Nye approached, a taunting smile curving his lips. Abram looked at him coldly and Nye's smile died. Turning away, Abram returned to the room to find Tempest curled in the blanket and sitting in the corner again. The chamber pot sat on the bed and she wore a cold, daring smile. He put the pot outside the door and went for a long walk.

When he came back, she was still crouched in the corner. She had stared at him in silence until her eyes closed against her will, and Abram had spent the night six feet from her, studying her while she slept. No amount of willpower had brought sleep to him.

Now, shifting in his saddle again, Abram glanced back.

She'd been watching him, for her head jerked away. He smiled slightly.

"It'll take two days to reach my land. It's up northwest."

Tempest said nothing. She looked back at the distant mountains.

Abram sighed to himself. Just let her be, he thought. She must still be wanting her father.

As he turned away, Tempest's gaze was drawn back to him again. She watched the way his body moved with the horse. He had a very broad back with muscles far more developed than Da's. When he leaned forward to give his horse a slap, the muscles rippled beneath the thin homespun cotton shirt. One blow and this man could kill her.

He took his hat off and wiped sweat from his forehead with his sleeve. Tempest studied the thick, wavy, chestnut hair that grew past his collar. It was like the healthy coat of a fox, not at all like the black, matted hair of her da. It would be soft, too. Abram Walker smelled different as well. Riding behind him yesterday, she had inhaled his scent, a mixture of earth, sweat, sun, and something else, something indefinable. She had liked it.

Nor was he stupid—unfortunately. She could untie her horse from the lead, but it would take time and he would see. If she wanted to get away, she would have to kill him. She had killed animals, but never a man. She wondered if she could.

They stopped alongside a creek and shared dried beef, dried fruit, and part of a loaf of hard-crusted bread. When Abram spoke to her, she ignored him. Finally he gave up. Leaning back against a fallen log, he watched the sun go down and seemed utterly content.

The old fears rose in Tempest as the sky darkened, and without her da, she stood alone against them. Abram's presence was a physical threat, rather than a comfort. She saw the surreptitious look he cast her way and remembered again the scene with the squaw by the river. He was a big man, too big.

"Are you cold?" Abram asked, seeing how she shivered, even close to the fire.

Their eyes met and held. He stood slowly and came around the fire. Leaning down, he picked up one of the blankets and held it out to her. She clutched it and pulled it around her upraised knees, watching him warily. He reached toward her and she stiffened, but he only rested his hand lightly on her head.

"Sleep, Tempest. We've another long day ahead of us tomorrow."

She relaxed as he went back to his side of the fire and stretched out. Leaning back against the log, his hands behind his head, he smiled easily at her. In a few moments, his hands slipped down to rest in his lap and he slept.

Tempest studied him in the flickering firelight. His hair fell forward over a broad, deeply tanned brow. He had a long, straight nose and a firm mouth. His jaw was square and firm, but there were creases in his cheeks that deepened when he smiled. His teeth were good, she remembered, not straight, but strong and white. Grudgingly, she liked his smile. His neck was thick, his arms powerful. She remembered how easily he had pulled her from her father and held her back; he hadn't even been breathing hard, while she had fought with all her strength. And he had known how to protect himself. This man of the earth was no simple fool like most of the others.

Walker's chest rose and fell in the slow, rhythmic breathing of sleep. His rifle lay close by, within easy reach of his right hand. His knife was sheathed and looped to his wide leather belt.

Tempest chewed on her lower lip. She could sneak up on a buck in the forest and put a knife deep into its jugular without the animal even hearing or scenting her. But could she move around this fire now and lay Abram Walker's throat open with his own knife?

The mountains were dark shadows in the distance. How many nights lay between her and Da? If he didn't want to be found, he wouldn't be. They had hidden before, for months at a time. He knew every Indian trick, and some of his own, to lose himself in the wilderness. And if she did manage to find him, what would he do to her for breaking his word to Walker?

She shuddered.

Alone, out there in the vast land, with only a fire to ward off the darkness and all the other things, she would go mad, madder than her father had ever been.

Da, why did ye do this to me? Her throat closed tightly. She tried to breathe slowly to ease the hard, swelling pain, but it didn't help.

Ye ken I could never get away once ye were gone, didna ye? Ye goddamned bloody bastard!

Her eyes burned, filled, and spilled over.

I need you! Where are you?

She rested her forehead against her knees, feeling the heat of the fire on her shins and forearms. On her back was the chill of darkness, and it grew.

She raised her head again and looked at Abram Walker. At least she was not completely alone this time.

The sun rose orange-pink above the eastern range of hills. Tempest was awake long before Abram. She rebuilt the fire, then saddled her horse and loaded the supplies back on the packhorse. Abram awakened and stood, alarmed when he saw her moving about near the horses. She came back and sat by the fire again. He stretched high then, fingers spreading, as Tempest watched. He smiled. This morning he said nothing, but set about making the tasteless gruel breakfast and strong coffee he had before. He handed her a plate. With a disgusted look, she ate it, scooping it up with three fingers.

Abram took a small round object from his saddlebag and went to wash in the creek. He rolled the object in his hands after wetting them, and Tempest watched him rub the froth on his face and then scrape it away. She'd seen other men shave at the fort and always wondered at the sense of it. The hair just grew back by the next morning. It was a great waste of time.

Rubbing his chin, Abram Walker grinned at her. "Much better."

The sun was warm on their backs as they rode on again silently. The land spoke to them from all around. Insects whirred from the tall grasses. The wind whispered. The horses' hooves drummed against the earth. There was no such thing as silence anywhere—for silence itself rang sweet. They stopped to eat again, then rode on.

"There it is. Fairfield Farm."

Against her will, Tempest's eyes lifted in curiosity. She squinted against the late afternoon sun and saw the dwelling place in the distance. Her heart began to pound heavily.

It was a cabin just like the other! Tempest's mind whirled with pain. Once again she saw flames, smelled acrid smoke, and heard the warbling war cries mingling with her mother's scream; she heard the hiss of an arrow and the horrid thud of impact.

"Tempest?"

She drew in a sharp breath and blinked.

"What is it?" Abram brought his horse close. "Tell me."

Tempest didn't answer. She pressed her knees against the horse's sides, but Abram kept pace with her. She could feel him watching her and her muscles tightened. Was he searching for her weaknesses? Her face became still and expressionless.

"What were you thinking about a moment ago?"

Silence.

"I'd like to know, Tempest," he encouraged.

She shot him a contemptuous look. "It's enough that ye own me, mon!"

A muscle moved in his cheek. "I don't own you."

She raised one brow. Her Scottish burr thickened and grew coarse. "Five dollars in gold and a bottle of whiskey—that says ye do."

"If I bought anything, it was your freedom."

Her lip curled back. "Ye bought yerself an Indian slave."

"No slave—a wife, my wife, part of me. If you're a slave, then I am, too." His mouth tightened ominously. "Forget the gold and whiskey."

"Goods have been exchanged." Her face had more hauteur than any aristocrat.

Abram's face darkened. "Your own father set the price, my girl!"

Her fixed expression slipped and then set again. Head high, Tempest rode on.

Abram cursed himself.

As they came closer to the cabin, Abram spoke again, more calmly. "It's not much, by Pennsylvania standards, but it's plenty comfortable. I'll need to build a barn before fall and, more important, a smokehouse. There's no glass in the windows, of course. It's too dear and has to come all the way around the Horn. We need other things more, like a wood stove. I constructed an *horno* over there." He pointed east of the cabin. "Sutter gave me the plans he learned from the Californios. We've got a Dutch oven. We can wait a few years for a stove."

Tempest stared at the small, neat, log and sod cabin with the flat roof. It was closed and dark. Her heart shrank, squeezing tighter and tighter until it felt like a stone in her chest.

Abram dismounted, his eyes sparkling as he talked of his home. Tempest remained on horseback, unmoving.

"I'm digging a well, but we've got more than enough water for now from our stream. It's only a quarter mile away, and there's a natural spring not far from here. I'd have built the cabin closer to that, but it's a low area and I didn't want to risk flooding. We're on high ground here."

Tempest slid slowly from her horse. She stood gazing at her new home with sick dread.

"Most of Kathy's things had to be dumped along the trail," Abram went on, opening the thick, oak-plank door and standing aside in a gentlemanly manner that was lost on Tempest. "Come on. Take a look."

Still, Tempest hung back. Abram went in without her, and after a moment curiosity made her follow. Abram moved to open the shutters and let air and light pour in. Dust particles swirled madly in the sunny glow; the place smelled strongly of cold earth, cut pine, and old smoke.

Her fear dissolved as Tempest caught sight of an enormous bed the like of which she had never seen. It was very wide and long and was covered by a colorful, patterned blanket. It was a wondrous thing!

"The bed is made out of the bottom of my Conestoga," Abram said, seeing her wide-eyed stare. "It's good and solid." He leaned down, pressing his hand into the moss-filled mattress. "It'll last us years."

Tempest approached, more interested in the blanket. Was it like her mother's that had burned? She had not thought white people were interested in their family history the way Indians were. Her father had never once spoken of his.

"It's a wedding quilt," Abram explained. "When Kathy and I announced our betrothal, all her friends got together and made this. Each square was sewn by a different woman and shows some experience shared with Kathy or me or some wish for our marriage."

Tempest bent and touched one of the brightly colored pictures and glanced at him in question.

"A barn raising. This one is a harvest festival. That one is a horse sale."

She touched yet another square. It showed two white bells intertwined by embroidered flowers and strange writing.

"June 7, 1836 . . . the day Kathy and I were married," Abram said huskily. Tempest looked up at him again. His face was pale, his eyes dull and seeing only the pretty patch. He bent and with one finger traced the writing slowly, then drew his hand away. He abruptly pointed to another scene. "That was our church with its high steeple and bell. This one is the apple tree behind my house where Kathy used to swing as a child."

Tempest's attention was distracted from the wedding quilt
as she watched Abram's expressions change. Each square
brought a different look: laughter, wistfulness, sadness. It had
great power.

Abram straightened and looked at her. "Anyway . . . look
around." He made a generous gesture.

This cabin was not so much like the other as she had first
thought. Here there were no hides and pelts, no traps and gear
hung about. There was only the great bed with its marvelous
quilt, a plank table, two hand-hewn chairs, a cupboard, and a
tall box with many brass handles.

"That's Kathy's highboy. Her folks gave it to us. We had
to dump everything else coming over the mountains, but she
insisted on keeping that. We left a brass bedstead, marble-
topped commodes, the harpsichord . . ." He shook his head and
sighed heavily, gazing at the highboy. He hadn't the heart to
discard it after Kathy had died.

Standing next to it, he ran his hand along the polished wood
surface just as Kathy had done so many times. Then he looked
at Tempest. "It's yours now, and everything that's in it."

"Mine?" She frowned distrustfully.

Abram pulled open the top drawer and took out a small
cardboard box. Opening it, he took out a round yellow object.

"Do you know what this is?"

She came forward and took it. It was smooth and hard.
Tempest sniffed at it and her eyes widened at the flowery scent,
in her experience previously limited to meadows in spring. She
licked it.

"No! Don't try to eat it!"

She grimaced and thrust the object back at him. Abram
didn't accept it, but ran his finger around the inside of his
collar. "It's soap. You use it to wash your hair and body."

She eyed him coldly. "Ye must have bees with a fine liking
to ye, mon, if ye make yerself smell like a flower field."

He smiled easily. "I use the plain stuff myself. This is for
ladies. I'd rather you smelled of lavender than of polecat."

Tempest's face reddened as her finger whitened around the
ball of scented soap. "Take yer soap and shove it up yer ass.
I wilna bathe!"

Abram's face registered none of his shocked feelings. He
drew in a slow, calming breath. "There's wood in the box over
there. Will you build a fire?"

"If it pleases me."

"And?"

She met his eyes. "It pleases," she said uneasily.

"Good. The flints are on the mantel. I'll be back in a few minutes."

Abram took up the two buckets outside the door and headed for the creek. He wondered how he was going to manage to get her clean without using brute force.

Dipping the buckets into the deep pool, he remembered how fastidious Kathy had been. She had always washed her face and hands morning and night, and she'd bathed twice a week. Back home she'd always kept a barrel outside to catch rainwater for washing her hair.

When Abram returned to the cabin, the fire was going strong. Tempest sat cross-legged beside the bed, fingering the stitchery on the quilt. She glanced up at him and stood quickly, putting her hands behind her back. Her eyes narrowed on the two sloshing buckets he carried. He emptied one into the big iron pot that hung on a hook over the fire.

"The water'll be warm enough in a few minutes." He took a large washpan down from a hook on the wall and set it on the table. "We'll start with your hair."

"Yer ears made of stone? I said I dunna bathe!"

"That's obvious, but you're going to start. *Now.*"

Tempest dropped into a crouch and spread her hands. Her eyes glowed darkly. "Try it and I'll slit ye from one side of yer neck to the other."

"Using what? Your fingernail?"

She blinked. Da had her knife.

Abram took a step toward her. She jumped back. He stood facing her, arms akimbo. "This'll be a lot easier on both of us if you cooperate."

"Go to hell!"

Using a cloth to protect his hands, Abram removed the steaming pot and poured water into the pan, then set the pot back on the iron hook. He took a ladle from a hook and laid in on the table. Then he pulled the chair out and turned it around. "Sit down."

Tempest didn't move. She was breathing hard. She wouldn't be able to make it to the door before he got her, and she knew he was too strong for her to fight successfully.

He grinned tauntingly. "I never thought McClaren's daughter would be afraid of a little soap and water."

Her chin jerked up, her eyes flaring. "I'm not afraid!"

"No? Sure looks like it to me. If you're not, come on over and sit down. I'll wash your hair for you. Next time, you'll be able to manage it."

She approached the chair grimly, her heart pounding in hard jolts. She sat on the very edge of the chair and Abram put a gentle but firm hand on her shoulder, feeling her tense.

"Relax. You're going to like it."

She gave him a bleak, mirthless smile. Her hands clenched and unclenched.

Abram untied the leather thongs wrapped around the ends of her braids and tossed them into the fire. Then he carefully unbraided her thick hair and let it hang like six black snakes down her rigid back. Each tress kinked tightly after the endless months in braids, and her hair smelled heavily of dirt and smoke.

Tempest stared straight ahead, her hands gripping her thighs.

"Relax and lean back," Abram instructed, urging her back with gentle hands on her shoulders. "Lean back." Finally she did, one shaking hand coming up to protect her throat. She stared up at him closely and flinched as he poured a ladleful of water over her hair.

"Oily as duck feathers," he murmured, smiling down at her. Her face was so taut, so grim, filled with distrust and resentment. Her pulse beat visibly in the hollow beneath her jaw. He trickled more warm water over her hair and gently stroked her scalp.

Taking the bar of soap, he rolled it in his hands and then began to massage the lather into her hair. Tempest gritted her teeth, her eyes darting up and trying to see what he was doing.

"Smells good, doesn't it?" he grinned. "Like spring flowers. My mother loved lilacs. This reminds me a little of her." He went on massaging and talking softly. Slowly she began to relax.

It did feel good. Lulled, she closed her eyes and sighed. He poured a little more water on and worked more of the heady scent into her soaked hair. His fingers were hard, yet not hurting.

"You like it?"

She wasn't going to admit it.

"Now, we rinse." He poured ladle after ladle of clean, warm water over the thick black cloud of hair. When he finally was satisfied that all the soap was out, he put his calloused hand behind her neck and helped her to straighten up. Then he dropped a cloth over her head. She jumped and yanked it off.

He grinned. "Rub it dry."

She eyed him angrily as she obeyed.

"Well? Was that so bad?" he taunted gently.

Tempest sat stiff-lipped, her hair in wild, tangled disarray around her small face and down her back. She shrugged insolently.

Abram laughed softly and lifted a handful of black hair. "Smell it." He put it in front of her nose. Her brows lifted. He rubbed the hair between his fingers; it was soft and silky, not at all coarse as he had expected an Indian's hair to be.

"A woman's crowning glory," he murmured.

Tempest drew her head back, pulling her hair from his grasp. He let the strands slip free with a light tug and then tucked his thumbs into his belt.

"You'll smell that good all over once you've had your bath." He could see defiance pouring hotly from her sparkling blue eyes.

"What's the purpose?" Her mouth was tight with mutiny.

"To be healthy, you have to be clean."

"Bullshit! I've never been sick a day in my life!"

Abram let his breath out slowly. "Then you've been lucky." He picked up the pan and tossed the dirty water out the door, then poured half of the water in the second bucket into the steaming pot. He set the large pan on the floor between the fire and the bed.

"You'll stand in the pan after you've taken off all your clothes. Get wet all over first and then lather yourself. All over. *Everywhere*. Once you've done that, rinse with this." He pointed to the bucket still half-full of cold water. "Understand?"

Her eyes were round. "Ye expect me to take off all my clothes?"

"That's the usual way you bathe."

"I wash once in spring—with everything on."

"You'll wash once a week with everything off." He raised an eyebrow. "And your clothes will be washed separately. Now, do you want to take them off by yourself, or shall I help you?"

She tried diversion. "Ye don't wash buckskin separate, mon. It shrinks."

"Won't matter." He was going to burn hers as soon as he got his hands on them.

"I wilna take off anything!"

"Oh, yes, you will." He looked at her squarely. Several moments passed.

"Not while you watch," she amended slowly.

"Fair enough. I'll wait outside." He saw a faint, sly smile light her eyes. "Believe me, Tempest, I'll *know* if you've bathed or not. Furthermore, I want your clothes tossed out in one minute. If they aren't, I'm coming back in for them."

The smile vanished, replaced by a cold, hard glare. "What about you, ye bastard? Do ye wash yer body?" she sneered.

"Every Saturday."

She snorted. Her eyes narrowed. "What do I wear when I'm finished if ye've got my clothes?"

Abram crossed the room, opened a trunk, and pulled out another quilt. This one had interlocking white circles against a pale yellow background. He dropped it on the table. "Wrap this around you."

Her chin tipped, her blue eyes burning, she watched him pause in the doorway. "One minute, then I come in and take your clothes off your back for you." He hoped she believed him. He left the door slightly ajar.

Tempest kicked it shut. She swore for a full half a minute before yanking off her buckskins and heaving them out the window at him.

Her arms wrapped around her body, she stared angrily at the wash pan. She hadn't been naked since her mother and she had bathed in the mountain stream. She felt vulnerable and unprotected. Keeping an eye on the door, she poured water into the pan until it was ankle-deep, then stepped in. Squatting, she splashed water hastily over her shoulders, chest, and legs. The warmth slid over her belly and back and down between her legs.

Lathering her hands as Walker had done, she began to wash quickly. Everywhere, he had said. *"I'll know if you haven't . . ."* Did he plan to sniff at her like a bloody dog? She swore again, under her breath.

The rich scent of lavender filled her nostrils. She grudgingly admitted that this was a ritual she might come to enjoy. She liked the feel of the slick soap on her body and rubbed it over her shoulders, arms, hips, and legs. Exploring further, she touched her small, firm breasts, her flat stomach. Her body was coated in white suds and lavender scent. Tempest closed her eyes and inhaled the marvelous magic of the small ball in her hand.

Everywhere.

She tucked her hands between her legs and quickly washed there as well. Then she squatted and splashed.

The water was sudsy and brown. After checking carefully to make sure Abram was not in sight, she cast it out the door and poured in a little more. Rolling the soap ball, she filled her hands with frothing white to wash her face. She had almost forgotten, and he'd notice that first.

Abram was in the animal shelter currying his horse when he heard Tempest screaming. Dropping the brush, he ran toward the cabin. When he threw open the door, he saw her bent over, clawing at her eyes, her hands covered with soap.

"Fool!" he shot out angrily. He should have warned her; why hadn't he thought of it? "Take your hands away from your face!" He grabbed up the bucket. Tempest howled in agony. Catching her arm, he swung her around and shoved her down into the chair. *"Keep your hands away from your eyes!"*

She clawed at them wildly, gasping between sobs. Abram caught her by the hair and forced her head down into the water bucket. She bucked and twisted, bubbles rising from under the water. He held on, his fingers deep in the black mass, the muscles of his arm standing out. He drew her head up. She gasped in air and screamed. One soapy hand left the bucket rim to go for his eyes as she twisted. He jerked back and she left stripes of red along one side of his neck. He gritted his teeth and yanked her around again, catching the offending hand and pulling it up behind her back for better leverage as he dunked her several more times. Then he grabbed her soapy hands and shoved them into the bucket to rinse them, dodging as she went for his arm with her teeth. He elbowed her back. Finally he let her go.

She sprang up, her legs spread and planted, her chin jutting out, and screamed profanity at him. Abram had never heard anyone so eloquent in the art. Some of it was unfamiliar to him and he guessed she'd learned Scottish curses and Indian ones as well. She was laying hell and worse on his head; she cursed everything from his wit to the size of his manhood, which she had not even seen yet.

He might have laughed had he not been so stunned. The words washed over him almost unheard as he stared transfixed at the young body glistening with water, the soft brown skin, the dark, erect nipples on small, perfect breasts, the tiny waist he could easily span with his hands, the slim hips, the long, shapely legs and slender feet. His eyes slid over her again, stopping once at the soft-lipped joining between her legs and the first wisps of woman's hair. He lost his breath.

"My God..."

Her black hair surrounded Tempest's face and flowed down her back like a heavy cloud, moving with each jerk of her head as though it had a life all its own. She railed at him like some sexually charged primeval woman.

And Abram's body responded just as primitively. The swelling and throbbing grew in his loins. He drew in a sharp breath, clenching his hands.

Tempest froze. She saw only the huge, white-knuckled fists and not the look in his eyes. Her heart stopped and then began again, thundering in her ears.

Abram grabbed the blanket from the table and flung it at her. "Put the thing around you!"

Round-eyed, she obeyed, clutching it tightly. His fist hadn't come at her yet, but there was a look in his hazel eyes that stilled her vile, flapping tongue.

For a long moment, they stared at one another. Abram, fully aroused, fought for control. Tempest sensed great danger, but not the sort that threatened her life.

Finally Abram swallowed hard and gave a shuddering sigh. He raked a trembling hand through his hair. "Next time," he said hoarsely, "don't get the soap in your eyes."

His words were wasted. "There'll be no problem because there wilna be a next time. I'll not touch the stuff again," Tempest spat. Her sight was still fuzzy.

Abram's mouth thinned to a narrow line. "You'll take a bath once a week just like I do. Only next time, you'll have enough common sense not to get the soap in your eyes!"

Tempest studied him and said nothing more.

Abram crossed to the highboy, yanked open the drawer, and pulled some things out. Laying them on the wedding quilt, he turned back to Tempest.

"These are for you. They'll be too big, but they'll do. My wife was heavier than you, but they're better than those buckskin rags."

Tempest stared, amazed. What were these strange things? Thin, white pantaloons with ribbons at the waist and lace around the ankles; a white skirt; a blue-flowered skirt; a little white sleeveless shirt with more ribbons and lace; and another long-sleeved white shirt. How many layers of clothing did white women need? She picked up a peculiar-looking thing with bones in it and stared at it curiously, wondering what it was.

"A corset," Abram said, and took it from her. He stuffed it back into the drawer. "You don't need it." His face was redder than the breast of a robin. Puzzled, she watched him run a forefinger around inside his collar.

"The pantaloons, camisole, and petticoat first, Tempest," he said, pointing them out. "Then the shirtwaist and skirt." He frowned and turned to the highboy again, pulling out more items. "Then stockings." He looked at the wide, worn leather shoes he held and then at Tempest's small, narrow bare feet. "I'll get your moccasins and clean them up for you."

He left in a rush, leaving the door open. Tempest shook her head slightly as she gazed after him. Then she dropped the quilt and bent to the clothes.

Abram turned back for another look and got a full view of her firm, brown buttocks. He gulped and stared like a poleaxed bull. She bent forward and the last bit of air jolted from his lungs.

Think about the plowing you'll do tomorrow. Think about feeding the oxen in the morning. Think about anything but what it'd be like to meld with that warm, moist flesh.

But telling himself did little good.

The pantaloons hung loosely on her hips, and she was fumbling in confusion with the buttons on the camisole. Resigned, Abram came back. He turned her to face him, brushed her hands away, and worked the buttons into their holes, burningly aware of the budded nipples so close to his fingertips. What would she do if he brushed them?

Probably claw my eyes out!

Tiny beads of moisture broke out on his forehead and along his upper lip as he stood so close to her, trying not to think about possessing her.

"What be wrong with ye, mon?"

Abram met her curious, indignant stare and blushed. He could almost feel steam hissing up from his damp shirt collar.

Sweat usually meant fear, but Tempest saw none in Walker's eyes. What she saw caused a quiver of uncertainty to run over her. Her muscles tensed. Why were his hands shaking so much? She glanced down and watched him fumble with the last two buttons. He took his hands away quickly and let out a sharp breath.

"These should be tighter," he said huskily, and pulled the

ribbons snugger at her waist, bringing the pantaloons up higher. Next he tossed the petticoat over her head and let the billows settle before securing it at her waist also. He held the shirtwaist while she shrugged into it and last of all threw the skirt over her head and buttoned and tied it at the back. The more she wore, the less nervous he seemed, but the more uncomfortable she became.

"I'm hot!"

"You'll get used to wearing these clothes. You look very nice."

"Trussed like a bloody turkey."

"Except your hair," he continued, ignoring her comment. "You'll have to brush the tangles out and do something with it." He opened another drawer and took out a boar-bristle brush, handing it to her. He used to brush Kathy's hair for her sometimes, but right now he had better get himself out of this cabin and cool off.

"I'm going to see to the stock. See what you can find to fix us for supper."

"Ye mean ye eat something besides dried beef and beans and that crap ye call—"

"See what you can find," he said, and left.

Consider your origin; you were not born to live
like brutes, but to follow virtue and knowledge.
—Dante
The Divine Comedy

Abram returned some time later and found Tempest
sitting cross-legged before the fire, working snarls from her
hair with her fingers. The brush was on the bed, along with
the petticoat and stockings. She kept her back to him.

Whatever she was simmering in the iron pot smelled good.
Abram peered in; it looked ready. He opened the cupboard and
took out two chipped china dishes, napkins, and pewterware.
Tempest turned slightly to watch him.

"Come and sit down," he invited.

She came and sat while he removed the iron pot full of
stewed dried beef from the fire and poured the steaming contents into a serving bowl. He set the empty pot on the hearth
and sat down.

"Bow your head and fold your hands for the blessing."

She looked at him as though he'd lost his mind. He showed
her how to weave her fingers together, then bowed his head.
"Lord, for what we are about to receive, may we be truly
thankful. Amen."

As he raised his head, he saw Tempest already chewing on
a piece of salted meat and starting to reach into the bowl for
another. With a swift motion, he caught her wrist.

"Hold it right there! We've a few things to get straight about
what's proper and what isn't."

She tried to yank free, but failed.

"You'll wait for me to finish the blessing, and you'll eat
with a fork." He lifted his own and wagged it in front of her.
"This is a fork."

Her mouth was a mutinous line. "I'll eat as I bloody well
like!"

"You'll eat with a fork or you won't eat at all." He let her

61

go. "Now, sit back and I'll serve you like a lady."

Abram spooned chunks of meat and gravy onto her plate and set it down before her. Her hands stayed flat on the table as he served himself. Then he took up the fork, speared a chunk of meat, and popped it into his mouth. He chewed and swallowed. "Simple," he said. "And no grease on my hands."

Tempest picked up a big chunk of meat with her fingers, popped it into her mouth, and chewed loudly, her cheeks ballooning out. She swallowed and then licked her fingers. "Simple. And no grease on my hands."

Abram remained calm. "It's polite to use a knife, fork, and spoon."

"Horse dung. Who gives a bloody damn?"

Her language made him cringe inwardly, but he didn't let her see. She was profane enough without encouragement. "I care. Now, pick up your fork."

Tempest looked at him with narrowed eyes, assessing him. He hadn't hit her yet in spite of much provocation. Da would have knocked her flat long ago. Maybe Walker didn't have the guts; there was one sure way to find out. She chewed hesitantly on the inside of her lower lip and then, holding her breath and watching him closely, she swept the fork from the table onto the floor.

"Suit yourself."

Abram reached across the table. Tempest pulled back sharply, but all he did was take her plate. He scraped her meal back into the serving bowl, and then went on eating his own. Her lips parted. She reached for her plate, but he pulled it out of her reach. She reached for the bowl and he moved it away. She drew in an angry breath.

"Give me some food!"

He went on eating without answering. She started to get up. His head snapped up, his hazel eyes hard. *"Sit down!"*

She sat. After a moment, he went back to eating.

"I want some food," she said through clenched teeth.

"You'll get some tomorrow morning if you agree to use your fork and spoon."

"I'm hungry now."

"Well, isn't that just too bad?" He scooped the last of the stew onto his own plate. "Maybe tomorrow you'll cooperate a little better." Smiling at her, he forked a large chunk of meat into his mouth and chewed, watching her angry, disbelieving face.

Tempest sat in grim silence, watching each bite he took until the last was gone. He soaked up the gravy with the stale bread left over from their journey from New Helvetia. When nothing remained, her shoulders slumped.

Abram leaned back in his chair and wiped his mouth with the napkin, then he tossed it on the table.

Stop feeling guilty. It's for her own good.

"I don't have many rules," he began softly, "but those I set you'll live by."

Tempest's stomach growled loudly in response. She glared at him and then looked down dismally at the empty serving bowl and plates. "How many rules ye got, mon?"

"When you eat, you use a knife, fork, and spoon. You don't lift your plate and drink from it, and you use a napkin to wipe your mouth and not your sleeve. You chew with your mouth closed."

"Anything else?" she spat.

"You wait for the blessing to be finished and you allow me to serve you. Last, the words 'please' and 'thank you' will be added to your very limited vocabulary of acceptable words."

Her lip curled. "It *pleases* me to eat as I like, and I'll *thank* ye to stuff yer orders up yer—"

"Try to eat as you like," he interrupted mildly, "and you'll go hungry." He stood up and stacked the plates. She didn't move from the table while he washed them in the water he'd brought in. She still hadn't moved when he put them away.

Moving his chair closer to the fire, Abram took down the big family Bible he'd carried across the continent. Kathy had always liked for him to read to her while she did her evening chores.

He glanced over at Tempest's stiff back as she remained at the table. Hate and anger poured from those blue eyes as she encompassed the room, and him, in one sweeping anathema. Nevertheless, Abram leaned back comfortably and opened the leather tome.

He began reading from the Book of Ruth. *"Now it came to pass in the days when the judges ruled, that there was a famine in the land. And a certain man of Bethlehem-Judah went to sojourn in the country of Moab."* It seemed the best of all places to begin.

Occasionally he glanced at Tempest as he read to see if she was listening to him at all. After a while, she relaxed and the hot, intense emotion dissolved from her face. He smiled to himself. She was listening, interested in spite of herself.

"Whither thou goest, I will go. Your God shall be my God . . ."

He read to the very end of Ruth and then closed the Bible slowly. He stood and placed it back on the mantel beneath the rifle mounted on the wall. "God's holy word," he told her, seeing her strange, bemused look.

"Whose God? Yers or mine?"

"I didn't know you had one," he said seriously. "Do you?"

She said nothing.

"There's only one God, yours *and* mine. He's called by different names, that's all. The Great Spirit or Jehovah, he's one and the same, Tempest. The Almighty One, the Creator of Life."

Tempest looked away, her face bland. Abram let the subject drop. He rolled his shoulders to loosen the tense muscles, then stretched his arms as he yawned broadly. He went to the highboy and took out a long, worn, pink flannel shirt and dropped it on the bed. "Your nightgown."

She looked from it to him. His eyebrows rose. "You put this on for bed."

"I'm wearing enough already."

"You take those off first and then put this on."

"Ye said these were mine!"

"I don't mean to take them away from you. You just take them off, fold them away, and put them on again tomorrow."

"Why?"

"Because you work in those and you sleep in this."

"Why?"

Abram sighed. "This is soft, loose, and more comfortable."

She eyed the nightgown, less than impressed. "I like what I'm wearing. I'd freeze in that."

His eyes crinkled at the corners in amusement. "You'll be plenty warm enough."

"Seems to me ye waste a lot of time getting in and out of clothes when ye could just leave them on in the first place."

"And wash them every spring in a creek?" One corner of his mouth lifted. "I'll be outside for a few minutes, so you'll have privacy."

"Privacy?"

"Being alone to get out of your clothes and into that."

"What if I dunna take these things off?" she challenged.

"That'll be your decision."

She smiled coldly, her eyes glinting.

He smiled back with deceptive gentleness. "Just like not using a fork to eat and not taking a bath."

"I want my buckskins!"

"They've been buried."

"What?!"

"Buried," he repeated, his thumbs hooked in his belt, meeting her glare squarely. "Now, what'll it be?"

Her stomach rumbled again, reminding her of one defeat already suffered. "I've always slept in buckskins," she tried one last time.

"When you were with McClaren. You're with me, now. You've got more than one change of clothes, and you'll use them."

There was no lessening of determination in his hazel eyes or the set of his jaw. Tempest was hungry and tired. She sighed.

Abram recognized her capitulation and left. When he came back after a long walk in the fields he would soon plow, he found her again sitting before the fire. She was wearing the nightgown.

"Why didn't you just get into bed?"

No response.

The silent treatment again, he thought wryly, and pulled his shirt free of his pants. She turned and watched as he unbuttoned the shirt and shrugged it off.

Kathy had never watched him undress, nor had he her. They had always turned away to allow for each other's modesty. Even when they had made love, they came together in the veil of protective darkness.

Yet here Tempest McClaren sat watching him boldly. Her gaze moved from his flushed face down over the fur of red hair covering his chest to where his hands rested on his belt buckle. She waited.

What would she do if he dropped his pants and let her see everything? What would she do if she saw a man fully aroused? For he was quickly getting there. Slowly Abram's fingers worked the buckle loose. But long years of ingrained modesty won out. "Turn around, Tempest."

She smiled slightly, but did. He sat on the edge of the bed and removed his boots and socks. Then, glancing back, he slipped his pants off. He stood and turned to push the quilts back, and she looked around at him. He slid beneath the covers and pulled them up to his waist, but his arousal had been clearly visible through the worn-thin long johns.

"The bed's meant for both of us."

"I'm no fool, mon."

He blushed like a virgin and cursed himself. He watched as she picked up the wedding-ring quilt and pulled it around herself like a snug cocoon.

"Come to bed with me, Tempest. I'm not going to force you to—"

"I dinna sleep with my da, and I wilna sleep with you."

"I'm not your da. I'm your husband."

She looked back at him again with narrowed, cold eyes. "Ye're nothing until I say ye are, mon, whatever ye'd like to think."

He studied her set face and then sighed. Lying back, he stared up at the beamed ceiling. Maybe she'd change her mind when the fire burned low and the night grew chill—but he doubted it. She'd spent too many years on the hard ground in the open to long for soft, dried moss and heavy down quilts.

Turning his head, he gazed at her. Maybe she was wiser than he. If she did come to bed with him, he'd be hard pressed to ignore the ache in his loins. It was hard enough to ignore now with her a room away.

She was watching him closely, her body tense as if she was ready to spring away.

He smiled gently. "Fair enough, Tempest. When you say." He saw the flicker of surprise in her face before he turned away.

Rome wasn't built in a day, and Tempest McClaren would not be had in three nights. Or four. Or even many more.

But Abram knew himself to be a patient man . . . or so he thought.

A soft answer turneth away wrath.
—Proverbs 15:1

Abram rose before dawn. The fire was low, the great oak log having burned down to red-gold and gray coals. Tempest was tightly wrapped in the quilt, only the top of her dark head showing.

He dressed quietly and then came across the room, hunkering down to gently fold back one corner of the quilt. He gazed at her. Her face was smooth, the long, black lashes scalloping her bronze cheeks. She shifted. A frown tightened her young features, and then she relaxed again. Her lips parted and showed the edge of her small, straight, white teeth. Carefully, so as not to awaken her, Abram brushed the loose, raven strands of soft hair back from her temples. Then he watched the slow pulse in her throat, the soft rise and fall of her chest. God, how he longed to lean down and softly kiss her awake.

Tempest's eyelids fluttered and opened. For a moment she gazed up at him with sleep-drugged eyes; then they cleared and widened. She gasped and drew sharply back.

Abram straightened.

Tempest looked up his entire, immense length looming over her. Her breath caught and her heart seemed to leap up to lodge itself in her throat.

Abram saw the darkness in her eyes and smiled in reassurance. "It's almost dawn. Time to get up." He moved away and heard the rustle of the quilt as she flung it off. When he glanced back, she was standing.

"The bed would've been more comfortable."

Her eyes narrowed. Her black hair kinked in a mass of riotous curls around her shoulders and down over her back. It framed her face, making the pale blue eyes all the more startling. He wanted to push his fingers into that mass of flowing hair, bury his face in it and his manhood in her.

"What're ye staring at?" she snarled.

"You," he admitted huskily. "You're beautiful."

"Quit looking at me like that!"

He smiled ruefully. "You'd better get used to it, Tempest. It's something that's never going to change."

Pouring beans into the coffee grinder, he began turning the crank and filling the cabin with the rich aroma. He set the grinder aside and took up the water bucket. "I'll fetch water while you get dressed."

Tempest pulled her clothes from the highboy and dressed as quickly as she could, but the buttons were difficult, for she was used to leather ties. She was still working on the shirtwaist when Abram returned. Her face reddened angrily and she swung away as she continued, baffling frustration. Finally she finished and turned back, watching him move restlessly about the cabin.

Her stomach growled loudly and he glanced at her, then gestured at the chair by the table. She sat, glaring up at him. He set a bowl of gruel and a pewter spoon before her and held out a napkin.

"That goes on your lap."

Her first impulse was to fling it on the floor, but she remembered the night before. She snatched the napkin from him and dropped it on her lap, still folded.

He sat down opposite her, folded his hands, and waited. She felt foolish, but imitated him. She watched him as he said the blessing. He glanced up when he finished and nodded toward her spoon. "Go ahead and eat now."

She took up the utensil in unaccustomed fingers and scooped up some mush. Closing her eyes in disgust, she chewed and swallowed.

Abram smiled slightly. "It's nourishing. If you don't like it, maybe tomorrow you could cook up something. Do you know how to use the *horno* outside? It's for baking bread, you know."

"I dunna bake bread."

"Don't speak with your mouth full."

"Then dunna be asking me stupid questions and expecting answers!" she flared. She looked down at her bowl again. "This is worse than the slop they feed the Indians at the fort!"

"Bread's easy enough to make. Flour, salt, yeast..." he continued, unperturbed. "I'll show you how before I go out to the plowing this morning. Don't look so grim. You're intelligent enough to learn."

She drew in her breath sharply.

Abram poured more coffee for them both. "How about the Dutch oven? You know anything about that?"

Her eyes glinted. She forced down another mouthful of mush before speaking. "I can cook over an open fire or in a pit. I can set traps and track and kill deer, bear, beaver, and otter. Smaller animals dunna count for much. I can skin and tan hides, but I *dunna make bread, and I dunna cook with a Dutch oven!*"

"You'll learn." He nodded. "I'm impressed by your other abilities, of course. I'm not much good at any of those things, so you can teach me. I'll teach you what it is to be a farmer's wife and we'll both be the richer for each other."

She stared at him, amazed. Then her eyes narrowed assessingly.

Abram met her gaze in silence. Hers fell away first and she went back to eating her gruel.

"Just a few things to start," Abram said, pushing his empty bowl aside. "Cleanliness is important. I won't bend on that, Tempest. When you work with food, you wash your hands with soap and water first. When we finish eating, you wash the dishes, pewterware, and pots with soap and water as well. There's a scrub brush over there for getting everything off. Do you understand?"

Her mouth twisted in a derisive smirk.

"Do you understand?" he repeated in a low, hard voice that brought a flicker of uncertainty to her eyes.

"Yes," she hissed.

"Good." He sipped his coffee. "The cabin floor should be dampened and swept every day, the fireplace cleaned of ashes and the fire relaid, the furniture rubbed down once a week with oil, and the chamber pot emptied in the outhouse every day." He paused. "When nature calls, Tempest, you go there to relieve yourself and not just outside our front door."

"The place stinks."

"Nevertheless—"

Her chin jerked up. "Ye canna tell me where to—"

"I can and I am," he said bitingly.

Her mouth tight, she glared at him.

He leaned back in his chair and watched her defiant face. "Can you remember everything I've told you to do?"

"Why dampen dirt?"

"So we won't eat, breathe, and sleep in it," he said reasonably.

"There's naught wrong with dirt, mon. Why're ye so afraid of it?"

"I make my living from it, but I won't have it coating my food or the inside of my bed." He'd eaten, breathed, and slept in dust for more than two thousand miles on his arduous journey to California. That had been more than enough.

Standing up, he pushed his hands into his pockets and rocked back on his heels. He nodded toward the corner. "There's the broom and bucket. You can dump the ashes out back, and I'll get around to working them into the soil. There's plenty of chopped wood piled by the corral. Try to keep the bin by the fireplace full." He let his words sink in and waited for her to respond. Her lips said nothing, but her eyes spat succinct profanity.

"I'll be plowing in the south field today. If you need me, you can find me there."

Hot silence, blue fire.

Abram sighed inwardly. "I'll be in at noon for dinner. Those sacks are beans," he indicated. "And there's still plenty of dried or salted meat in that tall cabinet."

Silence.

Abram looked squarely into her mutinous face. "Have you got everything straight or does it need repeating?"

After a moment, her chin tipped. "I heard."

He smiled. Leaning down, he placed his hands flat on the table. "Do you think you can remember everything?" he needled.

"Any fool could do what ye said."

"The question is, can you?"

Color filled her cheeks.

"Well, we'll see, won't we?" he said easily, and straightened.

"*If* I stay."

His body tensed and he felt his stomach turn over. For a long moment he said nothing, but just looked at her. "You can saddle your horse and leave while I'm working in the fields, yes. I can't spend every minute watching over you. But I don't think you will. Your own father won't take you back. He's gone. How many days and nights or weeks would it take you to find him even if he wanted to be found?" He had seen how she shook when dark fell, and knew by her wide, darkening eyes that he had hit on the truth. But he didn't want to make it a challenge and risk her taking up the dare.

"Here you're safe and warm and protected," he went on

more gently. "Here you're wanted. Here you'll be loved. But if you're stupid enough to run off, go ahead. However, in spite of your bad temper and foul manners, I'm hoping you'll decide to stay with me."

Tempest watched him leave. She went to lean in the open doorway as he walked to the animal shelter. A few minutes later he emerged leading an ox already harnessed to the plow. He didn't look at her. She turned away, frowning deeply.

The minor tasks Abram had given her were quickly accomplished. Still hungry, she munched on jerky while working. She sprinkled the floor with water she toted from the creek and swept it. She washed the dishes and pewterware and then sharpened the knives with a whetstone.

Tempest paused, glancing at the highboy and then out the door to where she could see Abram working in the distance, and, giving in to curiosity, dismissed her duties. She opened the top drawer and began to empty its contents onto the huge bed.

Each drawer revealed new treasures. There were three skirts—one dark brown, another black, and a third of dark, somber gray—half a dozen shirtwaists of cream colors and prints, camisoles, pantaloons, eyelet-lace-trimmed petticoats, the whale-bone corset, and several pairs of stockings. She found the clunky shoes in the third drawer, and at the back was a small metal box that fit in her palm. She looked it over, intrigued, and tried to open it but couldn't. She set it atop the highboy to figure out later.

In the drawer that held the flannel nightgown, Tempest found several cloth sacks with flowers and birds embroidered on them such as she'd never seen before. She pulled them out, tracing the wondrous pictures with her fingertip, delighting in the smooth texture of the silk thread.

A large, woven box occupied part of the bottom drawer. When Tempest opened it, she gasped. A myriad of brilliantly colored threads on small spools filled the top two trays. Beneath were swatches of cloth and other tiny treasures. She clutched them tightly, afraid of losing them.

She was so lost in her explorations that she didn't hear Abram approach the door at noon. He stood looking at her with Kathy's things spread all about her as she sat in the middle of the great bed, and felt a sharp pain in his chest. He cleared his throat.

Startled, Tempest glanced up. She froze for an instant, and

then leaped from the bed, spools, scissors, pincushion, and buttons scattering across the earthen floor. Her face was pale, her eyes huge as she stared at him. Her hands were behind her back, hiding something from him.

Abram approached her slowly. She backed up against the highboy, and her eyes grew enormous. When he stopped in front of her, she closed her eyes and gritted her teeth. Her body shook.

"What do you have behind your back?"

Her eyes opened slowly. She swallowed convulsively but did not respond. He put his hand out.

Her eyes grew dull and a soft, quivering sigh escaped as she brought her clenched hands around and dumped her little treasures into his palm. "I dinna steal them. I only looked—" Her voice caught.

Abram looked at the things in his hand, then at her. "You can't steal what already belongs to you." He selected one object. "Give me your hand."

She obeyed.

"It's a thimble," he told her, putting it on her middle finger. "You wear it when you sew. It protects your finger from being pricked when you push the needle through the cloth." He poured the other things into her palm. "These are enamel buttons. Kathy bought them at the fair. There weren't enough for a dress, but she thought they were pretty." He put his hand beneath Tempest's and closed her fingers over the things.

Tempest gazed up at him with wide, bemused eyes.

Abram caught sight of the little metal box on the highboy. "I'd forgotten about this," he murmured wistfully. He took it up and pressed a tiny catch. The box opened and music played. Tempest gasped and jumped back.

"Our only family heirloom," Abram said, smiling slightly. "It belonged to Kathy's grandmother. She brought it from Europe."

Fear forgotten in the wonder of it, Tempest came closer, staring at the amazing object in Walker's hand. The music slowed. He took a tiny key from inside the box and inserted it in the bottom, winding it around and around. The music tinkled more quickly then. He held it out to her.

"Take it. It's yours."

She backed up a step and shook her head. Her eyes were enormous.

"There's something in it."

His large, brown fingers took something from the delicate box, which he set on the highboy again. He looked at the thing in his hand and pain flickered across his face.

"I gave this ring to Kathy for Christmas the first year we were married. It's an aquamarine. Nothing expensive, but she said it was the most beautiful thing she had ever had. It was too small, so she never wore it, but she liked to take it out and look at it."

Tempest saw the deep lines around Walker's eyes and mouth, the moisture in his hazel eyes. An emotion new to her expanded in her chest. He knew loss, too.

Abram saw how she looked at him. "We're both alone, aren't we, Tempest?" he murmured, his mouth curving slightly, though the smile didn't reach his eyes. He looked down at the ring again.

"I'd forgotten all about this, but I want you to have it." He reached out and took her hand, the one that was not clutching the tin thimble and the bright red enamel buttons, and slid the ring on her finger. "All I have is yours, Tempest. Everything."

She frowned. "Why do ye give these things to me?"

"Because it's the way I want it to be."

"For how long?"

"For as long as we both live," he said softly.

"That's a high price for anything."

"We *need* each other."

"I had my da, mon," she said softly, no anger in her words this time. A deep bewilderment seemed to fill her young-old face.

"No, Tempest. I don't think you'd had your father for a long time. I don't think you've had anyone for a long time."

Tempest's eyes filled and she looked away to stare at nothing. Abram put his hand gently to her cheek. "You have me, now. You'll be happier with me."

He looked at Tempest McClaren and suddenly thought of Kathy. He remembered her heavy-boned, solidly muscled body, her plain, pleasant features and earth-toned coloring. She had been warm, modest, and gentle, and he'd loved her from boyhood.

Tempest was taller, delicately boned, and slender, not yet a woman. He had never seen her really smile, not a smile that lit her eyes as Kathy's smile had done. Nor had he heard Tempest laugh other than in insult and derision. She was as cold as a Sierra winter, as hard as Independence Rock, and as wild as the land in which they now lived. Yet she was also vulnerable, more vulnerable than Kathy had ever been, and one day she'd be incredibly beautiful.

Had he put the two women side by side, he'd have thought Kathy the stronger and healthier, the survivor. Yet she'd succumbed to the first fever that hit the wagon train. She hadn't even fought against it, seeing it as God's will. He sensed that Tempest McClaren would accept nothing as God's will. She would fight and she would survive.

God knew, he needed a woman like Tempest in this vast land. He needed a woman to bear him sons and daughters, a woman to share his life, to give him hope and purpose.

If anyone had ever told him he'd take a young half-breed girl, fathered by a mad Scottish trapper, to wife, he'd have laughed in their faces and believed them mad. Yet here, now, it seemed right and wise to do just that. He needed Tempest's spirit, her strong will, her wilderness wisdom, but he also needed her vulnerability. He wanted his woman to need him.

For all her strengths, this child-woman standing before him needed him far more than Kathy ever had, even in death. With time, maybe Tempest would understand that.

With time.

"Ye want another Kathy," Tempest said.

"No," Abram told her, putting a hard hand on her shoulder. "I want you . . . just as you are."

"Then ye dunna know yer own truth, mon. Ye lie to yerself. Ye already seek to change what I be. Ye should've taken heed of those at the fort who told ye I am a savage—a half-breed heathen who knows more about death than life. That is what I am. Not yer white woman Kathy."

She started to turn away but he caught hold of her upper arms, holding her there before him. "Savage, yes. Half-breed, yes. But who of us is pure of blood? I'm part English, part Irish, part German, part God-knows-what-else. And we're all savage underneath; it's part of man's nature. Some of us are a little more savage than others. If you think because I expect you to bathe and to eat with a fork or to clean my house and cook my food that I want to change what you are underneath, you're wrong—terribly wrong."

"Ye may be part of all those things ye say ye are, mon, but ye're all white, and that makes all the difference."

"It doesn't. I *chose* a half-breed wife. I hope for children from your body, children with your blood."

Tempest's mouth fell open and her face turned deep red. Then, jerking back, she glared up at him coldly.

"Ye want a bloody lot for five dollars in gold and a bottle of whiskey!" She shoved her treasures into her pocket while glaring at him. "Mon, I'll cook yer food and sweep yer bloody cabin. I'll oil yer damn furniture. But I wilna spread my legs and play the bought squaw! Do yer rutting at the fort!"

In a matter of half an hour, she managed to put together a meager, though nourishing, meal with what Abram had on hand. He ate, glancing at her over the rim of his coffee mug. He could feel her pale eyes watching him closely when he wasn't looking. "Aren't you going to eat?" he asked.

She made a simple negative movement with her head and remained silent.

Silence was a powerful weapon, Abram thought ruefully. He wished for the chatter of a woman. Kathy had talked incessantly, so much that sometimes he'd wished for her silence. Tempest's was too much.

He stood up and looked down at her dark head, pushing his hands deeply into his pockets. "I'll be in at sunset." Then, feeling resigned, he went out.

Tempest waited until he was well away. Then she slid the serving bowl closer and began to pick food out with her fingers. She lifted the bowl and slurped noisily at the remaining juices. She set it down and started to wipe her mouth across the back of her arm, but caught herself. Reaching across the table, she snatched up Abram's napkin instead.

Leaning back, Tempest let out a gusty, open-mouthed belch, while digging in her pocket for the thimble and buttons. She rolled them in the palm of her hand, admiring them.

"Never leave yerself in debt to any mon," her da had once told her when he'd been deep in his cups. How many loads of wood, how many days of cleaning this cabin and cooking meals and emptying Walker's chamber pot would it take to pay for these things?

He said everything he had belonged to her, but she knew there was a catch in the bargain. There was always a catch. At least he'd been honest about it. He said everything he had was hers, but he wanted everything from her as well. And she was damned if she'd give it to him at any price.

But she wasn't going to give up the thimble and buttons. Her fingers curled tightly around them for a moment, and then she tucked them back into her skirt pocket.

When Abram returned from a hard day in the field, the cabin was neat and swept. Whatever simmered over the fire smelled tantalizing. The table was even set, though the utensils were mixed up. He glanced at Tempest and smiled.

She noted the dampness of his forelock and his shiny cheeks and knew he'd washed again. The man had a great fondness for being clean, she thought.

He looked at her in frank question at her perusal, and she turned away, stirring the beans.

"I plowed a good portion today," he said to fill the silence, "but there're more rocks than I expected." It would have been enough to set Kathy off, but Tempest remained silent.

"How long before we eat?" he asked after a long pause.

Tempest took up a cloth and lifted the pot from the hook over the fire. She poured the beans into the serving bowl, set the pot aside, and put the bowl in the center of the table. She sat down, still without speaking.

With a sigh, Abram sat down as well. Tempest bowed her head, clasped her hands, and waited for him to say the blessing. She let him serve her. His eyebrows rose slightly.

Tempest tried to use the utensils as Abram did, but her clumsiness roused her temper. Finally it erupted when the fork slipped from her fingers onto the plate and splattered juice into her face. She inhaled sharply and then let fly a string of the foulest epithets Abram had ever heard.

He swallowed his bite of food and glanced at her. "Try again."

She leaned toward him and swore again, adding a few more choice Scottish curses.

"Keep it up, and I'll use the soap to wash out your mouth!" he warned her.

Her eyes glittered. She lifted her knife and Abram noticed that it, and his own, had been honed to an edge sharp enough to slice easily through wood. "I con use a knife right enough," she said through her teeth, and flipped it over expertly, then sent it hissing past his right ear. It struck the wall above the bed with a loud, vibrating twang and stuck there, quivering.

By the startled look on his face, she thought she'd frightened him, but when she reached for the serving bowl, he caught her wrist in a motion so swift that she gasped. His fingers tightened ruthlessly when she tried to yank free.

"The simplest white child of four can use a knife, fork, and spoon. I don't expect you to learn civilized manners in one or two meals, but *you will try!* That goes for everything else I tell you to do!"

Her eyes wide, she again tried to pull free. His hand tightened around her small wrist even more, cutting off the circulation.

"I can be patient," he said through his teeth, "but I'll warn you now—I will treat you with the same respect you do me. If you prefer things to be done by force, so be it. That's the way with stubborn, stupid animals, isn't it?"

Tempest felt the strength in his hand and saw the anger in his hazel eyes. She didn't move and said nothing, but the look on her face told him everything. He loosened his hold and let her slip free, but he still held her eyes.

"Now, you get up and go get that knife and sit down again," he commanded softly.

Tempest rose slowly and made a wide circle around him to the bed. She crawled across it and reached up to pry the knife free, then scrambled back across. Abram was sitting with his back to her, waiting. She clutched the knife tightly, her mind darting. One quick slash along the side of his neck and he'd die in seconds, his life's blood pouring out on the earthen floor. Or she could use both hands to bury it hilt-deep between his shoulder blades. She bit her lower lip.

Abram leaned back in his chair, still not turning around. He put both hands flat on the table, and, closing his eyes, said a short, silent prayer. "Well, Tempest, make up your mind."

He knew what she was thinking. Startled, she stared at his back. Slowly Tempest's hand lowered. *He knew and he sat there waiting.* Her anger dissolved, replaced by strong curiosity and grudging respect. She came back to the table and sat down, tilting her head to one side as she studied him.

"Ye're a madman—madder than Da."

He smiled slightly. "Maybe." He lifted his fork. "You hold it like this."

> Mutual aid is as much a law of animal life as
> mutual struggle.
> —Prince Pëtr Alekseevich Kropotkin

Boredom was Abram's greatest ally in working with
Tempest. She was used to constant travel, to struggle, and her
life on the farm was too easy, too slow. So each day Abram
added new chores. She learned to wash clothes by soaking
them in the creek and then using a wooden paddle to beat them
against a big flat rock, loosening the dirt. Then she soaked
them again in an iron pot over the outside fire. When the water
was hot, she put lye in and then stirred the clothing like a big
stew. With the paddle, she fished each garment out, went to
the creek to rinse it until the lye was gone, wrung the garment
out, and draped it over a tree branch or a low bush to dry.

Next Abram taught her how to use the sadiron. It took hours
of repeatedly reheating the iron over the fire to press out each
small wrinkle, using a thick pad in order not to scorch the
heavy, worn fabric.

"Ye should wear buckskin," she told him, her brow sweating
over the task. "Once it's properly tanned and chewed to softness, it wears forever."

"Until it smells like a dead animal and stands up in a corner
by itself," he responded.

Her list of responsibilities grew. Each new task was interesting until she mastered it.

When Abram tore his shirt while working, he took out the
sewing box and began instructions anew. She had a childish
love for the brightly colored threads and didn't resist him.
Threading the needle she quickly mastered, but no matter how
careful she was, she pricked herself, even when she used the

thimble. Worse, her stitches were large, as in her work with buckskin. She swore each time he told her to pull them out and try again.

Tempest balked at gardening. "Why dig holes for seeds when ye con gather what ye need from the land?" she demanded, hands on her hips in open mutiny.

"By planting, you have what you need at your hand and in plenty."

"It's at yer hand in plenty already, mon, but ye're too stupid to know what to look for and where!"

"Not potatoes, carrots, lettuce, squash, radishes, and cucumbers," he listed. "We can use what we need and then put up the rest for the long, rainy winter months."

"'Put up'?" she repeated blankly, but with the faintest, suspicious flare of her nostrils.

"Never mind." Abram knew there were some duties best explained at a later time. Besides, they hadn't the mason jars or wax to do it anyway. Some things could be dried and packed for storage, and he could build a cellar in the side of the hill. That would come later.

"We'll talk about that later, but for now, we need to turn the soil, hoe in fresh manure, make rows, and then plant the seeds." He showed her how to use the shovel and hoe and then left her to it.

"What if I dunna?" she yelled after him.

His lack of response left her with a curious foreboding. She swore vilely as she worked.

It was almost a week before she had the plot prepared to Abram's satisfaction. The rows and ditches were laid out in perfect, equidistant lines. He then doled out seed as if it were gold and showed her how to plant by digging shallow furrows and dropping seeds at even intervals, then covering them over, patting them down, covering them lightly with more fresh manure, and watering them. Kathy had made up the pockets back home and he'd carried them all the way across the country. He prayed hard that they would grow. Tempest frankly didn't give a damn.

By the end of the day the garden was planted. By dusk the birds arrived. They scratched and pecked while Abram came tearing in from the field, flapping his arms wildly like one of the feathered tribe that ascended quickly at his approach. The birds roosted in the surrounding trees, waiting patiently.

"Damn it!" Abram roared in uncharacteristic profanity. Tempest looked at him in surprise and then gave a hearty, appreciative laugh. It was the first time Abram had heard it and he in turn glanced at her in surprise. She grinned boldly.

"We learn from each other," she parroted impudently. Abram gave her a wry look.

"Stay here and keep the birds away," he said, and went to the cabin. He came out with some clothes and headed for the animal shelter. A few minutes later he came across the yard to where Tempest sat chewing distractedly on a piece of grass.

"What the hell is that?" she asked, glancing at what he carried under one arm.

"A scarecrow." He tied it up on a long pole and brushed off his hands. "That should do it." He winked at her and headed back for the field. She shook her head, watching him.

It helped for two days, and then a few brave birds returned. The smaller sparrows were easily frightened, but one great black crow was far more daring. He perched on the scarecrow's head and cawed a welcome to his friends. From the window near which Tempest was working on the dishes, she saw others drift in, and suddenly realized that all her work planting and mucking in the dirt and horse manure was about to be for nothing. She marched grimly to the mantel and then to the door. Standing just outside the door, she took careful aim.

Abram heard the gunshot and left the ox and plow standing as he ran for the cabin. When he arrived, breathless and concerned, Tempest was standing in the yard with one hand on her hip and the smoking rifle resting at ease.

"Who'd you shoot, for God's sake?"

Calmly and smugly, she nodded toward the garden. Abram glanced around and saw black feathers still floating down. *"That* should do it," she told him, and strolled back into the cabin.

Raking a hand through his hair, Abram measured the distance between cabin and garden with his eyes, judging it to be well over a hundred yards. He followed her in and watched her expertly reload. "I'm going back to the field," he muttered.

"Good-bye." She remounted the gun above the mantel without looking at him. Abram left, shaking his head.

That night, with the cabin cozy and filled with the lingering aroma of their usual dried meat and bean dinner, Abram sat in his chair and watched Tempest as she sat cross-legged near the fire. She was close enough to touch. All he had to do was lean down and put out his hand, but he didn't. He wanted so badly to talk that he couldn't think of anything to say.

Tempest glanced up at him curiously. "Do ye never eat anything but dried or salted meat and beans?"

His eyebrows rose. "Don't you like it?"

"Not when there be fresh at hand."

He smiled. "I hadn't even thought about hunting. I've been too busy trying to get the sections plowed in time for spring planting, and there's plenty of salted and dried meat left, and a big sack of beans."

"There be rabbits aplenty."

"I'm not much good at rabbit hunting," he admitted ruefully. "They're too fast, too smart."

Her look of incredulity was bald. "Smart? Rabbits are stupid. Ye dunna shoot them, ye snare them. Shooting them is a waste of ammunition. Same with raccoon and beaver, though they're quicker and more cunning. Ye build a trap. Ye save the gun for bear or deer or the big cats. Deer is good eating."

"Is that why you blasted that poor crow off its roost this afternoon?" Abram teased.

"He was looking at me and thumbing his damn nose."

"Beak," he grinned. "Gave you a personal challenge, did he?" His eyes laughed gently. When she didn't answer, he leaned forward. "Maybe I should leave the hunting to you, seeing as you're a crack shot. What do you think?"

"If ye canna even outthink a bloody rabbit, maybe ye should."

Abram laughed. He relaxed far back into his chair and smiled easily down at her. "Ah, Tempest, if you but lived in Pennsylvania for a year, you'd know what it is to have a chicken every other Sunday and a smoked ham for Christmas. Sometimes, even a turkey or a pheasant. But out here . . ." He shook his head. "You offer a bony rabbit."

Tempest's jaw set at his teasing. She stood up abruptly and went to the door, opening it with a hard jerk. Darkness was beyond and she stood at the edge of the light, not wanting to be inside with his laughter at her expense, but not daring to go out into the darkness either.

Abram came and stood behind her. He gently touched her shoulder, but she shrugged his hand off. He pushed his hands deeply into his pockets and leaned against the doorjamb. Studying her haughty profile, he smiled.

"Do you want to hunt again, Tempest?"

Her mouth tightened and her nostrils flared.

"Do you miss your old life?" he asked, his smile diminishing.

She looked at him coldly. "Would ye not miss this life if ye were torn away from it?"

He sighed and looked out into the darkness. "Yes, but this life is very different from my other back home."

She frowned. "Then why did ye come of yer own will?"

"For a *better* life," he said gently, smiling down at her.

"And what have ye, mon? This"—she looked around the cabin disparagingly—"that dirt out there, and a dead wife."

His breath stopped. "Woman, you wield words like a knife."

"Can ye deny any of it? It is the truth."

He leaned his head back and closed his eyes. "Leave it to a woman to show a man his truth," he said through thinned lips. He opened his eyes again. "I've a start on a home," he said simply. "And that land out there is more than I had before. Yes, Kathy is dead, but I have you."

Her eyes glinted. "Ye've naught, mon."

"Light the lamp, Tempest, and look around again." He leaned down closer to her. "Look at me," he murmured intently, holding her gaze.

Tempest started to turn back into the cabin, but Abram blocked her way with a white-knuckled hand against the jamb. She turned the other way, but before her lay the darkness. She looked back up at him with wide, anxious eyes.

"What do you see, Tempest McClaren Walker? Look closely."

Her breath caught. He raised his other hand slowly to touch her cheek, but she flinched away. His mouth curved ruefully. "How long before you let me touch you? How long before you touch me?"

He imagined lifting her then and carrying her back to the big bed, removing each garment as she lay acquiescent. He thought of weaving his fingers with hers and spreading her arms wide as he lay full on top of her and with his knees spread her legs wide and—

"When?" he rasped.

Her eyes were enormous, staring back into his. He straightened slowly and let his hand drop back to his side. His physical needs were at war with his reason. He leaned back again, looking down at her, and forced himself to focus on the years ahead rather than on this one aching moment.

"You want truth, Tempest," he said slowly. "You and me—that's truth."

"*Your* truth," she retorted, sensing that she was safe.

"The *inevitable* truth." He left her standing in the doorway and went back to his chair by the fire.

Tempest closed the door and came back to sit cross-legged before him. "I'm not afraid of ye."

He smiled. "Good. That's a start."

She frowned heavily. "I dunna understand ye, Walker."

"What do you want to know?"

"Why *me?* Why not the squaw who let ye?"

"Maybe that is the reason. She let me." He laughed softly. "I wasn't the only one, and a man wants to know his woman is his—and no one else's."

Tempest gazed into the crackling fire solemnly. Abram watched the firelight play over he perfect features. A hot, new sensation fired his blood as Kathy never had, and he frowned heavily.

"If Michael Nye had spoken for you, would you've gone with him more willingly?" Nye was a younger, more handsome man.

She glanced up sharply, her eyebrows high. "Nye?" She gave a snorting laugh. "Nye was scared to death of Da. He'd have filled his pants if my father had ever—"

"He wanted you."

"Aye," she nodded, "he wanted me, and he would've paid more than what ye did to use on me what hangs between his legs."

Abram blushed, but he persisted. "Who would you have chosen?"

"I wasna given a choice," she answered, her eyes narrowed and dark.

"*If . . .*"

She let out a hard breath and stood. "Neither of ye." Bending, she took another small log to lay on the fire. He stared at the smooth curve of her buttocks and then closed his eyes. He heard a loud burst of sparks and felt the heat intensify.

"What Nye wanted from me would've taken but a few minutes," Tempest said slowly. Abram opened his eyes. She sat down again and met his gaze. "But you, mon? Ye want everything from me. I'm not sure which of ye is worse."

"I don't want anything from you that I'm not willing to give back."

Her mouth twisted. "The only difference between you and Nye is he'd have taken what he paid for, while ye wait for it to be given to ye."

His face hardened. "Would you rather I took it?"

She blinked. "No."

He leaned forward and clasped his hands tightly between his knees. "Even a patient man can't wait forever."

Her expression grew watchful and guarded.

He leaned back again and smiled slightly.

Let her think about that for a while.

> Speak to the earth, and it shall teach thee.
>
> —Job 12:7–8

Early the next morning, as soon as Abram had gone to the fields, Tempest went to the shelter for her horse. She led him out and slipped the bosal over his head. Leaping onto his smooth back, she turned southwest. A white linen pillowcase decorated with embroidered hummingbirds and flowers and trimmed in fine crochet work flapped like a flag of surrender from the waistband of her hitched-up gray skirt.

Abram saw her riding away from the cabin and let go of the plow. He started to run, and then stopped. His hands clenched and unclenched at his sides for a long moment, and then he turned slowly and retraced his steps. He glanced up just once as she reached the knoll and then disappeared. Shoulders bent, he went back to work.

Tempest dug her heels into the horse hard and sent him surging over the grassy ground. She'd been cooped up too long in the closeness of the cabin with its smells of cooking, soap, wood polish, and beeswax candles. She needed the scents of grass, horse, and freedom. Taking deep gulps of the cool morning air, she raised her arms and spread her fingers as though to grasp the heavens and hold them. Her braids flew back, whipping against her shoulder blades with each stride of the horse. A broad smile lit her face and she tipped it up and closed her eyes to the brightness.

Spring.

The sights and sounds and smells of the sun-kissed, rain-soaked earth filled Tempest's senses. Had she had arms great enough, she would have embraced and held it close, drawn in the richness of it, taken new life from it. As it was, it surrounded her, soothed her, renewed her.

Soon the land would be covered with splashes of color: gold, red, purple, yellow, spring green.

She rode for miles, letting the reins lie loosely crossed and tucked beneath her slender thighs as her fingers dug into the heavy, coarse black mane of her Indian pony. The hard, rhythmic rubbing of her maidenhood against the warm, smooth back of the animal filled her with sighing exultation.

How much better was this freedom than the close, safe walls of that cabin and the dark, burning look of the man! For a few hours, she felt she could go on forever without him, without anyone. But knowledge is a hard master.

She reached her destination and pulled the horse to a stop, looking beyond at the great winding slough that came from the salt bay of Yerba Buena. Sunlight danced off the water, choked with tall grasses and cattails. Wild geese, cranes, wood ducks, and blue winged teal nested here. Short laughing and tickling cries came up from the bog where waterfowl roosted and played.

Tempest tossed the reins over the horse's head and slipped smoothly to the ground, tethering the animal to a branch. She tugged the pillowcase free and dropped it while she quickly divested herself of her clothing. Standing naked in the warm spring air, she took up the linen sack again and headed for the mire.

Slimy mud squished up between her toes and sucked at her bare feet as she waded in more than knee-deep among the tall reeds and rushes that grew in the green-brown, mossy water. As she moved farther from the shore, flocks of water birds ascended in a loud, flapping rush into the safety of the cloudless blue skies. Ducks raised frothy wakes across the marsh as they fled before her.

Moving slowly and sluggishly through the bog, Tempest parted clumps of reeds and searched. She pulled up plants and cut away the roots which she stowed in the pillowcase. Other plants she bound together in small bundles and slung over her shoulders with long grass twines. She searched further until she had found all she sought.

Her harvesting done, she worked her way back out of the thick, freshwater swamp and climbed the hill to where her horse still grazed contentedly. She lay back and dozed while the early afternoon sun baked the mud dry on her legs and arms. When she awakened, she peeled it away from her skin and then donned the garb of civilization.

Her return to the farm was less carefree. She rode more slowly, less exultantly, but with deeper satisfaction within her.

Pausing on the knoll, she looked down at the partially plowed field, the small, rough-built cabin, the animal shelter, and the oxen grazing in an open pasture. She sought for and found Abram, positioning a log, placing wedges, and finally swinging a mallet. The sharp thwack rang up to her on the hillside. She sat for several moments watching him and then pressed her heels firmly into the horse's sides.

Abram stopped. His head cocked and he turned, straightening. Even at this distance, Tempest felt the impact of his hazel eyes. He didn't move for several seconds, and then he returned to his work, his bare, bronzed back to her. She heard a crack as the log split into two eight-foot lengths. Abram set his mallet aside and heaved each section onto the growing pile of lumber he planned to use for the smokehouse. Then he gathered the wedges.

Watching him from beneath her thick lashes, Tempest dismounted. She set her sack aside and then removed the bosal from her horse. Opening the corral gate, she slapped his flank firmly and sent him in, closing the gate again.

When she turned, Abram was close behind her. He looked her over with a faint frown. Her hair had grass in it; her face was dirt-streaked and moist with sweat from a long, hard ride; her clothes were disheveled. The buttons on her shirtwaist weren't matched up properly with the buttonholes.

"Where have you been all day?"

She didn't answer, but bent to pick up the mud-stained linen pillowcase. One of Kathy's best.

"What've you got?" He set the tools down and held his hand out.

Tempest sashayed past him as he watched with a frown. "Come and see." She walked toward the creek and, curious, Abram followed.

She kicked off her moccasins and set the sack on the bank of the creek. Pulling her skirts up past her knees, she sat down with her legs spread apart and her feet in the water. Abram stared at the sleek, shapely calves, hardly aware that she was taking things from the linen pillowcase. She laid out small plant bundles, roots, and her last precious find.

"Eggs!" Abram exclaimed and hunkered down. "Where on earth did you find eggs?"

"In a duck nest at the marsh," she said dryly and bent forward to wash one carefully. There were six large brown eggs. Abram laughed softly.

"I'll be darned. I didn't even know there was a marsh near here."

She pointed southwest with a dripping hand.

Abram looked over the rest of Tempest's bounty. "What is all this stuff?"

"Arrowhead."

"Arrowhead?"

"Tule roots," she said, glancing at him. He picked one up and flipped it up and down in his palm, then smelled it. His expression was blank.

"Sutter calls them Indian potatoes," she explained, and washed the last egg.

"Potatoes?" He laughed again and sat down, leaning back on his elbow to watch her with growing respect. She took the tule root from him and began washing it in the creek. She looked very pleased with herself. "What else have you?"

"Wild rice." She pointed at the long green shoots. "And Da called those cossack asparagus."

"Never heard of it."

"Have ye heard of cattails?" she asked dryly.

"We're going to have cattails for supper?" he teased.

"Better than beans," she muttered, but her mouth curved.

Abram chuckled. Tempest finished washing the tule roots, then stood and let her skirts drop. Ducking under a low-hanging willow branch, she gathered her skirts again and leaped across the narrow creek. Bending down, she gathered several deep-green leaves and then leaped back. She dropped them on Abram's chest. "Taste one."

He did. His eyebrows rose. "Not bad."

"Indian lettuce," she informed him smugly, her hands on her slim hips. "There be food everywhere in this land. Over those hills are oaks with enough acorns to last ye yer lifetime. They can be ground, leached, and then made into cakes."

Abram grimaced. "But they taste foul, from what I've heard."

"With honey and wild mint, better than yer dried beans, mon."

He laughed. "You amaze me."

"Why?" Hands on her hips, she glared down at him.

His expression softened. "You know so many things. Where'd you ever learn all this? From your father? And where'd he learn it?"

"By watching the people who live on the land."

"Those Diggers at Sutter's Fort?" he asked in disbelief.

She tilted her head. "Yes, some of it. They ken more about staying alive than Sutter, or any of ye. They ken everything about this country, how to be one with it." She bent and snatched up the pillowcase to wash in the creek. "Ye whites never look; ye never listen. Ye think ye already ken everything, but without ye dried meat and beans and without ye guns, ye'd starve in a month."

Abram sat up. He plucked a blade of grass and chewed on it while watching her rigid back and sharp movements.

"You're right," he admitted slowly.

She wrung out the case and then looked at him. She was still pensive. "Ye say ye came here for a better life."

"Yes."

"Then why do ye all drag the old one with ye?"

He frowned, then smiled without humor. "I don't know."

She made a sweeping gesture. "Why this land? Why not higher in the mountains where there's more game? Why not closer to the sea? What is here?"

He looked at her. "Water, high ground, wood for building, and nettles."

"Nettles? Ye want nettles?"

"Nettles only grow in fertile soil." He flicked the blade of grass away and stood. Pushing his hands into his pockets, he smiled slightly. "Now, I'll bet that's something you didn't know."

"No reason to know it," she retorted, squatting down to put her harvest back into the clean linen pillowcase.

"We can learn a lot from each other," he repeated.

She straightened, sack in hand. "If we want to," she agreed with a shrug. She stepped into her moccasins. "I set snares near the brambles on the hillside."

He grinned. "You mean we may have rabbit for supper instead of salted meat?" His eyes sparkled with laughter.

"We could have venison. I saw deer droppings not far from here, and they'll be down soon to forage."

"It's almost dusk. The sun's setting."

"Da always hunted deer at dusk."

"Back home, we hunted just before dawn."

She gave him a droll look and shrugged. "Well, I hope there's a rabbit," she muttered. "I'm bloody sick of dried meat." She turned away, her skirt flipping up just enough before she walked away to give Abram a brief glimpse of her slender ankles. His mouth curved tenderly.

Stooping again, he washed up in the creek. He took his time walking back toward the cabin and was suddenly alarmed to see Tempest running down the hillside.

"What's the matter?" he shouted, rushing to meet her.

She had a large rabbit in one hand. Her eyes were wide as she gasped for breath. She gestured sharply southwest.

"What is it?" he demanded.

"Riders," she gasped out. "Many riders!"

The words of his mouth were smoother than
butter, but war was in his heart.
—Psalms 55:21

The riders moved across the land in a long column
like a great centipede. Tempest stood near Abram, having fetched
his rifle. Both watched intently.

"Are they Mexicans?" Abram asked.

"No." Tempest frowned, straining to see. They were closer
now.

"Who then?"

She tried to place the two men in front. She had seen them
before. Where? The smaller man was dressed in buckskins.
Beside him was a tall man with a proud bearing. Both rode
easy on their horses.

"Freeman," she murmured to herself.

"Who?"

"Fremont," she corrected. "He was here before, a few winters ago."

"John Fremont?" Abram asked, excited.

Her father hadn't thought much of the man. "Full of himself," he'd said with a sneer.

"The other is Kit Carson," Tempest said, relaxing. He was
a small man, lean and quiet, with intelligent gray eyes. At the
fort when she'd seen him before, he'd stayed to himself. He
said little, but when he spoke, men listened, even Fremont,
who seldom listened to anyone.

"Fremont is one of the most important men in the country,"
Abram told her. "He opened the way west for the rest of us."

Tempest looked up sharply and jerked her head. "Him! My
da crossed the mountains long before he ever did. So did a
hundred others."

"Yes, but they never wrote about it. They never shared their
knowledge. John Fremont did. He surveyed the land and then
went back. He and his wife, Jessie Benton, wrote about this

country so that others would know what was waiting for them when they came. His father-in-law is Senator Thomas Hart Benton, one of the great powers in our country."

Tempest had never heard of Jessie or Thomas Hart Benton and was unimpressed. She *had* heard of Fremont's ambitions while eavesdropping at Sutter's Fort. "This isna the United States. This is California—part of Mexico. What's the mon think he's doing, bringing an army here?"

"He's surveying the land."

"Why? It's not his land." She sneered as she saw Fremont riding forward. "Da said he was a puffed-up buffoon."

Abram glanced at her sharply. "Whatever your father said or thought about him, when he comes here you'll treat him with due respect."

"If it be due, I'll give it."

Abram grew stern. "Any person who crosses our threshold becomes our guest, and will be treated with hospitality. No matter who they are or how you feel about them. Do you understand?"

She started to turn away, and he caught her wrist roughly. "I mean it, Tempest. Don't try me on this, because you'll regret it."

Her chin tilted up and she gave him a hard smile. "Rest easy, mon. I wilna order the bastard out. I wilna say even a single word to him." She jerked her arm free and walked away. Abram watched her with a heavy frown and then turned back when he heard Fremont call out a greeting.

Tempest glanced back and saw the tall, erect man dismount and shake hands with Abram. Unease filled her. She went into the cabin and looked out the open window. The two men still talked while the long column of buckskin-clad soldiers remained on horseback, awaiting further orders. Fremont turned and called out to them and made a wide circular gesture. The men broke the column formation, dismounted, and began to ready camp.

"Damn!"

Kit Carson strode toward the two men and spoke to them. He shook hands with Abram, and then the three started toward the cabin. Tight-lipped, Tempest spun away. She went to the wood bin, picked up a heavy oak log, and heaved it into the fireplace. She kicked it into place and then stooped down before it to snap kindling and shove it into place so that it would catch among the coals. Golden flames licked around the log.

So much for my rabbit!

She snatched the spit down from its iron hooks as the door opened behind her. She leaned the spit against the stones. Brushing off her hands, she stood and turned. Abram met her fiery glance with one of grim warning. She let out her breath slowly.

"Gentlemen, this is my wife, Tempest. Tempest, this is Lieutenant Fremont and his scout, Christopher Carson."

Christopher! She almost laughed out loud. She looked at Fremont. He wasn't as tall or as broad as Abram, but his energy seemed to fill the small cabin. He removed his hat gallantly and smiled at her, then bowed slightly. "Mrs. Walker, it's a pleasure."

Carson nodded once, his eyes enigmatic. She met his gaze squarely, and her mouth curved in a slow, wry smile. *Aye, ye remember me, dunna ye, mon?*

"Please sit down." Abram gestured at the two chairs. The dead, gutted rabbit lay on the table, and he lifted it and put it on the counter by the window, then took a rag and wiped the blood away. He glanced at Tempest, opened a cabinet, and took out a bottle and three cups. Her eyebrows shot up.

As they began to talk, Tempest went to the counter to skin the rabbit. She could feel Carson watching her while Abram and Fremont talked. Taking up a small hatchet, she made four swift whacks and chopped off the rabbit's feet. There was a moment of utter silence. She turned and held her hand out, palm up. Abram unsheathed his knife and placed it in her hand, handle first. She turned back to her task and made several expert cuts, flipped the knife so that it stuck in the counter plank, and then pulled the whole skin free of the rabbit's body.

Carrying the stripped carcass across the room, she took up the iron rod and spitted the rabbit in one smooth thrust. With a sharp clang, she dropped the rod back on the hooks over the fire.

Turning around, she encountered the fixed gazes of the three men. Abram looked grim, Fremont stunned and questioning, Carson mockingly amused.

Abram cleared his throat.

"You're very adept at skinning and spitting a rabbit, Mrs. Walker," Fremont commented.

"If I'm not mistaken," Carson said slowly, "Mrs. Walker is McClaren's daughter."

Tempest grinned coldly at them.

"You're not mistaken," Abram said, setting his cup down and giving her a quelling look.

Fremont glanced sharply at Carson and then back at Tempest where she stood at the fire. She put her hands on her hips.

"You remember McClaren from our previous visit to California, sir," Carson murmured.

"I remember him."

Tempest's grin remained, her eyes glinting.

Abram sat forward. He gave Tempest a faint smile. "McClaren is one of the best trappers in this territory."

"Anywhere," Carson himself corrected.

"Aye," Tempest said boldly. She spoke to Carson. "He knows his animals, doesna he?" Then she looked from him straight at John Fremont.

The man met her look and smiled in wry amusement and understanding. "He had very little respect for me," he admitted. "I believe his words were 'encroaching bastard' and 'bringing forth the bloody purge of civilization.'" He even managed a creditable imitation of McClaren's burr and appeared little worried about ither accusation.

Tempest returned to the counter and took the roots, cattail stalks, and eggs from the pillowcase. She put the eggs into a basket and set them aside with determination. She'd spent too much time mucking about in the bog searching them out to share them with any bounder.

Tempest's rudeness brought heightened color to Abram's face. His knuckles were white as he clenched the handle of his cup and his jaw knotted as he looked at her stiff back.

Fremont seemed relaxed and congenial in spite of the reception. He even smiled. "You said you've held this land for almost a year?"

"Eight months." Abram forced himself to relax. He'd have to deal with Tempest's insurrection later. If he took her to task now, there'd be hell to pay.

"You're planning to farm?"

"Two sections. The rest I plan to use for cattle."

"We could see how much you've plowed already on the ride in. You've done a lot of work in a few months."

"This cabin is solidly built," Carson remarked. "I've seen some put up by settlers that won't stand the first rains."

"It'll do for a time," Abram agreed and then glanced at Tempest. "We'll need more room in a couple of years."

Fremont grinned. "You planning a large family, Mr. Walker?"

"Yes." Tempest glanced back at Abram over her shoulder and he smiled. She jerked around again and the knife came down on a tule root with a loud crack. Turning his head slightly, Abram encountered Carson's shrewd, amused eyes.

"You're a courageous man, Mr. Walker."

"Persevering, Mr. Carson."

"That's what makes a good pioneer." Carson grinned, and Fremont laughed softly.

Abram replenished the men's cups with wild grape brandy. "How far north you planning on going, Lieutenant?"

Fremont's face hardened. "Maybe all the way to Oregon Territory."

"But not so far we can't come back in a hurry," Carson added, turning his mug around on the table.

Abram frowned. "There's been trouble?"

"It's coming," Fremont said, shaking his head in disgust.

"I've had none here," Abram said, looking from one to the other of the grim-faced men.

Fremont's mouth drew down into a hard, unyielding line. His eyes were flinty and distant. "If Governor Castro thinks he can succeed in expelling Americans from this territory by a simple proclamation, he's going to find himself holding a bear by the tail."

Abram's stomach plunged into his boots. Stunned, he stared at the angry face of the young, hotheaded lieutenant. "What proclamation?"

"The one he made a few weeks ago when we arrived in Monterey," Carson responded.

"He ordered you out of California?" Abram asked, trying to make sense of it.

"Peremptorily," Fremont growled. "He seems to think I've come with an army and the intention of conquering California." He snorted contemptuously. "Everyone on the continent knows that we came to survey a route to the Pacific. Yet this fool orders me out of the territory when we come into Monterey to procure supplies for our move north!

"We didn't come to start a war with Mexico or to cause trouble for American settlers, so we left Monterey peaceably and encamped on Hawk's Peak. It's our practice to raise our country's flag and we did so, but Castro grew belligerent and crazed. He was ready to start firing, and we were ready to return the favor if he did. Thomas Larkin interceded, however, and smoothed things over enough so that we could ride north." He drank some brandy.

"We have word that Castro has called for volunteers and has raised a force of more than two hundred troops," Carson informed Abram easily.

"My God. Then we're at war."

Fremont shook his head. "It's me he wants. Let him come if he's fool enough. But I doubt he will."

"What happens to the settlers when you leave the territory?" Abram asked, worried about his own tentative position. He had not applied for Mexican citizenship, and he knew that nearly all those settlers who had legal, documented land grants from Mexico were not only citizens of Mexico, but also were or had become Catholics. Some had further strengthened their positions by marrying Californio women. Abram Walker was an American Methodist who already had a wife.

"Well, I came more than two thousand miles, and no proclamation will send me packing!" he muttered when Fremont offered no response.

Fremont smiled slightly. "Every other settler feels the same, Walker. You've all the advantage."

"How?" All he could think of were the two hundred troops Castro had raised.

"Your numbers are growing every month. In a few years, there'll be more Americans in California than Mexicans."

All the more reason for Castro to attempt an expulsion now, before the numbers became too great, Abram thought grimly.

"That's what caused the trouble in the first place," Fremont continued. "He saw me and my sixty men and thought he had an army on his doorstep."

"A threat to his authority," Carson murmured, a faint smile on his lips.

"Authority!" Fremont snorted. "He's a weakling! Mexico is in the same position here as England was with the colonies. They think they can rule the settlers without proper representation. But in this case Mexico is even weaker than England was."

Tempest was at the fire turning the browning rabbit. She listened intently.

"What about his two hundred troops?" Abram asked. "When

you leave, what protection do the settlers have?"

"Things may calm down when we leave," Fremont said, but his tone implied that he didn't really believe it.

"He's more concerned with us than with you," Carson said in encouragement, but Abram sat like stone. Tempest saw how pale his face was and how hard the muscles in his jaw were.

"Well, I'm not leaving." He glanced at Fremont. "If it comes to a fight, he'll have one. Where will you stand if war does come?"

Fremont lifted his cup. "First and foremost, I am an American and stand for her interests." He drained the last of his brandy and glanced at Carson with a gleam in his eyes. Then he stood and smiled at Abram. "But it may come to nothing at all, Walker. Once I leave California, he'll probably go back to Monterey and have a fiesta." He laughed contemptuously.

Fremont extended his hand to Abram as the three men stood near the door. "I thank you for your kind hospitality in allowing us to camp here for the night."

"You won't stay for supper, Lieutenant?"

Fremont declined graciously and issued a counter-invitation for Tempest and Abram to join him and his men in partaking of fresh steer. "We've learned to live well off the land."

Tempest knew what he meant. It was undoubtedly one from a Californio rancho; she wondered if Fremont had bothered to pay for it.

With a glance at Tempest, Abram was equally gracious in declining.

"We'll be leaving early tomorrow morning, so I'll say good-bye now. I wouldn't worry too much about Castro," Fremont said. "Things are sure to die down." He turned and made a slight bow to Tempest. "Ma'am." Carson nodded to her.

She watched the three men leave and heard their voices outside.

When Abram returned, Tempest had the table set and the rabbit pieced. His face was grim as he sat down. Tempest looked at him surreptitiously as he said the blessing and then served her coal-baked tule roots, steaming green cattail stalks, and a leg of the roasted rabbit. Then he served himself.

He didn't seem to care that she was even there, and oddly enough, that smarted. He said nothing as he ate, and she'd worked hard to set forth this banquet. After weeks of dried meat and beans, he ought to show more appreciation!

"I dinna know ye drank spirits," she attacked from the flank.

He glanced up. "Sometimes, when the occasion calls for it."

"Fremont's coming and causing trouble is occasion for it?" she challenged.

Abram released his breath and lowered his fork. "Any visitor would've been occasion for it. It's a thing called hospitality, something you've obviously never heard of or experienced!"

His sharp reproval hurt. She looked down at the meal of fresh vegetables and meat and felt her eyes burn. *Damn him! Damn Fremont! Damn the bloody lot!* Tight-lipped, she jabbed her fork into a chunk of the tule root. She chewed and swallowed and then looked at him again. "Tell me something, mon! If ye were faced with sixty men, well armed and trained and on ye territory, would ye not think ye faced an army?!"

Abram had thought as much himself. "The point is, he isn't."

Tempest's mouth twisted. "Fremont has already been here 'to survey a route to the Pacific,'" she said with pointed derision. "What's his bloody reason for coming back?"

Whatever the reason, Abram knew that a spark had flashed in Monterey, and a range fire was about to spread across the land.

She's beautiful and therefore to be woo'd
She is a woman, therefore to be won.
　　　　　　　　—William Shakespeare

Fremont took his men north, and the following week on the farm passed slowly. With the column's departure, Abram expected trouble, but none came. No Mexican troops arrived to force him off his land. Yet Abram could not dispel his unease, and he almost wished he had taken land closer to New Helvetia, or perhaps the new settlement of Sonoma would have been better. It was too late now. Grueling weeks of back-breaking work had already gone into plowing, and he would soon plant. No one could make him leave this land now—not without a fight!

Fear for his land was not the only problem confronting Abram. There was Tempest.

Her nearness and her ingenuous sensuality caused an emotional war within him. For some time now, whether he was working in the fields or relaxing in the cabin, Abram's mind would involuntarily resurrect the image of Tempest standing nude after her first bath, her black hair cascading down her shoulders and only partially concealing her beautiful breasts. The image would fade as he watched droplets of water fall from the soft wisps of hair revealing her maturing womanhood.

And now, seeming resigned to a life with him, Tempest no longer watched him with cold, wary distrust. But she still slept on the floor, leaving the big bed to Abram, who had no intention of forcing himself upon her. Something had to give. He was no longer satisfied with spending himself in the shadows out of sight of the cabin. His need was strong.

Tonight, Abram read the story of Meshach, Shadrach, and Abednego. This was a precious time each day, when he and Tempest were close. They never touched, but he had her rapt attention, and he savored it. He would read slowly, occasionally glancing at her as she listened. She never asked him to read, nor questioned him about the passages afterward. He wished she would—just once.

Finishing the story, he closed the Bible. With a sigh, he gazed down at her. She was so still, so beautiful. He cleared his throat before attempting to speak. "Did you like the story?"

She shrugged.

Abram felt a surge of frustration and anger. He stood abruptly and put the Bible back on the mantel beneath the mounted rifle, then pushed his hands deeply into his pockets.

"Mesh..ch, Shadrach, and Abednego," Tempest murmured. "Such strange names."

He took his hands from his pockets and sat down again, his heart beating faster. "Did you like the story?" he repeated with more determination.

She glanced at him with a faint frown and said nothing. His mouth tightened.

"Did you understand it?"

"There's naught to understand; it be but a tale," she said, sensing his mood.

"It's not a tale; it's true."

She sniffed. "Dunna be expecting me to believe three men could stand in a fire and live."

"They weren't standing there alone."

"No. They had a ghost with them."

"God—not a ghost."

"Whatever ye say, mon," she muttered and looked back into the fire. Abram heard the stubborn refusal in her tone. He sighed heavily and stood again, restless. He added another log to the fire, pushing it into place with his booted foot.

Tempest glanced up at him; she could feel his tension. He looked down at her, and the look in his hazel eyes made her muscles tighten. She remembered what he'd said a week past about a patient man having his limits. Thus far, he'd made no attempt to touch her in any way. But his eyes touched her now, gripped her.

A cold lump grew in her stomach as she looked up at him, and it spread chilly tendrils of apprehension through her body.

Abram looked away, gritting his teeth. His father had warned him as a boy that masturbation could lead to blindness and insanity. Better to risk them than to suffer this. He turned away from the fire and strode across the room, knowing that if Tempest's eyes moved any lower, she'd see the immense bulge at the front of his dungarees.

God, how he needed the tender touch of a woman. He ached for it, hurt for that moist, enfolding warmth, and if he didn't have it soon, he would go mad just as his father had prophesied!

Kathy's brush lay on the highboy. He fingered it distractedly, remembering how he used to brush her hair for her sometimes. It had crackled with each stroke, and he would gather it to one side and brush his lips against the nape of her neck. She'd liked that, and it had often been the prelude to their tender lovemaking, a quiet sign of his need.

There was still some of Kathy's hair in the brush. He pulled it free and rubbed it between his fingers. It was dark brown and coarse, and he remembered how she'd worn it coiled tightly on the back of her head so that it didn't get in her way while she worked.

Tempest never used the brush. She used her fingers. Maybe she had never used one, other than to curry a damn horse!

He took it up and looked at it, and thought of the silken texture of Tempest's hair when he'd washed it. Since that first shampooing, he'd collected rainwater and let her do it for herself. She no longer balked at bathing, but seemed to rather enjoy it now that she knew better than to get the soap near her eyes.

Abram turned slowly and looked at Tempest. She was watching him closely with a pensive frown. Her gaze dropped to the brush in his hand and she slowly stood as he came back toward the fire. All that wary distrust was back in her narrowed blue eyes.

"Sit down," he told her.

She straightened. "Why?"

"I'm going to brush your hair for you."

"What for? I washed it yesterday and it's braided until next quarter moon."

"You'll like it." He smiled. At her silence and anxious look, his smiled grew mocking. "Have I ever hurt you before? Why're you so afraid of me?"

Her chin tipped up as he'd expected. "I'm not afraid!"

"Then sit down before the fire again and let me take out your braids and brush your hair properly for you."

She sat down slowly, her muscles tense. He squatted down behind her, and she cocked her head to one side, looking at him from the corner of her eye. He hesitated, his breath shallow. Raising his hands, he put them lightly on her shoulders. She jumped, but this time he didn't take his hands away. He could feel her collarbones and the rigid tension in her slender body. He'd barely touched her since the day he'd held her head under the water to get the soap out of her eyes. He closed his eyes for a long moment and then opened them again while he gently massaged her shoulder blades with his thumbs.

"Relax. I'm not going to hurt you," he whispered. *I just want to touch you.*

Slowly, she began to relax. He removed the ties from her braids and began to unplait the thick, silky black hair. He loved the feel of it in his hands, the faint, lingering smell of lavender soap, cookfire smoke, and her. He finished loosening it and ran his fingers deeply into the mass.

"What're ye about, mon?" she demanded, jerking her head.

He let her hair slide free of his fingers. "Does a horse sweat with fear when you curry it?" he needled. "Stop fretting so much and enjoy it." He sat down behind her and stretched his legs out on either side of her slender hips.

She said nothing, going straight forward, her back stiff.

Abram applied the brush with long, slow strokes. "I used to do this for Kathy," he murmured. Tempest's rich black hair shimmered down her back. The more he brushed, the more it glistened. "I love the feel of a woman's hair." He put his palm lightly on her head as he brought the bristles through some tangles. He could feel her relaxing. At the next stroke, her back arched like a cat being petted. His pulse leaped.

He went on brushing her hair until his arm was tired. Then he set the brush aside and gathered the fan of silken tresses in his hands. "Kathy used to make one braid before she went to bed. I'm not much good at this..." he murmured, and with clumsy fingers wove Tempest's hair. "There," he said finally, lifting the soft plait and draping it over her right shoulder so that it fell against one firm breast.

Holding his breath, he stared at the little hollow at the back of her neck just below her hairline. He leaned forward and kissed it.

Tempest jerked forward and swung her head around to stare back at him.

He smiled slightly and then got to his feet. "Would you like me to read to you some more?" he asked, his hands deep in his pockets, disguising the evidence of his feelings.

A confusion of emotions surged wildly through Tempest as she looked up at Abram. She had enjoyed having him brush her hair, but when he'd put his lips lightly to her neck, it had felt like a jolt of hot lightning, frightening her badly. Now he stood there wearing that gentle smile of his. She didn't understand him at all. If her father had been strange, this man was stranger still, impossible to understand.

Her life was changing so rapidly. She tried to revive the memory of Da. She thought of riding with him, sitting for endless hours in the saddle, then staggering from the horse to gather kindling and cook meals. She remembered dropping near the fire and pulling a filthy blanket over herself, too tired to sleep and feeling the hard rock and earth beneath her. All the hunting and killing, the skinning and tanning—she could still feel the slick blood on her hands, remember the smell of death all around her.

All those frozen winters when she and Da had lived in whatever shelter or hole they could find came back to her in a rush of misery that overwhelmed her. Never a cabin, never a place like that other one in the high mountain valley—in her mind she saw Da's face, bleak, hard, distant, reflecting his own inner hell as he stared into the flames of a campfire.

Silence. So much silence. Endless silence.

How she had longed for him to touch her, to talk to her, to be as he had been before. *Before*.

Had he blamed her for her mother's death? Was that why he'd sold her? Had her mother's death been her fault? She could still hear Winona's first cry of warning. Why hadn't she heeded it and realized that those Indians had come to destroy? Too late, she'd understood. Too late, she'd run. If she had obeyed immediately, that arrow might have missed her mother. If she'd run faster, perhaps they might have escaped.

Or—if she had acted more quickly, the arrow might have struck her, instead. Was that why her da had turned inward and away from her until he'd finally rid himself of her altogether? Had he wished it had been Tempest who died that day instead of her mother?

That must be the reason. It must be.

Abram saw only the agony carved into the young-old face. Tempest's blue eyes were stark and raw. He hunkered down in front of her, and saw she was caught up in some hellish recollection.

"Oh, Da . . ." she moaned, her face clearing in some vague

comprehension as she answered an unknown question. "If only I'd run faster..."

Abram thought he understood, and despaired. A lead weight seemed to fill the pit of his stomach.

God, I did this to her. This pain is of my doing. I could have let her be, but all I could think of was my need, my loneliness, my dreams. I never really stopped to think about what she wanted.

Tempest focused slowly on Abram, kneeling in front of her, his face lined and pale. He had said that all he wanted was to love her, to protect her, to share his life with her. He had given her gifts, the most precious and beautiful of things that she still kept tucked in her skirt pocket where she could touch them whenever she wished. But this man had wrenched her from Da. He'd freed her and followed her. All those miles he'd followed, all those hours he'd waited—just to give her water and food and comfort when she'd run herself almost to death after a father who didn't want her anymore.

He'd taken her from all those things she had known so well—too well. Silence; long, cold winters; damp, dark-shadowed dwelling places; death; loneliness. Abram Walker had brought her here to this cabin—to warmth, tenderness, security, and human touch.

Tempest looked at Abram and saw him.

He's alive. He's not walking dead like Da. He is alive!

Abram watched her wide, startled eyes fill and spill over. He watched her lips part in faint surprise and wonder. "What can I do now?" he said hoarsely, his own eyes burning with remorse, his throat closing hotly. "What can I do?"

Tempest didn't know how to tell him. She had long since forgotten how to reach out to another, no matter how desperate she was, so when Abram rose and moved away from her, she merely watched him. Her body trembled inwardly at the loss, but she didn't know what to do about it.

Touch me, Abram. Hold me. Keep the demons at bay. Please ...please...

Lord, what fools these mortals be!
—William Shakespeare
A Midsummer Night's Dream

The change in Tempest's attitude was so remarkable that Abram didn't know what to make of it. She no longer fought his every dictate, no longer hurled insults at every opportunity; she simply looked at him solemnly when he instructed her, and then obeyed.

She went hunting and shot a twelve-point buck. Abram savored the rich feast of fresh venison, and she scraped the flesh from the hide and soaked it in a tub of water and wood-ash until the hair was loosened enough to be rubbed off. She snared more rabbits over passing weeks and stitched the pelts together into a soft rug that she put beside the great bed where his feet first touched the cold, earthen floor each morning. She foraged for nuts, roots, and wild vegetables, and roasted dandelion roots to stretch his coffee supply.

Her silence was different. Abram saw no burning resentment, no fiery hatred pouring from her watchful blue eyes. She was becoming more and more like the silent slaves of Sutter's Fort. When he looked at her, he saw mute appeal and inwardly writhed. He felt sick with guilt at the loss of her proud, defiant spirit, and spent long hours in the fields away from the house—away from her.

McClaren's gone into the high country. I can't even give her back to her father now. God, why can't she just accept me and forget him!

Abram had forgotten how a woman's silence could wear down a man's soul.

He stopped reading the Bible in the evenings. Each night

after dinner, he sat by the fire, staring morosely into the flames, brooding. Her blue eyes became duller, filled with a silent, growing grief, causing Abram to withdraw even further.

The first plowing was finished, but stones still had to be carted from the fields. Tempest came out to the field with him one morning and they worked until their faces were gray with exhaustion, until they couldn't think or worry.

"There's no need for you to work like this," he told her in confused anger. She plodded past him with an unearthed stone in her thin arms. She'd been at it since daybreak, hour after endless hour; back and forth she trod with the stones, stacking them on the wall he'd begun. Her look of grim determination brought a heaviness to his chest.

"I tell you, there's no need!" he called after her. Her shoulders were hunched as she carried the granite burden. She didn't stop, didn't speak.

Why wouldn't she stop? *Damn her!*

Abram raked his hand through his dusty hair and returned to his plowing, trying not to look at her. He'd never worried about Kathy overworking in the fields. Why should he worry about this stubborn chit? When she became too tired, she'd quit and go back to the cabin.

The sun rose higher, hot and heavy. When it reached its zenith, Tempest left the field and prepared a midday meal. Prairie chicken, acorn patties, barberry greens, and fresh bread from the *horno* were waiting for him when he came in after washing up. Tempest sat down, her back straight and her hands folded. When he bowed his head, she did also. He prayed bitterly, and then studied her with a dark frown.

"There's no need for you to work out there. There's more than enough to do around the cabin," he said as he filled her plate and set it down in front of her with a thump. She used knife, fork, and spoon with tedious effort and didn't spill a thing.

"Did you hear me?"

She blinked at his harsh tone and lowered her head to dab at her mouth with the napkin. "Do ye expect less of me than ye did of yer white woman?" Her burr was heavy.

Abram glared at her. "What do you mean by that?"

Her eyes were hooded. "Ye said yer Kathy worked beside ye, mon."

"I've got my oxen to work beside me now. I don't need you to," he told her, confused by her determination. Was this a new woman's punishment—cutting his conscience into ribbons?

Where was the fiery girl he had brought back here? *I've killed her.*

His lips pressed together. "Besides, Tempest, the work's too hard for you."

"Was it too hard for her?"

"She'd worked on a farm all her life. She was used to it. She knew what she was doing."

"I'll get used to it."

A muscle worked in his jaw. "Suit yourself," he muttered, and finished his meal in cold silence.

Tempest washed clothes and hung them on the bushes, and then returned to the field work.

Abram watched her as he replowed. She seemed driven to remove every stone he uncovered with his laboring. Sweat glistened on her brow and drenched the front of her bodice and the back of her dress.

The sun descended slowly. Abram could tell by her sagging shoulders and unsteady steps that she had pushed herself too far. Yet she stooped again and brushed dirt from another rock until she could grasp it and use her body weight to pry it up. He left his ox and plow and strode toward her.

"Leave it!"

She fell back and stared up at him. Her face was deep red and streaked with dirt and sweat, although she was so close to complete exhaustion that the perspiration no longer came.

"Nothing's done in a day. Now go on back to the cabin!"

Tempest rolled the stone from her lap and struggled to her feet. She kept her face averted as she staggered and then walked slowly toward the house, her shoulders quivering but her head high.

"Take in the wash or clean the cabin! Go hunting! Just leave the fields to me!" he shouted, and then rubbed the back of his neck as he stared after her.

Her body's going to make her pay the price for what she did today. She doesn't need me yelling at her.

Disconsolate, Tempest watched him from within the cabin. She drew back when he glanced toward her. Then she watched again as he paused at the end of a long furrow and wiped sweat from his face with his sleeve before bringing the ox and plow around again.

He's changed. He bought me to work with him, and now

he doesna want me anymore. Whatever he said before, he's changed his mind now.

By nightfall Tempest could hardly move. She managed to prepare a simple meal and waited. Her muscles stiffened even as she rested at the table.

Abram knew she was in pain when he entered the cabin and saw her pale, drawn face. She ate little, and after supper he left the cabin and went to the animal shelter. He brought back a bottle of horse liniment.

"Take off your shirtwaist and camisole and sit down on the bed," he told her flatly. She glanced up at him sharply and then saw the small brown bottle in his large hand. "You'll feel better once this is rubbed in."

She slowly unbuttoned the shirtwaist and drew it back off her shoulders. Then she unbuttoned and untied the camisole. As it slid down over the soft swell of her breasts, he averted his eyes, concentrating on the log and sod walls, the highboy. She sat down on the edge of the bed, the thin camisole clutched in front of her, and gazed at him pensively.

He came toward her slowly and sat down. "Turn around." She turned away, offering him her smooth, brown back. He poured liniment into his palm, set the bottle aside, and rubbed his hands together. Then he spread the liquid across her shoulders and down the chain of her spine. She made a soft, harsh sound in her throat as he began to rub.

"It'll help," he said gruffly, not wanting to hurt her. "Hold still."

Her skin felt as smooth as butter. He kneaded her muscles and she sighed.

"Why're you driving yourself?" he demanded.

"It's why ye bought me."

His hands stilled and his mouth thinned to a narrow line; then he sighed heavily and continued the massage. "You wouldn't be much good to me dead, now, would you?" he asked, trying to keep his tone light. It came out with grating harshness.

He worked over her back and even when the liniment was absorbed, he didn't stop. She was relaxed, her body pulsing forward under the firm pressure of his hands.

"Why do ye never read anymore, mon?" she asked quietly, and his hands stilled again.

"If you want me to read, you've only to say so."

She turned her head slightly so she could look at him.

"Please . . ."

Please.

So much in one simple word. Capitulation. Surrender. A hard, well-aimed blow.

"Which story do you like most?"

She thought for a moment. A faint smile touched her lips, seeping into her eyes. "The mon who collected animals?"

"Noah."

"Aye, Noah."

Abram stood and moved away from the bed. She shrugged back into her camisole and came to sit on the mat before the fire. He hadn't realized how much he had missed this time. He sat down and opened the Bible to Genesis 6:17 and began to read. Tempest stared into the fire until he finished. Her mouth curved.

"The Indians have a story about a flood."

"They do?" He closed the Bible and set it aside.

"Aye. They tell of a storm like Noah's, but yer story canna be true."

"Why not?" he asked carefully, hope trembling through him as she seemed to open to him.

"There's no boat big enough to hold two of every kind of animal. Even if yer Noah could build one, ye canna put a bear with a puma or a chicken with a fox." She shook her head. "No, it canna be true, but it makes for a bonny fine story, mon."

Abram leaned forward and clasped his hands together between his knees. "All things are possible with God."

She looked at him then. "Mon, if that be so, why dinna yer God just make men good in the first place and save himself all the trouble?"

Surprised, Abram laughed softly. "Well, I don't know . . . I guess he wanted us to have a choice."

"Then he shouldna be so angry when the people choose something other than him."

Abram rubbed the back of his neck and leaned back in his chair. How was he to answer that? He wasn't sure he understood himself.

"God is our Father, Tempest, and I expect that, like a human father, he wants his children to live according to his rules. When his children don't, they pay the consequences. Like the law in the Garden of Eden not to eat of the Tree of Knowledge. Eve took the fruit and shared it with Adam, and they had to pay the price of their disobedience by being cast out. Later, when the people sinned, God washed the earth clean of them, except for Noah and his family, who were righteous. It wasn't because God wanted to hurt them."

"But he hurt them anyway."

Abram sighed, not sure how to explain, aware that whatever he said would be far from adequate. "Maybe pain and sorrow are necessary for us to grow. It's true of the body; maybe it's true for the soul. I don't know, Tempest, but God's laws were made to be obeyed."

Tempest thought of her da. What law of her father's had she unwittingly broken that he had cast her out of his life forever? How could she overcome the growing emptiness at the loss of him—and now at the withdrawal of this man as well?

Abram leaned forward. He reached out and brushed his fingertips across her shoulder. "Tell me what you're thinking."

Her eyes were so solemn, guileless, and searching. She moistened her lips. "What're yer laws, mon? How will I know when I've broken one? What will be yer punishment?" She clenched her jaws so tightly that the muscles stood out.

"I won't cast you out, if that's what you're thinking. You're my wife . . . part of me. If I cast you away, I'd be cutting away part of myself, the part that's alive as long as you're here with me. Do you understand?"

An ageless sadness and wisdom filled her blue eyes. "Aye, mon, just as part of Da was cut away when my mother died." The dark memory of blood, fire, and smoke shivered through her. She drew in a whimpering breath and hung her head.

"What is it?" Abram lifted her chin.

She drew back from his touch and shook her head, hiding her face again. Abram saw her throat work.

"Talking sometimes purges . . ."

"Naught will purge some things."

Then let me hold you, Tempest McClaren. Let me give you comfort. But he had lost the nerve to offer himself.

They were silent for a long time, neither looking at the other.

Tempest's head bobbed drowsily. Abram yawned, and stood. "Let me rub some more liniment in, and then we can both get some sleep."

Her look was grateful. She stood and removed the shirtwaist and camisole, then unbuttoned the skirt and untied the

petticoat. She took her nightgown from the middle drawer and
slipped it on, letting it hang unbuttoned around her waist as
she drew down the last undergarments. When everything was
neatly folded away, she went to sit on the edge of the bed.

Abram watched each grimace, knowing that her body had
already stiffened up from her long respite by the fire. He was
mesmerized by the small, firm, dark-tipped breasts, the gentle
curve of her brown back, the slight curve of her hip beneath
the thin lawn nightgown.

"Stretch out on your stomach," he told her, taking up the
liniment again. He set the bottle on the highboy and leaned
forward, resting one knee on the bed as he rubbed his palms
together. The sight of her bare back down to the curve of her
buttocks and the clear outline of those buttocks and legs beneath
the soft layer of thin cloth made hot blood surge in his veins.
He gritted his teeth and bent to the task, trying to close his
mind to his body's urging. She groaned deeply, and he eased
the pressure of his hands.

"You'll be no good for anything tomorrow after what you
did today." He closed his eyes tightly and concentrated on what
he had to do, rather than what he wanted to do.

Her abused muscles loosened and grew warm beneath his
unhurried ministrations. Her head turned to one side and her
eyelids drooped. He watched the alertness in her face smooth
away. The gnawing tightness in his loins eased. He smiled
down at her.

Spreading his fingers and spanning her shoulders, he made
one last long, slow sweep over her back, then rested his hands
against the small curve, his thumbs on her spine. Leaning down,
he brushed his lips lightly against her temple. He closed his
eyes and kissed the tender hollow at the back of her neck.

He moved quietly away and undressed. Very carefully, he
drew back the bedclothes and slid into bed, drawing the blankets
up again over himself and Tempest. She had curled onto her
side and he fitted himself behind her, not so close as to touch
and awaken her, but close enough to feel the heat radiating
from her young body.

His heart thumping wildly, he lay still. If he touched her
. . . *Oh, God.*

She turned slowly and he drew back so that she wouldn't
brush against him. Her face was turned toward his and he could
make out her wonderful features in the hazy glow of the firelight. Taking the risk, he reached out and lightly touched her

cheek. Her eyelids trembled. He held his breath and prayed. She relaxed with a soft sigh. With the tips of his fingers, he traced every curve and plane of her face, the velvet softness of her lips, the slow pulse in her throat.

"There's a verse in Genesis," he whispered to her as she slept. "It says, *'Therefore shall a man leave his father and his mother and shall cleave unto his wife.'* Tempest, it's the same for a woman." His hand moved slowly lower over the small, firm, peaked breasts, the ladder of her ribs, the satiny skin of her hip, and stopped. His hand tightened and he inched closer until their bodies barely touched. He breathed in the scent of her.

"Forget your da, Tempest McClaren," he murmured, and brushed his lips against her hair. "Cleave unto me."

"Mon . . ." she moaned softly, and nestled closer.

Abram smiled. He could wait now. He could wait a little longer.

Weeping may endure for a night,
but joy cometh in the morning.

—Psalms 30:5

Abram slid his hand in quest along the moss-filled canvas mattress beneath the heavy quilts, encountering nothing, and his eyes opened slowly. Where was Tempest?

Soft domestic sounds penetrated his sleep-drugged brain, and he saw sunlight streaming in through the open windows. Sitting up, he rubbed his face and yawned.

Tempest was standing by the fire, stirring something in the iron pot suspended over the glowing coals. She had been watching him, but now she turned her back and bent to her task again.

"Mornin'," he mumbled with the huskiness of a good night's sleep.

It was late, long past dawn. Frowning, he shoved the bedclothes back and stood. Stepping into his dungarees and shrugging on his shirt, he stared at Tempest's bent back and the gentle curve of her hips.

Had those hips been curved back into his own last night, or had he imagined everything? When he'd run his hand along the mattress, he'd expected to find her beside him, not fully dressed and working over the fire, more silent and withdrawn than ever. Disappointment and frustration brought a hard frown and a glint of temper to his face.

"You should've awakened me earlier. I've lost a couple of good hours of work."

She didn't look at him, but poured out a mug of coffee and set it on the table next to his bowl. Then she took up the bowl and went back to the pot over the fire and began spooning up his breakfast.

"Did you sleep well last night?" he demanded. Why wouldn't she look at him? What had he done wrong? "I'd like an answer."

She set his bowl on the table. Her eyes grazed his briefly. *"You* should've awakened *me*. I wouldna have stayed the night in yer bed."

His anger mounted. "You didn't sleep through, girl, don't pretend you did. I felt you moving around." And he'd been hard pressed to contain himself. "You could've gotten up then, but you chose to stay put," he snarled.

"I'll no crowd ye agin, mon," she said, turning away. Abram had never heard her brogue so thick.

The stiffness of her back told him more clearly than words that the stone wall growing outside was nothing compared to the one she was building up between them. Last night seemed as far away as if it had never been. His breath came in a sharp jerk of anger; color mounted in his face.

She has no right to do this to me! He had wanted her until his guts had curled into aching knots, but he hadn't taken her. How many other men would have been this patient? How many other men would have rubbed her back, let her sleep in a warm bed, and not rolled her onto her back and forced her legs apart? How many men in their right mind would have put up with her long, punishing silences, her stubborn willfulness and simmering defiance?

No *man!*

"Goddamn it, I've had enough! I made a mistake thinking I could make a wife of you! Oh, you eat with a fork now instead of jamming food in like an animal! You're not filthy. You don't smell like horse dung, dirt, and death; the stinking buckskins are gone. Every other word isn't a foul one. But beyond that, *what in hell are you?"*

He came forward and put his arm on the mantel, leaning down to look at her, wanting to see some of his own pain in her face. She refused to look at him, continuing to stir in the iron pot, making bigger, slower circles in the gruel.

Frustration coursed through Abram strong and hot, building up and driving him. His voice came out choked and shaking.

"You're just like your da, you know that?" he snarled. "What did you say about him? *Walking dead.* I should've listened to the men at the fort. I should've waited for another wagon train. I wanted a wife—a woman, someone warm, someone able to share with me. But I saw you and went a little crazy. I thought there was something in you, but there isn't. I should've left you with the Mad Scot."

He stalked out of the cabin, slamming the door behind him, and strode angrily across the open yard and into the quiet stable. "Damn!" He struck his hand against the post and raked shaking fingers through his hair.

Kathy had never driven him to such rage. He had never in his life spoken to anyone the way he had just now to Tempest. He had wanted to hurt her! The hot, bitter words had done nothing but drive his own anger even higher, his frustration even deeper. He raised his hand and watched it shake, then clenched it into a fist until the knuckles turned white. He could feel the blood pounding in his head.

Last night she had murmured *mon* and he'd been filled with foolish hope. This morning, he'd opened his eyes again. *Nothing has changed.*

Abram understood Tempest less now than he had that first moment he had seen her. He had felt something move inside him, had sensed her vulnerability. God, how wrong could a man be? Tempest McClaren was hard, unrelenting, and cold—colder than a mountain winter, colder than death.

"To hell with her." He yoked the oxen.

Abram didn't return to the cabin until midday. Tempest was coming up from the creek with a bucket of water, so full it sloshed over the rim and dampened the hem of a dark skirt Kathy had once worn.

Kathy.

How could he ever have thought Tempest McClaren could take her place?

Tempest's head was down, her face concealed. Abram went into the cabin, fully expecting to find a cold hearth and nothing to eat but congealed mush from breakfast.

The table was properly laid and the rich aroma of rabbit and wild vegetable stew rose from the iron pot that bubbled over the fire. He glanced around and took in the tidied bed, the swept floor, the oiled furniture. Beside his place was a folded shirt. It was one he had torn a week ago, It was mended, bright red stitches crossing the fabric like small, irregular bird tracks. A poor job, and one no primary girl in Pennsylvania would have wanted to be seen.

A movement at the door made him turn. Tempest stood there, looking at him solemnly. She lowered her head and put the bucket just inside the door before going back out. He frowned and glanced at the table again.

One place setting.

Standing in the doorway, he called out to her. "Have you already eaten?"

She took up the hoe and walked toward the garden.

"Well, are you going to come in and eat now or not?"

She shook her head.

Abram stood watching her for a long, tense moment. She bent to the work, her back toward him. "Fine," he snarled, and went back inside. He served himself, scraped the chair back violently, and sat.

A woman has her ways of tormenting a man for his harsh words, he thought as he ate by himself in the silent room. When he had said something in anger to Kathy, she'd look at him with martyred patience, then let him stew in guilt for hours before she agreed to forgive him—even when he'd been right. Yet she had never made him feel unmanly. She had never driven him to rage.

Tempest emasculated him.

He ought to be used to her silence by now, but he wasn't. He doubted he ever would be. He was no closer to her today than he had been the first day he had brought her back here.

He remembered how hard he'd worked to build this cabin for her. He had cut every tree and dragged it back, mixed the adobe and grass to fill in the spaces between the logs, split the shingles. Hope. Want. Need. The dream of Tempest McClaren being with him.

He had brought her back here and created his own living hell.

Shoving his empty plate aside, Abram put his elbows on the table and rested his aching head on the heels of his hands. The sound of the hoe was faint. After a while it stopped. He stood and went to lean against the doorjamb. Tempest was in the field again, toting rocks. She bent and pulled, finally hefting a bulky stone in her arms, then trudged across the broken earth to drop it on the wall. Again and again, stone after stone.

He almost hated her.

He stood and watched, his arms crossed over his tight aching chest, a grim frown creasing his face. Finally he turned away. He'd go hunting and get his mind off everything for a few hours, get away from the plowing and planting. Get away from *her!*

Abram didn't look at her as he brought his horse out and saddled him. He didn't look at her as he shoved his rifle into the holster and swung himself up. He didn't look at her as he gave the animal a sharp kick and galloped away.

Riding aimlessly, not really caring if he found game or not, Abram took comfort in the sun's warmth on his back. He slowed his mount to a leisurely walk. Game there was, but the rifle remained sheathed. He saw little of the rolling, wild-wheat-covered hills, the oaks, the brush, the marshland where Tempest had come. He raised his head and saw the cloud-shrouded mountains in the distance. He'd come across those almost a year ago. Every foot had been a fight, every mile a battle.

All those grand hopes and dreams he had had: what had happened to them? Had everything died with Kathy a thousand miles before he reached this murderous range? Had he buried everything with her? Should he have stayed in Pennsylvania and been satisfied with what he had had there—a few acres, a meager living? He had more now, yet less. *Less.*

Kathy hadn't wanted to leave Pennsylvania. She had raised so many arguments—found so many reasons to stay. *"Abram, what if I get pregnant on the way? What about Mama and Papa and our aunts and uncles, Cousin Mary. You know she's in a family way. Why can't we just work harder to buy land little by little until we have all you want? California is so far away. It's a wilderness."*

But he'd brought her around to his way of thinking.

She'd counted the graves by the trail while he'd dreamed his dreams. And he buried her beneath a pine overlooking a valley in the Rockies.

Why did I come?

Abram didn't even realize he was crying. Tears streaked his face as he rode on.

"Oh, Kathy . . ."

God, I'm so lonely. I wanted space, but this land is so vast, so empty. How many miles must I ride to find a neighbor?

Loneliness ate at him, seemed to swallow him whole. *I should have stayed home in Pennsylvania. Why did I come? Why did I think the dream was worth the risk? I never expected to lose you, Kathy.*

Nor had he expected to lay all his hopes on a wild, half-breed girl.

When he came back, the sunset was reflected orange-pink against the distant hills. He paused on the rise above his fledgling farm and looked down at it, longing for the promising beauty of it to penetrate him, rouse his eagerness. Somewhere beyond in the wilderness, a lone wolf howled. Abram sighed, his gaze traveling slowly over the expanse of the plowed earth.

A forlorn figure sat huddled in the middle of the plowed field.

Tempest.

The anger had long since left Abram and there remained only a deep weariness. He urged his horse forward and rode down the slope, his heart tripping at a pace as fast as the hoofbeats. Tempest's head lifted and turned, her face white in the deepening dusk. Nearing her, he drew in and the animal sidestepped, tossing its head as Abram held the reins too taut.

"What're you doing out here?" he demanded.

She was trembling. She struggled to stand, swaying.

"Have you been out here all day?"

She said nothing, and anger pulsed through Abram again, along with a quick feeling of shame and resentment. "Go back to the house!"

In the distance, the wolf howled again and was answered. He would have to secure the horses for the night. He left Tempest standing in the field and rode toward the animal shelter. Unsaddling the horse, he brushed him down, forked fresh hay into his stall, and poured a liberal amount of oats for him. There was plenty of water in the carved-out log. Closing the door and securing it, he headed toward the cabin.

The cabin was still warm from the afternoon sun, but Tempest wasn't there. Abram stormed outside, his eyes scanning the field in the growing darkness and finding her sitting again on the ground. He strode toward her.

"Damn you! Get up!"

When she didn't move, he grabbed her arm and dragged her to her feet. Her body sagged, her head lolling back, and he saw something in her face that made his body suddenly go cold. He lifted her and held her close as he hurried back toward the cabin.

Kicking the door open, he entered and carried her across to the bed. He put her down gently and then went to rebuild the fire. When he turned back, Tempest was standing, swaying as though someone were pushing at her. Her face was dirty and streaked, her eyes red-rimmed and swollen. She stared at the open cabin door unblinkingly. He closed it and dropped the bar.

"Sit down before you fall." He took her arm, forcing her backward. Her knees buckled against the edge of the bed and she sat down hard, her back stiff.

"What'd you do?" His hand tightened. He shook her slightly. "Did you work out there all day? Why? To make me feel like a miserable bastard?" he said harshly.

She shook her head slowly. "I wanted to please ye."

"Please me?"

She looked up at him, her face working. "I canna...I canna..."

"What am I supposed to do? Patience wears thin after a while." He stepped away from her, afraid of the power of his own emotions.

"I canna go now, mon," she murmured brokenly. He stopped short and turned back to stare down at her. She looked up at him with grieving, frightened eyes, and he frowned.

"But I thought... I thought that's what you wanted. To go back. To be with your da."

Her mouth quivered. "With each moon ye like me less... while I try harder. I canna..."

Abram gazed at her, almost stunned. "Is that how you've seen it?"

Her hands clenched tightly. "It's the way it is."

He came closer. "Because of what I said this morning?"

She lowered her head. "Ye canna change truth."

He crouched down before her and grasped her wrists. The tendons were stretched tight. She was cold, so cold. He saw the tight line of her jaw, the way her lips pressed together, the raw look in her blue eyes.

He had been right after all. She needed him. God, she needed him worse than he had known.

He let go of one of her wrists and tilted her chin up. "It wasn't the truth, not all of it. I was angry. People say cruel things when they're angry. Lord, I can't even remember half of what I said to you this morning."

She looked straight into him. "I canna be yer Kathy."

The air was punched from his lungs. All day he had longed for Kathy, longed for her simplicity, her quiet manner, her woman's acceptance, while he'd cursed this girl for being what she was. *Strong*. But was she? And how far into a man's soul could she see with those strange eyes of hers?

"Kathy's gone. I miss her, yes, but she is gone." Tempest

turned her head away, but he put a firm hand beneath her chin and turned it back again. "We've been over this before. It's old ground, long since turned."

"Old ground," she repeated, and looked at him again. "I canna be white for ye. I canna even be Indian. I am what I am, mon. Putting me in gingham doesna change what's inside."

Abram released her and stood slowly. "What happened this morning? Last night, I thought everything was coming round for us, the way I'd always hoped it would. You whispered my name last night. Did you know that?"

He had never seen Tempest blush. He watched in surprised fascination as color mounted her neck and filled her face. Her eyes glistened. She looked away, her chin trembling.

Abram pushed his hands into his pockets, wanting so badly to touch her, but knowing that if he did he wouldn't be able to quell the feelings rising in him. He gritted his teeth against the desire to hold her.

"Things have to change," he said. "You're going to sleep with me in our bed. You're not going to lie in front of the fire like a family dog."

She said nothing, her head bent.

"I think you were more comfortable with me than you're willing to admit. Otherwise, why did you stay beside me all night?" He paused, waiting, and then plunged on. "I think you liked it when I touched you, too," he added, wanting desperately to believe it.

Still Tempest kept her head down, her shoulders hunched.

"Didn't you?" he rasped.

She raised her head and looked at him. Two huge tears slid slowly down her cheeks. "Aye," she whispered brokenly. She had liked it very much. Looking up at him now, she acknowledged the many things she had come to like about this strange man. She liked the way his reddish-brown hair fell forward on his tanned brow. She liked the way his hazel eyes crinkled at the corners when he smiled. She liked the deep creases in his sunburned cheeks. She liked the sound of his deep, calm voice as he read from the big black book. She liked the sight of his bared, hair-covered chest as he worked, liked to watch the muscles move beneath the bronzed, glistening skin. She liked the smell of him.

Strength, life—Abram Walker.

She had liked most of all the feel of his arm weighting her

down into the softness of that bed, his leg thrown over hers. She had felt safe, protected, cherished.

Warmth, human comfort, closeness, softness—things she'd not felt in so many years that she could scarcely remember them at all.

When Abram had galloped away, she thought he was leaving her—just as Da had left her. She had started to run after him—just as she had after Da. But when she'd reached the rise of the hill and seen him riding toward the mountains, she had stopped. It had done no good before—her da had only ridden faster. *Faster*. Abram Walker would, too.

So she'd gone back and worked, trudging back and forth with stones until she couldn't take another step, couldn't lift another burden. She'd sunk down, the last stone heavy in her lap, and, in final, tearful desperation, prayed to Abram Walker's God that he would come back, that she wouldn't be left alone.

Alone. *Again*.

Then the wolf had howled.

She had remembered her mother lying dead as the buzzards pecked out her eyes. She had remembered the blackened walls of the fireplace.

She had remembered McClaren striding into the dark cave, the bloody sack in his hand and death in his eyes.

"Tempest?" Abram saw the stark emotions in her face and came to her. He gripped her shoulders. "Tempest..." he murmured hoarsely.

Her mouth quivered. Her eyes filled with tears and with him. "Dunna leave me... dunna go away and leave me..."

"Oh, God—I won't... I won't," he promised, and drew her close.

She came against him hard, throwing her arms around him, clinging tightly. Abram closed his eyes and rested his chin on her head. He could feel the tremors running through her. *How long I've waited for this... just this.* And he held her closer.

"I dinna fix ye anything to eat..."

"I don't care," he murmured against her hair. Her body grew warmer, melting against his. "Let's just sit by the fire."

They drew apart, suddenly shy. Abram reclined before the fire, bracing himself on one elbow as he watched the firelight play across Tempest's young, still-troubled face as she sat on the woven mat.

She's so incredibly beautiful, he thought, *so different from anyone I've ever known.* The white blood showed in her blue eyes, her high cheekbones, her straight nose. The Indian blood revealed itself in her thick, raven hair, her light-brown skin, the square line of her jaw, her full mouth. He'd never tire of looking at her, not as long as he lived.

She didn't move when he reached out and ran his hand down along her arm until he grasped her hand. Lifting it, he pressed it against his lips, his eyes drooping partly closed as he continued to watch her. Sitting up slowly, he took her hand in both of his. He opened her fingers and turned her hand so that the palm was against his own.

"So small," he whispered. Her head was lowered, her arm outstretched to him as he held her hand. "Look at me, Tempest," he pleaded.

She raised her head slowly, looking at him openly, waiting.

Waiting for him. Instinct told him everything. Warm, tingling surges began in his loins and pulsed in swelling beats. He swallowed hard. *Just like that, after all these long, agonizing weeks. How? Why?*

But he knew.

His hand trembled as he reached out and clumsily unbuttoned the front of her dress. His breath came hard as he revealed the thin camisole beneath. Tugging gently at the ribbons, he watched the garment fall open and reveal creamy mounds of nubile flesh. His heart thundered and a flush of urgency spread hotly across his skin, then focused and hardened into an aching pain.

"I won't hurt you," he murmured hoarsely, and slowly put his hands on her breasts. She closed her eyes tightly, but she didn't protest or flinch away. She waited, acquiescent. He saw the erratic pulse in her throat.

"Please . . . don't be afraid."

Her breasts quivered as he slid both hands further into the open camisole and sought the dark peaks with his work-roughened thumbs. Her hands curled into hard little fists resting on her thighs.

"You're so soft," he gasped, his eyes closing rapturously. When he opened them again, he looked at her in the firelight— her golden skin, the pallor of her face, the look in her eyes— and found he couldn't ignore what he knew was true.

"You're making it a bargain, aren't you? You're afraid if you don't let me . . . I'll leave," he murmured bleakly.

She didn't need to answer. Why couldn't he make himself see this as acknowledgment of her need for him? She was giving herself to him; all that mattered was her willingness. But he felt he was somehow breaking her spirit.

Drawing the edges of the camisole back together with shaking fingers, Abram met Tempest's fixed gaze with a gentle smile. She frowned slightly as he stood up. She stared at the bulge in his dungarees and she blushed, turning away. "We've both been through a lot today. Let's sleep on things. We can talk about everything tomorrow."

"Why do ye not take what belongs to ye?" she asked softly.

"Because you don't. Because I don't want a sacrifice."

The woman in Tempest was far wiser. Life itself was sacrifice. Without it, there could be no rebirth. It was time.

She watched him prepare for bed. When he slid beneath the quilts, she stood and slowly removed her clothes. She left the nightgown in the drawer. When she came into the bed beside him, she brought her hip against his.

Abram knew then that he was only a man. He hadn't meant to touch her again, but he turned and pulled her close. He only meant to kiss her once, to show her he understood—but one kiss wasn't enough. Nor was a second, or a third, each more urgent, each quickening his pounding pulse, his ragged breathing. She didn't fight him. He rolled her onto her back and pressed his knee between her soft, slim legs. They parted.

"Oh, God . . . I wish it were different . . ."

Yet how else could it be? he thought as his lungs strained, his heart thundered, and his body burned with the feel of her soft form beneath his, her legs on either side of him. He pressed forward. She gasped and arched against the invading hardness, the pain.

"I'm sorry," he moaned, meaning it. But he couldn't prevent hurting her. There was no other way. Her hips bucked up and he drove forward again, harder, feeling the protective membrane stretch and then tear. She cried out again and her fingernails dug into his shoulders. He caught her wrists and held them back against the canvas mattress. He wanted to stop and then go on more slowly, more gently, but he couldn't. It had been too long. He needed her too much.

Tight, moist warmth closed around him as he went into her with a deep groan. His weight held her pinioned as his hands left her wrists to grip her hips. Her heaving movements to dislodge him merely served to drive him faster, bring him to the edge and push him over into mindless ecstasy more quickly. He gave himself up to her with a deep, wrenching cry.

Tempest went still beneath him. "Mon?"

Another, softer groan sighed from Abram's parted lips. His breath came hard, fast, rasping—like a dying man.

Her young arms clasped him urgently. "Mon!"

It was done.

Abram felt so light, almost as if he might float up from her warm softness unless he held on tightly and kept himself locked inside her. His convulsive shuddering died away and his body slowly began to relax, to recover from the agonizing, pulsing heat that had spiraled through his mind and body. He no longer felt light. Was he crushing her? He couldn't move yet. The relief of release went clear through him and down to his toes. Sagging, he turned his head against her shoulder.

"I love you," he whispered, and kissed her neck.

When he was finally able to roll away, Tempest sat up and looked down at him. The deep lines around his eyes and mouth were softened; his eyes were dazed, warm, glowing. He smiled and raised a hand to her cheek. She covered it with her own.

"It hurt ye," she murmured. "It hurt ye as much as it did me."

He felt so spent. The hard, fast beating of his heart hadn't slowed yet. All he wanted was for her to lie down beside him again, to be there with him. *Always*.

"Why do ye want to rut if it hurts so much?" she asked, wanting to understand.

Abram was thankful for the heavy shadows that obscured his face from her intent perusal. "Lie with me," he whispered. "Please."

She slowly stretched out beside him. He drew the quilt up.

"There's a narrow boundary between pain and pleasure," he said, his voice still husky, unlike his own.

"I dunna understand."

He knew. Oh, God, he knew, and wished he didn't. Turning his head, he looked at her openly. It saddened him that she didn't know. There was no way she could understand until she experienced those heightened sensations for herself, and that couldn't happen until he learned how to breach all her barriers and reach inside her, touch her very soul. And that might never happen.

Mating was a kind of pain. Passion had sharp, hot claws that dug into him, pulling at him, embracing him, sucking him dry. For one instant, everything was gone in the inner explosion, the outward gift. A part of himself, the creative male part, was drawn out and absorbed by her; then life came back, renewed and right.

It wasn't easy. It was pain. Yet it was good—and it was necessary.

How could he ever explain to her?

"I need to be part of you, Tempest. It hurts me not to be part of you. It hurts a man not to join with his woman."

Tempest's face filled with an odd kind of pity. She moved closer. Putting her arms around him, she pressed her warm body against his.

Surprised, Abram remained still. Was she trying to comfort him? He let her, thinking how good she felt, how natural. He brushed his lips against her dark hair.

"You smell good," he murmured.

Earth and woman.

Life.

Longing for that lovely lady
How can I bring my aching heart to rest?
—Han Wu-ti

The fields greened with awakening crops while Tempest's garden birthed radishes, onions, squash, potatoes, and tomatoes. She still preferred to reap the bounty of the wild, treating Abram to the unfamiliar delicacies of burdock, cattail-pollen hotcakes, clover steamed between hot stones, dock mash, wild grapes, and a variety of sweet berries. Most of her finds came from within walking distance of the rough cabin.

Abram worked on building a smokehouse. When it was finished, Tempest shot a large buck, strung it, gutted it, and brought it back for butchering. This accomplished, she hung the meat in the smokehouse, keeping a low and even fire going for a week.

Abram thanked God daily for having Tempest, and at night, with her curled warmly against his side, he lay in joyous silence, filled with purpose. As soon as she became a woman, he would fill her with child.

In addition to tending the growing crops, Abram moved fieldstones and began laying a foundation for a corncrib. When Tempest wasn't working in the cabin or gathering food, she carried out his simple instructions for thinning and hoeing the corn rows. She piled and pulled plants for stock feed.

"Trappin's easier," she grumbled.

"We're doing fine, and in another year or two people will come pouring into this land. We'll be having house and barn raisings and husking bees and holiday celebrations just like back home. These newcomers will need corn to tide them over while they get started." He swung his ax, deepening the notch in a big log, readying it to be set into position on the south wall of his new corncrib.

He watched the horizon, remembering Fremont's warning, but no one came to try to expel him. They were alone. Sonoma was a day's ride to the west and New Helvetia was almost two days to the east. He wondered whether he had made the best decision, settling between the two instead of close to one or the other. He'd wanted space. He hadn't come across a con-

tinent to build his farm right next to another man's. He wanted
room to spread.

Yet Fremont's words remained in his memory. The fear had
been planted, and it grew.

Abram looked out at the foot-high corn. After the harvest
he would take bushels of it and of wheat to trade at New
Helvetia. He wanted cattle, just a few head to start. He'd always
made his living from the earth, but he'd seen at Sutter's Fort
how the two endeavors could be combined to good profit. And
hadn't God himself preferred Abel's gift of the fatted calf to
Cain's of golden grain?

This was a new land. Perhaps Tempest was right. Leave
the old life behind and find a new way of doing things.

During one of her foraging expeditions, Tempest found a
bee tree. It was close enough to the farm to be of benefit to
them. Abram wanted it even closer.

"We con smoke them into a stupor," Tempest suggested,
thinking that he only wanted to steal the honey.

"Good idea. We'll do it this evening, just after dusk." He
spent the rest of the day hollowing out a section of log and
devising a matching hatch with leather hinges. He carried it
along as they hiked up the hill.

Tempest built the fire inside the old, dead trunk and then
threw on moist leaves to make heavier smoke. The angry bees
buzzed loudly overhead, then gradually quieted as the smoke
drugged most of them.

"Stand back," Abram told her.

Tempest's eyes shot open. "What are ye doing, mon? Are
ye mad?"

The first powerful whack of Abram's ax roused the bees
again.

Tempest swore at him. "Ye've only to climb up and steal
what ye want, ye fool!"

Some bees burst forth and swirled in confusion. Appalled,
Tempest stared up at the growing dark cloud of infuriated
insects.

"Out of my way!" Abram shouted as she leaped across to
stop him.

"Ye bloody ass! Get out of here! Get—OUCH!" A bee sting
burned the side of her neck and she swatted the creature. Abram
shoved her roughly out of his way again and with two more
chops toppled the tree. He jumped on it and split it straight

down the center. The cloying smell of honey permeated the night.

"Holy Jesus!" Tempest cried in fright, seeing disaster hovering above Abram's head and him oblivious. She tore off her skirt and whipped wildly at the air as the bees started to attack. "What in hell are ye doing?!" she screamed at him, debating leaving him to his fate as half a dozen bees found their mark on her. She yelped, swinging her skirt faster.

"Got her!" Abram exclaimed, holding the main honeycomb housing the queen bee in his hand. She heard the hatch of the hollowed section of log slam. "Let's go!"

"What about the bleeding range fire ye've started?" she roared in vexation at his retreating back. He ran back, stomped up and down on the small blaze and kicked dirt about in a frenzied dance while waving his arms around, and then ran like hell.

Tempest laid every curse known to her on Abram's head as she ran ahead of him. Abram dumped the makeshift hive at the edge of the cornfield as they raced between rows. Most of the bees paused, swirling in a black mass around the man-made hive, seeking their queen.

Others pursued like black pellets of shot, diving on Tempest and Abram alike. Tempest reached the cabin first. Abram plunged in after her and she slammed the door. He was laughing breathlessly. For the next few minutes, Tempest was fully occupied with murdering the enraged bees who had managed to zoom in with her. Abram sagged against the door, dripping honey.

The hard blow to his right eye took him completely by surprise. "Hey!" Another connected with his midsection that was harder than any he had gotten from the boys he'd fought as a youngster. She hurled a kick at his shin and was aiming for his left eye when he caught hold of her.

"Hold up!" he shouted. She attacked him with teeth and fists. Abram held her tightly around the waist, hauling her roughly against his hard, heaving chest. "Stop it!" She bit him in the fleshy spot just next to his armpit and earned a yelp and immediate release. He just managed to parry another swing and catch hold of her wrist. He twisted it sharply up and around. He had never thought he'd be using a wrestling hold on his wife, but he held her tightly with his forearm locked around her throat. Tempest squirmed violently, thrashing and screaming profanity.

Finally, he spun her back around, grabbed her shoulders and shook her violently, shouting right into her face. She went limp, her head going back and he saw the swelling stings across her face and down her neck.

"Oh, Tempest," he groaned.

She sniffed indelicately. "Ye fool! All ye had to do was grab what ye wanted. But *no!* Ye had to chop down the tree and get the bees riled enough to kill!"

"We've got our own hive now."

She voiced her sentiments in one short, crudely descriptive word. He pulled a stinger from her cheek and she gasped, her eyes hot. "Hush," he pleaded. "Let me get them all out for you."

She slapped his hand away, grimacing as she got covered with honey. He lifted his hand and took a long, slow lick while watching her teasingly. "Hmm, tastes like they've been in clover." He offered his hand to her placatingly. She eyed him balefully, then capitulated and took a lick herself. She gave a grunt of pleasure and lapped more honey, sucking greedily at each of his fingers, her eyes half closed.

A fire began in Abram's midsection and grew heavy.

"Worth it?" he said hoarsely.

She bit down hard on his pinky and he jerked his hand out of her grasp with a sharp gasp. She grinned broadly. "Ask me tomorrow." She went to the door and listened against the planks. Then she opened it cautiously. "They're gone."

"Where're you going?" he asked, sucking at his throbbing finger.

"To the creek."

"What for?" he asked, following curiously when she didn't answer.

She took off her clothes as she went, dropping them heedlessly. Her skirt was somewhere up on the hill, dropped and forgotten when she'd run from the swarm. Abram's heart was pounding as he watched her in the moonlight. She crouched down by the creek and began slapping globs of mud on her face and neck and arms. "It'll draw the poison," she told him.

Exploring gingerly, Abram found three lumps on his head other than the half a dozen Tempest had given him. His right eye was almost as swollen as her left one. He smiled slightly, bent down, and flicked mud at her. Tempest, not knowing how to play, took up a handful and flung it in retaliation. Her aim was better than his, and he spat mud, wiping it off his face and out of his eyes.

Something more to teach her, he thought, rinsing his hands in the creek.

She was dabbing mud on a swelling just above her right breast. The moon made her skin look pale. Abram's mouth went dry as he watched. She raised her head slowly and looked at him.

"No," she said simply. "I hurt all over already. I dunna need ye pawing at me."

Abram blushed crimson.

Still she gazed at him curiously. "I canna understand ye wanting to do it so much."

So much! he thought ruefully, gritting his teeth. It had been four days since the last time. She had been exhausted from field work, as dry as the desert. It had been an ordeal just to enter her.

"I haven't been bothering you overmuch," he growled defensively.

"Not because ye dunna want to," she responded bluntly. She shook her head. "Ye always groan and cry out, and I con see that look on yer face at the end of it."

Sweet Jesus. Does she lie there on her back and watch me the whole time? he wondered despairingly. Good God! He closed his eyes, mortified.

Why didn't she just keep silent? Why wouldn't she allow him the chance to regain his self-control? Kathy used to say she was close to her time of the month and it pained her, or she was too tired, or she had a headache. But she had never used a verbal hammer on his manhood.

Tempest watched Abram's face. He opened his eyes and looked at her with a slight, bitter curve to his mouth, his eyes shining with hurt in the moonlight.

He knew well enough that she didn't enjoy coupling, that she submitted to his lust only when his need was too strong to ignore any longer. He usually managed to finish quickly, while Tempest lay still beneath him, stroking his back gently while he regained his breath.

From her standpoint, Tempest realized that sometimes he wanted her badly but didn't bother her. Then, other times, his own physical needs were so strong, so pressing, that her feelings didn't matter at all.

Like now. For the moment, her words had discouraged him. The look in his eyes was grim as he stood up.

"Let the mud at least dry, Abram."

She stood up and saw how hard he tried not to stare at her breasts. But the moon was shining fully. He seemed to be holding his breath and she saw the faint sheen of sweat on his forehead and upper lip.

Resignedly she held out her hand. He looked at her with a faint frown. Then, not wanting to question her, he took her hand firmly and led her back to the cabin.

Lying on the bed beside her, spent and relaxed, Abram tried not to think he had failed her. She sat up. He knew his seed drained from her in her cross-legged position; that hurt him almost more than anything else. Did she do it on purpose? *I'm expecting too much too soon,* he told himself.

Tempest lay down again beside him and quickly fell asleep. He stayed on his back, staring up at the ceiling. *It'd be easier if I loved her less.*

His thoughts gradually turned away from Tempest and wandered to the troubles Fremont had heard of in Monterey. Or started, as Tempest had said. Maybe she was right.

He wished he knew what was happening. With the corn and wheat planted, maybe he should take a few days and make a trip to New Helvetia. But what if McClaren were there? No, it was unlikely. He'd gone back to the mountains. He wouldn't return until winter at the earliest.

Tempest grew restless, and Abram turned slightly to watch her. It happened often. The nightmare came as though the darkness in her mind broke free with the darkness of night. He wondered what she dreamed about when she whimpered and her hands clutched into tight, white-knuckled fists. She began to thrash, breathing in soft, gasping cries. What was she fighting?

Her thrashing slowed, and he knew she would begin to sob softly. "Hush," he whispered, turning onto his stomach and putting his arm across her, drawing her closer. "Hush . . ."

Her breathing slowed again and he felt her body relax. Her face turned toward him, her eyelids trembling but not opening. He should have closed the window, but the cool air felt so good after a long, hot day. Faint moonlight streamed in and let him study Tempest's face. Her taut features twitched and then gradually relaxed into the smooth face of an angelic child.

"Be a woman for me, Tempest McClaren," he whispered, and closed his eyes for sleep.

Nothing can be done in California without the
sanctifying influence of the spirit.
—Dame Shirley

Tempest was collecting acorns for coffee from beneath the ancient oaks above the farm when she spotted several
riders coming from the northwest. They were moving together
at a brisk canter and would reach Abram before she could.
Cautiously but quickly she moved down the hill, hiding among
the brush as they approached. She saw Abram go for his musket, which was leaning against a log close at hand.

There were about a dozen men, all but two dressed in buckskin. They looked to be all Americans but for one, and he rode
straight-backed, his head high like a soldier, and wore the dark
pants, pale shirt, and bolero of a Californio gentleman.

Tempest drew in a startled breath as she recognized Marianno Guadalupe Vallejo. Another man rode close beside him.
Both of them were unarmed, while the others carried their
muskets at the ready, prepared for trouble.

She had seen Vallejo several times when riding with her
father. They had gone to his Sonoma hacienda to trade otter
pelts and Tempest had gleaned information about the Californio
by listening in on fireside conversations among the rough Yankee settlers and even Vallejo's own people, who never tired
of proudly relating the glorious tales of their revered *patron*.

Governor Figueroa had sent Vallejo north in the thirties to
end Indian insurrections, block Russian expansion, and secu-
larize the mission lands. Vallejo, a young and ambitious man,
had packed up his entire family and moved them north, together
with his in-laws, the Carrillos. Then he had sent out his younger
brother, Salvador, to teach the Sotoyomi tribesmen a lesson.
In one series of battles, more then eight hundred braves lay
dead and three hundred more were taken slaves, without the
loss of a single Californio. In establishing the Petaluma rancho,
Vallejo's caballeros had dragged leather lariats over the ground
and marked out 15,000 square leagues of land for Vallejo.

Then he built an adobe fortress on a hillside overlooking the rich valley land. With hard work, that land had come to produce vast amounts of barley and wheat and fed thousands of head of longhorn cattle, which Vallejo raised for the hide and tallow trade.

As for the Russians, he had outlasted them, and they sold their holdings to Sutter in 1841 and sailed north to Alaska. The otter had played out almost at the same time that the Orient's demand for their pelts had dwindled. All that had remained of their venture was a few cannon, some livestock, equipment and supplies, and thousands of healthy gophers that ate everything planted in the rich coastal soil. But then, since Sutter had paid mostly in promises, he had gotten his money's worth.

So what were these Yankee trappers and settlers doing with Marianno Vallejo? How had they dared to take such a man from his rancho at gunpoint? How had they managed to take him at all, considering Vallejo's almost limitless powers, as well as the hundreds of caballeros at his command? And what reason could they have other than to start trouble?

Tempest scanned the horizon for Californio riders but saw none. The pillowcase holding the acorns lay forgotten on the hillside as she headed down toward Abram.

The men were dismounting before the cabin. Abram already stood there, musket in hand, though the barrel now pointed at the ground. Vallejo was moved off between two armed men accompanied by his unarmed companion, whom Tempest now recognized as Jacob Leese, the German immigrant who had married into the Californio's family and often acted as his translator in dealing with English-speaking settlers and trappers.

"It's war," Abram told her as she reached his side. "Men, this is my wife, Tempest. Tempest—William Ide, John Grigsby, Ezekiel Merritt, William Knight, Robert Semple . . ."

Tempest didn't care who they were. All she wanted to know was whether they were all drunk or just plain mad. Several indeed looked as though they were suffering the ill effects of too much whiskey or wild grape brandy.

"They've taken General Vallejo prisoner."

"I con see, mon."

"They're on their way to Sutter's Fort in hopes of meeting Fremont."

Fremont!

"Fremont has nothing to do with our actions," William Ide was quick to put in. "This is our own act of revolution."

"But what has it to do with Vallejo?" Abram asked. "I thought he was no longer an officer in the Mexican Army. Didn't he resign his commission as commandant-general and disband his men?"

"Nevertheless, he's still Mexico's supreme power in the north," Ide insisted. "We received word a few days ago that Castro has sent men north to obtain horses to outfit his men. We already know of his plans to try to expel us from the territory. That left us with no choice but to seize the herd before he got them first."

"But we couldn't stop there," Grigsby put in. "William pointed out that if we stopped with taking the horses, we'd be branded horse thieves."

"By taking Vallejo," Ide cut in proudly, "we have established ourselves as patriots, rather than outlaws or renegades. I've written a proclamation of independence stating our reasons for what we've done." He took it out of his pocket and handed it to Abram, who glanced through it quickly.

A sallow man with bloodshot eyes produced a piece of folded cloth from his saddlebag. He unfolded it carefully and held it up. "Behold our flag," he said, grinning broadly.

Tempest stared at the piece of cheap white cotton. It bore a red-printed star and stripe, something that vaguely resembled a grizzly bear, and, across the bottom, black-inked letters. It didn't look at all important.

"California Republic," Abram read aloud. Tempest glanced up at him and wondered whether what she saw in his eyes was triumph or fear.

The man holding the flag began refolding it. "We thought the star might give them all a little reminder of Texas."

"But what do you plan to do with Vallejo?" Abram persisted. "Didn't he go before Castro and speak against seeking military aid from England or France? I thought he argued that California should divorce herself from Mexico. By all accounts, he should be our ally and not our enemy!"

"We only took him prisoner to establish our own credibility. We'll take him up to Sutter's Fort to accomplish the same thing, and then release him," Ide reasoned.

"But since we are able to take a man of Vallejo's power, Castro will think twice about riding against us," Knight explained.

"Vallejo hasn't given us any trouble to speak of," Semple remarked.

William Ide slanted an irritated glance at him. "He was being entertained by all of you swilling his brandy, rather than promoting an agreement. We sent John in to find out what was going on, and he also fell prey to the general's hospitality." He gave Abram a wry smile. "By the time I went in, the rest of them were so befuddled with Vallejo's brandy they couldn't have thought of terms of capitulation, let alone written or signed them."

"We're grateful for your abstemiousness, Brother William," Ezekiel Merritt commented dryly.

Ide had the good grace to look embarrassed.

"We've founded a republic," Semple said. "Now we've got to hold onto it."

"And for that we'll have to enlist Sutter's help. Fremont's, too," Grigsby added.

"We'd be grateful if you'd let us camp the night here. We'll be heading out at first light tomorrow," a subdued Ide said.

Abram smiled broadly. "We'll share what we have with you, and if it's agreeable, we'll ride with you to the fort. You might need reinforcements should Castro's men give chase."

"You might want to leave your wife behind," Ide said with a frown.

Abram laughed and glanced down at Tempest. "Gentlemen, my wife is a better shot than any of you."

Considering what she'd seen of Yankee shooting, Tempest wasn't overly flattered.

The ride to Sutter's Fort was swift and uneventful. Vallejo remained calm and talked congenially to the men by means of his interpreter, Jacob Leese. When they arrived, Sutter greeted the Californio as an honored guest and friend.

Tempest drew in her horse before entering the high walls and looked toward the river where she and her father had often camped when trading at New Helvetia. It was summer now and she knew he would still be high in the Sierras, trapping beaver and river otter. The soonest he would return would be fall, and more probably winter.

Abram waited, his horse moving restlessly beneath him, sensing his unease. Tempest glanced at him and he saw the fathomlessness of her blue eyes. *Does she hate me again?* he wondered, knowing that she was thinking of her father. Their relationship was still so new, still changing, her need of him growing stronger with each passing month. Yet if McClaren arrived, Abram knew he wouldn't be able to hold her. She would chase her father across the hill again, this time until she died.

Work inside the fort came to a halt with the news of the revolt and the arrival of Marianno Vallejo. The bear flag was run up the pole to the jubilant cheers of American coopers, blacksmiths, wagoners, chandlers, and farmers, while Sutter had the cannons fired in celebration.

"Probably thinks he'll be the first president," Tempest muttered, perched on a barrel outside the storage room. She chewed on a stalk of wheat, watching the men pass a jug of wild grape brandy around.

"What if Castro manages to get his horses from the south and rides on us here?" someone shouted amid the buzz of triumph.

"Let him come! Fremont's up on the Butte."

"Gentlemen, gentlemen," Sutter interposed quickly, trying to keep order. "We can manage this revolution ourselves, without the intervention of the United States."

"We're settlers, Captain, not trained soldiers. Fremont has sixty men, armed and ready. He told us what we could expect after the Hawk's Peak incident."

"The quarrel there was with Fremont riding into the territory as if he owned it," Sutter said. "Raising the American flag on Hawk's Peak was tantamount to a declaration of war!"

"If Thomas Larkin hadn't acted as mediator, there would have been war," another man put in.

"War, hell!" a grizzled mountain man interjected. "I hear Fremont snuck away in the night!"

"Nevertheless," Grigsby said more quietly, "Castro wouldn't have sent men north to get horses for his troops unless he planned to wage war. Ezekiel was right! We had no choice but to take the herd before the Mexican Army got to them. The bastards mean to force us out of the territory!"

"You mean *try*, don't you?" someone else shouted angrily. "We'll throw *them* out first!"

"While you hold Vallejo here, Captain, we're going to have to ride back to Sonoma and fight to hold what's ours!"

The brandy-loosened tongues wagged far into the summer night. Tempest and Abram left them to it and bedded down in the emigrant quarters near the southeast bastion.

She knew that when Fremont arrived, trouble would follow as surely as it did when two bears met on the same trail. What some of these men had forgotten, or perhaps had never known, was that there was bad blood between the Swiss captain and the American lieutenant of the "nonmilitary" Corps of Topographical Engineers. During Fremont's earlier expedition in 1845, he had accused three of his own men of stealing sugar. Sutter, acting as Mexican magistrate and the only real law around, had presided over their trial and found them not guilty. When he promptly hired all three to work for him at the fort, Fremont had taken the incident as a personal affront. McClaren had laughed long and hard over that one: "The bleeding son of a bitch doesna understand a thin'! He thinks Sutter was slapping him in the face when all he wants is able-bodied men to work for him!"

Fremont nursed the "insult" like a dog licking an open wound.

As soon as the American glory-hound had smelled the fresh meat of revolt, he'd come running and panting for his share of the feast, thought Tempest.

Her snort of derision drew Abram's interested glance as he pulled off his boots. "What're you thinking?"

She began unbuttoning her shirtwaist. "I be wondering who's going to be governor general of this fine new republic of yers," she said dryly. "Be it yer wagon master, William Ide, with his grand words and bonny hand? Be it Sutter for being in the territory longest and giving space to every newcomer who crosses over the mountains in one piece? Or Fremont with his men and guns to take it away from the lot of ye?"

Abram frowned. "I don't know."

Perhaps being a republic wasn't their safest course. Perhaps they should quickly annex themselves as a territory of the United States of America. It would be a fine thing to be on American soil, not just a squatter on Mexican land.

Watching Tempest pull off her clothes, Abram stopped worrying about who should take command. "Come to bed with me, Tempest," he bade softly.

She looked at him, her eyes clear. "Ye wouldna even need the tin to have the squaw."

He'd seen the squaw rub herself while looking at him and had hoped no one else had witnessed it. For a few moments, he had seriously considered her offer. It had been a long time since he had gone into a woman who wanted him more than he wanted her. A long time.

He said no more, and Tempest studied his set, angry face. She came to bed and was surprised when he turned his back to her.

Fremont's arrival changed the jubilant mood at the fort. The animosity between Sutter and Fremont thickened when the American lieutenant took absolute command of the fort that belonged to Sutter and began giving all the orders. Vallejo was no longer treated with consideration. The furniture Sutter had put in his quarters and the other amenities due a man of his status were removed. Armed guards were posted outside his door.

"He is not an honored guest!" Fremont raged when Sutter was removed bodily from Vallejo's quarters after spending a congenial evening playing cards and sipping brandy with the well-respected Californio. "He is a prisoner of war, and will be treated accordingly."

"You do not have Colonel Castro locked in those quarters, but an admired civilian who himself argued for annexation to the United States!" Sutter fumed, somewhat less loudly than the younger man.

"You are no longer in command of this fort, and you will not dare to interfere with my command. Is that clear? Or shall I lock you up as well?" Fremont snarled.

With armed men to back Fremont, there was little Sutter could do but wait and hope to resume control of his own settlement soon. Even his mistress, Manuiki, could not bolster his dismal spirits and resurrect the affable gentleman everyone had come to know. Had his bulldog still been alive, Sutter would undoubtedly have set the animal on Fremont.

Finally Fremont announced his plans to leave enough of his men behind to hold the fort and guard Vallejo while he took the main body of his soldiers west to block any retaliatory action by Castro against the Bear Flaggers.

Abram decided to ride with him.

"Mon, be ye looking for a fight?" Tempest demanded.

"We've a better chance fighting with Fremont than going back to Fairfield and trying to hold our land by ourselves," Abram reasoned with her while packing what he would need in the way of supplies.

Tempest cared nothing about the farm. Had she had a choice, she would have led Abram toward the peace of the mountains and waited out the revolution there.

As it was, it didn't last long. Had they but known, the outcome was already decided. In February 1845, the American Congress had passed a joint resolution inviting Texas to become one of the United States, and President John Tyler signed the resolution on March 1, three days before the inauguration of President James K. Polk.

Mexico promptly broke off diplomatic relations, although President Herrera made a last effort to avert war and bloodshed. Polk took the hint and sent John Slidell to Mexico to handle peace negotiations, only to learn that Herrera had been overthrown by the Mexican militarist General Paredes, and that the American minister had been dismissed.

Polk called on Congress to declare war on Mexico.

By the time Castro sent men north for horses to outfit his troops, General Zachary Taylor had already crossed the Nueces and occupied the disputed land north of the Rio Grande. General Kearny had received orders from Polk at Fort Leavenworth to go forth and occupy New Mexico and had successfully marched on and taken Santa Fe. That accomplished, he was on his way to California with three hundred trained dragoons and the expectations of war. Commodore John Sloat was sailing north from Mazatlán to claim California by sea.

The Bear Flag Republic was about to meet a far greater conquering force than the ineffectual Mexican colonel struggling against a politically ambitious American lieutenant.

It was about to meet Manifest Destiny.

The higher the baboon climbs, the more he
shows his butt.
—An American saying

Fremont decided to pitch camp in the hills a day's
journey from his destination. Leaving the bustle of the camp
behind, Tempest headed toward the nearby creek for Abram's
and her supper. She walked along the bank until she found two
pools below the branch elbows of a fallen log. Gathering her
gingham skirt tightly around her, she tucked it securely between
her knees and then slowly eased out onto the dead tree. Stretching out on her stomach, one arm wrapped around a branch to
keep her from falling, she slowly lowered her other hand inch
by inch into the water. She concentrated on the large trout
gently waving in the water, holding its place in placid rest in
the cool shade beneath the log. When her hand lay beneath it,
she closed her fingers like a vise and thrust upward, heaving
the flapping fish onto the bank. Tempest straightened, took
three running steps, and leaped to the sand. She grasped the
eighteen-inch trout, holding it captive while she brought a rock
down on the back of its head, quieting its agonized struggle.

A hundred feet upriver from the first pool, she caught another equally large fish using the same method.

"Well, if that don't beat all," someone murmured in an
awestruck voice. Tempest glanced up sharply to see one of
Fremont's young, buckskin-clad surveyors standing beneath a
tree watching her. He had thick, wavy brown hair that grew
almost to his shoulders, and a thin mustache and long mutton-
chop sideburns added age to his otherwise youthful face. His
brown eyes studied her with friendly male interest. Straightening, he walked down the slight incline to the bank where
she still held the dead fish.

"Can you do that anytime you want, Mrs. Walker?"

"Only where there be fish."

He laughed at her cold rebuff. "Only way I've ever done it

140

was with a line or a net. Heard tell some folks can do it with a bow and arrow, but this is the first time I've seen a fish caught with bare hands."

She returned her attention to the catch, making two swift, expert cuts and pulling the innards free with one tug. She tossed the mess at the surveyor's feet, then rinsed both fish in the cold creek. Slipping a reed through their mouths and gill slit, she stood and tied it to her belt.

The man still stood watching her. When he accompanied her as she began to walk toward camp, she glanced at him warily. Tension rippled along her muscles as she noted the admiring curiosity that darkened his eyes.

"What's your secret? How do you catch them like that?"

Perhaps if she told him, he would leave her alone. "Keep yer shadow off the water and move slowly so ye dunna scare away the fish."

"Sounds easy enough." He moved closer to her and she backed up sharply, alarmed. Abram called out to her. "Here!" she shouted, relief loosening her muscles. She looked straight into the young man's eyes and gave him a cold smile.

"I meant you no harm, ma'am," he said softly.

"I see you've managed supper again," Abram laughed. "As long as my wife's with me, I'll never go hungry," he said to the young man standing between them.

"I was just trying to learn her secret. All she'd say is to keep my shadow off the water and move slowly."

"Could you show him how to do it?" Abram asked her.

She shrugged. "We'll have to go upstream." As they walked, the young man called to others to follow. By the time she found a likely spot, a dozen men stood on the bank watching her. Abram winked, and she moved out into position on a large, flat rock below which was a swirling pool. She could see another fish as big as the two she had already caught. Trying to ignore the watching soldiers, she moved slowly and carefully and managed to fling the fish onto the bank.

"I've got to try that!" one of the other men announced. "Looks easy enough!"

He copied Tempest's position and movements, fixing his eyes on another trout. As he made a grab for the fish a few minutes later, he toppled unceremoniously into the creek. The trout darted downstream like a silver streak of light while the man spluttered and splashed to his feet, accompanied by his friends' uproarious laughter. "Ho, Bundy, your fish went thataway! You better swim mighty fast! 'Bout time you took a bath!"

Bundy regained his feet, if not his dignity. Tempest grinned broadly. "Yer shadow touched the pool and ye moved too fast," she told him. More laughter followed. He muttered under his breath and strode out of the creek.

Tempest refilled both their canteens and the woven Indian basket with water. Abram looped the canteens about his neck and held the fish while she gathered clover and Indian lettuce into the basket of water. "You enjoyed that, didn't you?"

"Aye."

"Could we spare the poor fellow a fish?"

Her smile dimmed. "If it be yers, mon. I wilna give him mine." Someone had snatched up the third she had tossed onto the bank.

"One's enough for both of us," Abram said solemnly, and took the largest trout from the reed tie. Tempest watched angrily as he approached Bundy, whose buckskins were steaming as he sat close by a fire to dry them. The surveyor gratefully accepted the fish, amid more laughter from the others.

Muttering to herself, Tempest marched over to their campsite and squatted down to begin building a small cookfire. She would never understand Abram Walker—never. He was not predictable like her da, whose actions she could anticipate in every situation. Abram she could not comprehend. She poked rocks into the flames, swearing vilely under her breath.

Abram returned and stretched out against his saddle to watch her as she rolled a hot stone out of the fire, picked it up with two sticks, and dropped it into the woven basket. Its heat made water boil, cooking the greens. She cocked her head to one side to look at him. Then she pointed her knife in Bundy's direction.

"Had that son of a bitch caught a dozen fish, he wouldna have shared nary a one with ye."

"That may well be so."

"Then why give him yers?" she demanded hotly.

In answer, Abram told her the story of how Jesus had used seven small loaves of unleavened bread and a few fish to feed a crowd of four thousand.

And though she still did not understand him, Tempest divided her fish and shared it with him before the evening ended.

As they lay beside each other beneath the Indian blanket

and the stars, Abram brushed his mouth against her cheek and murmured, "I knew you wouldn't let me go hungry."

The following afternoon, the cavalcade was intercepted on its way west by a hard-riding Yankee settler waving his long-rifle in the air. He drew rein before John Fremont.

"By God, we sent Castro's men a-runnin', sir," he shouted exultantly while his horse sidled nervously. He pointed back the way he'd come with the barrel of his gun. "They come at us from the south, a good fifty of 'em! Shot two of us, but, by God, we got three for every one they hit of ours. They're hightailing it south again, probably right back to Castro hisself!"

"Where're your troops? How many of you are there?"

"Same bunch that took the governor's horses to begin with, plus more from around the area. We're down near the Olompali Indian village where we had the battle. Not ten miles from here!"

"Ride back and tell your men we're on our way. We'll join forces with you on the Marin peninsula at nightfall."

As the settler rode off with Fremont's orders, the latter consulted with his adjutant, Lieutenant Gillespie. Word quickly passed among the men that they'd all cross to the presidio.

Tempest moved her Indian pony close to Abram as they quickened their pace once more to reach the peninsula. "Why in bloody hell does he want to cross to the presidio? There be no garrison there. 'Tis naught but a ruin!"

"I heard mention of cannon there."

"Cannon!" Tempest laughed. "Oh, aye, there be cannon. But they've not been fired in years! Not in my lifetime at least. You think cannon be left about if they be worth anything? Castro's not a complete horse's arse! If the one that's leading us about wants to fight Mexicans, why doesna he go back and raise his bleeding flag over Hawk's Peak again! 'Tis sure I am he'd be obliged to do a little fighting there if he stayed around long enough to find out!"

They joined forces with the Bear Flaggers as planned and crossed the bay by boat to the windswept settlement of Yerba Buena, which was merely a few adobe and wood houses and a pier. It was bitterly cold.

Fremont led his force into the little ruin of the presidio and gave orders for the ten old Spanish guns to be spiked. Tempest stood by her horse watching as the Yankees unquestioningly followed their grand leader's orders. Abram came to stand next to her and saw her laughing silently at them all, her body shaking with malicious mirth, tears streaming from her blue eyes.

"Just once, hold your tongue," he told her.

That evening Fremont named the entrance of the bay Chrysopylae—the Golden Gate. Tempest heard about it while sitting huddled in a damp blanket as close to the breeze-whipped fire as was safe. She looked out at the gray hills, the white capped gray water, the gray sky.

"Golden Gate," she muttered, curling into fetal position, trying to conserve what little body warmth she had left.

The next day Abram and Tempest recrossed the bay with the Bear Flaggers. Fremont agreed to follow shortly when he was sure that the area was secured. Tempest wondered if the heroic John C. Fremont was delaying his move north because he was afraid Vallejo's caballeros might be ready for a fight and he wanted to be sure Sonoma was secure before he arrived to join in celebration of the Yankee Fourth of July.

As Abram and Tempest rode north to join in the festivities planned at Sonoma, Tempest glanced at Abram. "Mon, what's Fremont going to do now that he's spiked the guns and named the entrance to the bay? Is he going to rush north and roust the Russians next?"

Abram knew well enough that the Russians had been gone for years and that she was merely making her contempt clearer to him. He was beginning to understand. He'd heard from one of Fremont's own men that when Kit Carson had neglected to post guards while in the Oregon Territory, their camp had been raided by Indians. Fremont had retaliated by massacring an entire Indian village consisting mostly of women and children. It hadn't mattered to him that they were not even the same tribe that had raided his camp in the first place. One Indian was the same as any other in Fremont's opinion.

> Thou shalt love thy neighbor as thyself.
> —Leviticus 19:18

Abram knew he had a problem when he saw several women he had known from the wagon train clustered before the Sonoma trading post. They were watching the triumphant, exuberant entrance of the Bear Flaggers—and had seen him with Tempest. He could sense what they were thinking, and avoided looking directly at them.

All were good women of fine, moral upbringing, married to God-fearing men who toiled on the land just as he did. It had been Barbara Parr, still wearing the same, faded brown dress and prim bonnet, who had helped him nurse Kathy through her last days. Her husband, Roger, had stood with him beside the grave beneath the mountain pine. Sarah Hastings had held school in the back of one of the Conestogas. Hope Dreikurs had given him her last chicken, roasted and stuffed with pine nuts, and kind words of solace for his loss. All good friends.

But now these same women stood rooted, staring with unveiled hostility at him and his child-woman, half-breed wife. Barbara's brown eyes were wide, her finely shaped mouth agape. Hope had one hand to her mouth as though to stifle an audible gasp. And Sarah looked ready to faint.

For one crushing, mortifying moment, Abram saw himself through their eyes—a man in his early thirties with a girl in tow, an Indian girl for whom he continually lusted. He could feel the heat coming up his sweating neck and filling his face.

Barbara leaned toward the other women and they whispered together in a tight circle. Abram wasn't sure what to do as he passed, so he pretended he hadn't noticed them.

Men were shouting news of the Battle of Olompali and Fremont's brave spiking of the presidio cannons. The settlers milled about, calling out questions, laughing, cheering, whooping with victory and congratulations. California was now a republic!

Tempest turned in her saddle and looked back at the three women who had been staring at her as though she were an abomination. They were still staring, though more surreptitiously, when she met the tall, brown-bonneted woman's eyes.

Glancing at Abram as she turned around, she raised a querying brow. His face was hot as a sunset and rigid as stone. He didn't look at her at all. She might not have been there beside him.

"Friends of yers?" she asked bitingly.

"Yes. They're all good Christian women."

Tempest thought of a yellow-haired woman in a faded gingham dress and said not a word. Her heart pounded dully.

Roger Parr, Tom Hastings, and Henry Dreikurs were among the curious spectators shouting questions. They surrounded Abram as he sidled Dusty into a place at the hitching post in front of the grange. He always felt clumsy when he dismounted in normal fashion, while Tempest seemed to melt from her horse and stand with proud, silent bearing.

The men noticed her immediately. What man wouldn't? Their questions about Fremont and the fighting were silenced as they stared with far more interest at Tempest McClaren, who was obviously with Abram. Abram heard Tom's softly audible exclamation and saw Henry's admiring look.

"My wife, Tempest," was all he could manage by way of introduction.

There was no protecting arm around her shoulders as Tempest stood facing the three men, all similar in their solid features, strong bodies, and worn farm clothes. Like Abram. And like the women, she saw their shock, though it was more quickly concealed.

She wanted to hide behind Abram, but didn't. His face was hard as he looked at the men. "Tempest—Roger, Tom, and Henry," he said curtly.

Roger was the first to speak, his swamp-water green eyes hesitant. "Ma'am, it's a pleasure." The other two men added their greetings. Tempest said nothing to any of them, seeing what a pleasure it was, but moved to one side and began loosening the saddle cinches. Abram cleared his throat.

After a few uncomfortable seconds, conversation began again. She heard one of the men murmur, "You sly old dog, Abram." Another added teasingly, "Marry 'em young so you can train 'em proper." More words passed back and forth between the men, and Abram said gruffly, "I want children.

Seemed a good idea to marry again." More hushed words. "Oh, don't worry about it," Henry said, slapping Abram on the back. "They loved Kathy, but they'll accept that you need a woman. A man can't be alone in this country." "You loved her," another said, "but you can't mourn forever."

Tempest's throat was tight. She didn't hear Abram come around the horses to stand near her. "We'll camp over there," he told her, pointing toward some wagons in the meadow beyond the settlement buildings. "I want you to get to know my friends."

She lifted her head and looked him straight in the eyes. "Ye think they want to know me?"

Abram heard the coarsened brogue and knew that the cold indifferent expression on Tempest's face was in self-defense. She looked capable of taking anything, but he knew her vulnerability. The trouble was, he also knew that if one of those church-reared women should hint an insult, Tempest would blast her with both barrels of her vile, heathenous tongue. They were no more ready for Tempest McClaren than Tempest McClaren was ready for them.

But what could he do? He loved and needed her desperately, but he acknowledged that he needed his friends as well. He needed to be in touch with his old life, the old ways.

"They'll accept you if you give them a chance," he told her firmly. "Treat them as you would have them treat you, and everything will be just fine."

She stared at him, amazed. He really believed it!

"Just try, Tempest. Please. That's all I ask of you. It means very much to me."

She saw just how much it did mean, and ached inside. She had come to believe she was nearly the only thing of importance in this man's life, she and his land. It was a frightening blow to find that she wasn't, after all. If she failed him now, what would he do to her? Cast her out? He had said he would never do that, but if her own da could, then how much easier it would be for Abram Walker, who was not even a blood relation.

"There's nothing to fear," Abram assured her.

"I'm not afraid," she snarled, jerking her hand away from his.

He didn't argue, even when he saw how she moistened her dry lips and looked quickly away from him. He put his hands on her thin shoulders. "When I introduce you to the ladies, all you have to say is, 'I'm pleased to meet you,' and try to smile

nicely. Everything will be fine after that. You'll see. It won't
be hard at all."

She remembered how the women had looked at her. Would
they talk in front of her as the other yellow-haired woman had?
A hard, cold heaviness grew inside her, but her eyes burned
like fire.

"Will you do that much for me, Tempest?" Abram pleaded
softly.

"Aye," she agreed bleakly. But it wouldn't make one damn
bit of difference.

It was worse than she feared, though not at all what
she had expected. After her softly murmured greeting and
Abram's departure with the other men, no one said a word.
The women stared at her and she stared back, terrified and
trying to hide it. They blushed, forced smiles, and fidgeted.
Tempest clenched her jaw and put on her Indian face. The three
women rather too brightly suggested that they ought to get
things ready for the men's return.

"They're probably going to buy brandy at the trading post,"
Hope said, and the women laughed in reproving camaraderie,
which cut Tempest out completely.

Tempest couldn't even manage a smile. Her heart thumped
in sickening beats. Where was Abram? All the white men in
Fremont's cavalcade and those who'd looked at her with dark,
hungry eyes at Sutter's Fort had not roused the fear that these
three simple women did. Only a woman knows what another
woman is capable of.

With dusk coming, the women began working together
around the cookfire. Tempest escaped to the creek to dig tule
potatoes and gather Indian lettuce and wild herbs to cook with
the dried beef Abram had brought along. She took her time,
but finally she couldn't postpone her return any longer.

As she approached the small circle of four Conestogas,
which had been rerigged for trade rather than cross-country
travel, Tempest heard the women talking. She crept closer,
hiding herself behind one wagon, straining to hear what they
said, to hear if they were talking about her.

"What can she be digging for in that creek muck?"

"Heaven only knows."

"She's very pretty, isn't she, for an Indian."

"She sounds Scottish. Henry said Abram told him she's part

Scottish anyway. Her father was a trapper."

"Crazy as a loon, too. Tom heard of McClaren when we were at Sutter's Fort."

"She frightens me. Did you see how she looked at us? I don't know what she was thinking."

"She's certainly a far cry from Kathy."

"Well, you *know* why Abram took her back to his land with him, don't you?"

"Men are just disgusting at times. Kathy hasn't even been in her grave two years. You'd think he could wait a bit longer to have another *wife.*"

"They can't be married. I've never heard of a minister at Sutter's Fort, or anywhere else in California. And Abram's not Catholic."

"Good heavens, Barbara! You mean Abram's living in sin with this girl?"

"She can't be more than fifteen."

"Oh, Hope, do you suppose that makes any difference?"

"I never thought Abram was like that."

"*All* men are like that."

"Corinne would be so much better suited to him. They were such good friends, Abram and Kathy and Corinne and John. With John passed on now and her all alone . . ."

"Maybe if Abram had known before, Sarah, but what can he do now that he's stuck with this girl?"

"He could give her back to her father."

Suddenly someone laid a hand on Tempest's arm, startling her into a sharp gasp. "There's nothing more cruel than a good Christian woman, is there?" came a softly amused, feminine voice. Tempest flung off the gentle touch and ran back toward the dark shadows of the cottonwoods by the meandering creek. She heard the woman approaching her once more and scrubbed wildly at her face to get rid of the tears.

"I'm sorry you heard them," the woman said, sitting down nearby.

Tempest tipped her chin defiantly and glared at her. The woman was older than she, probably in her mid-twenties, with fine, clear features, a full mouth, dark-arched eyebrows and sparkling eyes. She was wearing a simple, pale shirtwaist and a gathered skirt. Beneath the hem heavy boots showed. The woman crossed her feet at the ankles and rested slender, work-callused hands in her lap.

"I'm Linda Breeden, and they didn't approve of me either, at first." Her smile was wry. "They don't mean to be cruel. They just . . . talk." She shrugged.

"Bullshit."

Linda's eyes widened and then she laughed. "Well, you *do* speak your mind after all, don't you?"

Tempest looked away, unable to contain an audible sniff and hoping Linda Breeden didn't see how she surreptitiously wiped her nose on her sleeve. She didn't care about her sleeve, only that this stranger might suspect that she was crying.

"Tempest, you're very pretty and you've got yourself a grand man. I'm not laughing at you. Believe me, I'm not."

Tempest drew her knees up, hugging them tightly against her chest, and gritting her teeth while she managed to swallow the lump that was choking her. "What was wrong with ye?" she challenged.

"Me? Oh, well . . . I worked for my living before I married. Not that I don't work now, mind you," she added with a soft, lilting laugh. "I was a secretary for a lawyer. I recopied his reports, kept his books, and made good coffee. Ladies don't do that sort of thing. But he was my cousin."

"Why dinna they approve of that?" Tempest asked, curious.

"Most improper, you know," Linda said airily, then grinned. "A woman's place is in the home. Only. They disapprove of what they don't understand, but they do eventually come around."

"Who gives a bloody damn?"

"You do, or you wouldn't have been standing there eavesdropping and crying over what they were saying about you," Linda said bluntly.

Tempest glared at her with open hatred.

Linda smiled. "You're very young." She adjusted her skirt and then pointed down to the creek. "What were you digging, by the way?"

"Roots."

"To eat?"

"What do ye suppose I planned to do with them?"

Linda sighed and gave her a patient look. "How did you meet Abram?"

"He bought me from my father for five dollars in gold and a bottle of whiskey."

"Oh, Lord. Don't tell anyone else that!" Linda said, stunned.

She leaned forward. "Did he *really?* Abram actually *bought* you?"

Tempest bit her lip and stared at the ground, wishing she hadn't said anything. Who was Corinne anyway?

"Abram, of all people," Linda murmured, and laughed softly. "Well, still rivers do run deep, they say. Five dollars in gold isn't chicken feed. It's enough to buy him a new plow or a good horse. Poor old Dusty is ready for the boneyard."

Tempest turned her head slowly and looked at the chattering woman. Linda smiled at her. "He must love you very much, and how you came to be with him doesn't matter to me at all, Tempest Walker." She held out her hand. "Welcome."

The woman was almost as strange as Abram, Tempest thought, but oddly enough, she trusted her. Reaching out slowly, she shook Linda Breeden's hand.

Woe unto them that are wise in their own eyes.
—Isaiah 5:21

The Fourth of July hit Sonoma with wild, celebratory force, lauding both American independence and the new Republic of California. Fremont arrived to take his share of the praise and partake in the festivities as guest of honor. He rode in with his troops like a victorious Caesar, rather than what he really was—an untried lieutenant whose greatest strength was his political connections.

Toasts were drunk until most of the good men of Sonoma—roving hunters, trappers, runaway sailors, and rough-tongued, hard-living frontiersmen—were laughing and filling the air with ribald cheers and self-congratulations. Even the farmers and their Christian wives joined in the exciting ruckus.

Those who lived in the settlement opened their homes and built their cookfires higher. Soon the smells of good, down-home, country cooking permeated the air. Tempest tasted her first piece of American apple pie, prepared by the able hands of Linda Breeden.

Dozens of pairs of feet tapped to the music of harmonicas, fiddles, guitars, and mandolins and the dancing ranged from polkas and a Virginia reels to just plain kicking up one's heels in uncontained, drunken jubilation.

Tempest met Corinne Anderson.

She was round, soft, and warm, and Abram hugged her in happy greeting. He even kissed her on the cheek and told her how sorry he was to hear of her husband, John, passing on. Corinne's face turned bright pink as she gazed up at Abram. Tempest felt cold and stiff inside at what she saw in the woman's eyes.

The other women surrounded Corinne in protective welcome. Linda kept Tempest company until she was pulled into the dance by her laughing, thoroughly inebriated husband, Parker. Tempest watched them whirling about, dipping and swaying.

Abram caught hold of Tempest's hand as several of the other men claimed their wives. "Dance with me, darlin'."

She could smell wild grape brandy on his breath and was amazed. "No."

Abram swung her around anyway, tugging her close, a firm hand at her slender waist. "Do what I do."

"Bloody hell I will," she growled, and pulled free in a panic. "I'll not make an arse of meself!"

His eyes darkened. "Fine." He swung away angrily and walked straight over to Corinne. She'd dance with him gladly. She smiled brightly at his invitation and went straight into his arms without hesitation. She reminded him piercingly of Kathy—acquiescent.

Tempest felt swift pain clutching at her as she watched. She melted back into the shadows.

Abram saw her retreat and felt instant remorse. Of course she wouldn't dance with him; she didn't know how. She didn't know much of anything except how to survive in the wild. He wanted to go after her, but he could hardly leave Corinne standing there in the middle of the fracas. He should have been more patient with Tempest, should have understood her embarrassment. She was fiercely proud, not wanting anyone to see her weakness.

"You're a fine dancer, Abram."

"Pardon me?"

"I said you're a fine dancer."

He saw the look in Corinne's eyes. Where had Tempest gone? He couldn't see her anymore. She had backed up next to the people near the wine keg and then disappeared completely.

She won't leave. Where would she go? Where could she go?

But all he wanted was for those drunk fiddlers to stop so he could go find his wife. He had been so caught up in the celebration, in seeing and talking with his old friends, in the new republic, that he hadn't given much thought to Tempest and how she had fared with all this. Linda Breeden seemed to genuinely like Tempest, but the rest . . . what of the rest? Why hadn't he bothered to ask?

Because he knew. There was nothing he could do about it except let Tempest find her own way with the other women. Any interference from him would only rouse ill feeling and make matters even worse.

When the music finally ended, he took Corinne back to the others and then went looking for Tempest. He found her standing with the same young surveyor who had followed her down to the creek when she fished. They were just on the edge of the light.

"I've been looking all over for you," he said tightly, hot jealousy churning inside him. The young man was handsome and obviously intrigued by her.

Tempest didn't look at him.

"Quite a celebration, isn't it, sir?" the man asked politely.

"Yes." Abram looked at him, but saw that he was looking at Tempest again.

He's only a few years older than her—just about the age difference between me and Kathy. While I could be Tempest's own father . . .

"I'd better get back, I guess," the young man said, and left. Tempest still hadn't said anything. What had she been thinking just then when she looked at him with those shadowed, bleak eyes? She had looked past him as though expecting someone else to be there.

"What'd he want?" he asked, nodding his head toward the young man who was walking away.

Tempest shrugged. "I'm sorry I dinna dance with ye."

He wondered at her tone. Was she treating him to more of her sarcasm? "I did my dancing," he told her, wishing he had stayed beside her instead of squiring Corinne for that seemingly endless reel. He sensed a new vulnerability and uncertainty in Tempest, could almost feel her fear. But why should she be afraid?

"It's late. Maybe you'd like to turn in," he suggested. He wanted to hold her so badly he ached. But people were wandering everywhere, talking and drinking and dancing, and he could hardly do what he wanted here in sight of them. Out there in the darkness around the wagons, before the others came back, he could make love to her, reassure her. God, how he needed to hold her again.

Tempest's eyes narrowed. So, he wanted to be rid of her so that he could go back to the other woman. The others would approve. *He thinks he can just send me back to Da.* Even if McClaren could be found, she knew he wouldn't take her back. He had given his word, and he never broke it.

"No," she told Abram coldly, and saw how his expression fell in disappointment. They went back to the gathering and

Tempest suffered it in silence. It was late when everyone began heading off to their sleeping places.

Abram laid out their bedding while the others climbed into their wagons. The sounds of low voices and creaking wood drifted through the air as they moved about and finally settled.

Lying beside Tempest beneath the stars, Abram tried not to think about her body, how good it felt to go into her. He tried to concentrate on the four wagons nearby with the couples inside, together with their seven assorted children. It'd been too many days since he'd made love to Tempest, and no matter how hard he concentrated on other things, the sum of every day and hour of that time seemed to be forming a hard, throbbing knot in his loins.

"What'd ye say, mon?" Tempest whispered. She thought she'd heard him swear. Abram never swore—almost never. The only time she had ever heard him curse was when the crows had come to peck at the seeds his white woman had brought across the country for him.

"Nothing. Go to sleep."

He was angry. She could hear it in the bite of his voice, almost feel the rigidity of his body, though he didn't touch her. He was trying to keep a distance between them when before he had always shared his warmth. *He doesna want to touch me. It's their fault, these friends who surround him and remind him of his Kathy.*

"I dunna want to sleep," she said resentfully.

"Tempest, for God's sake."

He glared at her. She could see the shine of his eyes in the moonlight. *They'll take ye away from me.* Anger and fear made her breath quicken. She hated his friends with their shared memories, their shared way of life. Would he sell her off to someone else and have his money for a plow? A fierce desperation gripped her.

He saw it in her eyes and reached out to touch her soothingly. She moved closer, her leg brushing his, and he drew in his deep breath sharply. She looked at him and he stared back. She heard his unsteady breath and knew then how she could keep him hers, however the others might want to tear them apart. She'd do what she had to do.

She slid her hand beneath the blanket, groping. She touched his hip and he jerked with surprise. Still he gazed at her, shock widening his eyes. She stroked as she looked into his eyes.

"No," he managed to gasp in a harsh whisper, pushing her

hand roughly away. "The others..."

Angry, Tempest turned onto her side and moved closer still. She touched him again, determined.

"Tempest," he choked. Then he couldn't breathe at all as he felt her hand move again, working at the buttons on his dungarees. He closed his eyes tightly and gritted his teeth. His back arched suddenly. "Don't," he hissed, and an agonized, uncontainable moan came from his parted lips. His heart was pounding so hard and fast he thought he was going to pass out.

Tempest felt her own power growing as he grew under her hand. It excited her. Her hand tightened, grew rougher. He groaned, trembling violently, and then moved suddenly, shoving her hand away and rolling her onto her back. She felt his hands pulling at her clothes and helped him.

Sweet Jesus, she's not dry. He gripped her tightly, hardly aware that his weight was crushing her into the hard ground beneath the single blanket under them. He couldn't think of anything more. He could only feel his body sinking into hers and hers opening wide to him.

She caught hold of him fiercely. *She's dead, Abram Walker, and I'm alive. Ye're mine now. Mine.* She wrapped her arms and legs around him tightly and dug her fingernails into his back.

Hang onto it, Abram thought, trying desperately, wanting the moment to last. But when he felt her legs go around him and her nails dig in, he couldn't hold back anything. He cried out, the sound harsh and primitive, carrying in the night air. It ended too soon. His body shook in the aftermath.

Tempest knew it would be a few moments before he could move off her. The heat and the weight of him was somehow comforting.

She had hoped. Now she knew. Those people in the silent wagons were no threat at all to her. Nor was his dead Kathy, or the comfortable Widow Anderson.

She heard soft whispers.

Abram raised his head, kissed her briefly, rolled from her, and adjusted his clothes. He whispered hoarsely, "I love you," and promptly went to sleep.

Tempest lay listening to the shocked stillness that had fallen over the wagons, knowing that they had heard Abram quite clearly—just as she had hoped they would.

She smiled coldly into the darkness, satisfied.

Then saith He to Thomas, reach hither thy
finger, and behold my hands; and reach hither
thy hand, and thrust it into my side: and be not
faithless but believing.
—John 20:27

It had been more than three weeks since Abram and
Tempest had left home to accompany the Bear Flaggers with
Vallejo to Sutter's Fort. Abram wasn't sure what he would find
on their return. He had had nightmares about the Californios
burning him out; he had feared the crops would be dead from
lack of care. When he rode over the last hill and looked down
on his land, he was amazed.

"Look at it!" he cried out joyously. Below, the corn grew
green and healthy, swaying in the gentle breeze. The wheat
rippled like a golden inland sea. "This place is Eden!" The
serpents who had dared try to deny the Americans their opportunity had been routed. If they pressed further, it would be
they who were expelled from this new land.

Tempest watched Abram's exultant face. She had overheard
the men talking at Sonoma, had seen their carefully nursed
anger, their prejudices against the Californios. They had forgotten already who had given them their land through Sutter.
They had forgotten how long Vallejo and Noriega and a dozen
others had been here, taming this land, building this land.

Fremont *made* them forget.

Once blood was let, friendship was forfeit. For all Abram's
talk of the Bible and God's word, no man could turn the other
cheek when a blow came. It wasn't natural. The blow had
come and hatred already burned. For how many years, how
many generations?

Because of one arse who wanted glory, Tempest thought.
But why should she care? The Spanish had stolen the land from
the Indians, who had been here since time began, so the Cal-

ifornios were now getting what they had given.

Hatred for those who possessed something they wanted was the one thing the Mexicans, the Californios, and the Americans shared, the one thing they had in common. They all wanted land, and hated those who had it before them.

Stirred from her thoughts by the realization that Abram was already halfway down the hill, Tempest rode after him.

Abram threw himself into his labors the next morning. He was up well before dawn working in the fields. Tempest could hear him singing loudly, ". . . bringing in the sheaves . . . bringing in the sheaves," and didn't know what he meant. He came in to eat breakfast and went back out again, working on past noon.

Abram was possessed by an inner, burning joy. The feel of the earth on his hands made his blood warm. Late in the afternoon, he worked on notching the stacked logs for the barn walls. He seemed tireless.

"The sun's gone down."

Startled, Abram glanced over his shoulder and saw Tempest standing by the remaining pile of logs, watching him curiously. He smiled. "I'll set this log and then wash up."

She waited for him. His rust-brown hair was plastered to his damp forehead. His face was dark red from exertion. He swung the ax once more and she watched his back muscles ripple. His arms bulged as he lifted the log and carried it to the barn wall and banged it into place. Then he dusted off his hands and grinned at her.

"That's it," he announced.

She gave him a direct look. "Will ye be reading this evening?" She had missed that most of all.

"If you want," he agreed, understanding. She was a child in many ways. "What's for supper?"

"Pheasant. A fat one."

He squeezed her shoulder lightly and kissed her cheek as he passed. "And I'm ready for it." He expected her to go back to the house, but she followed him toward the creek. He glanced at her as she ducked under the cottonwood branches and leaned against the big white trunk. She looked at his body as he stripped off his shirt. He was embarrassed by her scrutiny of his hair-covered chest.

"Ye're a strong mon, Abram Walker."

Strong and stupid, he thought, wondering what she was

about this time. He knelt by the creek and washed his arms, chest, hands, and face, then bent low and put his head completely into the pool, roughing his hair. Straightening, he shook like a dog. She smiled slightly as he stood and turned.

"Should I be washing, too?"

Their eyes met. Abram was profoundly aware of her fingers toying with the top buttons of her dress. He knew she'd felt her woman's power that night after the celebration of Sonoma. He hadn't been able to regain any semblance of control. The men had teased him down by the river the next morning; their wives had been stonily silent and refused to meet his eyes at all.

She's practicing her newfound strength on me, he thought. Her smile deliberately provoked his lust. He remembered schoolgirls back in Farmington who had looked at him with feline assessment the first summer they were out of the classroom and ready for a husband. Kathy had once looked at him in that way—curious, pensive, aware, a silent promise offered in exchange for a promise. A woman's game of advance and retreat.

His body told him to unbuckle his belt and drop his dungarees right there and take her. Tempest was his wife, after all. Yet his mind told him to tread very carefully. Given full knowledge of her power over him, she could become a tyrant.

He smiled indolently. "Food first, sweetheart."

Tempest considered him for a long moment. Was he challenging her or teasing her? She straightened, her hand dropping to her side. Scooping the low-hanging branches up out of her way with a flourish, Abram grinned at her. "After you, my lady."

Watching the sway of her hips as she preceded him to the cabin, he wondered if he had made a mistake.

After their evening meal, Tempest took the big black Bible from the mantel and placed it in Abram's lap as he sat in his chair by the fire. "Something I havena heard," she requested.

He laughed softly, watching her as she went back to washing the dishes. He thought about reading Samson and Delilah but decided it wouldn't do for Tempest's present frame of mind. He began on Exodus.

Tempest learned how the children of God became slaves, how their numbers grew, and how, frightened by their increased number and growing power, Pharoah ordered all the boy babies slaughtered. Abram stopped with the birth of Moses.

She shook her head grimly. "There's a bloody lot of killing in that book."

"They were hard times."

"Naught's changed," she murmured under her breath, picking up her sampler and folding it away.

Abram spent the next week of evenings reading the Book of Exodus. Tempest listened, appalled at the power of Abram's God as he sent plagues of blood, frogs, gnats, flies, boils, hail, and locusts down on those who would not free his people. The worst was the plague of darkness and the death of the Egyptian first-born, while God's people were passed over.

"So they got their revenge after all," she murmured.

When he read of Moses' journey into the desert, his parting of the Red Sea and closing it over the pursuing Egyptians, and then the celebration of Miriam, Tempest wondered where the kindness was in God's people. They were as cruel and ruthless as their masters before them. Worse!

The Ten Commandments left her feeling even more grim. She wished Abram would go back to reading the simple, exciting tales he had before.

"If using God's name in vain sends us to the hellfire place ye told me about, then I'm well on my way." She had broken other laws as well—worse ones.

Abram smiled slightly. "I've broken that law myself on occasion."

"Then ye'll be burning right along with me."

"No. God forgives us anything if we believe in Jesus Christ as our savior."

"Anything?"

"Anything."

She shook her head. "I dinna understand it before, and I understand it less now. This God of yers makes laws, but he will forgive if ye break them. Why bother making laws at all then?"

"We're supposed to try to live according to what Jesus taught. If you do that, you won't break the laws."

"Ah, but he'll forgive ye nonetheless," she mocked. "I find no sense in this. Ye read to me about a God who rains down plagues, murders hundreds of babies, and drowns an entire army. Then ye tell me yer God is loving and kind. Ye say he thinks of us as his kin. He canna be both ways, mon. He is either bloody hard, or he is soft. Which one is he?"

Abram leaned his head back, feeling inadequate to answer

her questions. His minister back home would have had some answer; he wished he knew what it would have been. Too often he himself had been told, "You must believe; you must have faith." Tempest wasn't going to be satisfied with that, and it had been years since he had asked himself those selfsame questions. He couldn't remember how he had worked it all out in his own mind to satisfy his own doubts. Perhaps he had just come to believe, to have faith, as he had been instructed to do.

He sighed heavily.

"Well?" she demanded impatiently.

He sat forward. Still silent, he raked his fingers through his hair and scratched distractedly.

"Ye have no answer," she sneered, her burr strong with angry disappointment.

He glanced at her and knew that he had better say *something*. "God is hard on those who are against him, but kind to those who are not." It was the best he could do, and it drew a derisive snort from Tempest.

"That's why he let the Egyptians take his people as slaves and allowed them to kill all those children in the first place."

Abram stared at her, appalled. He thought again that she was nothing like his Kathy, who would have died before voicing such blasphemy, or even daring to think it. Tempest wanted to know, demanded to know. It was in her eyes. *Tell me something I can believe and hang on to,* they said fiercely. She would believe nothing just because he told her it was so. She would accept nothing on faith alone.

"I don't know how to explain it to you," he admitted bleakly.

"Because ye dunna ken yeself," she told him, and sighed heavily. She studied him critically. "But ye believe it all, dunna ye, mon? Every damn word."

He could answer that. "Yes. I do."

"Why? *How?*"

"Because I *feel* the truth of it."

She sat there on the pallet, frowning. Once, in despair, she had cried out to Abram's God, and He had answered. "Yer God is here. I just dinna ken what He *is*." She was afraid.

Abram saw her fear and wondered at it. Perhaps it came from what he had been reading to her. Tomorrow he would find something else in the Old Testament. The Psalms, perhaps.

Tempest stood and put the Bible back onto the mantel. Usually she undressed for bed first while Abram waited in his chair by the fire, his face averted. Tonight, though, she stood in front of him. He saw the uncertainty in her face, but wasn't sure of the cause. He held out his hand and Tempest slid hers into it. She came forward willingly when he tugged and sat on his lap. He was startled when she gently brushed her fingertips against his sunburned cheek, her eyes solemn.

"Ye may be wrong, mon, but ye've more answers for me than Da ever had," she whispered. She curled against him, resting her head on his shoulder, and he heard her sigh.

Abram's throat worked and he closed his eyes tightly. He rested his hand on the curve of her hip. If they sat this way forever, he would be content.

Answers, she said. What he had to offer wouldn't be enough for her, he knew. Not forever.

The ear of jealousy heareth all things.
—Wisdom of Solomon 1:10

Summer passed. The crops grew high and ripe, until the corn was taller than Abram's six-foot frame. The wheat waved gold.

Abram waited.

As he planned his harvest-time, Commodore Robert Stockton had already mustered a California Battalion of Mounted Riflemen and marched south to enforce his bombastic proclamation that California was now a territory of the United States of America. Fremont and Gillespie, for their services in "conquering the hostile territory," were promoted.

Colonel Castro in Santa Clara and Governor Pio Pico in Los Angeles both told their people that resistance was hopeless and left promptly for the safer climes of Mexico. Cowardice was not limited to Fremont.

Stockton reached Los Angeles and left Gillespie in charge of a garrison and the Angelenos. Gillespie took the bull by the horns, set down strict rules and a curfew, and created rebellion where none had been before. Fort Hill was besieged as a result.

Jose Antonio Carrillo dug up a cannon from Señora Inocencia Reyes's garden, lashed it to the running gear of a wagon, loaded it with homemade powder, and blasted the hell out of the Americans in the Battle of the Old Woman's Gun. The Americans retreated, their tails between their legs, to San Pedro, where they licked their wounds and counted their casualties. The Angelenos enjoyed sovereignty for three months.

Then General Kearny arrived. Kit Carson had intercepted him en route and told him that California was at peace, so the general had sent two hundred of his trained dragoons back to New Mexico and decided that one hundred was enough for California.

Weary, half-starved, and in no fighting mood, Kearny and his men encamped near the Indian village of San Pascual north-east of San Diego and then learned of the rebel occupation. Kit Carson assured Kearny strongly that all Californios were cowards and fools who couldn't and wouldn't fight. Kearny roused his men and they went to steal fresh horses. In a ten-minute battle, twenty-two Americans were killed and sixteen wounded. Not wanting to be responsible for a complete carnage, the Californios withdrew honorably from further slaughter of the dragoons.

Since they were the last remaining on the field, Kearny declared the victory to the Americans. Kit Carson and Lieutenant Edward Beale hightailed it to San Diego to bring relief forces.

Rather than lack of honor or bravery, it was shortage of powder and dissension within their ranks that defeated the Angelenos and allowed Stockton's and Kearny's joined forces to recapture Los Angeles. Andres Pico surrendered to Fremont and the terms of the Capitulation of Cahuenga were set. Full pardons were given to all the rebels through Fremont's magnanimity.

So ended the war with Mexico and the rebellion of the Californios against Manifest Destiny, but the battle of power had just begun. Kearny, Stockton, and Fremont all wanted command of California. With his customary pomposity and haste, Fremont chose to ignore his orders from Kearny and accepted the preferred ones from Stockton to become governor of California.

Abram's friends came to help with the fall harvest before the issue of California was yet settled. He rode to greet them while Tempest put on coffee and laid out loaves of bread and pots of honey. She was determined to make Abram proud of her.

There were four wagons. The Driekurs wagon was the first, their children bouncing excitedly in back. Next came the Hastings. Tempest felt better when she saw Linda and Parker Breeden, but her heart sank when the last wagon revealed Barbara and Roger Parr and, sitting in the back of the loaded-down wagon, the Widow. She was gazing at Abram as he stood laughing and talking with the men now lifting their wives and children down. He reached up for her and her face brightened.

While the children ran wild, the women insisted on helping Tempest prepare the evening meal. She had already planned to serve smoked venison, tule potatoes, garden carrots, and squash, but the women had brought jars of beef and potato sausages in pig casings.

"Everyone's so tired of venison," Hope said.

"We've apples. We can make some pies in a jiffy," Barbara said, already going through the cupboards.

Tempest's hands clenched, but she tried to control herself. It wouldn't do to strangle the woman.

The gay chatter annoyed her. The cabin wasn't small, but with Hope, Sarah, Barbara, Linda, and Corinne all trying to help, they bumped into one another repeatedly. Tempest's face became tighter with each passing moment.

Linda stacked dishes on the table. She glanced at Tempest and smiled. Tempest didn't smile back.

"We should set up a long table out front," Barbara said, taking command. She took some things from the cupboards and set them on the counter. "Where do you keep your saw-horses, Tempest?" She was busy poking her nose into Tempest's lower cupboards as she asked.

"Not there," Tempest informed her coldly.

Barbara stood. "Do you even know?"

When Tempest didn't answer, she glanced away and rolled her eyes at Sarah and Hope. The two women lowered their heads and laughed softly. Barbara turned to Corinne. "Why don't you go out and ask Abram about setting up? You know what to do, and he will be more than willing to help you."

Corinne gave an uncertain and embarrassed glance at Tempest, then left. Barbara closed the cupboard door and looked at Tempest. Her smile was unpleasantly smug.

"Helping, are ye?" Tempest said, meeting her eyes squarely.

"As much as I can." She leaned back against Tempest's counter and looked about the room with contemptuous disdain.

Tempest put her hands on her hips. "Her best and yers together wilna be good enough."

Three women caught their breath. Tempest looked at each in turn and then smiled the Mad Scot's smile.

Barbara paled and drew herself up. "Well, then, maybe we should just leave you to do everything yourself." She moved stiffly toward the door.

"Oh, I think I con manage, thank ye very much!" Tempest said loudly to the woman's back. Sarah and Hope still stood frozen in the cabin, staring. Tempest turned and impaled them with a look. "Ye want to help, too, ladies?" she asked. She jerked her head toward the door. "Go shuck corn!" They fled the cabin almost at a run.

Linda sat down heavily in the straight-backed chair by the table. Tempest turned on her. "Why're ye laughing? What's so bloody funny?"

Linda's shoulders shook and she started to hiccup, tears streaming from her hazel eyes. Tempest slumped into a chair opposite her, imagining Abram's face when he heard what she'd just done. She leaned her elbows on the table and put her head in her hands.

Linda touched her hand then, her mirth under control. Tempest raised her head. "Tempest," Linda said, her lips twitching slightly, "I like you better and better."

Tempest grunted ungraciously, her eyes bleak.

Linda put her hand over Tempest's and squeezed. "You haven't a thing to worry about."

"Abram will—"

"Abram *won't*. And you're right about them. Abram Walker is *all* yours. Anyone who looks at him when he's looking at you knows it. And you declared war that last night, didn't you?" She laughed and patted Tempest's hand before standing. "Shall we get busy on those apple pies?"

Tempest sniffed. "Ye con make the pies. I'm going to get the side of deer." She stood up, glaring at the open door. "They can stuff their damn sausages."

Everyone sat down to a long plank table laden with a good, hearty meal of venison steaks, bowls heaped with the tule potatoes, garden vegetables, and four golden-brown apple pies. There were vats of cider at each end of the table so people could help themselves to as much as they wanted. When the sun went down, the children were settled into the backs of the wagons to sleep while their elders sat about the barnyard fire reminiscing about their journey west. Parker broke out his mouth organ and the group sang familiar songs and hymns.

Tempest stacked dishes in the cabin and listened to the music. When she heard Abram's strong baritone join in harmony with Corinne's soprano, she ground her teeth. Everyone else stopped singing to listen to them, and when they stopped, gay talk filled the air, then Abram's laughter. Tempest slammed the cupboard door.

She was already undressed and in bed when he came in. She pretended to be asleep.

"Why didn't you come out and join us?" Abram asked, taking his clothes off and sliding beneath the counterpane.

"That widow would have made ye a proper wife," she snarled.

"Probably," he agreed tightly.

She turned her back on him.

"At times like this, Tempest, you remind me that I married a child." He put his hand firmly on her shoulder, forcing her to turn onto her back. "I don't like feeling like a cradle robber."

"How do ye think of yer widow?"

"Her interest is flattering." Tempest turned her face away, but he forced it back, angry yet hopeful as well. "Your jealousy is even more so," he said frankly. "It gives me hope that someday you'll actually love me." He let her go and she turned away from him again. He lay on his back and stared at the ceiling.

"I do . . ."

"Don't say it, Tempest. Don't you dare say it now. You'd only be lying, and I can't abide that." He turned his head and gazed at her as she rolled over to look at him. "You've a certain fondness for me. You *need* me. But you don't love me, not yet."

She saw the sad curve of his lips and felt a heavy weight on her heart. They lay beside one another, silent. She reached out and touched his face. He was right, but she did feel something for him, something more than fondness and need. She *liked* him. She *respected* him. For Tempest, that counted for a great deal.

His fingers entwined with hers tightly. "It's all right," he said huskily. "You don't have to prove anything."

She drew his hand over and placed it on her breast. Abram stopped breathing for a moment. He felt the bed shift as she moved onto her back and looked at him. He let out his breath shakily, closing his eyes tightly. "You know just how to undo me, don't you?" He rolled toward her, seeking.

All the men, women, and children helped with harvesting the two crops. A wagon was drawn alongside the rows of corn. The pickers snapped off the ears and tossed them against the bang-board to drop neatly into the wagon bed. Later the loaded wagons were emptied at the corncrib where the women sat shucking the ears. Linda and one of the older children worked the corn shellers, grinding the dried kernels off so that they spilled into big sacks which another girl stitched shut. The cornstalks were then stripped, the leaves bundled to be collected later and stored in the barn for rich winter fodder for the stock.

Then came the wheat. The men swung great arcs with the sickles, harvesting it, then pitched it into wagons to be dumped in the yard. The children threshed the wheat by leading the oxen around on it, and then the adults winnowed it as an afternoon breeze came up. The wind carried the chaff away, leaving the wheat thick and golden on the ground to be raked and sacked.

Within a few days, the work was done. Abram's crops were harvested, sacked, marked, and loaded into Parker's and Tom's wagons, ready for the journey to Sutter's Fort. Abram reimbursed his helpers with a percentage of the crops, as well as large quantities of the smoked meats Tempest had hunted.

Abram and Tempest accompanied them on horseback. Tempest said almost nothing the first day out, and that night she pressed as closely to Abram as possible. He tried to sleep, but he kept worrying about McClaren. Tempest moved restlessly and whimpered, and he knew she was having the nightmare again. It had been a long time since it had come. He stroked her and whispered soothing words and she quieted again.

They started out just after dawn the next day. She was silent, more silent than the day before, seeming not even to hear the antics of the children as they ran beside the wagons or the men and women talking to one another from the wagon seats. Linda called out to her, but she kept riding, her head straight forward.

Abram brought his horse up beside hers. "Talk to me." She glanced at him, then away. The look in her eyes bothered him. "It's too early for your father to be down from the mountains." He hadn't intended it to come out so sharply. He saw the muscle tighten in her jaw. "What if he is there?" he asked more gently.

She frowned, but didn't answer.

"What would happen?" he demanded.

"It'd depend."

His heart sank. "On what?"

"On what he wants. On what ye want." She didn't look at him again.

"You're staying with me," he told her in a low, warning tone.

"If Da wants me back, I wilna be."

"You'll go back to that bastard over my dead body."

She looked at him then with wide, haunted eyes. "Maybe."

"Is that what you're hoping for?"

"He is my *da.*"

"You're *my wife,*" he said fiercely.

"I'm just the half-breed ye bought and took home to yer bed."

"Damn you," he breathed, his eyes burning. He wanted to knock her off her horse. "Do you want to go back to the way it was with him?"

She didn't know. Her chest ached as though someone were standing on her. Which one? Da or Abram? What did it matter?

She felt safe and loved with Abram Walker. She knew by now what to expect from him: she knew what he would try to do, what he wanted from her.

Yet a part of her longed achingly for McClaren. She closed her eyes and tried to see her father's face. All she could conjure up were his eyes—blue, cold, and devoid of life. Did she want to go back to him? To that?

Just the thought last night had brought back the dream. But none of that changed the fact that she still loved her father more than any other human being, that she was linked to him by more than flesh and blood.

Then there was Abram. *Could* she leave him? Her throat closed, dry and tight, as she thought of being away from his care.

"You don't know, do you?" Abram said roughly.

She looked at him.

He hadn't seen her cry since the day he had followed her when she'd run after her father. "Do you?" he repeated raggedly.

"It wouldna matter what I wanted, mon. It'll be between you and Da what happens to me. I've no say at all, have I?"

Abram knew she was right. "He'll have to kill me before I'll give you back."

What you do not want done to yourself,
do not do to others.
—Confucius

New Helvetia was growing.

Seven dusty, tattered Conestogas rested in the meadow beyond the open gate of Sutter's Fort. Cookfires were going, the acrid smoke curling up into the heavy, warm afternoon air. A thin woman in a faded brown gingham dress and sagging bonnet bent wearily over an iron pot, one hand pressed to the small of her back while with the other she stirred slowly. Another woman sat slouched in the cool of a wagon, nursing a baby. Her shadowed face was turned in placid concentration toward a frail, dark-haired boy in patched dungarees who was drawing in the dirt with a stick. Three more children were crouched in the high golden grass watching the Indian laborers sweat in Sutter's fields. A tall boy crept along the edge of the field and threw a rock.

Tempest knew the wagon train was newly arrived, for the grazing oxen still had protruding ribs, not having had time to fatten up yet after the long continental journey.

"Wonder where they hail from," Abram said.

Tempest was more interested in the four oaks near the river where she and Da had camped many times before when they had come to trade at the fort. If he had come, he would be there.

Someone was.

She strained to see, but all she could make out was a horse grazing and the faint, curling smoke of a campfire. She dug her heels into her horse sharply and rode toward the river.

"Tempest!"

She ignored Abram's shout in her excitement and bursting joy, seeing only the shadowy shape of a man sitting with his back to the massive old oak trunk, a jug in his hand.

Abram's old Dusty thundered after her.

The man beneath the oaks turned his head slightly, and Tempest uttered a faint, choked cry. She slowed. Abram rode up next to her and reached out to grab hold of her reins. She drew back sharply, her teeth bared, and brought the leather straps around and slapped them across his chest. He gasped and caught hold of them on her second swing and yanked them from her so sharply that she was almost unhorsed.

He looped her reins tightly around his saddle horn, glaring from her to the man down by the river. "Is it him?"

"No."

"How can you tell this far away?" he snapped, turning their horses back toward the others, who were watching them in stunned interest.

"There be only one horse grazing, not a string, and the fire's too big." Long years of outrunning murderous enemies had made her father a cautious man, even when he was this close to the thick adobe walls of a fort or the cluster of houses in a settlement. Besides that, the man sitting beneath the oak hadn't even stood up, so easy was he in his thoughts. At the first sound of horses riding toward him, McClaren would have been on his feet, rifle or knife in hand.

Abram relaxed slightly, but the vein in his temple was visibly pounding. "Just as well." He rode toward the Breeden wagon.

"What was that all about?" Linda asked without restraint. She looked from Abram to Tempest with speculation.

"Nothing. Just a little family tiff."

Linda and Parker both noted the reins secured and out of Tempest's hands.

They all rode into the fort and drew up in front of the commissary office. Sutter came out, his rotund, bewhiskered face wreathed in welcoming smiles as he took in the loaded wagons. Tempest could almost see him mentally rubbing his hands together as he saw the goods.

The women quickly abandoned the wagons, leaving the men to talk business while they went back out to greet the new arrivals. Linda motioned for Tempest to come along, but Tempest remained at Abram's side, her mouth tight. She wondered if she'd hear news of her father.

The sacks of corn and wheat were unloaded and tallied. Tempest leaned close to Abram and whispered firmly, "Dunna take the mon's word or his notes. They aren't worth horse

dung, and ye already have plenty of that on Fairfield Farm."
She yanked the reins from his hand. "I'll see to the horses
while ye see to him." She nodded curtly toward the amicable
Swiss.

Abram watched her walk away and shook his head, smiling
wryly. Though crudely put, he knew her advice was sound.
Sutter was already known to have overextended himself by
purchasing the Russians' Fort Ross on the Pacific coast north
of Yerba Buena. Only a small amount of money had exchanged
hands and the rest was in a promissory note that Sutter was
unlikely to ever fulfill. "They will have to come back for it,
and it is a long voyage," he had said over brandy one evening.
Nevertheless, he didn't miss an opportunity to short a farmer
or a trader in his rush to accumulate wealth.

Abram bartered his harvest for several head of cattle, half
a dozen hens and two roosters, and a pair of boots each for
himself and Tempest. He was well satisfied with the agreement.

"We'll get a good night's sleep and head back in the morning," he told her as they set up camp just beyond the walls of
the fort and within a few hundred yards of the wagon train and
the Sonomans.

"I thought ye'd be wanting to sing and dance all night with
yer friends and the widow."

Abram gave her a long, perceptive look and his mouth
curved slightly. "We can hear the music right here where we
are. If you've a mind to do some dancing, just say the word."

She began clearing grass before making a fire. "Any word
about my da?" she asked without looking at him.

"He's high in the Sierras trapping beaver," Abram told her.

Tempest could feel him watching her as she laid the kindling
and scratched the flints to spark a fire.

"Someone else said he's headed for the Oregon Territory,"
he added more slowly. Rumors abounded.

Tempest's hands stilled. *So he's running again,* she thought
miserably. *We came as far west as the land went, clear to the
ocean. Now he is going north without me.*

Her hands shook as she picked up several twigs and placed
them on the fire. Swallowing hard, she ran the tip of her tongue
along her dry lips. Abram hunkered down on the other side of
the fire, his shoulders hunched. "You don't need your father
anymore, Tempest. You have me now."

She raised her head and glared at him with glistening eyes.
"Ye'll just have to do then, won't ye?"

"Yes, I will." He was trying to be patient.

She stood and brushed off her hands. Abram stood as well. "Where're you going?" he demanded when she turned away.

She glanced back at him, her expression forbidding. "To the bushes. Ye want to come along and watch to make sure I dunna run away?"

His face filled with color. "Keep talking to me like that and I'm going to wash out your mouth with soap!"

But all the defiance had already drained from Tempest. Her eyes welled and spilled over. Abram took a step toward her and she covered her face. "I love you. Don't you know that yet? Isn't that enough?" he said hoarsely.

"Ye canna understand yet, con ye, mon? I loved *him*. He's all I had."

Abram's face fell. "I know, but you couldn't stay with him forever. You couldn't live like that as a woman."

"It would've been grand to have some say in the matter," she said, and turned away.

Abram shoved his hands deeply into his pockets and watched her until she disappeared into the bushes. Then he sat down by the fire and put his head in his hands. Sighing shakily, he rubbed his face and moist eyes fiercely with his hand and then stared off toward the wagons where his friends were. He saw the women sitting on the tongue of a wagon. Laughter drifted in the cooling evening air. Someone began playing a harmonica—probably Parker again. The familiar strains of "Nearer, my God, to Thee" floated across the cool dark space to him.

Moving on the edge of the light he saw Corinne. She was looking toward him. He couldn't see her face from this distance, but he didn't need to. Corinne had a sweetness about her, a melancholy shadow in her blue eyes, a soft, pink mouth that curved naturally into a faint smile.

She'd have been easy. She would have come willingly to my bed, worked beside me in the fields, made a good home for me in the cabin, given me half a dozen children, probably all boys.

His life would have been as smooth as sitting in a rocker watching the corn grow in good weather. Marrying Corinne would have been like marrying Kathy all over again.

Corinne Anderson would never have sworn at him, called him vile names, questioned his requests, blasphemed God's Holy Word by doubting, or denied him his rights in bed. She would have cooked three big meals a day. She would have made him apple pie when they had apples, and oatmeal cookies when they had oatmeal. She would have made him shirts with perfect, even stitches and worked in the vegetable garden without complaint. She would have shucked corn and gotten on with the other woman.

He smiled slightly.

Corinne Anderson would not have known what to harvest from a mire, let alone ventured to set foot in one. She would never have been able to put meat on his table. She wouldn't have made him think about what he read from the Bible. She would never have thought to challenge his authority as a man because she would believe it was his God-given right. Nor could she ever possibly have hoped to arouse him so fully that if he touched her he might come off like one of those rockets at a county fair.

Abram didn't see Tempest until she was standing within the ring of firelight. She saw the way he smiled, and looking out she saw the widow as well.

"You move so softly," he said, startled.

"Ye dunna ken how to listen."

"I guess not." He laughed, easy with himself. He watched her prepare their simple meal while the stars came out and the crickets began their nightly serenade. Tempest served him first, her eyes downcast. It was as close to an apology as she was likely to come, he knew. They ate in silence, sitting on opposite sides of the fire. He felt her distance.

Laughter and music came from the wagons. Tempest looked toward them pensively, then at Abram in open question.

He had no desire to be there. He wanted only to be here, near the fire with Tempest, preferably on the same side with her beside him or in his arms. One simple sentence from her meant more to him than an evening of talk with anyone else. One heartfelt laugh from her would have brought him the most intense joy.

He smiled at her, everything he felt in his eyes. Hers softened.

He got up and came around the fire to sit down next to her. She didn't move away. He leaned back on one elbow, studying her smooth, golden face as she looked back at him. When she was angry or pensive or concentrating on some task, she had the face of a woman. Yet now, her eyes shadowed with weariness, but relaxed and trusting him, she looked incredibly young. How old was she anyway? A child still.

"What do you think about when you're so quiet?" he asked.

Her eyes flickered and her expression grew wary. "I dunna think. I look. I listen."

His smile was lopsided and disbelieving. "You're the think-ingest woman I know. You think all the time—too much, sometimes." She said nothing. He prodded. "Tell me. What were you listening to a moment ago?"

"The soft wind in the grass, the insects, the fire, yer breath-ing, those people over there. Ye dinna hear me when I came to the fire because *you* were thinking. All ye could hear were yer own thoughts. Ye see what is around ye, but ye dunna understand anything."

His brows rose. "So. What did you learn by listening?"

"Much."

"What?" He was curious.

"Had those women free will, they never would have come out here."

Abram sat up. "What makes you say that?"

"The look in their eyes, the way they stand over a cookfire, the way they move. Listen, mon, and ye'll hear that it's the men who laugh and sing. Not the women. They sit by and talk among themselves. They turn their faces east."

Abram frowned. He stood up and moved into the darkness beyond the firelight, listening and watching. What Tempest said had been true of Kathy. Was it as true of the rest? Not for all of them, surely—not for the ones without children, for the ones who had not been so close to their families back home, for the ones who had a restless, questing spirit.

He came back to the fire and sat down glumly. "Maybe you're right. Partly. They'll be happy as soon as they're settled. Remember Sonoma? The women laughed and sang and danced there."

"Because it was like before."

"What do you mean, 'like before'?"

"Linda told me. As soon as they staked out their land, they began to build houses like the ones they left. They planted seeds from their other gardens. They recreated what they had lost. Just like you, mon, they dragged the old life with them all the way across the plains and mountains and desert and mountains again until they reached here."

He sat in silence for a long moment, rubbing his forehead. Then something occurred to him. He lowered his hand and looked at her steadily. She didn't like that look, for her brows drew down and her mouth became a hard line.

"You have a lot in common with those women, then."

"I dunna have anything in common with them," she spat fiercely.

"Oh, no? You drag your old life around on your back, too, just like they do." Tempest said nothing, her face wooden, but Abram knew he had made a good thrust. "Maybe you listen and watch because you're afraid to let yourself think too much."

Her eyes ignited. She glared at him for a pulsating moment and then stared into the fire, her mouth grim.

"You've a lot to learn about getting on with people, Tempest. A lot to learn about life."

She laughed sharply and glanced up at him fiercely. "I dunna need them."

"We all need other people. You needed your father. Now you need me, don't you? Admit it. Just once, admit it to me."

"Only you," she conceded grudgingly.

"Part of the joy of life is needing other people, having them need you. Working together, helping one another . . ."

"The more people I meet, Abram Walker, the more cruelty I find. Ye can expect naught but that from *needing people,*" she told him with the air of someone who knows only too well.

"If it's what you expect, what you look for, yes. But not if you live by the Golden Rule. 'Do unto others as you would have them do unto you.' It's what Jesus taught us."

"Fine words," she sneered.

"More than words, Tempest. A way of life that works."

"The way it did for yer Jesus? Ye told me yerself how his own people nailed him to a cross and watched him die in agony."

She always defeated him with her logic. Not this time! It was too important. Maybe she wasn't ready to understand Christ's sacrifice, but she was damn well ready to understand Abram.

Abram rose and came around the fire. Tempest drew back slightly. He crouched down close to her and reached out slowly to cup her cheek. Her eyes flickered. "I treated you with love and kindness when you wanted nothing more than to see me dead or gone, or both. Now, most of the time, you treat me with respect, even consideration, and sometimes, thanks be to God, fondness. One day, maybe more. *That's* what I mean, Tempest. What we give, we receive. What we sow, we reap."

She searched his face. He caressed her smooth cheek with

his thumb. "You sit. You listen and watch, but you *think* about that." He let his hand drop to his side as he stood and moved away a few feet. He laid out the blanket, positioned the saddle, and then stretched out comfortably to look up at the starry sky. He glanced at Tempest after a while and saw that she hadn't moved. She was gazing toward the wagons, her brow puckered, and her mouth soft. That hard, young-old face could be agonizingly vulnerable at times.

He watched her for a long while, loving the very sight of her. Finally he said, "Tomorrow will be a long day. We'd better get some sleep."

She rose, and Abram looked at her slender body as she bent to put another log on the fire, sending up a burst of sparks that rose high into the darkness and then winked out. The night was getting colder.

"Are you still afraid of the dark, Tempest?" he asked as she sat down on the blanket, her hip not quite touching his. She drew the blanket up over them both as she lay back beside him. He turned his head and looked at her, waiting.

"Not as much," she admitted. She rolled onto her side and edged back until she pressed into his side. Abram turned and brought his legs up so that his thighs were behind hers, her back against his chest. He put his arm around her and pressed her body even tighter back into his, then cupped her breast gently. "We'll keep one another safe and warm," he whispered, breathing in the scent of her.

Tempest relaxed and slept dreamlessly in his protective embrace.

A maid that laughs is half taken.
　　　　　　　　　—John Ray

Work resumed at Fairfield Farm as soon as Abram and Tempest returned. They spent several days clearing the cornfield of stalks, and then Abram plowed the land until it was smooth and dark. Tempest grumbled as she pulled the seedy vegetable plants out of the garden and hoed the weeds. Then she shoveled and raked new rows and mounds until Abram was satisfied and doled out several more seed packets from Kathy's hoard for a winter garden.

Rains began to fall intermittently and the farm went into a lull. Abram spent the wet days making plans and working in the barn. Next year he'd plant beans at the base of the dried cornstalks and they'd have three crops to trade instead of two.

The longhorns grew fat on the shucks and the chickens multiplied in spite of a persistent weasel who defied Tempest's traps. Finally, in frustration, she laid in wait and shot him through the head.

Each evening Tempest would lift the Bible down from the mantel and Abram would read. He read Job, Joshua, and Proverbs. She asked many questions he couldn't answer, but he tried and she listened, and she learned.

Sometimes when they lay side by side in bed, Abram could hardly remember his life without her. She had become a necessity to him, physically, mentally, and emotionally. His need for her frightened him. He had never felt this way about Kathy. He had felt joy with his first wife, but never this worry about whether she was happy, whether she was satisfied with her life or with him.

On a windy day, Tempest would stand on their hill with her eyes closed and let the chill winter air caress her face until her cheeks were red. Abram would watch and wonder what she thought about at such times, but was afraid to ask, sure he knew the answer.

Sometimes the sheer loneliness of the land made Abram

seek Tempest's warm, soft woman's flesh. She no longer denied him, and making love to her renewed his spirit and gave him hope. Yet she never once surrendered any part of her inner self. He wondered if she ever would, or even could.

"I wish I could make you feel it the way I do," he murmured huskily against her neck one night after having spent himself in her, his heart still hammering.

"'Tis not important." She put her hand on his head consolingly. He shifted his weight from her and raised himself on one elbow to look down at her. Pushing her loosened hair back from her temples, he smiled sadly.

"It's very important to me. Just once, I'd like to make you cry out."

"The way ye do?"

"Yes." He wasn't embarrassed as much by her bluntness now. She drove him to ecstasy without any response from her at all. How much better would it be for them both if he were able to touch that secret place, that spark in her? He sighed, knowing instinctively that he couldn't. "At least you don't hate it anymore."

"No. Sometimes I like it."

"You do?"

She gave him a faint, woman's smile. "'Tis the only time ye're not my master."

It wasn't the answer he wanted to hear. "There should be more pleasure in it for you than that."

She frowned, serious. "I dunna think I'd like to feel what ye do."

"Why not?"

"Because when ye come off, ye aren't really there."

His brow puckered. "Not there? What do you mean?"

"Ye're turned inside out, or something else takes control. Ye have the same look on yer face that an animal does when it dies." She didn't tell him that a man looked the same way . . . or a woman.

Abram lay on his back, his forehead creased in thought. He and Kathy had always made love in the dark, so he had never seen her face when she'd reached her crisis. He didn't have any idea how she looked.

"Maybe you're right," he conceded, though dubious. "But however a person looks, that feeling is the way it was meant to be between a man and a woman."

Tempest didn't argue. She couldn't agree, either, at least not until she had experienced it for herself. Maybe she couldn't. Abram didn't know enough about woman's bodies or minds to guess. All he did know was that there was a large part of Tempest McClaren that wasn't his, that probably never would be his. He would have to learn to accept that, because he could not seem to change it.

October was warm, but November came cold, gray, and barren. Abram and Tempest went hunting to replenish the diminishing hoard in the smokehouse. Two miles from the cabin they were caught in a rainstorm. They huddled against a great, denuded oak, hoping to wait it out, but after half an hour they decided they had better make a run for home.

Abram took a chill. Tempest brewed him bark tea and rubbed a homemade remedy on his chest, but the head cold sank into his chest. The ailment, though not confining, persisted through November and Thanksgiving, when they would have gone to Sonoma to celebrate with his friends. Tempest certainly was not disappointed, but Abram missed the grand gatherings that reminded him of home, the cheerful chattering crowds of family and friends. The isolation was almost too much to bear.

Abram found that the humid chill of a California winter sank into his bones and lingered more tenaciously than the freezing weather of a snowy Pennsylvania winter. His cough continued to plague him, and he didn't dare compound the ailment with another chill. With the steady rains upon them, it was too wet for comfortable travel to Sonoma, so Abram set his mind to a quiet Christmas at home with his wife. Unlike Thanksgiving, the Holy Day was not going to pass them without some celebration and tradition.

He reasoned that McClaren, being the heathen he was, had probably never even celebrated the birth of Christ. Tempest had never heard of Him other than in the form of a curse before Abram had taken her home with him. Abram was determined to give Tempest a proper Christmas. To this end, he spent secret hours whittling small gifts. One special gift he worked on every afternoon in the barn, keeping the project covered with bundles of shucks so that it couldn't be seen upon entering the barn. His excitement grew as Christmas approached.

One of Tempest's duties was finding the eggs. Abram was working on the roof of the smokehouse one day when he spied her heading for the barn. "Hey!" he shouted, but she was concentrating on some tracks and didn't notice.

Turning, he slid down the shingled roof, muttering under his breath, then dropped to the ground with a jarring thud. "Tempest!" He straightened hastily and ran.

She was poking around the shucks when he skidded into the open doorway. "What're you doing over there?"

She straightened sharply and looked back at him in surprise. "Looking for eggs." She eyed him curiously.

"There are no eggs over there, now go on out of here."

"The red hen sneaked in here and then strutted out. There be eggs in here. And this be the best spot to roost. See, her tracks come right over here." She turned and bent, poking again. A couple of bundles of shucks toppled.

"I don't want everything turned upside down for a couple of eggs," he said. "Now, go on out and look in the garden where the hens usually lay."

Tempest straightened again, her blue eyes shining fire. "I beg yer bleedin' pardon!" She dropped the small woven basket she carried, stomped on it, and then stalked past him into the yard. He watched her until she slammed into the cabin so hard that a shingle slid off the roof and landed with a splat in the mud.

Scratching his head distractedly, Abram wondered how he was going to get back into her good graces after that. He went into the barn and restacked the bundles. No more than a foot from where Tempest had been hunting eggs was a cache of them. He put them in his hat.

When he came out of the barn, Tempest was swinging the hoe viciously in the vegetable garden. His mouth curved ruefully. He approached with caution and she stopped working and eyed him angrily. He came closer and held out his hat. "I was wrong about the hen. I'm sorry."

Surprise blossomed on her face. She leaned the hoe against the string-bean bush and took his hat. Then she cocked her head and gave him a curious look. "What're ye hiding in the barn, mon?"

"What makes you think I'm hiding something?"

She looked at him again, then set down the hat and took the hoe and went back to work. Never dare a woman's curiosity, Abram thought. He knew that the moment his back was turned she'd head for that barn like a shot. "I'm making a new tool," he said, and smiled cajolingly as he saw a way to thwart her. "It's made of wood and requires a lot of sanding and rubbing until it's smooth. If you wouldn't mind..."

"Oh, no!" she said angrily. "I've well enough to do! Ye're the one sittin' in front of the fire when it rains while ye still expect yer meals cooked, yer shirts ironed and sewed and this mucking about out here!"

He held up his hand, hiding his amusement and satisfaction. "All right. Never mind. I guess I'll just have to do all the work myself," he muttered in a pained tone, turning away. His mouth twisted. She'd avoid the barn for a few days, and that was all the time he needed.

Abram had everything ready the day before Christmas. Unsuspecting, Tempest went about her usual duties. She spent the morning down by the creek washing clothes, worked in the garden following their noonday meal, then ironed until dusk and supper.

While Abram sat by the fire, she mended his dungarees again. He still had not convinced her that the thread should match the material and the stitches should blend and not stand out. It was no longer a matter of obligation with her but one of choice, for with hours of practice she had become quite adept. She enjoyed this chore and never complained about doing it. Someday she hoped she would be skilled enough to copy the hummingbirds and flowers of Kathy's fine pillow-cases, or maybe even create designs of her own.

She sat cross-legged on the woven mat while Abram read. He chose the Gospel according to Matthew, telling the story of Christ's birth and the gifts of the three wise men. Then he yawned broadly and suggested that they go to bed.

"It's early. Why dunna ye read some more?"

"I'm tired. Had a long day."

"I've another shirt to sew."

"Leave it for tomorrow."

She lifted her head and gave him a speculative look. He knew what she was thinking and smiled, his eyes teasing. "I said I was *tired.*"

He tried not to doze while he waited for her to fall asleep. When her breathing was slow and even, he slipped silently from the bed, crept from the cabin, and went to the barn. By dawn the cabin was just the way he wanted it. Unable to contain his excitement, he heaved a heavy log noisily onto the fire.

Tempest moaned softly and rolled over. Abram stood beside the bed watching her awaken. Her eyes opened slowly, melt-

ingly blue, and she yawned and stretched like a young cat. He
laughed softly.

"Come on, sleepyhead, wake up. I've a surprise for you."

She yawned again, so broadly he could see right down her
throat. Then she sat up and rubbed her face.

"Merry Christmas!"

She looked up at him blankly. He gestured across the cabin
and her gaze traveled to the small pine tree that stood in the
far corner. Her eyes widened. She kicked off the counterpane
and padded across the cold earthen floor to look more closely.
He had decorated the branches with corn-shuck dolls and whit-
tled soldiers, rocking horses, and birds. She touched each carved
toy, walking around the tree, her face open, amazed, and glowing like a child's.

"This is for you," he said, unable to wait for her to notice
on her own. He put his hands on her shoulders and turned her
toward the fireplace, where he had hung red-berry boughs just
beneath the mantel. Opposite his own chair was another, made
of young willow branches woven and secured by thick rawhide
strips. He let go of Tempest and went across to lightly touch
the back of the chair, which set it rocking.

Tempest stood motionless, staring at it, her lips slightly
parted. Then they closed softly and she looked at him. Something different was in the clear, overbright blue eyes. His heart
tripped crazily.

"So you won't have to sit on the floor anymore. And someday you're going to have a baby to rock," he said huskily. "Try
it."

She just looked at him. Her eyes filled.

"Don't cry," he said, alarmed. "Why are you *crying?*"

Shrugging, she grimaced, the tears running freely. She sniffed
and wiped her nose with the back of her hand. Then she shook
her head again, her expression pained. "I dunna know, mon."

Then she started to laugh.

Stunned, Abram stared.

It was the first natural, unbidden, joyous laugh he had ever
heard pass Tempest McClaren's lips. It rippled through him
like birdsong after a silent day, a bubbling creek in a drought-
dry summer, a rousing hymn in a crowded church. A huge
lump grew in his throat. Pain had never felt so good.

The land of darkness and the shadow of death.
                                                —Job 10:21

Over the next three soggy months of winter, Abram and Tempest had two visitors. The first was Bull Jaeger, a wagoner from Missouri who had come west with Abram and Kathy on William Ide's wagon train. He had started a business in Sonoma, but it was not prospering as he had hoped. Knowing that Sutter was looking for more men to join his enterprises at the fort, and not having a wife, Bull joked that he could move again without fear of reprisal.

For all the brawn and gruffness that had earned him his nickname, Bull was shy of women. He sat on the edge of the straight-backed chair while he talked to Abram and kept a surreptitious eye on Tempest as she prepared dinner. She was equally curious about him, for every time she looked at him he turned bright red. It started at his neck, which was as thick as Tempest's thigh, and spread up over his anvil jaw and ruddy cheeks, past his startled gray eyes, across his pale forehead, and right up to his receding hairline. He couldn't sustain her glance, and would clear his throat and look around the cabin as though searching frantically for a cupboard or corner big enough to hide him. Finding none, he would look at her again and say for the dozenth time, "Hope I'm not putting you out too much, ma'am."

To which Tempest finally replied, "Depends on how much ye eat."

Abram laughed softly, gave her a stern look, and leaned across to pat Bull on the back. "She's teasing."

Tempest's brows shot up in challenge, but she held her tongue.

Bull brought news rather than provisions, which was more precious to Abram than the latter would have been anyway. He related that since Vallejo's release after his two-month incarceration by the hostile Fremont, he had returned to his hacienda a far less friendly American ally.

"He's not starting a war, mind you, but he ain't exactly hospitable either." Bull shrugged. Tempest shot Abram a telling glance and went back to slowly turning the spitted venison. Rain pattered on the shingle roof.

Besides Vallejo's changed sentiments, there were the usual family squabbles, community politics, gossip, and additions to the population to discuss over dinner. The Doherty brothers had split, one going north to Oregon, the other south to Yerba Buena. William Ide was claiming to have conquered California, and so was John Fremont. Barbara Parr had had another baby, her fourth, and Linda Breeden was expecting.

"Poor girl looks like death warmed over. Her husband's right worried about her," Bull commented.

Although Abram offered him space by the hearth, Bull chose to sleep in the barn. Before he left Fairfield, he helped Abram construct a *carreta* for taking his produce and sacked grain and corn to market. Bull's cart was not as clumsy as its Mexican counterpart; it was light and easily controlled, yet large enough to carry half as much as an altered Conestoga.

After Bull departed for New Helvetia, Abram hooked Dusty to the cart and raced the thing around and around the farm, shouting like a drunken Indian scout. Tempest watched, forcibly reminded of her da after he had consumed the better part of a jug of whiskey.

A few weeks after Bull Jaeger left, Wesley Saticoy arrived. He was on his way to Yerba Buena from Sutter's Fort. He came in late afternoon, his packhorses loaded down.

"I've a hankering for the sea again," Saticoy grinned. He was a tall bean-pole of a man with a crinkly bronzed face, golden hair, and an outgoing manner. "Being landed isn't all it's cracked up to be. Bejesus! In the summer it's heat and flies, and in the winter it's mud. Nothing ever smells clear like good salt-sea air. Besides that, the work's enough to get any good man down."

Among his provisions were jugs of Sutter's wild grape brandy. He uncorked one to share with Abram as they sat outside in front of the cabin. The news Saticoy brought was not grounds for celebration, but tragic fare.

While Abram and Tempest had been sheltered, warm, and well-fed, eighty-six members of the Donner party had been trapped by the killing snows of the high Sierras.

"By the time the rescue group reached them, half were dead,

frozen or starved," Saticoy related somberly. "George Donner was too weak even to leave with the first group and his wife, Tamsen, wouldn't budge without him. They sent their three daughters on through, but by the time another party reached the train, the rest were dead."

Saticoy downed more of the strong brandy and wiped his mouth on his sleeve. He offered the jug to Abram, but Abram wasn't about to try to keep up with the seasoned drinker. Saticoy shrugged. "They brought some of them to Johnson's Ranch, some to Sutter's Fort. Skin-covered skeletons. Bejesus! And their hollow, haunted eyes . . ." He swilled more brandy.

"Forty-six dead, and it's that son of a bitch Lansford W. Hastings that ought to be called to account for it. If they hadn't believed his worthless reports, they'd have come through before the snows hit. But as it was, they took Hastings' Cutoff and *got* cut off. Some of 'em was smart and wanted to go another way, but they spent too much time haggling and fighting. A man even got kilt over it. Jim Reed was almost lynched for stabbing a fellow that beat him about the head with the butt-end of his whip. They was going to lynch him, but then they decided banishment would be worse. It was Reed hisself who led some of the rescuers back to get the survivors out. He was right all along."

"Where are the rest now?"

"Spread out." Saticoy tipped the jug and his Adam's apple bobbed several times. He wiped his mouth again. "Lots of orphans, widows, and widowers." He glanced at Abram with red, hesitant eyes. "But that ain't the worst of it by far, Abram."

Abram frowned. "What do you mean? How much worse than forty-six dead could it be?"

Wesley Saticoy grimaced. A look of revulsion twisted his features, and he swigged brandy as though trying to wash away a foul taste.

"What do you mean?" Abram demanded in a low voice.

"They was eating each other." Saticoy's speech was heavily slurred, but his eyes were horrifyingly clear and sober. "In one family . . . Jesus . . ." He shuddered. "The children was eating their own dead mother."

"My God," Abram breathed, sickened.

A small, inarticulate noise came from behind him and he glanced back sharply to see Tempest silhouetted in the doorway. The firelight was behind her and he couldn't see her face. There were some things no woman should hear, and it hadn't been intended for her to hear this. He wished that he had quieted Wesley, or that Tempest hadn't chosen that precise moment to eavesdrop on their conversation.

"They're all going to hell for sure," Wesley murmured, and fell silent, shaking his head and muttering.

Abram stood and strode to the door. He put his hand on Tempest's shoulder. She was shaking violently. "Why don't you go back inside?" he told her gently. He saw the bright sheen of her eyes as she looked up at him blankly. Then, without a word, she turned away and went back into the cabin. He closed the door.

It was a couple of hours later when he came in. He had listened sadly as Wesley poured out the tale of the horrors the rescuers had found, then helped the sodden man to the barn to bunk down. When he entered the cabin, Tempest was in bed, curled on her side beneath the covers. He moved quietly, stripping down to his long johns, then slipped in beside her. It was a long time before sleep claimed him against the roiling thoughts brought on by Saticoy's story.

It was longer for Tempest.

The dream came, dragging at her weary body, sucking her down into hell just as Saticoy had said. Once more she saw her mother pierced by arrows and pecked by gluttonous ravens, heard the wolves snarling and lunging, pawing away the pile of stones. She moaned and writhed but didn't awaken. Abram slept innocently beside her.

The wolves went away and Da was there, towering above her with his dead-cold eyes, eating the human flesh, forcing her to join in his grotesque meal.

Then the Indians came again. They were standing on the hill above the high mountain valley. They slowly walked toward her. She tried to run, but her feet sank into the grassy soil and stayed rooted. She fought wildly to free herself, clawing at the ground, digging and digging, but she only sank in farther, the earth mounding around her. The braves were all around her and she could smell the terrible stench of dead flesh. Where their chests should have been were great, gaping, bloody caverns.

She tried to scream, but no sound came. She was choking. Da was gutting a bear over by the rebuilt cabin, his back to her. Close, but deaf, unaware, beyond caring. Mad. She tried to huddle low in the dark hole, to hide from the dead, but suddenly her feet were free and she floated up. She clutched at the earth, trying to cover herself, but it was almost as though the air itself drew her upward. Hands dripping rotten, stinking flesh reached for her. She heard a hellish moaning and sighing. And their faces—

Tempest screamed, her body arching bolt upright.

Abram was jolted awake, his heart hammering. He stared into the darkness, trying to see or hear whatever it was that had slashed his deep sleep like a knife.

Tempest was sitting up in bed shaking violently, her breathing harsh and loud as if she had been running full-out.

"Tempest?" He put his hand on her back soothingly. Her gown was soaked through with sweat. He sat up and reached for her, but she lunged from the bed and stumbled toward the door. Kicking off the quilt, Abram followed. "What's wrong? Are you all right?"

She was on her hands and knees a few feet from the open door. He could hear the wracking dry heaves and see the way her back curved sharply, trying to expel whatever she had eaten that had made her ill.

Nothing came. Abram bent over her, holding her braced. The spasms finally stopped and the night air feathered her hair against her hunched shoulders. "You should have awakened me and told me you were sick," he said thickly, frightened. He began to gently massage her shoulders, knowing how her body must ache. "When did this start?"

She turned and gripped him so tightly that it hurt. He pried her arms loose from his waist and pulled her up. "Easy..." he whispered and lifted her. She started to sob, clinging to him, her body trembling violently. "You'll be fine. It's all right. Just sleep... sleep and it will be all right by morning." He shouldered the door closed and carried her to the bed. When he tried to lay her down she wouldn't let him go, so he came down beside her, holding her close, bringing the quilt up over them. He stroked her and murmured loving words. Gradually, she relaxed in his arms.

But it was Abram who slept. Tempest held onto him, staring into the terrifying darkness.

A child of our grandmother Eve, a female, or,
for thy more sweet understanding, a woman.
—William Shakespeare
Love's Labour's Lost

For several days following Saticoy's visit, Tempest remained silent. Her face was leeched of color, her eyes dull and turned inward. Abram understood on the second night with the recurrence of the nightmare that what ailed Tempest was not physical, but a sickness of her soul.

He wondered what had caused the return of her dreams with such awful force, but when he broached the subject, she wouldn't even look at him, let alone answer. Finally Abram had no choice but to let the matter alone and hope that the situation would soon ease. He wasn't sleeping enough, either.

She slept close to him, her body pressed warmly into his, and gradually the nightmares became intermittent, occurring less and less often until they only came when she was overtired from strenuous farm work or when some inner, secret connection with her past life reared its ugly head.

McClaren had a lot to answer for, Abram thought savagely.

Winter exhausted itself into sleep and spring awakened. Abram began the plowing and Tempest cleared more rocks. She hated field work; it was grueling, dull labor fit only for the dumbest beasts. She straightened with a large stone in her dirt-crusted hands and glared at Abram. He was beginning to lay out the long rows for planting by driving in stakes at the end of the field.

He loved this life; it shone in his face. He sang. He smiled. He relished the feeling of dirt under his fingernails, smudged on his face, coating his clothes, even though he always washed himself free of it at the end of the day.

Tempest sighed heavily as she trudged to the stone wall and dropped her burden with a thunk. Hunting and trapping had been more challenging, and far less torturous to the body. She had used her cunning to outwit the animals. She had had to watch, and listen, and learn from the prey she hunted until she thought as it thought.

With farming, she was a beast of burden. Like Abram's oxen—slow, plodding, dull-witted. And working hard and doing things right brought no guarantees of success. Abram courted God by praying morning, noon, and night for just the right amount of rain, falling gently and not pounding his newly planted crops; for sun, warm but not blistering. And how many bleeding hours had they spent last year walking the rows and checking each corn plant for bugs, smashing the unwanted visitors until their fingers were caked with insect guts?

"By next year, there won't be a single stone on our land," Abram called to her as she rested against the wall.

"Praise God," she muttered.

She put her head back and closed her eyes, feeling the soft warmth of the morning sun on her cheeks. A meadowlark was singing close by, and she smiled slightly. Sometimes before dawn came golden-rose, she would lie in the embracing folds of Kathy Walker's quilt beside Abram's hard body and listen to the land. She could hear the air stroke and kiss the low, green grasses.

Then Abram would rise, hitch his plow to the ox, and turn the earth. Birds would land just behind him as he worked, feasting on the pale, writhing worms uncovered by the blade. Where the soft, sweet-tasting grasses had grown spread a great, brown scar.

She hated the digging, the manure spreading, the weeding, the endless hours of back-breaking work that made her feel crabbed and old. Sometimes, by dusk, she was sure that if she just closed her eyes, she would fall over dead—and be bloody grateful for the rest.

Today was worse than usual. There was a dull ache in her vitals and in the small of her back that no amount of rubbing or stretching would ease. She sensed something not right in herself, some secret difference. It wasn't exactly pain, for it was bearable, yet the persistence of it agitated her.

It's toting these bleeding stones that's doing it, she thought, pushing away from the wall and walking along the furrows again, resenting Abram's good spirits. He was singing "Bringing in the sheaves" again, whatever that meant. *A body's meant to be straight, not bent like a willow.*

Abram's mallet pounded behind her, driving in another stake. The sound grated; her temples pounded. She swore under her breath as she stooped to lift another rock. It didn't weigh much, so she turned and heaved it back toward the wall.

Something opened inside her. She drew a sharp breath, straightening cautiously, and felt a heaviness in her belly. Almost hysterical anger and fear rippled through her. "Yer God put these bloody damn stones here!" she screamed at Abram. "And I'm leavin' 'em where they lie!"

Abram straightened and stared at her.

She glared back at him and then stalked across the field, swearing as she went. She didn't look at him again but went straight to the cabin. Slamming the door made her feel better, but only briefly. She puttered, swiping the oiled rag over the highboy, bedstead, table, and chairs, sprinkling water over the earthen floor, sweeping—anything to distract herself from the dull ache.

Abram would be coming in soon for a midday meal. She wasn't hungry, but she should prepare something for him. Had she eaten breakfast? Maybe that was the problem. Yet no hunger pangs had ever felt like this, and she had been hungry before.

She bent over the iron pot and felt a sudden warm, moist rush between her legs. She dropped the big ladle with a clang and grabbed up the folds of brown gingham. Her heart stopped. "Oh . . ."

Fear throbbed through her. How had she hurt herself there? She was bleeding from inside where she couldn't be fixed. "Abram," she moaned. *"Abram!"*

He saw her running toward him, crying wildly. When she held out her bloody hand, his eyes went huge and he dropped the mallet. "What'd you do to yourself? Where're you hurt? Jesus Christ, where?" he demanded, his face ghastly white.

"Here! Here!" she sobbed, and pulled her skirt high. "It's coming from the vitals."

He stood rooted, staring. "Oh, God," he muttered, his face going a bright, hot red.

"Don't stand there! Do something! I'm bleeding to death and ye just stand there gaping."

His eyes fell away and he raked his hand through his hair, heedless of the crusted dirt on his fingers. "There's nothing wrong with you, Tempest."

"I'm bleeding from inside and ye say there's *naught wrong?*" she cried, stunned at his indifference. "Yer damn rocks did this to me!"

"No, they didn't. It's just the woman thing. The curse."

She bunched her skirt up to stop the flow, and stared at him. Why was he standing there with his neck and face all red and his hands idle rather than helping her? "Do something," she pleaded, her eyes round.

"There's nothing to be done. It's going to happen to you every month."

She stared at him, openmouthed. "What're ye saying?"

He swallowed, ran a shaky hand around the back of his neck, and looked at her self-consciously. "Remember Adam and Eve?"

"I dunna need a bloody tale, ye dumb arse!"

"You have to understand what's happening to you. It started with them, you see. It's the curse God laid on women because of what Eve did in the Garden of Eden. At least, that's how Kathy's mother explained it to her. I—"

"Ye're bleedin' mad!"

"It's going to happen every month from now on until you're too old to have children."

What he was saying was horrifying. "Because of *Eve?*" She tried to take it in. "I'm bleeding because she gave some fruit to that mon?"

He stood there, as dumb as an ox.

Tempest glared at him. She wasn't dying; she was cursed. "I dinna give that apple to that fool, so why is God punishing me?"

"It's not exactly a curse," he said lamely. "It's also a . . . a kind of blessing."

"Blessing?" she hissed.

"It means you've become a woman. It'll be possible for us to make a baby now." She backed away from him sharply, her eyes huge. "I didn't mean *right* now," he told her, his color deepening, and sighed. "I'm not quite that depraved, Tempest. Go on down to the creek and wash. I'll be there in a minute with what you need."

Tempest stripped off her soiled skirt beside the creek and sat in the cold water. It swirled about her waist and washed all the blood away. She thought about what Abram had said and shook her head grimly. She heard him approaching and watched him duck beneath the cottonwood branches, carrying another skirt, underthings, and some ragged cloth.

"What ye told me makes no sense," she said from where she sat. "Ye've been trying to make a baby in me for a full change of seasons, mon, and haven't yet. Why should this make a difference?"

He hadn't thought she could embarrass him anymore. He cleared his throat. "I don't rightly know," he said gruffly. "It just does. It happens to all women. It'll stop in a few days."

"And come back in another moon?"

"Yes."

"Yer God has a long, mean memory, Abram Walker."

He smiled slightly at that. "I'm just not much good at explaining."

She considered him for a long moment. "Ye're glad."

"I've been waiting for it to come."

"If ye ken it was going to happen, why dinna ye warn me about it?"

Abram held a rag out like a truce flag. "Embarrassed," he said frankly, and looked it. He busied himself folding the cloth while she dried herself. When she finished, he showed her what to do.

She sighed heavily, the rags in place and the clean skirt donned, and regarded him with her hands on her hips. "What'd God do to Adam for eating that apple?"

"Cast him out of the Garden of Eden and made him toil for everything he needed to stay alive." He smiled at her. "So you see, women got the best of the deal."

After working since dawn in the fields, hauling rocks, cleaning the cabin, and cooking meat she'd hunted herself, Tempest couldn't agree with him.

Saint-seducing gold.
—William Shakespeare
Romeo and Juliet

Through correspondence and reports from such men
as Thomas Larkin, John Fremont, John Bidwell, and numerous
government agents and officers sent to the west coast, word
spread throughout the east that California had good, open land
that was now protected by America. More and more wagon
trains were organized and settlers surged west to the new frontier. Each month brought an increase in California's American
population by one hundred, two hundred, and more.

Abram and Tempest found themselves with neighbors in-
creasingly closer than the previous twenty-five miles. When
they returned to New Helvetia in late September to trade their
crops for goods and stock, they saw two frontier towns growing
up, one around Sutter's Fort and another downriver, established
by Sutter's estranged son, John. It was called Sacramento.

An enterprising Mormon elder, Samuel Brannan, who had
arrived in San Francisco on the *Brooklyn* at the end of July,
had already set up a general store with his partner, Charles
Smith, just beyond Sutter's walls. The sawmill James Marshall
was building under contract to Sutter was fast nearing com-
pletion up at Coloma. Soon milled lumber would be available
in quantity and a building boom would begin.

McClaren hadn't returned from the mountains. There was
no word from the Mad Scot.

Parker and Linda Breeden packed up and left Sonoma, stopping by Fairfield on their way north. Tempest sat on the bed
and watched Linda nurse eight-month-old Matthew. The baby's
wide blue eyes had closed in blissful pleasure as his small,
rosy mouth worked avidly at his mother's white breast. "Parker

194

says Sonoma's no place for raising a family," Linda explained. Dark circles showed beneath her usually sparkling eyes, and a rueful curve twisted her full mouth. "The town's still mostly rough frontiersmen, army deserters, and sailors, and as for the others . . . well, I never really got on with them." A faintly wicked smile lit her face.

"Widow Anderson's got herself a man," she told Tempest, "so she won't be after yours. She latched onto a Kentucky widower with six children." She laughed. "Barbara Parr was writhing in moral indignation when Corinne admitted that she was already in a family way after only three weeks of marriage. Indecent to be about it so quickly, is what she said," she added, mimicking the dulcet tones of Barbara Parr. "This Hutchins fellow that Corinne married is planning a big spread south of Sonoma someplace, and of course he needs lots of boys to help him work it. His first wife, God rest her poor tired soul, gave him three girls. So he's out to see what he can get from his second."

Tempest was scarcely listening. She had eyes only for Matthew. She watched the baby's tiny fist pushing against Linda. She had seen babies before, but only at a distance. This one looked so fragile that she longed to touch him, yet he frightened her, too.

Linda fell silent and smiled.

"Is he always so hungry?" Tempest asked.

"Always, more so at night." She laughed softly. "He's got two hollow legs, haven't you, Mattie darling? But you're done now." She drew him away and covered herself, then glanced at Tempest. "Here. You do the honors." She held Matthew out.

Tempest drew back sharply. "Me?" she gasped. "No!"

"Oh, come now, Tempest. You weren't afraid of the ladies of Sonoma, so how can you sit there shaking over a mere baby? He won't bite. He hasn't got many teeth."

Tempest's heart raced frantically as she took Matt and held him awkwardly. "Cover your shoulder with this cloth, then put him up there and pat him gently on the back," Linda instructed. The baby was warm and soft and squirmy. She was afraid to pat him, so she gingerly stroked his back. He relaxed and gradually she did too, enjoying the feel of him against her.

"He smells good." She nuzzled his neck.

"Now," Linda grinned. Matt raised his head slightly and

gave a hearty burp of approval. Linda burst out laughing. "Oh, your face!"

"I think the little blighter's spitting up on me," Tempest gasped.

"Undoubtedly," Linda chortled, and took her son back. She handed Tempest a clean diaper. "And that's not all he'll be doing in a minute."

"Do I have to learn everything at once?" Tempest asked, and then grinned at Linda's wry expression. "He's a bonny fine lad."

"He is, isn't he? Gave me quite a time, but he was worth it." After he'd been changed and lulled into drowsiness, Linda tucked the baby into the large woven basket in which he slept. The two young women sat watching him for a long time. Finally Linda looked up. "You'd like a baby, wouldn't you?"

Tempest shrugged, noncommittal.

"Abram would," Linda said, more to the point.

"Aye."

"Well, you know babies don't come in a package at Christmas. You've got to do some work about getting one," she teased.

"Since I got the mark of a woman, he's worked harder on me than he has on his fields."

"Oh!" Linda's face bloomed with high color.

"He thinks it's something wrong with him. Could it be?"

Linda put a hand to her warm cheek. "I don't know. Why does he think that?"

"Because his first woman dinna have a bairn, either."

"Well, that doesn't mean there's something wrong with him. These things take time."

"How much time?"

Linda laughed. "I did start this conversation, didn't I? That'll teach me." She let out her breath and chewed on her lower lip in concentration. She shrugged. "I don't know what to tell you. Sometimes it takes a long time. I knew a couple who wanted a baby for ten years. When they finally gave up hope, that's when they had one. Maybe it's a matter of not worrying so. Sometimes wanting something too much puts a damper on getting it. Just relax. God answers in his own time."

"I am relaxed," Tempest said. "It's Abram who's all hot and bothered about it."

Linda's face softened. "If any man deserves a son, it's Abram Walker." She reached over and put a hand on Tempest's. "Maybe if *you* prayed for one . . ."

Tempest had prayed once in despair, and had been answered. It had left her with an awed sense of acceptance that she was afraid to chance again. Whatever Abram said about God's mercy and love, she was terrified that if God took another look at her, he'd do something awful.

The Breedens stayed a week. Linda said nothing on that last morning, just looked at Abram, and then at Tempest. Tempest stood silently, her face blank, her heart hot and heavy. Linda came forward and hugged her, not letting go for a full minute. Then she gently touched Tempest's cheek, gave her a watery wink, and turned away. Parker lifted her up onto the seat of the Conestoga. She glanced back into the wagon to check on the sleeping baby and then turned away, her eyes straight forward. Once they started off, she didn't look back.

Abram put his arm around Tempest's shoulders and gave her a squeeze, then let her go. "I've got work to do in the barn," he said thickly, and walked slowly away.

Tempest stood alone in the yard until the Breedens' wagon was over the rise and out of sight.

Even with winter upon them again, there was more work to do about the farm. It seemed that the better things went, the heavier the workload got. They now had eight head of cattle, a flock of chickens, and two pigs, one expecting a litter. Abram slaughtered the ornery male, and from it they got lard, crackling, and two hundred pounds of salted pork. Tempest had never tasted bacon or ham, and she wasn't sure she liked either. She kept thinking of the nasty beast from which the meat came.

"Dinna it say in yer book that we werena to eat it?"

Abram had a hard time talking himself out of it. They had ham for Thanksgiving and again for Christmas. Abram cut another pine tree and decorated it with the corn-husk dolls and wooden toys he had made the year before. He added strings of beads he had traded for at Sutter's Fort, and gave Tempest a mirror to hang on the wall so that she could brush her hair before it. She gave him a fringed buckskin coat with rabbit-fur lining.

Not until the middle of March did they hear the first rumors that gold had been found in the tailrace just below the sawmill at Coloma.

Abram gleaned more information as gold seekers passed by,

stopping briefly for water and sometimes a meal. Rumors ran rampant. James Marshall had discovered gold on the American River. He had ridden to Sutter and they had tried to keep it quiet, but one of the children of Mrs. Wimmer had told a teamster. To prove that her son was not a liar, Mrs. Wimmer had told all, and soon Marshall's crew was digging gold, rather than finishing and working a sawmill.

Sam Brannan suspected something when he saw Marshall and Sutter riding back and forth between Coloma and the fort, talking in secret and looking flushed from something other than the usual wild grape brandy and time with the squaws. When gold began crossing Brannan's general store counter, he started buying up all the available mining gear between Los Angeles and Oregon. As soon as his shelves were well stocked, he rode to San Francisco armed with a jar of gold dust, and proclaimed, "Gold! Gold! Gold from the American River!" Even skeptics such as Edward Kemble, the teenage editor of the *California Star*, succumbed to the mania and rushed for the diggings.

San Francisco was deserted, Monterey empty. San Jose was closed down, and even the jailer, Henry Bee, had taken his ten Indian prisoners, two of whom were murderers, to the diggings. Sailors and soldiers were deserting by the hundreds, making more in one week of digging and panning gold than they could in five years of service to their ship or country.

The contagion took Abram in the spring. One minute he was thinning seedlings; the next he was marching toward Tempest where she was hanging wet wash on some bushes by the creek.

"Get some things together! We're going to the gold country!"

Her eyebrows shot up. "What? Why?"

"Because everybody's getting rich, while we stay here and I work my tail off for cornmeal." He headed toward the house, almost running.

"These things wilna be dry for a couple hours!"

"Then leave them until we get back," he shouted impatiently, not even stopping to glance back. "I'll buy you something new and pretty with the gold I pan!"

"Bloody hell! If ye find gold, ye fool!" she muttered, snatching at the damp shirtwaist, skirt and shirts. "Should've told me ye were going out of yer mind this mornin' before I did the bleedin' wash!" she snarled under her breath, slopping the clothes back into the woven basket and lugging it back to the cabin. Abram was tossing supplies onto the table in a frenzy of motion.

Tempest set the basket down and stood watching him. She'd never seen him so crazed, even in bed. His motions were jerky as he snatched open cupboards and drawers, pulling out clothes and sacks of beans, peas, and lentils.

"Nobody has come by in the last three days," she reminded him calmly, "so what made yer brains boil over this morning?"

"Just that," he puffed, scouring the cupboards for other useful items. "No one's *left!* Everybody must be up on the American River. We're going to have to harvest the crops on our own, husk and grind and sack them on our own, and take the load to the fort. And then there probably won't be a soul around to even trade for it. What then? All the work, and nothing to show for it, while the rest of the men in the country are filling their pockets, pants, packs, probably *wagons,* with gold dust!"

She shook her head grimly. "I remember ye saying yerself that all those gold diggers are going to have to eat. The price of food is going to go up. The corn and wheat will be worth their weight in gold dust," Tempest said in broad imitation of Abram's own relaxed speech.

He cast her a dark look, his red-brown brows drawn down over narrowed eyes. "It's true enough, but it may not happen *this* year, and there may not be as much gold as they think there is, and we may not get our share if *we don't go right now!*" He jerked his chin. "Get yourself ready."

"Ye dunna want me here to keep the home fires burnin'?" she quipped.

"If you want to stay and harvest for me, I might consider it."

She drew in her breath sharply. "'Wither thou goest, I will go,'" she quoted Ruth hotly.

Abram laughed. "Well, then, you'd better get a move on, because I go!"

"If we're going to the high country, ye dunna need what ye're putting out. None of it."

He stopped. "What do we need?" She would know.

Tempest began tossing things at him: the buckskin coat she'd made for him, the rifle, ammunition, a sheathed hunting knife, a second shirt, dungarees, socks, a cast-iron frying pan that made him grunt as he caught it, and two blankets, rolled and tied. "And yer horse," she said drolly.

"And a pick and shovel. What about food?"

"There's the land. I'll see ye dunna starve, mon." She glanced at the table and grimaced. "Leave yer dried beans behind."

Hundreds of men lined the banks of the American River. At night, they came together in convivial gatherings. They cooked, washed, sang, and shared tall-tales in friendly revelry around the fire, while jugs of wild grape brandy pressed freely from hand to hand.

There was gold enough in California for everyone, and none of them worried about getting their fair share of it once they were in the fields and on the streams.

Tempest was noticed, for she was the one woman among hundreds of men, and a rare beauty at that. Men looked but kept a respectable distance.

Tempest found herself once again under the open sky and the stars. She had forgotten the sense of freedom it gave her. They moved south and east onto the Cosumnes, and then farther south onto the Mokelumne when word of another strike came. She returned to the old ways, hunting, fishing, trapping, digging wild roots, and gathering the natural bounty, while Abram raped the stream of its treasure.

When darkness came, the old fear came with it, and she stretched out close by Abram's hard, protective warmth. The grueling work of harvesting gold exhausted Abram's energies yet did not succeed in obliterating his deep need and desire for his wife.

"Oh, oh, ohhhh!" he cried out, and she closed her eyes, accepting the small price she paid for a dreamless night in his arms.

By July, two moons had passed without blood. Tempest told Abram.

"God be praised!" he cried, tears streaming from his eyes as he held her hands tightly. "You're with child!" The firelight made his face shine gold—more golden than that which filled his pockets, pants, and the bottom of his pack.

Yet still they remained on the banks of the Mokelumne.

The Lord gave, and the Lord hath taken away;
blessed be the name of the Lord.
—Job 1:21

During her morning foraging one day, Tempest found a fern grotto between three-hundred-foot-high redwoods. In the center was a flattened space, still warm from the body of an animal. Setting aside the woven basket filled with roots, bark, and greens, she sank down, nestling into the green curling hideaway, and stayed very still.

Insects buzzed all around her, and the rat-ta-tat-tat of a woodpecker echoed in the forest. Mingling with the whispering rush of pine branches was the roar and shush of the river where Abram panned. Two squirrels chitted loudly, and Tempest lifted her head and watched as one raced across a limb after the other, which darted straight up the side of a redwood giant and then disappeared.

She breathed in the pungent richness of red soil, fern, pine, morning dew, and high mountain air. Her head was light with it.

She waited for a long moment, listening. Then, sure of her solitude, she slowly unbuttoned the faded gingham dress so she could look down at herself.

Her body was changing. Her breasts were full, and below them was the bulge of her belly. She had already had to alter the gingham dress until the waistline came high above the swell of her abdomen. As her stomach protruded more and more, the skirt had inched up until Abram asked her to take down the hem in front to hide her ankles. She had complied but now when she walked, the skirt hung in tatters around her moccasined feet. Abram refused to let her go back to buckskin.

Tempest looked down at herself, faintly amused and anxious at the changed shape of her body. Spreading her hands over the creamy brown mound, she waited. The child moved inside her. Her lips parting slightly, Tempest sat up anxiously, and

201

again the child moved. Lifting her head, she closed her eyes and smiled exultantly. A filling emotion surged over her, a feeling so incredible, so new, that it frightened her.

Happiness.

"Flesh of my flesh, bone of my bone," Abram had said to her. She had recalled that it was from the story of Adam and Eve. It wasn't a curse after all.

Gazing down again, Tempest stroked the unborn child through her flesh. The weight of it pressed down against the joining between her legs, making her ache sometimes. She lay back slowly and stretched her arms above her head, letting the sunlight streaming through the high branches caress her. Again the child moved, this time with a vigorous punch of limbs and then a nudging, easy roll. Tempest laughed softly.

Raising and spreading her knees, she eased the pressure on the small of her back. It felt so good just to lie there quietly, listening to the earth, smelling it, feeling it at her back. But she couldn't linger long. Abram would worry. During the day he returned frequently to their camp above the river just to see her. Sometimes she resented his possessiveness about the child: the babe belonged to her, lived in her, lived from her. Abram's part in the creation had been brief.

But that feeling never lasted, for the glow in Abram's eyes matched the one in Tempest's heart. If he was proud of what he had given her, she was grateful.

"All I have is yours," Abram had told her at the beginning, and he had given her the very best part of himself.

Every night, Abram rested his head against her belly, listening. Then he would raise up on one elbow and smile down at her. "Our child has a good strong heart," he reassured her, and himself. He kissed her and then leaned lower to kiss her belly.

"We'll raise corn and wheat and children," he had laughed that first night, and through his eyes, Tempest saw herself surrounded by their offspring, heard their laughter and saw them running down the rows of corn.

"Tempest!"

Jarred from her reverie, Tempest raised herself onto her elbows. She heard the fear in Abram's voice and quickly sat up, pulling the gingham dress back over her shoulders and buttoning it. She stood, bending down for her basket. When she straightened again, she saw him just down the hill. He was starting off in the wrong direction, his body rigid with tension;

he had no wood-sense at all. She smiled indulgently.

"Here, Abram!"

He swung around, spotted her, and began running up the hill. "Are you all right?"

She descended from the fern grotto and met him halfway down the slope. "Fine, mon. Easy now."

"Don't laugh at me! I was worried." He reached out and took the basket. Then he gave her a brief kiss and smiled. "Were you hiding in there?" He nodded toward the ferns.

She shrugged, but her eyes shone brightly.

She was so beautiful at that moment that Abram wanted to take her back into the ferns again just to lay her down and touch her all over. Even in the faded, ragged gingham dress that hung around her swollen body like a sack, she was the most beautiful woman he had ever seen. He had not made love to her since learning she was with child. Yet even now in her bloated condition he wanted her, ached to have her again, and felt shamed by the desire to go into a pregnant woman.

He walked beside her, glancing at her frequently, but not touching her again. "It's time we left."

Tempest glanced up quickly, questioning. "Ye've done well lately. Dunna ye want to wait until the first snows come?"

"No. The baby should come by Christmas. If we wait much longer, you'll be in no condition to ride comfortably." He stopped and turned her toward him. "I have more than enough now, anyway. Enough to keep us comfortable for a long time. Tempest, I want to go home again. I want to sit by our fire and read to you. I want to lie beside you in our bed again." He smiled slightly, his eyes teasing. "And I want to watch you get even fatter than you are right now."

She laughed. Her haunted look was gone.

They began walking again, hand in hand. "We'll sit tight at Fairfield until spring," Abram went on. "By then the baby will be strong enough for a journey to Sutter's Fort, where we'll buy more stock and a better plow, and some pretty cloth for a nice dress for you."

She looked at him. "Will ye also buy Indian slaves?"

He was startled by the question. He hadn't thought about it, but he had gold enough to buy a dozen. He looked down at her and shook his head. "No. What I can't do with my own hands or with your help, I won't do. Later we can hire help if need be."

"Ye're a rare, fine mon, Abram Walker."

He laughed. "I'm just like any other. I'm hungry and want to know what's for supper."

They left the Mokelumne early the next morning. It took five days of riding to reach Fairfield. Abram's fields were overgrown with weeds, the corn rotten on the stalks and the wheat beaten flat by the fall rains.

"What a waste," Abram muttered in shame, dismounting and staring over his land.

"Ye've more gold in yer pack than ten fields of corn and wheat would have brought ye at market last year," Tempest told him.

"That's true," he agreed, then bent to fill his hands with earth. "But all the gold in my pack doesn't make me feel as good as this. I've my work cut out for me getting the place back into shape again."

And Tempest saw plainly that the prospect made him happier than he'd been all these months in the mountains seeking gold.

Upon opening the door, they knew immediately that people had used their home in their absence. Nothing was missing, but things had been moved. Someone had relaid the fire carefully so that all Abram had to do was strike his flints.

Tempest sank down wearily onto the bed. She ran her hand over the wedding quilt and sighed contentedly. Abram straightened from lighting the fire and looked at her tenderly, then came across the cold room and sat down on the bed, reaching out to put his hand on her belly.

"We're all home, safe."

Tempest couldn't keep her eyes open. She felt Abram's lips brush lightly against her eyelids and then her mouth. "Sleep well, my love."

She groped until she found his hand.

Abram spent November and December clearing and mulching the crops back into the soil to enrich it for the spring planting. The work was dirty and grueling. He even worked on rainy days, trying to make up for lost time.

The animals had fended well, feeding on the deserted crops and growing fat and lazy. The sow had gone wild. Abram shot her in a gully three miles from the farm and dragged her back by horse. Her meat replenished the smokehouse stock that had been shared with passing gold seekers. Abram also butchered one of the longhorns. They had enough meat to last them through spring, summer, and fall.

At night, while Tempest rocked in the chair he had made for her and sewed his shirts or dungarees or worked her sampler, Abram sat by the fire and read aloud.

Life was good. They had land, home, food, gold, each other, and a child coming. They could ask for nothing more.

Then Abram became ill.

He stumbled in from the field early one afternoon, pale and sweating. His hand was pressed to his right side. Tempest came to him, her eyes wide and alarmed. "What be wrong, mon?"

"Just a bellyache," he dismissed it, and sank down onto the bed, but his voice told her he was in pain. "It'll be right by morning. Thought it would let up by now," he muttered, "but it's been there since morning."

She wiped the sweat from his face with shaking hands, eased him back onto the bed, and removed his boots. He tried to stifle a groan as he rolled on his side and curled into the fetal position.

The pain worsened by nightfall. Warm compresses didn't help. Cool ones didn't lower the rising fever. He was conscious and lucid, and when Tempest knelt down by the bed to speak softly to him, she saw fear in his eyes.

"Ye'll be all right," she said firmly, but his fear was contagious.

"Tempest . . ."

"Ye *will* be all right." She took his hand and squeezed it strongly.

At dawn the excruciating pain subsided. Abram sighed deeply and slept for several hours. But when he awakened, his eyes were bleak and knowing, for he knew the respite would be short-lived. He remembered his older brother Luke and knew what was coming for him as well.

Oh, God, why now? Why at all?

"Lie with me," he whispered raggedly, and Tempest got up from where she had been sitting on the floor beside the bed. Her eyes heavy-lidded from worry and no sleep, she rested beside him, her arm across his hard chest and her head against his shoulder, their baby against his side.

"The pain's gone," he told her, trying to reassure her, at least for a while. His eyes burned. *How do I tell her it's not finished yet? God, how do I tell her?*

"Ye said ye would be fine come mornin'," she murmured huskily. Abram always kept his word.

He said nothing, but his arm tightened painfully around her.

By the following evening, Tempest knew that whatever ailed Abram had gotten worse, not better. The pain was returning. The fever rose in sudden bursts and then dropped slightly, only to shoot higher again. By the third day, Abram's abdomen was swollen taut and his skin was turning gray. Death resided in the house, waiting.

Abram reached out and she clutched his hand. He tried to smile, but couldn't, and his eyes filled. His hand tightened and he tugged her closer to the side of the bed, then let her go and reached out again. She put her hands over his as it trembled on her abdomen. He wanted to feel the baby.

She closed her eyes tightly, her lips clamped together and her teeth gritted, holding his hand against her belly.

I prayed to ye once and ye answered. Answer me now, God. Answer me now! Dunna let him die! God, dunna let him die!

Abram turned his hand in hers. "Sit," he whispered hoarsely. She slowly sank onto the bed, clutching his hand tightly. He saw her fear and understood it. "I've still a few days," he murmured.

But what would those days be like for her, he wondered. He just held her hand, not speaking at all, only thinking, praying.

Why when she needs me so much and knows it do You take me away? Why when the child I've wanted for so many years is coming?

Tempest stayed at his side through another day. Abram's body was rotting from the inside out, and he knew he was going to die whimpering and crying and finally screaming just the way Luke had. He knew also what it was doing to Tempest as she sat by helplessly, watching over him, trying to give him some small comfort from compresses and bark teas.

"Be strong for our baby," he pleaded.

In another day, only the pain mattered. He cried out because he couldn't help himself. "I wish it would end! *God, let me die! God, make it stop!*"

Nothing helped the pain. In her mind, Tempest swore at the heavens. She swore at Almighty God Himself. But if He heard her, He was doing nothing. Not to her. Not for Abram. He wasn't going to save Abram, and He wasn't going to grant him a merciful death.

Late in the afternoon, Tempest left the cabin while Abram lay semiconscious, writhing. She heard him moan her name, but steeled herself and closed the door behind her. She went directly to the barn and worked there over the grinding wheel for almost an hour. When she came back, Abram was still lucid. She came to him and took his hand with her left one.

"I knew you wouldn't leave me," he gasped harshly.

"I wilna leave ye again, mon. Not until it be over," she promised him.

She was afraid, terribly afraid. Sweat broke out on her forehead and her palms were damp. She was shaking badly.

Abram smiled tenderly. "There's nothing to fear. In God's house there are many mansions, Tempest. That's where I'll be—in God's house."

Even now, he believed. Even now, he thought of her fear and not of himself. Her throat closed hotly.

And I must think of him.

Whatever God would or wouldn't do, she knew what she must.

Abram watched her face, frowning. "I should've let you be. I should've let you stay with your father. At least then you'd have—"

"No, Abram." She leaned down close to him.

He looked up at her, gritting his teeth against the ceaseless pain. There was something in her eyes he'd never seen before. His heart thumped. Her mouth was trembling, but it curved slightly as she tried to smile at him. Tears welled and spilled from her eyes.

"I love ye, Abram Walker." She meant every word of it.

"I know," he said huskily. His own eyes filled and grew bleak. "I'm sorry."

She brought her right hand around from behind her. Her left tightened on his, holding it tightly and out of the way. With one sure, swift stroke of her sharpened hunting knife, she sliced through Abram's jugular and carotid. If there was one thing Tempest knew, it was how to kill quickly and painlessly. Da had taught her that much.

Abram's blood sprayed across her breasts and face. His eyes flickered in surprise, then dulled. If he felt anything at all, it had lasted only a split second.

The last thing Abram Walker saw in this life was Tempest's face and the love her eyes held for him.

> For dust thou art, and unto dust
> shalt thou return.
> —Genesis 3:19

Tempest sat beside Abram, holding his limp hand, waiting. The laws Abram had read to her from the black book were very clear. "Thou shalt not kill." "An eye for an eye." She expected death, a death more horrible than the one Abram would have died had she not ended it for him.

Yet she didn't die.

God took her child instead.

Within minutes of Abram's death, the pains began. They were swift, almost ruthless. The child was born on the earthen floor beside the wedding-quilt-covered bed where Abram lay with his throat laid open.

A stillborn son.

"Why not me?" Tempest screamed over and over.

When she could cry no more, she cleaned the baby carefully and wrapped it tenderly in one of Kathy Walker's best embroidered pillowcases. Then she placed it in the crook of Abram's right arm.

She went to the creek and washed. When she came back, she dressed in a black skirt and a dark-blue flowered shirtwaist. She lay down in the left arm of Abram and prayed to die. She stayed there for a full day, waiting. At the end of that time, she knew that God didn't want her.

She thought of taking her own life, but was terrified of where she would go if she did. At least here, on this earth, she knew what hell she faced.

Tempest trudged back and forth to the barn many times and brought back bundles of corn shucks, stacking them carefully around the bed. She dragged the wedding quilt from beneath the bodies and then gently arranged it over them. She put moist, rich soil in Abram's left hand and a sack of gold at his feet, and placed her aquamarine ring in the palm of the baby's hand.

She opened the music box and left it at the head of the bed, above them. Then she kissed them both and lit the fire.

Before she left the farm, she opened the barn door wide and unlatched the paddock gates. Then she rode her Indian pony to the top of the hill and sat astride it, watching until the cabin was a black, smoldering rubble. Turning her horse slowly away, she rode back toward New Helvetia.

All Tempest took with her from Fairfield Farm was a handful of enamel buttons, a tin thimble, and a big black book.

PART II

Sodom and Gomorrah

All the mines look hard and dreary
Everywhere I roam,
Oh, miners, how my heart grows weary,
Ne'er a cent and far away from home.
—Anonymous

Dropping his pile of gear, Jared Stryker straightened just outside the front door of the overcrowded immigrant cabin where he'd rented an uncomfortable bunk the night before. For one dollar he had gotten a slab of hard, splintered wood too short to accommodate his six-foot frame. There hadn't been a blanket, but he wouldn't have used it if one had been provided. The smell of sweat, dirt, wet canvas, and a communal chamber pot permeated the place. Between that and the five snoring, grunting, groaning forty-niners he'd shared the place with, he had gotten little rest.

It was a far cry from his bedroom back in Charleston with its cherry-wood French bed, fresh linen, brick fireplace, and bellpull, which with only a tug brought one of the black servants on the run. Within minutes, he would have had hot grits and ham served on a silver platter and warm water for a shave and a bath. But that was then . . .

Stretching his sore, cramped muscles, Jared gave a deep, relieved sigh. At least he'd been out of the rain, he thought ruefully, seeing that others had had to make do on the crowded hillside around Sutter's Fort.

It was still drizzling. The sky frowned pale gray with morning.

Beneath the oaks and sycamores that lined the American River were fewer than a hundred solidly built houses and a few stores. Some of the latter were little more than sheds with plank tables and shelves which displayed mining gear and supplies that sold for exorbitant prices. Several tall-masted ships that had come up from Yerba Buena were moored back at the Embarcadero on the Sacramento River.

Across the American, Jared could see the rough huts of the Kadema Indian village. A gristmill was on this side, farther down, and a cemetery up on the hillside behind him.

A few hardy, or foolhardy, men continued panning gold in the now snow-covered mountains. Most had come down into the valleys to sojourn through the cold winter months. Those who had gone up to the streams before '48 had long since returned to their farms or settlement towns.

Jared had arrived in Spring of '49 with thousands of others.

If I'd only come a few months earlier, I'd have my pockets full by now, he thought angrily. Now he'd have the long rainy late fall and winter months to go through before he could dip his pan again. How was he going to get by on what little gold he had?

Despite winter, more men poured into the territory every day. Those that were coming down from the mountains were met by those coming up from the sea. By next year, the Sacramento and American rivers, as well as all the tributaries that filled them, would be lined shoulder to shoulder with miners. Jared thought of the odds of making a strike and his mouth hardened into a white line.

There has to be an easier way to get rich. A faster way.

Clapping on his wide-brimmed, sweat-stained hat, which had protected his dark head from sun and rain during the six-month ride west over prairies and mountains and desert and more mountains, Jared reached down and hefted his heavy pack. It contained everything he needed, and all that was left from the hard journey from North Carolina. Some things had worn out; other things he had dumped along the trail. What remained was his bedroll, several changes of clothes, shaving gear, cooking equipment, a bowie knife, an ivory-handled pistol that had belonged to his maternal grandfather, his sack of hard-earned gold dust, and a well-worn deck of cards. Lashed to the pack were his pick, shovel, gold pan, and rifle, which was snugly fitted into a leather scabbard.

Shifting the considerable weight until it lay with reasonable comfort on his strong back, Jared bent cautiously and lifted his saddle and silver bridle. Laden like an overburdened pack mule, he started down the muddy slope toward the river where, for two bits, he'd stabled Alexander.

Laughing softly, Jared thought again of the day he had left home.

"Damn your impudence, Jared!" Charles Stryker had roared, his face holly-berry red, his brown eyes flashing with high Irish temper. "Get off my horse. I told you to stay off him!"

Alexander had reared, his ears flattening back and his nostrils flaring. The animal had a vicious streak and Jared had held him strongly. "Rest assured, Father. I'll take good care of him," Jared grinned.

"By God, I'll not have you racing that stallion against those rogues you call your friends again!" he bellowed, referring to several plantation owners' sons with whom Jared had been schooled in England. His merchant father had wanted him to rub noses with the blue bloods of Cooper River society and learn their ways, in spite of his own humble beginnings and his criticism of upper-class decadence. Roar he might about money spent or risks taken needlessly, but Jared was well aware that every time he played poker with a group of gentlemen and took the pot or ran a race and won, his father gloated. Jared knew that his father's one dream was to own a white-pillared mansion and cotton fields right alongside those same men he claimed he detested.

Jared's own dream was the same.

He had leaned down and slapped the great, black neck of the pacing horse. "Winnings from that last race will buy the supplies we need for the journey, eh, boy?" he had laughed.

"You're not going anywhere! I need you in the business!"

Jared turned the proud animal away. "Wish me luck in the gold fields."

"California?"

Jared grinned back at his parent unrepentantly. "I may bring back enough gold to buy you that plantation you've always coveted, Father."

"The hell you say! *Come back here!*"

Jared rode down the street.

"You're stealing my best horse, damn you!" his father had shouted after him.

"Hang me!" Jared had laughed, and then spurred Alexander to a brisk canter down the cobblestoned street.

The stallion had done him well in his travels across the continent. Alexander was a strong, proud Arabian who could run like the wind when Jared gave him his head. He wondered how the stableman had fared with the touchy animal.

Jared saw the sign for Smyth Stables just beyond a row of shanties. The rain began again, patting his hat with large, splattering drops. He tipped it slightly so that the water wouldn't run down the back of his neck. He could smell his damp buckskin coat, the wet grass, mud, horse dung, and the slow waters of the river.

The barrel-chested, redheaded hostler was weighing out gold dust on a small scale set up on a stump, while a young, weary traveler stood by watching him carefully and holding the reins of an old nag. The horse worried the bit and nudged at the boy.

Smyth spotted Jared and gave him a nod of acknowledgment. "Be right with you, mister." Then he stood and quickly poured the gold dust from the scale into a cloth, folded it, and tucked it neatly into his pants pocket as he reached out for the reins of the young man's horse. The boy walked away with a decided slump to his shoulders.

"I'll bring your devil around after I tuck this one in," Smyth said, leading the nag away.

While he waited, Jared slung his saddle over the hitching rail and shrugged off his pack. He pulled up his coat collar, then hunched back against a corral post and took another slow sweeping look at the hillside below Sutter's Fort.

Smoke curled from some of the shanties. Everything was quiet as most of the displaced miners and travelers waited out the rain in tents, lean-tos, and makeshift cabins. Jared wondered what Geneva would make of all this.

His lids lowered slightly as he thought about her—her corn-silk hair perfectly coiffed in a mound of thick, rich curls that seemed almost too much weight for her slender neck to support; her eyes a soft gray-blue, wide and innocent; her mouth with its slight smile, temptingly full but with a hint of unawakened sensuality. He remembered her mouth most of all—how he had longed to kiss it! Yet she was so far above him, the daughter of a plantation owner. He had felt honored when she had talked with him each time he managed a meeting, at the opera or the house of a mutual friend. She had always been gracious, faintly teasing, breathtakingly beautiful and aloof. She reminded him of a Botticelli angel.

And now she was married to that bastard Duprés.

If I had had money and land, she'd be mine now, Jared thought, closing his eyes tightly for a second, then opening them onto the dismal scene of a rainswept California hillside smothered by greedy humanity.

"Here's your horse, mister," Smyth said, recalling Jared's

grim attention. "I ought to charge you double. He took a bite out of my side when I turned my back on him."

"You won't do it again," Jared drawled with a mocking smile.

"Well, he's a damn fine animal, but he's meaner than the Mojave with no hat."

Jared swung the saddle up into place and reached under for the cinch. "How'd he treat you, boy? Like royalty, I'll bet, eh?" Alexander blew out and shook his silky mane. Jared laughed and slapped the beast's neck. Turning his head slightly as he worked, he caught sight of a small, roughly built hut of sticks and mud set off by itself beside the river. He straightened as he saw someone emerge from it.

A girl!

She was slim but shapely and wore a faded dark skirt, blue flowered blouse, and heavy boots. She straightened and let the hut's flap fall back into place and then started up the hill. Jared stared after her until she disappeared between the rows of shanties.

Smyth came out of the stable with a pitchfork and Jared glanced at him across Alexander's saddle. "Am I dead and in heaven, or did I just see a white woman down there?" he asked in his thick southern drawl.

"No white woman—a half-breed, but she's a right good looker."

"Who is she?"

"Don't know. She stays down there between rounds of the fort."

Jared grinned. "She's a whore, then." He hadn't been with a woman in several months and would richly enjoy the solace of a woman's flesh.

"No, sir. Heard tell one man offered her a bead necklace and a tin looking glass and she almost slit him from cock to Adam's apple with her knife. She don't just wear it for show, so if you're looking to get laid," he said, grinning licentiously, "then I'd tread mighty careful before I jumped on her."

"If she's not drumming business, what's she doing wandering around town?" Jared asked as he began tying his pack and gear behind the saddle.

"She hits all the whiskey holes looking for someone named McClaren."

"Husband?"

"Couldn't tell you. Why don't you try asking her?"

"Maybe I will." He glanced in the direction the girl had gone and mounted his horse.

"Tame as a kitten with you, ain't he?" Smyth remarked, watching the way the stallion responded to Jared's light touch.

"When occasion calls for it." Jared grinned and turned away. He was the only person who'd ever been able to manage Alexander, his father included.

Jared followed the muddy street up the hill, searching for the girl. She was nowhere in sight. "Well, we know where she lives, boy. We'll save her for another time. First we've got to find a place to live for the winter, and a way to *make* some money rather than *spend* what we have."

Jared thought of possibilities. He had a good script and a quick mind for figures, but he didn't cotton to the idea of being anyone's clerk. His father might have started that way, but Jared didn't plan to follow in his footsteps. That was one of the reasons he had left Charleston, and he hadn't traveled all the way across the continent to do the same thing in California that his father had expected of him in the family import-export firm.

So what could he do?

First he needed to feed the wolf growling in his belly.

He read the painted signs up and down the rows of shelters, sheds, businesses, and cabins. *Herbal cures—$1. Dry goods— chep.* A hitching rail with bloody rags wrapped around a post out front advertised a barber-cum-dentist: *Shave—25¢, Tooth Extrakshun—$1.* As Jared rode by he heard a loud yell and prolonged swearing. Several establishments showed a touch of humor. A sagging shack with shuttered window openings and a mud-splattered front door boasted, *Savoy Palace Hotel, Bunks—$2, with blanket—$3.* Another blithely stated, *California Or Bust—Busted Hotel, Bunks—50¢, Bedbugs Free.* The place was the only one he'd seen here with real windows, but they were steamed up from the breathing of numerous bodies inside.

Winding his way down toward the Embarcadero, always on the lookout for the young woman and a place to eat, Jared saw nothing holding any promise of a livelihood. Finally he spotted a sign reading *Sally's Fine-Home Cooking* and tied Alexander to the rail.

Sally turned out to be a robust, ruddy-faced Kentucky butcher named O'Sullivan, but the food was hot and the number of miners crammed into the place attested to its quality.

"'Fraid there's not much work around," Sally answered Jared's inquiry while replenishing his tin cup with steaming coffee. His sleeves were rolled up to show brawny, hair-covered arms.

Jared asked how Sally himself had gotten started, and the man admitted to rustling steers from the Californio ranches nearby and using that beef to start his eating place. "'Course, now I can afford to buy it." His grin showed a missing tooth.

Jared understood why when he paid out five dollars in gold for a rare steak, scrambled eggs, and a large, hot, sourdough roll. "Mulligan stew for lunch," Sally told him when Jared paid up.

"At your price, I may be eating one meal a day," Jared remarked wryly.

"One's better than none," Sally said, grinning.

The rain had stopped. The gray clouds grudgingly allowed sunlight to peek through and touch the sodden land. Men had come out of their shelters and were milling around.

Almost immediately Jared spotted the young woman again. She was up the hill from him. Men stopped what they were doing or saying to stare at her as she passed, but she didn't look at any of them and kept walking, even when several called out to her.

Jared followed, intrigued. She walked with her head high, her hair in one thick black braid that hung down her stiff back. Her tiny waist was cinched by a wide leather belt, and he could see the thick handle of a hunting knife protruding from the right side of it. He was far more interested, however, in the sway of those slender hips.

"What I can see looks pretty damn good, boy," he murmured to his horse, trying to follow her up the hill through the thronged street. She turned to the left into another lane of tents, huts, and buildings. Jared lost sight of her. His impatience grew as every man on the hill seemed bent on blocking his way.

"Move, dammit!" he ordered imperiously as two staggering men tried to cross the road in front of him.

"What's your damn hurry, mate?" one snarled as he held the other upright with one arm around the fellow's waist and a firm hand on the wrist draped over his shoulder. "Can't you see he's sick!"

"Sick, hell. Drunk, more likely."

The man's companion issued a loud hiccup as though to confirm Jared's contemptuous statement. His defender let him drop face-down into the muck with a loud splat. "And I say he's sick!" came the slurred, belligerent challenge.

"Suit yourself, but he'll be dead from drowning if you don't get him up," Jared remarked indifferently. The big sailor lunged and Jared brought up his foot, planting it in the middle of his attacker's chest and sending him flying backward. The man hit the mud and skidded. The man lying face-down in the street lifted his head enough to cough and groan. Jared touched his heels to the horse and Alexander stepped over the man gingerly and proceeded up the hill.

By the time he reached the next row of tents, the girl had disappeared once more.

Let's talk of graves, of worms, and epitaphs.
—William Shakespeare
Richard II

Four horses thundered along the wide muddy street above the river, racing between the rows of rough shelters and cabins. Miners thronged the sidelines, shouting wildly, jumping up and down, and waving their hats. Tempest watched the riders go by. One of the horses was a magnificent black stallion the like of which she had never seen before and he was ridden by a young, dark-haired, laughing man. He had a good lead on his nearest rival, who was whipping at his roan frantically in an effort to catch up. She watched the race for a moment, then turned her eyes to the crowd and searched among the faces for one with blue eyes and long gray-streaked hair and beard. A man big enough to stand out in the writhing mob of men.

Da wasn't there.

All the faces she could see were fairly young, though some were bearded, some prematurely lined. Most of the men wore heavy cloth coats, dungarees, and boots, not filthy buckskins and moccasins.

She turned away, walking up the hill, stopping again at every place that served whiskey, searching among more faces. Frequently men tried to stop her and talk to her, but she passed them without a look. All those faces seemed to melt together in her mind. She could see only two clearly. *Da. Abram.*

Don't think, just look, she told herself, stopping again and making a slow, sweeping glance along the plank bar on which a dozen miners leaned as they tipped shot glasses. Then she walked to the next place.

When she became hungry, she ate the cold slices of cooked tule root she kept in her pocket, or chewed on a piece of smoked rabbit. She would have to leave the area for a day again soon to hunt. Her food supply was low and needed replenishing. Perhaps tomorrow.

Another bar, more faces, and on again until she had been to them all. Then she returned to the hut by the river, tired and

220

afraid. With thousands of men and half a dozen women around her, she was completely alone. Huddling close to the small fire inside her hut, Tempest tried to warm herself. The smoke sought escape through the small opening at the top. It was raining again, drops hissing into the fire as they crept through. If it rained much more, the river would rise and sweep this shelter away.

She knew she should have built it on higher ground, farther back from the heavy, deceptively slow-looking waters. Yet this was the very place where she and Da had camped before, and somehow it gave her hope. If he came back, surely he would come here.

Or would he take one look at the throngs on the hill and flee to his mountains again, never to return? She tried not to think of that possibility.

Each day when she walked through the forest of tents, buildings, and lean-tos, she went in hope of hearing McClaren's mad laugh, seeing him tipping a jug, trading pelts, swearing at someone. Better a devil she knew than no one at all.

She tried not to think of Da, or of the men who stared at her as she passed them, or of the sounds in the darkness of the night, or of the feel of walls closing in around her.

Or of Abram.

Yet the aching longing she fought had become physical pain. It formed a hard knot like a malignant tumor in her chest and throat. Surely she would die of it. Please.

Just find the food ye need, the wood to keep the fire burning, and look for Da, she told herself over and over.

She rolled a few fist-sized stones from the fire, wrapped them in buckskin, and pressed them close about her as she curled into her blanket. She heard the Indian pony whicker from outside where he was securely tethered beneath an inadequate shelter. She reached for the saddlebag holding the big black book and slid it beneath her head. Staring into the orange glow of the fire, she tried to think of the stories Abram had read to her: of Noah or John or Ruth, of Rachel or Daniel or Meshach, Shadrach, and Abednego. She couldn't. She could only think of *him,* of the child, of Da.

"God," she whispered brokenly as she stared at her small fire and felt the shadows gathering, "please keep the wolves away."

But they came when she slept, as they did every night.

A lucky man is rarer than a white crow.
                    —Americanism

When next he saw the girl, Jared was sitting on the dealing side of a blackjack table beneath his own tent. Her back was to him as she stood just across the muddy street outside the doorway of a saloon. Jared flipped out cards to five patrons, then concentrated on her. *Turn around, lady, and let me have a look at you!*

Her head turned from left to right very slowly as she searched, and then she stepped away. Jared held his breath, excitement throbbing through him. "Hey, I said hit me with another card," one of the men demanded.

Jared caught the briefest glimpse of the girl's profile before she was lost to view. He nearly got up from the table to peer out after her.

"Hey, goddamn it!"

"Keep your pants on," Jared muttered, and flipped over another card, stung by the urge to close down play at the table so he could go after the girl. Of the five men playing against him, however, only one had any card sense, and the others were simply killing time. So, for the moment, common sense and simple greed won out over Jared's interest in the half-breed girl.

He was determined to win enough gold to begin building a small casino, hire another dealer, stock a bar, and hire a bartender. Now, hoping to fog any too-quick wits, he poured rotgut whiskey for his customers. His own private jug rested on the plank table. It was watered.

Jared was a good actor when it was called for. Whenever he let his eyelids drop and began slurring his sentences in a seemingly drunken haze, the bets jumped higher. He would then lose just enough to encourage careless betting, and finally, with cunning and consummate skill, would quickly empty the other players' pockets.

And so far his winnings from racing Alexander against any

and all comers had doubled and doubled again. He wouldn't need to go back to the gold fields in spring. He'd hit his own bonanza right here in the shadow of Sutter's Fort.

Paying one man and taking winnings from the four others, Jared replenished the whiskey glasses before dealing a new round. "At this rate, I'll be cleaned out by nightfall," grumbled a player no older than nineteen.

"If not before," another smiled wryly. Most of the men on the hill were young. Jared himself was only twenty-three, but he felt far more experienced than many of those he had met and played against. Some were no more than dumb farm boys never before off their land or out of their hometowns. A few had never even held a deck of cards, and some hadn't tasted whiskey, let alone gotten roaring drunk on it. He doubted if most had even had their first woman.

Jared, on the other hand, had been sent abroad to school. He had traveled throughout Europe on a Grand Tour, and had been playing cards since he was old enough to have change in his pocket. He could tell the difference between a fine wine and a pretender just by color, smell, and rolling a sip on his tongue. And he'd lost his virginity at fourteen to his mother's best friend, a forty-year-old widow.

Compared to these young men, Jared felt a hundred years older and wiser, and his knowledge gave him a faint arrogance that awed the others.

The younger miner lost again. He pushed back his stool and stood up. "That's it for me."

A Georgia cooper hurriedly took his place at the table.

Jared finally closed down the table at dusk, ushering the other men out and then dropping the flap. He stretched and then washed up. Measuring out a small portion of the gold dust into his drawstring leather pouch, he poured the bulk into another pouch to be delivered to the iron safe in the assayer's office, just around the corner. Once that was done, he walked down the hill to Sally's for a hearty meal.

The place was packed as usual. The long plank tables and benches were overcrowded with miners sitting elbow to elbow. The din of clanking cutlery against metal plates and the talk of bonanzas, home, and miner trouble was deafening. Jared hung his hat and buckskin coat on a nail just inside the door and shouted his order across to Sally. Then he slung his leg over a rough bench and sat down to wait.

"Keeerist," one young sandy-haired and -bearded man said. "Don't you think everybody else is in the same way, but there ain't no women in this damn territory. None except Mexicans and Indians."

"What I'd give for a little . . ." another man started, and his voice dropped as he whispered to the men around him, a bawdy grin on his face. They all laughed.

"What about that girl down by the river?" someone asked from Jared's right, and his attention sharpened in annoyance. He leaned forward slightly, resting his forearms on the table as he looked down the line of men and listened. A brawny sailor was answering.

"She's no whore. She's a widow lady."

"Widow! Keeerist! She can't be more than sixteen."

"Age don't matter much. I heard she married some settler in '46, right here at the fort."

"Keeerist!" The other swore, shaking his head. "That'd make her about thirteen or fourteen when she was snared. Who performed the ceremony? Sutter ain't no preacher."

"Don't know." The other man shrugged. "Didn't ask."

"Where's her man?" another asked.

"If's she's a widow, he must've got himself killed."

Laughter rippled up and down the benches. The man who'd asked returned pointed attention to his meal, his neck bright red.

"She's looking for someone," a big farm boy put in.

"A good man," one suggested lasciviously.

"She asks for McClaren when she asks for anything."

"Who's McClaren?"

"Keeerist! Who knows? Anybody know?"

Everyone shook heads and shrugged. Ale was drunk.

"Anyone ever just gone on down to her hut by the river and . . ."

Jared's steak was served. He glanced up. Sally grinned and extended his thick hairy arm to pour hot coffee into a battered tin mug. "Widder talk again. Horny bastards."

"A lot of talk about her, then?" Jared said as noncommittally as he could.

"Every time she walks up this street, the men stand like flag poles with colors waving." He glanced back as someone shouted. "Ah, shuddup. It's coming. It's coming." He shrugged and gave Jared a gap-toothed grin. "Heard you were doing all right for yourself."

Jared smiled wryly. "I'm getting by, Sally," he drawled, then laughed softly. "I see you're building on already."

"Running out of space in here. Gotta build on."

"Where're you getting your lumber?"

Sally grinned and gave him a conspiratorial wink. "South side of Sutter's Fort."

Following his meal, Jared went up to the stables to check on Alexander. The stallion was being well, if cautiously, tended, but he was growing restless from lack of exercise. No one could ride him but Jared; no one would have dared even to try.

He fed the horse a handful of oats, then began currying the already sleek back. "Need to run, eh, boy? Sorry, but I've been busy lately. We'll do some hard riding tomorrow morning and stretch out these fine legs of yours." He slapped the high, deep chest and Alexander stamped his hoof.

"Maybe we'll ride around the hill and see about that girl again, hmm? Before one of those other fools gets to her first," he murmured, thinking of the conversation he had overheard at Sally's. A widow was bound to be lonely, and lonely people needed comfort. "I've never seen her face, but her backside looks real nice." He laughed and slapped Alexander's hard rump. The stallion snorted disdainfully. "Don't want to share my affections, is that it?"

The horse turned his head and nudged Jared, who produced a small dried apple from his coat pocket and held it out in the palm of his hand. "Best I could do. Sorry it's so small. Not much around and this cost a fortune, so enjoy it." The stallion munched the treat while Jared scratched the underside of the animal's huge head. He slapped him again and then left the stall.

Walking around the fort, Jared noticed that most of the boards from the main gate had been torn away. In fact, whole sections of wall were being torn away. He thought of what Sally had told him about building on. Shaking his head, Jared laughed softly. Desperate men resorted to desperate measures.

Walking down the hill to his own tent, he thought about the young widow by the river. He built a small fire in the pit, hooked the tent's flap back, and opened his gaming table for business that would last until dawn.

There'd be plenty of time for thinking about the girl later.

Is this the noble nature whom
passion could not shake?
—William Shakespeare
Othello

"Damn!" Jared muttered. The girl was gone. He had
suspected as much the moment he spotted the empty shelter
where the pony had been tethered. Lifting the buckskin flap,
he bent and looked inside the hut. Empty. She'd left nothing
behind, so she probably wasn't coming back.

Who could blame her? Or perhaps she had finally found the
man she'd been searching for? Jared swore again.

He glanced around the interior of the dirt-and-stick dwelling.
It was large enough to accommodate two people, a few things,
and a good-sized fire, but barely fit for any savage. How could
a woman live in a place like this? Hadn't her settler husband
left her anything at all? He looked at the ashes of the fire in
the center of the floor and wished he had come sooner.

He backed out and dropped the flap. Sighing heavily, he
scanned the area, hoping to catch some glimpse of her. Men
everywhere—men and filth and shanties. Maybe that was why
she'd left, if it wasn't that she'd found the man she sought.
Maybe she'd been too afraid of the crowd of randy men watching her, getting ideas.

Her reasons didn't make any difference. She was gone.

Jared mounted Alexander and rode him down along the river
away from the settlement. Even when he'd gone several miles,
there were still men lining the banks of the American, panning
for gold while the sun still shone. He was well over four miles
from the milling camp when he finally felt free of it.

Loosening the reins and digging in his heels, he gave the
stallion his head. The horse galloped exultantly across the
winter-greened grasslands, and Jared felt his own throbbing
excitement grow. They raced together, giving in completely to
the lust for movement, speed. One mile, two, three; the animal

226

seemed tireless. Jared's own body was tense with the joyous passion of the moment. The land opened up wide before him. Out here in the open, away from the hordes at the settlement, there was no one, and the sense of freedom was almost better than the feel of a heavy sack of gold dust. It laced his blood and heightened his senses better than fine brandy.

He finally slowed Alexander to a canter, then leaned down and patted the thick damp neck. "Needed that, didn't we? Too damn many people." He laughed, straightening in the saddle, his eyes shining. The laugh stopped short as he spotted an Indian pony grazing in an open area just beyond the shadows of a grove of sycamores, white oaks, and cottonwoods.

The girl!

Jared's hands tightened on the reins, and Alexander's head came up sharply. "Sorry, boy," Jared muttered, loosening his hold again and turning the horse toward the trees and brush that made a long meandering line suggesting a creek.

Dismounting, he tethered the stallion to a low branch of a white oak. The pony raised its head once at their approach, then went back to cropping the grass shoots that had sprung up from the rains.

It was so quiet that Jared felt vaguely uncomfortable. He could call out to her, but a loud voice in this peace seemed somehow sacrilegious. He walked among the trees looking for her. Just below him was a muddy creek clogged with cattails.

He saw smoke farther down along the creek and wove his way through the brambles to investigate its source. He found a small cleared area and a banked, smoky fire above which was a lattice woven of sticks bearing meat and fish strips stretched out for smoking. Near the fire were baskets mounded with acorns, berries, tubers, and green plant stems.

Birds burst into the sky with a violent rush, startling Jared. He turned, looking for the cause of the flock's alarm. Leaving the fire he headed downstream. Suddenly he spotted the young woman.

She stood not more than fifteen feet away from him. Her back was to him as she worked among the cattails and reeds, her skirt raised and pulled snugly toward the front. She bent and pulled something from the muck. Jared looked at the shapely brown calves and the backs of her knees and smiled. When she bent again, he became acutely aware of the firm, gently rounded backside outlined clearly beneath the taut, faded black material. His mouth pursed in silent admiration.

He stood staring, his body tensing with desire. She straightened fully and he saw how small her waist was, cinched by a wide leather belt on which was a sheath for the knife he knew she carried.

Holding an uprooted cattail, she worked quickly. Jared saw the flash of a blade just before she cast away the stalks. She bent to rinse whatever she kept and Jared's heart hammered as he gazed at her womanly form bent over in that position. She straightened again and tucked her find into the front folds of her threadbare skirt.

Jared moved, pushing his way through the last of the brush.

The woman froze. Her shoulders stiffened and her head jerked up and cocked to one side. She reminded him of a deer sensing a threatening presence, poising herself for flight if necessary.

"Hello," he said, and was dismayed at the rough huskiness of his voice.

She whirled around, half-crouching, her arms spread and one hand clutching a long hunting knife in a whitened fist.

Jared caught his breath at the suddenness of her action and stared into a pair of wide, amazingly beautiful blue eyes. His pulse soared. His eyes wandered over the rest of her. "Oh, and I let you walk right past me," he murmured softly.

Tempest's shock was no less profound. Ready for an attack, she found herself looking into the luminous dark-brown eyes of the most beauteous man she had ever seen. He was tall and leanly built, but the open white shirt he wore revealed a well-formed, bronzed chest covered with dark, curling hair. His breeches were fitted and tucked into knee-high, shiny black boots. His hair, black and glistening with health, fell across his tanned forehead almost to the arched brows. He had a straight nose and a well-shaped mouth, which just now was curved into an incredulous smile.

He moved toward her. Tempest drew back, her heart thundering.

"I won't hurt you," he told her; he had a drawling accent she had heard before among the populace around Sutter's Fort. His was smoother, like rich wild honey.

He was not as big as Abram, but what he lacked in muscular breadth was more than made up for in his aura of youthful strength and the sheer virile grace of his body. She judged him to be a good bit younger than Abram as well. He didn't look like the hundreds of miners camped near the settlement. He was cleaner, and there was a look of arrogance about him.

He was looking at her body, his brown glowing eyes moving from her exposed throat to her full breasts and down to her waist and hips and knees.

She assessed him again, evaluating which way he might come at her and how she might best parry any attack.

Jared let out his breath slowly. "You *are* beautiful."

"Am I supposed to be flattered?"

A Scottish burr, for God's sake! Jared laughed softly in surprise, and then saw how her eyes narrowed coldly. She looked straight into his eyes without coyness or fear. That direct look made him even more aware of her, more aware than he'd ever been of a woman. He hadn't felt such immediate arousal since his mother had left the parlor and Alicia Hampton had put her jeweled hand in his virgin lap.

"My name is Jared Stryker, ma'am. And who may you be?"

She lifted her chin and didn't respond.

"I've seen you several times walking through the camp. You're looking for McClaren."

That got a reaction. Her eyes went very wide and eager. She sheathed the knife in a swift, expert motion and waded toward him through the murky water. "Ye ken him, mon?" she asked. "Have ye seen him?"

"No." He saw her expression fall and become grim. "I know nothing about him, in fact, other than you've been seeking him. Who is he?"

"My da." She had stopped a few feet from him.

"Who?" he said blankly, not understanding.

"My *father*." She moved again, wading out of the creek and walking past him. Turning, Jared watched as she went back among the brambles along the reed-choked creek bank and headed toward her fire. After a moment, he followed. The sway of those slender hips mesmerized him and he now had an even better view of her shapely legs and fragile, muddied ankles.

Sensing his gaze, she glanced back over her shoulder at him. His smile did strange things to her vitals. She tugged her skirt hem free of the wide leather belt and let it drop, roots and stalks scattering. Her mouth tightened. Kneeling, she gathered them into a pile and began sorting them in her baskets.

"Does your father know you're at the fort?"

He was a fine one for questions, she thought. Shrugging, she didn't answer or look up at him. If she ignored him, he would go away. His presence made her uneasy.

Jared looked down at her, noting the stiffness of her body. He could sense her tension and distrust. She probably had good reason not to trust a man. "Are you out here on your own today?"

Still she remained silent.

He squatted down near her. "Who are you?"

She lifted her head slightly and looked at him. "Tempest McClaren Walker," she told him simply.

"Tempest," he repeated. She was an enigma with her Scottish accent. "Have you family near by?"

She looked down again, her small hand whitening around a gnarled, brown-crusted root. "No." She slowly put the root into a basket.

Jared reached across into the basket. She jerked her hand back to keep him from touching her. He picked up the bulbous root and looked at her, amused by her defensive action. "Is this what you've been living on?"

Her eyes flashed. "I eat better than those creatures on the hills."

He knew she had taken insult and strove to make quick amends. "No doubt," he agreed with a smile. "They wouldn't know where to reap a harvest."

She gave him a sardonic look. "That be why ye're here, of course. To reap a harvest."

He laughed. "I've been luckier than most and can pay for my meals at a tavern." He tossed her root back into the basket. "Maybe I can help you, Tempest."

She raised one eyebrow. "Now, why would ye be wantin' to help me, mon, unless ye be hopin' for somethin' in the bargain?"

He could imagine how many times she had been propositioned and winced inwardly at the way he had opened the conversation. She couldn't be more than sixteen and was incredibly beautiful, even muddied and wearing an ugly, ill-fitting, faded shirtwaist and skirt. Hard knowledge shone in her blue eyes. He sensed a depth to her that he never had in any other woman. His curiosity grew.

"I meant no disrespect."

He looked sincere. She studied his angular face, intrigued by him in spite of her wariness. He was a fine sight and made her feel strangely shaky inside. It was not a loathsome feeling, but neither was it comfortable. She gave him the benefit of the doubt and returned her attention to the sorting.

"I'd like to help you. This is no way for a woman to live."

She thought of Abram as he blocked her way through the wide gate of the fort; he had said much the same thing. She remembered running until her body ached and her feet were bloody. Then collapsing among those rocks, and Abram's gentle, callused hand on her, his rough yet tender voice. He'd put the canteen in her lap and later curled the warmth of his big, hard body against her back. She remembered other things as well— Abram singing as he plowed his fields, the smile on his face when she'd told him of the baby. Most of all she remembered his hazel eyes dulling as his life poured out.

Jared wondered at her stoic silence and the dully placid look on her face. He saw her face take on a look of pain and reached out to gently touch her cheek. She drew in a sharp breath and recoiled from him.

"I won't hurt you," he assured her, and saw the vein in her throat pulsing violently. "You've no need to be afraid of me." Had her husband been some brute who'd beaten her?

"Leave me be."

Her harsh, curt command shocked him. No woman had ever treated him this way. A deep, primitive anger rose in him, as well as the desire to force her back against the sandy ground and take her right then.

She sensed something of this and her eyes went wide.

Appalled by what he felt, Jared drew back from her and stood. He stared down at her, stunned by the effect she had on him. He moved a few feet away. His heart was racing, and he resented the loss of control even while reveling in the fire pounding through his veins. He'd never met anyone like her, and certainly no woman had ever done this to him before.

Silence stretched between them. Each was intently aware of the other.

"What'll you do if your father doesn't return for you?"

"Wait."

"For how long?"

"As long as necessary."

Jared came back and hunkered down again. She watched him closely. "Tempest, aren't you afraid of all those men around you?"

She was, but they were preferable to the silent darkness away from them. Only a few had bothered her, and her chilling, formidable silence was usually enough to discourage them.

Only one had required the flash and prick of her knife.

"You should have someone to take care of you."

Tempest had heard that before, several times, in several ways. She raised her head and looked at Jared.

Her look was answer enough without a single word. He smiled slightly. "I take it you've had the offer before."

"Aye, once or twice," she said, and stood up. She moved away from him and bent over the smoky fire to check her meat and fish strips. Using the grimy folds of her skirt to protect her hands, she removed the lattice and set it on the grass so the dried meats could cool. Then she began stacking the baskets onto a blanket in preparation for tying it into a secure bundle.

She could feel Jared Stryker standing there watching her every move. Glancing at him once, she saw his gaze moving down over her body again, lingering on her breasts and hips. Strange sensations stirred in her body. Disturbed, she returned her attention to making a secure pack.

"I'll ride back with you," he told her.

Wary of his effect on her, she looked at him coldly. "I'll no be going back till night."

"Where will you be going from here?"

"To get more food." And bathe and wash her clothes.

He thought of her standing in another muddy creek grubbing for tubers. She was surviving the same way those ignorant, heathen savages did up around the fort. He studied her more carefully, searching for resemblances between this girl and the Indian women he'd seen around the Kadema, Sek, and Pujuni villages near New Helvetia.

Tempest Walker's features were too refined. She couldn't be a Digger even though she lived like one. Her looks bore evidence to better breeding than that, though savage nonetheless. And surely, had her mother been one of those Indians, she would have gone back to a village and not lived on her own in a wickiup instead.

She intrigued him. He imagined her clean and dressed in a fine gown, and knew she would rival Geneva's beauty.

He felt an instant of shock at the very idea that an ignorant little half-breed, no matter how beautiful, could rouse such a treacherous thought. Geneva was more than beautiful; she had *breeding*.

It was the breeding that had distanced her from him. He had to remember that. She was several thousand miles away, and beyond that physical distance, she was married to another man. He had to forget her.

Tempest Walker hefted her neat pack.

Jared put his hand on it. "Here. Let me carry it for you."

"I con manage."

"Allow me, ma'am." He took it firmly. The way she followed him through the brush and up to the meadow made him wonder if she thought he planned to steal her hoard of roots and stems.

She stopped as they reached the clearing. "So ye be *him,*" she muttered cryptically, and he glanced back at her and saw that she was looking across at his horse. She smiled. "I saw ye running him by the river."

"He wins every time." He carried her bundle toward the grazing Indian pony. He laughed and turned slightly to tell her how he'd stolen him, but Tempest was no longer following him. Looking around, he saw her walking up to his stallion. Alexander stepped back, his body quivering with the warning that always came a bare second before a vicious attack.

"Jesus!" Jared dumped the pack and sprinted toward them. *"Look out!!"*

Too late! The great black neck bunched and then stretched out in a strike more swift than a snake's. His white teeth bared and open, the horse went straight for the girl.

I begin to smell a rat.
　　—Miguel de Cervantes Saavedra

　　Tempest fell back with a cry as the stallion's teeth snapped shut on her shoulder and ripped away part of her dress. She stumbled back out of the way of his hooves.

Jared shouted at the animal. He paused just long enough in his headlong run to snatch up a heavy fallen branch before diving between Alexander and the girl. He swore, enraged at the beast, and went for him with the club.

"No!" Tempest cried out.

Alexander backed nervously, his black eyes rolling from the man to the girl and back again.

"He deserves it! Vicious-tempered son of a bitch! I should've taken a whip to him long ago!" Jared swore at the horse, but heaved the club aside.

"Seems to me ye're the one with the vicious temper," Tempest said, sitting down.

Jared noted her pale face. He knelt down. "Goddamn it, but he got you, didn't he?" he said grimly, seeing blood oozing between her fingers.

"Aye, he did a wee bit," she agreed, and laughed.

"How can you laugh? He could've killed you!"

"Oh, ay, he could've at that, but ye saved the day, laddie, dinna ye?"

She was mocking him and he straightened angrily. "I'd better get the canteen and see to that shoulder."

"'Tis fine, mon. Stop yer fussin'."

"You're bleeding."

She nodded toward the stallion. "He's a fine beast, Jared Stryker. Done ye well, I bet."

"He's earned me enough to start my own casino." He glared across at the animal now placidly cropping grass. "He's a miserable fiend," he muttered.

Tempest stood up slowly, gaining her equilibrium while

Stryker's attention was on his horse. Her head swam. Jared turned and reached for her, but she stepped back.

"You'd better sit down before you faint."

"I dunna be the faintin' kind."

"Just sit down," he ordered, his eyes darkening. He went across to get his canteen of fresh water and came back again. She was still standing, a look in her eyes he'd never seen in a woman's before. His brows lifted slightly. He took out his linen handkerchief and dampened it.

"Ye dropped something," Tempest said, stooping to pick up a small envelope that had fallen from his pocket. The golden design on the back intrigued her, as did the smear of red wax that had been pressed there.

Jared saw the precious parchment envelope in her dirty hand and quickly took it from her to tuck into his pocket again. A muscle clenched in his jaw as he looked at her. She raised one eyebrow. He stepped forward to press the dampened handkerchief to her shoulder but she hit his hand away. He held it out. "All right. You do it if you don't trust me to," he said grimly.

She saw to it herself.

When she finished nursing her shoulder, she handed him back the soiled handkerchief. "Thank ye." Turning, she walked away toward the bundle he'd dropped.

Jared stared down at the linen swatch in his hand and muttered an expletive before tossing it aside and following her. "Tempest!"

She glanced back. "Go on yer way."

He couldn't just let her ride off after being bitten like that. Whether she admitted it or not, she looked shaken.

When he kept coming, Tempest swung around to face him, her hand going to the hilt of her knife. "Don't ye be tryin' to put yer hands on me," she warned.

Jared paused. "I wasn't." He saw the tension in her svelte body and the wide pupils darkening her pale blue eyes. "How can you laugh at almost being killed and be afraid of *me?*" he asked.

She backed a few steps and then relaxed slightly, though she still kept her steady gaze on him. "Cautious. Not afraid."

"I suppose you have reason," he said. "I think you should sit for a while. You mount up now and you're liable to fall right off."

She took her hand away from her knife and put both hands

on her hips. "There be a fine joke," she said, grinning broadly. Laughing, she turned away and strode toward her Indian pony.

She wasn't as assured as she pretended. She knew Jared was following her again. The man wouldn't go away. She quickly gathered up the bundle, wanting to be quit of him.

"How long have you been without a husband?" Jared asked.

She shot him a startled look. "Ye seem to know a bit."

"Not enough," he said, smiling. He searched her face. "You must have been very young when you married."

"I had no choice in the matter." She hefted the bundle to her back.

"Let me—"

"I've done well enough on my own," she said sharply, giving him a glinting hostile look.

"I only want to help."

She turned her back on him. Jared watched as she approached the pony and set the bundle down. The animal raised its head and whinied softly. Tempest ran a gentle hand over his side, slapping him on the rump before she stepped a few yards away to retrieve an Indian blanket, a saddle, a bosal, and a saddlebag that looked heavy with something big and square inside. He heard something rattle as well. Beads?

Within a few minutes, she had expertly saddled and packed her horse. She knew what she was doing. He doubted he could have managed the same task in twice the time she took, nor half so well.

Curiosity prodded. "Don't leave, Tempest—please. I'd like to talk with you for a while."

She looked at him coolly. "Why?"

"Well, you're not like anyone I've ever met," he admitted with a wry smile, moving slowly toward her, not wanting to startle her into sudden flight. He stopped a few feet away. "How do you come by your Scottish burr?"

"What be wrong with it?" she said, her eyes flashing.

"Nothing. It's charming."

"Da was from Scotland." Why had she told him anything? Jared shifted, his body hardly moving and remaining in an indolent stance, and she felt her lungs tightening. She became acutely aware of the exposed expanse of tanned male chest, the narrow waist, the long, firmly muscled legs splayed so that she felt almost drawn to the joining. Stryker looked at her openly, steadily, a look that brought to her mind what a man did with a woman.

Somehow Abram, pressing her down into the moss-filled mattress, his body burrowing itself in hers with uncontrolled, hard thrusts, had never made her feel this deep, quivering woman's trepidation. She felt Stryker's interest. And his want.

Jared saw how Tempest's gaze flickered nervously over his body and then rose again to meet his. Her expression grew oddly pensive and bemused. He knew that she was as aware of him physically as he was of her.

Alicia had told him once about widows, having been one herself twice over. "I'd go mad without this," she had gasped against his neck, her hands kneading his bare buttocks. "Oh, God, it's like ambrosia. Once tasted, you can't go without..."

Looking at Tempest, taking in her wild beauty, he wondered how she would be in bed.

Primitive.

He tried to divert his thoughts. "You said you had no choice in the matter of your marriage. Were you happy?"

She stiffened. "Ye ask a lot of questions."

"How else do people get to know one another?" He searched her face. "Were you happy?"

"Aye."

That could work for him or against him. "How old are you?"

She shrugged.

They stood a few feet apart, looking at one another with primeval recognition. Jared had experienced sexual attraction before and reveled in the coursing heat and tightening sensations. But Tempest was uneasy with them.

"I'll ride with you," Jared told her softly.

Tempest blinked. "No," she said after a slight pause. She turned away and mounted her horse in a motion so smoothly graceful and agile that Jared stared.

He gave a soft laugh. "No, I don't think you would fall off." He stepped closer and saw her slender leg tense in command. Her horse sidled. Jared stopped. "Just give me a minute—"

"I said no," she repeated firmly, her back rigidly straight as she looked down at him.

Her vehemence annoyed him. "Mind explaining why not? I only mean to look after you."

He had a right quick temper, she noted. "I've work to do," she said simply, shifting the reins lightly. "Ye'd be gettin' in my way."

He gave her a mocking bow. "As you wish, my lady."

Straightening, he gave her a bold look that took her in from her exposed shoulder down to her ankle. Meeting her eyes again, he smiled slowly. Her face darkened.

"What ye be lookin' for, laddie, is to be had across the river from the gristmill. A tin looking glass is all ye need."

Jared thought her eyes were colder than a dock whore's at that moment, but she had all the pride and arrogance of a southern aristocrat. Standing with arms akimbo, he smiled to himself as he watched her ride away, heeling her pony into a canter, her long black braid bouncing against her back.

She couldn't be much older than sixteen, but she was definitely *all* woman.

"And you're going to be mine, Tempest Walker," he murmured after her.

The world wants to be deceived.
> —Sebastian Brant
> *Ship of Fools*

"Tempest? Are you in there?"

She recognized Jared Stryker's voice immediately, even through the muffling of stick-and-mud walls and the haze of exhausted sleep. She'd ridden far and worked hard gathering what she needed yesterday and hadn't returned until the lights before the miners' tents and shanties glowed in a wide golden chain around the high walls of the fort.

Sitting up slowly, she looked toward the flap of her hut. Sunlight turned it pale yellow and she knew it was well past daybreak.

What was he doing here?

"I came by last night, but you hadn't returned yet. Are you listening?" he asked. "Can I come in?"

"No." She edged back farther away from the doorway.

"You're still angry," he said simply, and there was amusement in his tone.

Her heavily pounding heart and trembling stomach were not signs of anger. She knew what anger felt like. This was something alarming and incomprehensible. Fear? No, not exactly fear either, for she had been afraid many times and it was different altogether: fear always gave her the needed strength to flee or fight. This new feeling seemed to weaken her.

"Tempest, I'm coming in," Stryker said imperiously, obviously annoyed by her refusal to talk. He raised the flap.

Tempest lunged for her hunting knife.

As Jared stooped and entered through the small doorway, he saw her swift roll, the flash of a blade, her bright, wild eyes. She pressed herself back on the other side of the glowing embers of her fire. The dirty blanket was twisted around her slim hips and the lunge she'd made for the knife had torn the

239

bodice of her dress further, revealing what his gaze raptly took
in for a breath-stopping instant.

He let the flap drop behind him and raised his hands, palms
up. "Easy. I'm not going to hurt you." Very slowly he edged
in and sat down cross-legged, his eyes never leaving hers. She
was tense and ready to spring, and the way she held that knife
told him she was no novice at using it.

He forced himself to keep his eyes up off her body, sure
that if he gaped, he would be in serious difficulty. He spread
his hands again in a reassuring manner meant to calm her. "I
swear I won't touch you, Tempest."

She shifted slightly, inching back farther, and this time Jared
couldn't prevent his gaze from dropping again. She saw and,
with a sharp jerk, covered herself.

"Ye con get yer bleeding arse out of here," she hissed, her
teeth bared almost in a snarl.

Stunned, Jared stared at her. No woman in his wide ac-
quaintance had ever spoken in such a profane manner. Tempest
was definitely not a lady. But neither was she a whore, he
thought in slightly amused disappointment.

Belatedly, he realized that the young girl now staring him
down was an unknown quantity. He had foolishly walked right
into this wildcat's den thinking that he entered the mud hut of
a defenseless girl. *Defenseless!* He had the distinct feeling—
no, the instinctive *understanding*—that if he moved even a
fraction of an inch closer, she would remove some part of his
anatomy with that gleaming knife of hers.

Retreat, however, was unthinkable.

The very threat of physical danger from her hand and the
look of her wildness quickened Jared's senses. He loved a hunt,
and the smell of woman was strong in the warm hut. His blood
stirred, grew hot and heavy. He felt a strange impulse to tell
her in equally coarse language just what effect she was having
on him and what he wanted to do with her right now.

Tempest knew. She stared into the burning, dark-brown eyes
with growing physical awareness. She saw how Jared's chest
rose and fell, how his breathing came more rapidly, faintly
audible in the small, dimly lit hut. She swallowed hard.

The wall of the hut was hard at her back. Hunger blazed in
the face before her. Her palms began to sweat, slicking the
bone handle of the knife she clutched. She waited, her heart
thundering, blood singing in her ears. She dampened her dry
lips with the tip of her tongue and saw how Jared's hands

resting on his hard male thighs shook and then tightened into white fists as he drew in a breath through gritted teeth. She saw more, and her own breath caught as her body froze.

Jared saw where her eyes were fixed. He tried to defuse his arousal, embarrassed more by his own lack of control rather than what she could see plainly outlined. What was this girl that she could make his body feel like it was stretched on a rack over high flames?

"Damn," he murmured tightly, partially closing his eyes so as not to look at the girl just out of reach across the fire. The blade flickered as her hand trembled.

Now she is afraid, he realized, and was angry because of it. He knew how he must look to her, with his lust pouring out of his eyes, his body evidence of what went on in his mind. *Tell her now you only came to talk!* He forced himself to breathe more evenly, dredging his mind for something to cool his heavy ardor. He seized frantically upon the chilling memory of his mother arriving at Alicia's house to visit at the same moment that he was in the parlor, Alicia's head bobbing in his lap.

He uttered a gasping laugh as he felt the same shattering effect wash over him again. His passion ebbed.

"Put down the knife, Tempest," he said, and smiled mockingly. "I won't move."

Slowly her hand lowered and her knuckles lost the whiteness of fierce strength. She watched him closely, still poised for attack should he be lying.

"I have a proposition to make that will be beneficial to both of us," he said in a steadier tone. "Every time you walk through the camp looking for your father, every man on the hill stares at you. You're beautiful, Tempest, and there can't be more than a few women around here and hardly more than one to every twenty men in the whole of the territory. Men are starving for a look at a woman."

He saw well enough that she didn't like the turn of the conversation one bit, but he wanted her to see the advantages of her sex and the attention she commanded.

"I've started a small casino. It's just in a tent at the moment, but I've almost enough gold now to begin building something more suitable." He paused. "I'd like to offer you a percentage of my profits if you'd just come and pour whiskey and sit in the tent while the games are going on."

Her blue eyes glowed with fiery scorn. "What for? So ye con cheat?"

He stiffened. "No. I'm good enough to win honestly," he said without bragging.

"Then why do ye need me?" she asked contemptuously.

Jared smiled. "To keep the men's minds off their cards," he told her frankly. "With you around, they'll be too busy looking to concentrate heavily on the game. I make more money; you make more money."

Her mouth curled. "So I just pour whiskey and stand about while the men gawk at me?"

They gawked at her anyway, so she might just as well get paid for it, he thought angrily, but knew he had better not voice that thought—not with the banked fire glowing in those eyes. Better to attack from the flank.

"How much chance is there really of you finding your father?" he demanded, and saw that she didn't like that question either. He plunged ahead. "Suppose he doesn't come back for you. Suppose you don't find him at all. What then, Tempest? What're you going to do here—keep gathering what you need from the land? What happens when a couple of men decide looking just isn't enough?" Even saying it made him faintly sick. The possibility was all too realistic. Surely she knew that already.

He leaned forward intently. "Are you going to live like this forever?" He jerked his head derisively, indicating her primitive shelter. "This isn't a way for a woman to live. I'd look after you, make sure you were safe. You'd have good food, a warm place to sleep, gold of your own to spend. It'd be a far better life than what you have here."

She grinned, a slow, cold baring of her even, white teeth. "Ah," she said smoothly, "now we be gettin' down to it, mon. Aye?" She leaned forward as well, resting her forearms on her raised knees, her eyes bright with a shrewd intelligence. "A moment ago it was pouring whiskey and standing about where the men con stare at me, but now it be something else. *You* taking care of *me*," she sneered. She laughed softly, mocking him. "A warm place to sleep? Gold of my own? What ye really want is a woman in yer bed."

He smiled easily. "The thought had crossed my mind, of course," he drawled. "But I'm not looking for *any* woman." He heard the air whistle between her teeth and grinned back at her. "Relax. That's not part of the proposition." Then he added more seriously, "Every man on the hill wants you in bed, but with me you'll have a choice."

"I've a choice now," she snapped. "I sleep alone."

"For how long? That knife of yours will hold off one, but what if several decide to take you down?" It was a form of coercion, he knew, but it was also the truth. He'd overheard conversations that made the threat quite explicit.

"I'd manage to do some damage before they got what they were after," she told him with a jerk of her chin.

"Granted, but the damage you did could cost you your life." He saw that she clearly understood what he was telling her. A woman could fight for her honor, but that might enrage an impassioned man so much that he would kill.

"Tempest, with me, you would be the one to say when our relationship changed." But change it would. He knew women well enough to see the effect he had on her.

"Ye sit here and tell me ye'd wait?" she said derisively. "Ye were hardly in my hut when ye were as hard as a pine log and shaking like ye were havin' a fit."

She certainly didn't pare her words. "I didn't say I wouldn't want you, or that being near you wouldn't be a bit wearing on my nerves," he agreed, and laughed softly. "But I think I could manage to control myself." She made a disbelieving, indelicate grunt. He leaned forward, his eyes holding hers. "Hard and ready, yes," he said crudely, "but you're not sprawled under me right now, are you? You're still sitting safe across the fire from me."

"Because of my knife, laddie, not yer honor," she spat, flashing the blade again.

Jared hadn't played poker since boyhood without learning how to bluff. His smile grew bold and self-confident. "Don't think that stopped me."

She studied him narrowly, her body rigid, the pulse visible in her throat. Then she called him. "Try if ye dare," she whispered coldly. When he didn't move, she very slowly raised herself to her knees, taking a defensive stance. "Come on, laddie, try," she said again, laughing at him coldly when he still sat there staring at her pensively.

He was no fool. He smiled at her, a slow, sensual smile that had its desired effect. "You don't look willing," he drawled softly, "and I never use force."

She was uncertain. He didn't look the type to know how to use a knife as she did, but his eyes were dark and unafraid. He was calm and watchful, too easy. He didn't once look at her knife, but looked instead into her eyes. It was that about him that made her finally relax.

She raised one eyebrow and sat down again, tilting her head to one side as she studied him with an enigmatic expression.

"Just think about my proposition. You could become the richest woman in California. Think about it." He raised himself slowly to a squatting position. "We'll talk about it again. All right?"

She shook her head. "I be no mon's whore, Jared Stryker," she told him in a soft, absolutely unyielding tone.

"Who said you were?" She wasn't a whore, but she would make him a damn fine mistress. She was his woman whether she knew it yet or not.

He lifted the buckskin flap. Just before he went out, he glanced back at her and grinned. "You were shaking, too, Tempest," he said. Then he left.

> My days are past.
> —Job 17:11

Jared left Tempest alone to think. She was intelligent and observant; sooner or later, she would decide on the only course open to her for her own safety. In the meantime, Jared kept a possessive eye on her by hiring an Ohio farm boy who was waiting out the winter to oversee whoever went near the hut. "Discourage them," Jared ordered.

Each day at about the same time, Tempest passed by his casino. She never once looked at him, and his impatience grew in direct proportion with her seeming indifference.

Gold poured steadily across Jared's poker table. He had enough now to contract a crew of carpenters to begin building his new casino near the gristmill owned by Samuel Brannan. With men desperate for work and a means of support while panning was impossible with winter on them, labor was plentiful and work progressed rapidly. Jared's large cache of gold dwindled as the two-story, many-roomed structure grew. He worked longer hours and took bigger risks, and his uncanny luck paid off.

But never once did he lose sight of his desire for Tempest McClaren Walker. It grew into a nagging physical need.

Jared's experience had taught him young that the quickest way into a woman's bed was through a man's purse strings. Even his beloved Geneva had succumbed to money, marrying it to save her father's Cooper River plantation.

Jared lay on his cot holding the small envelope that contained her last message to him. He knew her words by heart.

Jared, dearest—

Please try to understand and forgive me. The choice was never mine to make. You are forever the one in my heart.

Geneva

Money—gold—that was the all-important thing in this world, Jared thought bitterly, putting the envelope back into his breast pocket. Even someone as genteel as Geneva had sacrificed herself for it—just to insure familial honor and security. Had he himself had enough of it three years ago, Geneva would be his wife now and not that of a man twenty-five years her senior.

Gold—*gold!* That was what made all dreams possible.

What was Tempest's price?

Right now he didn't have the time to find out. He had a business to build.

Tempest stood beneath the bare cottonwood branches a few yards from her hut, currying her Indian pony. Her food stores were low again, and her horse was growing thin from lack of proper grazing and oats. She would have to ride out to find what she needed to survive, but she hated to leave the huge camp for fear Da would return in her absence and be gone before her return.

She was hungry all the time now. She had had only a strip of smoked rabbit and a small roasted root since morning, and it was dusk. She had been back and forth through the camp again today, and had seen no man who even resembled McClaren. When she had passed by Jared Stryker's casino, she kept her eyes averted, not wanting to look at him. He was far too disturbing.

Yet even without looking, she had felt him watching her. He had come to stand in the doorway of his enlarged tent, which he had made of heavy ship sails held together by strong ropes and tall pine poles. He had stood there staring after her as she walked up the hill. She had glanced back once and seen how he angrily flicked his cheroot into the street before going back inside, and her heart hadn't stopped pounding until she was around the bend of the muddy street. Was he still waiting for her to come to him? He had not pressed her since that first visit. Once he had ridden by and stopped long enough to try to give her a new dress. He said it was to replace the one his stallion had torn, and apologized for its tan color.

"It should be blue to match your eyes," he had said, his own eyes darkly holding hers as his mouth curved into that slow smile that made her stomach quiver.

"Ye owe me naught for that, mon," she had told him, holding out the package.

"Then accept it as a gift—a token of my esteem."

"A gift accepted is a debt owed. Take it back." She had thrust it into his hands and turned away, ducking back into her hut. She heard his muttered curse and then the pounding hooves of that black beast as he rode away.

In a few more days her firewood would be completely gone. If she didn't find more somehow, she would have to sleep in darkness. The mere thought made her body go cold.

"Are you McClaren's daughter?" came a deep, gruff voice from just behind her. Tempest spun, the curry brush raised, and faced a tall, burly mountain man in well-seasoned buckskins. She could have smelled him if she had not been thinking of Jared Stryker and her troubles.

His heavy beard was graying and his shoulder-length hair hung in greasy tangles beneath a coonskin cap. His narrowed, marsh-brown eyes surveyed her without expression.

"Aye," she said hoarsely, hope quickening her breathing and heart. "Who be ye?"

The man had a bundle under one arm. He took off his cap and then held the bundle out to her. "We went to your farm to winter and found you burned out. He said if you were still alive you'd be here at the Sacramento in the shadow of the fort."

A sinking sensation began in her chest and didn't seem to stop. "Where is he?"

He put his cap back on without answering.

"Is he coming here?"

He handed her the bundle. "He only give me that to give to you if you were here. It's done."

Her throat constricted. She caught hold of the man's arm, clutching his buckskin sleeve fiercely. He looked from her hand to her face. "He's gone, girl. Headed north." He put a calloused hand over hers briefly and then pried her fingers loose.

She clutched the bundle and watched him walk away, then stooped and went back into her hut. Setting the bundle down, she stared at it. Finally, she carefully untied the leather thongs, removed the thin buckskin wrap, and saw what lay rolled inside.

It was the finest, largest otter pelt she'd ever seen, six feet long and over two feet wide at the middle. Tempest put her shaking hands deeply into the rich, glistening black fur. "All the time, ye were at the sea, Da. Not in the mountains."

Close. He had been so close all the time.

Her throat burned. She rubbed the fur, dug her fingers into

it, unable to draw a breath through the hot tightness of her chest. *So close.* She tried to reroll the amazing pelt, but her cold hands trembled. Then she glimpsed the small markings on the tanned side and flipped it over. What did the writing mean? It wasn't in pictures she could understand, but in small scratched symbols.

Maybe he wasn't gone after all. Maybe he was waiting somewhere for her beyond the crowded hillsides. But where? North or south, east or west? On the American or the Sacramento? How would she know? Why hadn't he drawn a map she could understand?

Abram could have read the message to her, but Abram was dead.

Then she knew who could tell her. She quickly rolled the pelt, stuffed it beneath her arm, and ducked out of her hut. She ran up the muddy street. It was just past dusk and the soft glow of kerosene lanterns within the canvas tents and rough shelters dimmed the harsh reality of the mining camp. It might have been a carnival instead of a slum.

Tempest ran all the way up the hill until she reached Jared's tent casino. She plunged inside and stopped, her chest burning painfully. Men glanced up at her arrival and sat staring at her. She searched the faces until she caught sight of Jared standing by the long pine-plank bar at the back, speaking with the same young man who stood watching her hut every day. Jared was frowning as the young man spoke to him.

The hush drew his attention, for he turned his head and she felt the startled impact of his gaze. He brushed the young man aside and came toward her.

She met him halfway, uncaring of the curious stares they were receiving.

Jared saw only that her face was red and running sweat, her chest heaving from exertion. Her fingers were white as they clutched some bundle. "Come with me." He put a supportive hand beneath her elbow and led her to the back of the casino, drew back a flap of canvas, and ushered her into a private area. She scarcely looked around.

"You're too thin," he accused. "You take better care of your horse than you do of yourself. Why didn't you come to me before this?" He caught her shoulders, forcing her to sit down on a brass bed. He sat down beside her, pulling out his clean linen handkerchief and forcing her chin up and around so that he could wipe the sweat from her cheeks. A fierce tenderness filled him as he looked into the raw blue eyes staring up at him. "Who was that man who came to your hut? McClaren?"

She jerked her head back from his touch, her eyes closing tightly as she shook her head. Her mouth trembled. She drew in a ragged, gasping breath and looked at him again. "Con ye read?"

"Of course. Why?" He frowned, uncomprehending.

She stood abruptly, turning and dropping her bundle onto his bed. She unrolled a black pelt, underside up, and spread it out with shaking hands.

"Read this."

He glanced down briefly, surprised to see the perfect script that indicated the hand of an educated man. "What is this?"

"A message from my da."

"This? I thought you said he was a trapper."

"Please," she begged. *"What does he say?"*

Jared looked down and read the message aloud:

> The otter's time is finished, and so is mine. You are strong, daughter. You can find your own way. Seek not Absalom, for in him lies your own destruction.

At the end of the message was a large, clear handprint, the fingers splayed wide. It looked as if the writer had laid his hand against the cured hide carefully and then leaned heavily on it before dragging it away again.

Jared leaned closer, studying the writing and the print more closely, frowning slightly, disturbed. *The man must have been mad.*

McClaren hadn't used ink to write his daughter out of his life. Neither Jared nor Tempest could have known that it wasn't an animal's blood the Mad Scot had used.

It had been his own.

Thank you for nothing.
—Miguel de Cervantes Saavedra

"Sit down, Tempest," Jared said, seeing how her skin was the color of ashes. Her mouth was curved into a strange smile. She ignored him and stepped forward, close to his bed, and slowly put her own hand down onto the print of her father's. Tears welled and streamed silently down her cheeks. He had never seen a woman cry that way. Usually they sobbed, whimpered, or sniffed delicately into their handkerchiefs. Somehow the way Tempest cried was far more unsettling; it went much deeper.

Jared felt a swift, hot anger at McClaren. "He must have been a real bastard," he muttered under his breath, pitying her and not wanting to. Pity and desire were ill-mated emotions.

Tempest slowly turned the pelt over so that the black fur showed. She rubbed her hands into it. "Look at the size, mon," she whispered. "This was an old animal, one that must've been cunning enough to survive when all the others were taken. This was no easy kill for my da. It was a long, hard hunt." She rolled the pelt very carefully, with the fur on the inside, then picked it up as she might have a newborn child.

"I dunna ken who this Absalom was, but I ken what the message means. I know more now than I did two years ago when Da sold me to Abram for five dollars in gold and a bottle of whiskey."

"Jesus." Jared winced.

"Thank ye for reading it to me, Jared," she told him quietly, and turned toward the canvas flap that opened into the noisy casino.

"No," he said hoarsely, and laid a hand on her thin shoulder to detain her. "What're you going to do now?"

She stood with her back to him, her eyes closed, unable to breathe. She felt him move close behind her and her heart quickened. "Find my own way," she said shakily.

"Doing what?" He put his other hand on her arm and lowered

250

his head to nuzzle against her neck and kiss her. She jerked away, shrugging his hands off and facing him with wide, alarmed eyes. His patience snapped. "You can't go back to that damn hut!"

Her blue eyes became shrewdly cynical.

"Tempest, for God's sake," he ground out, coming close again. "You're living on roots. You're dressed in these damn filthy rags. Where are you going to get gold to buy wood for a fire to keep you warm? Don't you possess any common sense?"

She arched one eyebrow coldly. "Do I take it right that ye still be wantin' me to pour yer fine whiskey and stand in there," she jerked her head toward the flap, "so those men con look me over and forget their bloody cards?"

He gritted his teeth. Said in just that way, the proposition made him feel like a bastard. "I made the offer to get you here. You don't belong in that . . . wickiup."

"I ken what ye wanted, mon—me in that bed. Dunna pretend otherwise."

He let out his breath. "If it's straight talk you want, you've looked at me in that way sometimes."

She stiffened angrily.

He stared hard into her eyes. "Don't expect a man to apologize for going after what he wants."

"Buying what he wants!"

"The way your husband did?"

He regretted his retaliation as soon as he uttered it. He'd inherited the Strykers' lack of tact. After years of hearing his father's outbursts of temper against his genteel mother, he'd always sworn he'd not do it. Easier said than done. He sighed heavily. "I'm sorry." He came closer. "Tempest, stay with me," he urged roughly. "I'll see that you're protected. I'll give you a decent place to live, good food, nice clothes, everything a woman needs . . ." Desire husked his voice. "Whatever you want," he added, catching hold of her shoulders and giving her a soft shake.

She looked up into his burning eyes and felt weakened. A buzzing filled her ears and thrummed through her body, and her heart drummed heavily. She tried to keep her head. "Abram offered me everything he had."

Jared laughed coldly and let go of her. "You're after my casino?"

"Gold is the only language ye ken," she retorted with an arrogant, disdainful lift of her chin. "Mon, I'll try to put it in a way ye understand. *He* never took from me what I wasn't willing to give."

Hot jealousy gripped Jared at her words. He wanted to look on her as a passionate woman, but *not with another man.* Just the thought of it made him want to hit something. "I won't either," he ground out.

She gauged his darkened face with cold, blue eyes. "Everything I need or want, ye said."

He wondered what she did want. "That's what I said."

"'Tis a generous offer," she told him, her expression unreadable.

Her detached assessment grated on his pride. "Have you a better one at the moment?" he mocked.

"I have my freedom," she said seriously.

"I'm not asking to buy you for five dollars in gold and a bottle of whiskey," he said, incensed. "You wouldn't be my little Indian slave."

Deeply, fiercely angry, she said nothing for a long moment. Then, tilting her chin, she said, "Neither was I Abram's. I'll make *you* an offer, Jared." She smiled dryly. "I'll pour yer whiskey and wear that dress ye tried to give me. I'll stand in yer casino. My price is twenty dollars in gold—each day. And if I *choose* to come to yer bed, I will. I wilna be whore to any mon—be his price a cheap tin looking glass and a handful of beads, five dollars in gold and a bottle of whiskey, or *everything I need and whatever I want,*" she said, sneering his own words back at him. Then she shrugged. "Now, Jared Stryker, con ye accept *my* offer and take yer chances? If so, we con do business."

She was a fine red bitch, he thought, and could use a slapping down, but she excited him more than any other woman ever had. He wanted her so much it was all he could do to clench his hands and not haul her back to the bed and set her off her heels once and for all.

In good time, he thought.

He smiled. "You've got yourself a deal, Tempest," he told her silkily, and saw the way her eyes dilated as he looked into them. In good time, he thought again, assured. He held out his hand. "My word and offer stand."

She didn't shake hands with him but held up her own, showing three fingers. "In my life, this many were true to their given word: Da, Abram . . . and God. Dunna insult any one of them if ye ever want my respect."

Jared's smile flattened out. "I'm a gentleman, and a gentleman's word is his honor," he said stiffly.

Tempest looked calmly into his eyes and then turned and walked to the canvas flap. Lifting it, she glanced back at him again, one eyebrow raised in challenge. "We will see, wilna we?" She smiled faintly and let the flap drop back into place behind her.

And he received the gold at their hand, and
fashioned it with a graving tool, and made a
molten calf; and they said, "These are your
gods, O Israel, who brought you out of
the land of Egypt."
—Exodus 32:4

While Tempest went down to her hut with the farm
boy Jared had hired to watch over her, Jared had another of
his men help him put up a canvas divider splitting his large,
comfortable quarters into two smaller private chambers. He
hoped that the barricade would soon come down, and her de-
fenses with it.

"Put the wooden tub in there," he instructed, sure that Tempest would welcome a bath. He shoved his hands in his pockets
and contemplated his big brass bed.

The deep rumble of voices within the casino died down to
a mere mutter, and Jared knew that Tempest had come in again.
He lifted the flap and watched her proceed across the room,
her head high, her eyes straight ahead.

She walks like royalty, he thought in amusement. She didn't
look at him until she was within a few feet and even then it
was the barest, coldest brush of blue eyes before she walked
beneath his raised arm and entered the private area. He let the
flap drop and heard the voices rise again as rumor exploded.
They'd be betting on them already. He wondered if it bothered
Tempest.

"This area is yours," he told her, sliding the canvas partition
back on the pole that had been rigged. She looked at the wooden
tub. "I thought you might enjoy a hot bath."

She remembered her first bath, the lye burning her eyes,
Abram standing there staring at her body like a poleaxed ram.
"Aye, 'tis a fine pleasure I've not had for a time," she said,
and smiled at Jared. She set her heavy saddlebag on the earthen
floor, still holding the rolled otter pelt. The farm boy had put

254

another bundle inside before leaving.

"Is this everything?" Jared asked, surprised by her pitiful lack of possessions. He would change that.

She lifted her chin. "I left the baskets and yer mon took my horse to the stables."

She takes offense so easily, he reminded himself. *She's a proud woman, too proud.* Though why she should have any right to be he didn't know, poor, hungry, and ignorant as she was.

"I know this isn't much to offer," he said, indicating the small space in which there was a table that held a hammered tin candle holder and several candles and a simple cot near the tub. "But it's a little better than you've had."

"I've been warm."

Was she laughing at him? "Oliver is bringing in a small heater and a supply of wood. When you need more, just let me know and I'll have it brought to you. I should also have a chest of drawers for you by tomorrow." He glanced at the small bundle containing her clothing. There wasn't enough in that leather pouch to fill one drawer. He looked at her again, thinking of how she would look in silks and lace, satins and ribbons.

All in good time, old boy, he told himself. Pushing his hands into his pockets, he rocked back on his boot heels. "We do have one small problem."

She cocked one dark eyebrow.

"Only one bed, and it took me three weeks to get it shipped up from San Francisco!"

She grinned coldly. "And ye think I might prefer sharing it with ye rather than sleeping on that," she said, indicating the simple cot.

He grinned back boldly, his eyes moving down over her slim, curved body. His grin died as she placed her things deliberately on the cot and smiled.

"You're not going to get any sleep on that."

She put her hands on her hips and laughed softly. "I'll be getting a mite more sleep there than I'd be getting in yer brass bed." Her eyes swept down over him pointedly. "And I could sleep on the ground, which is softer than some things I can see, mon."

He was taken aback by her frankness and measuring look. "If you're worried about it, I guarantee to keep my hands to myself. We could put a board down the center of the bed so it'd be evenly divided between us. You on one side, me on the other—simple."

She laughed. "Now, if I were fool enough to believe that, ye could call me a horse's arse. And if ye believe it, yer body dunna ken yer own mind."

He smiled slightly, half-teasing, half-challenging. "I give my solemn word."

"Ye've given it once already."

He approached slowly until he stood right in front of her. Her smile died, but she didn't draw back from him. Her eyes were fathomless as they watched him. He ran a caressive finger along the soft curve of her cheek. "I told you what I wanted for you." Her skin was softer than rose petals and the color of calf suede.

"Aye. Ye did. And I told ye what I'd take from ye," she said quietly, and moved away from his touch.

He had seen the flicker of her eyes as he had touched her; they had darkened enough to tell him that the attraction wasn't only his. "It's up to you." He shrugged. "I'll do what I can about getting you a decent bed. Whatever you say, I don't want you spending much time in that thing."

"I'd like a bath and then, if ye still have it, the dress ye offered once."

"I still have it."

"Where do I get water?"

"I'll have it brought to you. Don't worry." He grinned. "I've an agreement with the proprietor of a bathhouse just up the street, and I'm sure a couple of those gentlemen at the bar will be more than eager to fetch and carry for you."

"How long will ye be wanting me to work at the bar?" she asked. She looked tired and distracted, with a sad pensiveness about her, a private, grim resolve.

His smile softened. "Just unpack what you have and then rest, Tempest. We'll talk about that tomorrow."

"We've already talked about it."

"You've had one helluva day," he told her firmly, irritated by her stubbornness. "You don't need to take on that riffraff at the bar on top of it. All I want you to do tonight is take it easy. You're dead on your feet. You need a long, leisurely, hot bath, fresh clothes, a good meal, plenty of sleep . . . some time to think things over."

"Thinking con be a grievous pastime, mon," she murmured, her eyes shadowed.

Any other woman with half Tempest's troubles would have been crying her woes on his shoulder by now, he thought. Admiration stirred in him. He looked into her wide blue eyes and then down over her ragged blouse and skirt. Rough, uncouth, and wild, yet somehow entirely feminine—and vulnerable. If she could look this precious in filthy rags, how much grander would she be when he was able to dress her in silk and lace?

Walking to his trunk, he threw back the top and lifted out a teal-blue frontier dress. He laid it across his bed. "While you're in your bath and then having a thick beefsteak from Sally's, you think about our agreement. You're not going to be hungry or cold or alone anymore, Tempest. You've got me to take care of you now."

He left her alone and hired two men at the bar to bring in buckets of warm water from the bathhouse. He sent another to Sally's for a platter of food. A few inquiries quickly discovered a pile of blankets.

Tempest was having her own difficulties adjusting to her new situation. She wondered if she had made the right decision in leaving her hut by the river. There, at least she had had privacy.

Two men delivered four buckets of steaming water and stared at her speechlessly as they poured it into the oak tub. Next came a man with a covered tray from Sally's, compliments of the house. Two more ogled her as they delivered a pile of blankets.

Last of all, Jared arrived unannounced with a bottle of French wine, hoping to sit with her while she partook of her meal, before she'd even gotten into the tepid bathwater. Instead, he got the broadside of her tongue.

"*Bloody hell!* Who else is going to come marching through here?" she railed at him. "Ye got Fremont's battalion lined up out there just waiting for a bleeding look at me?" She shoved past him and strode out into the silent casino. Every man in the place had heard her shouting and looked up from his cards or whiskey to listen raptly. She proceeded directly to the bar, thumbed a man off his stool, and used it to leap up onto the bar.

More than a hundred men stared at her as she walked from one end of the plank to the other. "Ye want to look! Well, take a bloody good one, because when I go back in there again, the next laddie—" she looked straight across at Jared "—whoever he be, that comes in is going to lose his family jewels!" She glared at them all, hands on her hips, her legs splayed. She let her words sink in for a second and then jumped down from the bar and walked back across the room between the tables of gaping men.

Jared stood at the canvas flap, the bottle of wine in his right hand, two glasses in his left. Tempest looked up at him. "I dunna drink whiskey."

"It's wine."

"Or wine *or* ale," she added firmly, and snapped the canvas flap closed behind her. She lifted it again and poked her head back out. "And don't be bringing me any water either, or ye'll be leaving half a mon with the best part in ye hand!"

"Yes, ma'am," he drawled, restraining a laugh.

"Just so we understand each other."

It was four in the morning before Jared laid down his cards and went to his quarters. A candle was still burning, casting a golden glow through the canvas partition between his bed and Tempest's cot.

"Tempest?"

No answer.

He slid the partition aside and peered in. She was sleeping, her hair a wild raven mass around her smooth face, curled on her side like a child. He thought about how she had climbed up on his bar and strode from one end to the other shouting at the randy men, and smiled.

An uncovered tin tray revealed a chewed bone and an empty tankard that had held milk. The dirty bathwater was still in the tub. She'd washed her clothes in it and hung them over one end of the canvas partition to dry. He was going to throw them away and dress her properly. There had to be someone in this godforsaken mining camp who was a tailor, someone who could make her some decent clothes.

He walked quietly to the cot and looked down at her. She'd washed her hair, for it was shiny and curled in swirls. He lifted one silky tress and felt it. He longed to push his fingers through the mass and use it to tilt her head back so that he could press his mouth to the hollow of her throat and then move down to her breasts.

What was she wearing under that blanket? Temptation prodded and he slowly lifted the edge to see. A creamy shoulder showed and then the paler curve of a smooth mound of female flesh. She shifted restlessly, making a soft, feminine sound, then moved her head and murmured something incomprehensible and rolled over onto her back, the blanket twisting from Jared's hand and dropping down to completely reveal her breasts.

He caught his breath.

How long since I've had a woman? Staring down at her, he knew it had been too long. What would she do if he lowered his mouth to hers and filled his hands with—

He *knew* what she'd do.

You gave her your word, Jared.

He was going to go mad with her barely six feet away from him. But how else could he have gotten her to agree to live with him? She needed time. He needed patience. He had seen how she looked at him; he could wait.

Yet looking down at her as she slept innocently, all he could think about was having those long, slender legs wrapped around his hips, her arms clasping him around the shoulders. His body throbbed with his imaginings, making known a painful masculine need that wouldn't go away, not without being buried deeply in a woman's flesh. *Damn!*

Tempest moved again. How could a mad trapper and a squaw have begotten this beauty? She was a survivor. He'd seen her fierceness and pride, recognized her quick intelligence. He didn't know another woman who could have survived on her own the way this girl had, with no husband, no father, no one at all. Most women would have gone looking for a man to take care of them and paid whatever price was asked for that care.

Too bad Tempest wasn't cut of that mold, Jared thought ruefully. He wasn't fond of the theory that if something was worth having, it was worth hard work and a fight to obtain. Especially where women were concerned, Jared liked things nice and easy, pleasurable, carefree, but exciting.

Studying Tempest's smooth, beautiful face, he thought again of all the rage that had poured from her pale blue eyes. He remembered how she'd sworn at him, that provocative, soft mouth spilling out words no woman should know. He thought of her striding along his bar, her hips swaying, the knife secured in the wide belt around her tiny waist, those full, high breasts firmly outlined, her head tilted proudly, daring them all, him included, to intrude on her again.

This would be no easy mating. Tempest wouldn't lie placidly beneath a man while he had his way; all that wildness and ferocity would explode in passion for the right man. She'd take more than she would give and in so doing, would receive more than she took.

He knew it. He sensed it about her just as he knew he was going to be rich—richer than Midas.

Tempest would be worth his patience. She would be worth whatever he had to give, whatever he had to do to have her.

O, what may man within him hide,
Though angel on the outward side!
—William Shakespeare
Measure for Measure

Tempest poured a shot of whiskey and slid the glass across the plank bar to a dark-eyed, mustachioed young man who wore a pale linen shirt and dark leather vest. He looked better off than most, and she'd already seen the pouch of gold dust he kept inside his shirt. "Two bits," she told him, setting the scale in front of him.

He smiled and poured out the requested amount. "I'll give you ten dollars in gold for a night in your bed," he said in a low, intimate tone. She poured the gold dust into a tin trap and tipped it into the pouch on her belt. By late night, the pouch was always heavy.

Without answering, she walked down the bar to replenish another glass for a sandy-haired boy of about nineteen. "Evening, Miss Tempest."

"Evening."

The first man had downed his whiskey and was calling for more. Her mouth grim, she complied.

"Twenty dollars in gold for an hour." She just looked at him. "Fifty then," he persisted, his eyes narrowing angrily.

"No."

"A hundred, and that's my last offer, but you'll have to allow me to have what I want."

Tempest leaned her forearms on the bar and grinned. "Now, laddie, what would ye be wanting to do?"

Men along the bar were grinning at one another. The customer leaned closer to Tempest and whispered, then straightened again and looked at her, waiting. He moistened his lips licentiously.

She patted the plank bar. "Sit up here, mon, where I can get to it."

He stared at her.

She took her knife from its sheath and patted it in the palm of her left hand. "Meat be better eating when it's roasted over a high fire. We'll start with the little bit ye mentioned."

He turned dark red from his worn collar up. Men guffawed all down the bar. Laughter spread across the crowded casino as her words were passed along from man to man. The man sitting beside the embarrassed patron showed big, white teeth. "Save your breath, mate. You'll have more luck bucking the tiger."

Tempest slipped her hunting knife back into its leather scabbard, picked up the half-full whiskey bottle, and walked along the bar replenishing glasses and collecting gold dust again.

"You tell 'em, ma'am," one called to her, laughing.

"The way I told ye yesterday?"

Laughter rippled along the bar, which was lined two-deep with men waiting for her to pour whiskey or just watching her for the pleasure of it. Most wanted nothing more than that—just the opportunity to see a beautiful woman. Others came to tease and pester her like horseflies.

"I'd give you my whole poke for one kiss, Tempest!"

"Ye've already spent yer poke at the monte table."

Another grinned. "If I refuse to give you the dust, will you come over the bar and take it out of my hide?"

"No dust, no whiskey."

"You ain't got a heart, Tempest!"

"And ye wilna have one if ye donna pay yer two bits!"

Sometimes Jared left his table to come to the bar and watch the fun. He'd stand at the end and rest his forearms on the plank while watching her parrying remarks and passes. The fifty men at the bar who taunted her, angered her with intimate requests, and made her laugh outright at their stupidity and assumptions did not unnerve her half as much as he knew he did.

She saw him standing at the end of the bar, watching her with that catlike smile. She didn't look directly at him, but slowly worked her way down to where he leaned. Reaching under the bar, she produced a bottle of fine red wine from a marked crate that was reserved for him. He never drank whiskey while he was gaming. Later, in his office, he would have a snifter of brandy. Sometimes when he came to talk with her after hours, he drank bourbon. She set a glass down in front of him and poured the wine. She didn't meet his eyes, but could feel his gaze fixed on her, warm, questing, magnetic.

"I heard you added another scalp to your belt a while ago," he remarked in amusement.

She shrugged. She glanced at him then and the impact of his dark, dancing eyes made her heart leap, then sent it racing out of control. She looked away again, her mouth tight.

She couldn't relax, not with the way Jared looked at her. She was far too aware of him as a man—how tall he was, how broad his shoulders were, the way the white linen shirt and dark vest fitted him so perfectly, the way his black hair brushed against his forehead, the way the grooves in his tanned cheeks deepened when he smiled at her, as he was smiling now. The way her own body warmed and pulsed with his closeness . . .

Reaching across, Jared put his hand lightly on her arm to detain her. Warmth radiated outward from where he touched, spreading up her arm and then across, downward into the woman part of her.

"You haven't said much to me in the last week," he said seriously. His hand slid down until it covered hers.

"What would ye have me say?" She withdrew her hand from beneath his, moved away, and bent to return the wine bottle to its crate, thus escaping his disturbing touch and the sensations it caused. When she straightened, she kept her distance.

"What're you afraid of, Tempest?" His brown eyes teased her.

She tipped her chin defiantly. "I'm not afraid."

"Then why do you jump every time I touch you?"

He was looking at her mouth. She leaned forward slightly, eyes glinting as he raised his again. "Because no man has a right to put his hand on me until I tell him so."

His gaze locked with hers. "Fair enough, but my hand wasn't on you in quite the way you mean. If it had been, you would have known."

She straightened sharply. "I've work to do to earn my keep."

"Tempest!"

She heard the imperiousness in his low expletive as she walked away from him. She reached the far end of the bar and dared a glance back at him. He was glowering at her, a muscle working in his cheek. He tipped the wineglass, downing the contents like whiskey, and then slammed it down before turning away to the gaming tables again.

This wasn't the first time she had angered him, she knew. Every time he came close to her and she moved away, she saw temper glittering just beneath the surface of his brown eyes. He wasn't at all like Abram, who had understood exactly how she felt and been patient.

She would have been safer living at her hut and only working for him. As it was now, he was always close, across the room, at the bar, in his office paying her the wage of twenty dollars in gold dust, pacing on the other side of that canvas partition. She felt him looking at her constantly. Often their eyes would meet across the room and hold for the briefest span of time—but long enough for her heart to respond wildly.

Sometimes she would lie there on her cot at night, the candle burning brightly on the small table, and hear Jared move about restlessly. She remembered how pleasant it had been to have Abram there, warm and solid, his comforting arms around her in bed. What would it be like to be held by Jared Stryker? Not *comforting*, she knew.

The closer he came to her, the more tense she felt. It wasn't a secure feeling he aroused. She didn't feel safe with him, didn't feel in control of her simplest emotions and instincts. Her body trembled, her breath caught, her heart raced, and warm, disquieting tingles stimulated her body.

Best to stay away.

He was watching her now; she could feel it. She didn't look across the room at him, but worked the bar, pouring whiskey, retorting to the men's ribald needling.

"Another, Miss Tempest," the young, sandy-haired miner said, gazing at her with soft hazel eyes that reminded her piercingly of Abram.

"Ye've had enough, Casey."

His hand was shaky as he withdrew his small pouch of gold dust. She reached out, pushing it back. "No." She leaned on the bar, her face close to his. "Another whiskey, and ye'll have yer face on the bar and another man's hand on yer gold."

He stared back into her eyes with soft bemusement. "Maybe you're right, but if I stop drinking, I lose my place. I don't want to lose my place." His grin was lopsided.

It seemed to be the established rule among the men that if you weren't drinking, you gave up your position at the bar to someone else. There were always men waiting for a chance to get closer, to get right up to the plank and have Tempest pour for them. Some, like the young miner, drank themselves into a stupor just to stay there and watch her.

"There be other nights, laddie," she said gently, and straightened. "Go home and sleep it off."

"Home's three thousand miles away. Take me a long spell to get there."

"You'd be sobered up by the time you made it," another man remarked from beside him with an insulting laugh.

Casey turned. "Mind your own business," he said, slurring his words.

"Nothing worse than a sloppy drunk, I always say, " the man commented insultingly.

"Who says I'm drunk? You?" Casey demanded belligerently, glaring with bloodshot eyes at the older, bigger man standing next to him.

"Me. You ain't man enough to hold your liquor, boy. Best drink sarsparilla."

Casey's arm swept around in a clumsy swing, sending the empty shot glass flying. The attempted blow was easily blocked and then the dark-haired man caught him by the throat with hard fingers. Gritting his teeth, he squeezed, and Casey's eyes went wide, his mouth gaping open like a grounded fish as he fought to free himself.

"Let him go!" Tempest ordered.

The big man squeezed even harder, uncaring how the younger man clawed wildly at his brawny forearm, his body jerking and thrashing in the fight for air.

"Let him go!"

"Hey, the kid's wetting himself," someone protested, but still the man squeezed, his eyes glowing with feral excitement.

The hazel eyes so much like Abram's glazed, and the boy's movements were slower, less coordinated.

Tempest acted. Her hand flashed to her belt as she lunged. A growl came from her throat, and the attacker's breath hissed in as she pressed the sharp point of her hunting knife into the hollow beneath his right ear and the angle of his jawbone.

"Let him go now, ye son of a bitch," she whispered coldly.

His hands loosened. The boy sagged free, dragging in a rasping lungful of air, then retching violently. The only sound at the bar was the young man vomiting up his six shots of whiskey on the earthen barroom floor.

"I let him go, Tempest," the man said, still frozen, his hands raised conciliatorily. "You're sticking me," he protested weakly.

Her mouth curved in a chilly smile. "Then dunna move."

"Easy, Tempest," Oliver, the other bartender, said from behind her.

She jerked her head. "See that the lad gets home safely."

"Put the knife away."

"When I'm ready."

Oliver gave a piercing whistle and signaled for someone to take the boy out.

"The little bastard deserved it," the man grumbled, Tempest's blade still at his throat.

"Maybe," she said, watching as the boy was half-carried out. Turning her knife, she laid the flat of the cold blade against the side of the man's neck. "But ye needed a lesson in manners." She swung back to her side of the bar and slipped the knife expertly back into its sheath. Then she reached for a bottle and slammed it down in front of the man. "Two bits'll buy ye another shot of whiskey; otherwise, get out."

"Maybe you'd better hightail it, Hugh," someone suggested with a soft laugh.

Hugh looked squarely into Tempest's eyes and grinned. "Fill her up again, ma'am," he told her, and produced his pouch of dust from his vest pocket. Tempest complied. She gripped the bottle tightly so that her hand wouldn't shake, but she felt sick.

"Good thing I don't hold grudges," Hugh remarked. He leaned forward slightly and rested his elbows on the bar. "Tell me true. Would you have stuck *him* if it'd been the other way around?"

"We'll never know," she said coldly, and moved away.

Jared was standing at the far end of the bar. He flipped up the gate and jerked his head to indicate for her to come with him. She handed Oliver the bottle as she passed.

As soon as they were alone in her quarters, Jared turned on her. "What was going on out there with that kid? Who was he?"

"Casey," she answered blankly, her nerves stretched taut from the incident and the look now darkening Jared's face. He was furious, the color seeping up under his skin, but something more than anger was stirring behind the dark, smoldering gaze he fixed on her. She could feel the tension in him as he stood blocking her way, his hands on his hips.

"Casey *who?*"

"How in bleedin' hell do I know! What's it matter?"

"It mattered to you! It mattered so much that you drew your knife on a man to protect that stinking little bastard! Now, who is he?" He grabbed her arm, yanking her close. She tried to pull loose.

"A lad," she hissed.

"Lad, hell! He's been sitting there all week waiting his chance to prove he's a man on you!"

"So how's he different from any other mon here?" she challenged derisively, glaring into his black eyes, anger firing her as well. "And that's why ye put me behind yer bar, remember? To bring the bastards in, line 'em up like dumb beasts, fill 'em up with whiskey, and then turn 'em over to ye so ye con clean out their pockets!"

Jared was breathing through gritted teeth.

"What would ye've had me do? Stand there while he was choked to death?"

"Oliver would've handled it!"

"Oliver had one hand up his nose and the other down his pants!"

He let her go abruptly. "You've got the mouth of a pig, you know that?"

His condemnation hurt more than a slap across the face. She tilted up her chin. "But then ye dinna hire me to be a lady, did ye?"

"That's for damn sure! You're cold enough to slit a man's throat without a second thought, aren't you? You act like a damn savage!"

Tempest froze inside. She just looked up at him for a blank moment, then turned slowly away. Silence filled the quarters. Her hands curled into tight fists and she clenched her teeth, her lips pressed together.

"You're shaking."

She felt Jared's firm hands on her shoulders and cringed away. "This be my side. Get out."

"You're forgetting where you are," he said, angry again. When he touched her again, his hands were hard, unyielding, hurting her. He forced her to turn around. "You look at me."

She kept her head down. He muttered an angry expletive and forced her chin up. Suddenly all the anger left him. "You're crying!"

She jerked her chin away and shrugged his hands off in a violent gesture. "Leave me be."

"You're not quite as hard and cold as you pretend, are you? You couldn't have done it. If it had come right down to it, you'd have lost your nerve for it."

"Dunna ye believe that, mon. I could've done it right enough." Her mouth trembled.

Jared smiled slightly. "Whatever you say," he murmured. He stepped in front of her and cupped his hands around her face. "Whatever you say," he whispered, his thumbs stroking her high cheekbones as he watched how her eyes went wide. He bent his head, brushing his mouth gently against hers. Her eyes closed slowly and then opened as he raised his head. He studied her face, and then put one arm firmly around her waist, pulling her body against his own while with the other hand he cupped the back of her head. His mouth descended again.

Tempest felt a sudden plunging sensation in her stomach, just as she once had when she'd leaped off a cliff and sailed downward toward a deep pool at the base of a mountain waterfall. She was going in over her head.

Jared lifted his mouth from hers, arching her even closer. He caught hold of her long braid, pulling her head back so that his hot breath was against her throat, traveling up along her throbbing pulse. "Tempest," he growled in a deeper, husky voice. She gasped, clutching at him, drowning from the sensations swirling in her body. "That's it," he whispered harshly. "That's it . . ."

He took her mouth again fiercely, pressing, taking. Cold shock washed through Tempest's body just as if she had finally made the full, frightening descent and hit the icy mountain pool. The water closed over her and she clawed frantically for the surface. She wrenched herself free of Jared's arms and stepped back quickly out of his reach.

"What d'ye think ye're doin'?" she cried between panting breaths.

Jared's chest rose and fell with his own labored breathing. His face was flushed, his eyes black and faintly glazed. "Jesus," he swore. *"Kissing you!"* Explaining was the last thing he had in mind.

"Putting your tongue in my mouth? Yer bloody mad!"

He was sharply, painfully aroused and moved restlessly, reaching for her. She jumped back, startled. He let out his breath and swore softly. "Didn't that husband of yours ever kiss you?"

"Aye, but not the way you did," she said from the other side of the room. She watched him warily as he rested his hands on his hips and breathed in a more controlled way. Her eyes lowered slowly, taking full notice of his arousal. When she met his gaze again, he smiled at her.

"Maybe he just didn't know any better," he suggested. "I learned how to kiss like that from a Parisian courtesan."

"I dunna care how ye learned, ye'll not be doin' it to me!"

His smile broadened. "Not tonight, apparently." He rubbed the back of his neck and looked at her from beneath lowered brows. "Tempest McClaren Walker, you're a woman of great potential. But right now, I need a good, stiff drink."

As soon as he was gone, Tempest sank down onto the stool by the table where the candle flickered. She was shaking violently.

Raucous laughter came from the bar. Someone was pounding on the planks and shouting. The low rumbling roar of an ocean of voices seemed to fill every space around her.

She pressed her hands to her ears. Her heart finally slowed to normal and she was able to breathe again.

> We secure our friends not by accepting favors
> but by doing them.
> —Thucydides

If Tempest had avoided him before, she was doubly cautious now, Jared realized with increasing frustration. Ever since he'd kissed her, she had kept a wary eye on him whenever he came near her. She didn't even accept the small pouch of gold dust from his hand when she could avoid doing so.

At first her reticence had amused him. But then he'd realized that it was a faint repugnance that glimmered in her eyes—not fear. That made him angry, for he had felt her body's response when he had held her and kissed her. He had heard her slight, indrawn breath, felt the soft trembling and the pulsing movement of her female muscles, heard her soft moan when his mouth took hers.

She had wanted him. Maybe she didn't understand her own body's messages where he was concerned. She must not have been aroused before, and certainly not by her farmer husband who knew nothing about how to kiss a woman passionately. She didn't know what to expect of real lovemaking, so she was having none of it at all!

Jared wondered if Abram Walker had been the type to fumble for a woman in the dark and have a swift release. Stupid bastard. Yet the idea of being the one to awaken Tempest wasn't unpleasant. In fact, it was unbearably exciting.

He tried to concentrate on his cards, but couldn't. If a simple kiss could make her fire up the way she had, how much more responsive would she become when he took more adventurous liberties?

He thought of Alicia. He thought of the Parisian courtesan. He thought about teaching Tempest everything those two libertines had taught him when he was Tempest's tender age.

He lost the hand of poker.

Disgusted with his level of concentration, he threw in his

cards, paid out the gold dust, and signaled for Edwards to take his deal. He wandered through the casino like a caged lion, checking monte tables, poker games, and blackjack, issuing curt orders.

The laughter from the bar grated on his nerves. He watched a new dealer working a table and didn't have to glance across to know that the men were vying for Tempest's attention. Young men, many of them good-looking, some well educated, some with money to spend, all with more time than he had. Some of them came in and spent the entire night leaning on that damn bar just to be near her.

He walked across to take his own place there. Tempest was wearing a plain brown skirt and a soft, doeskin shirt belted at the waist, but she would look beautiful even in sackcloth.

Watching her, he saw that she was learning how to play the men along. Four weeks behind his bar had taught her how to let the bawdy remarks and propositions slide off her back like water off a duck's feathers. She even smiled, though with more derision than friendliness.

He studied the men. Most were young, barely in their twenties, few much older than that. California was a young territory.

More than half the men standing at the bar were in love with her, at least for tonight. They competed for her attention as she walked back and forth, pouring whiskey. Every other young girl of her age would have died to have such admiration, yet she seemed to hate it.

Tempest was an immeasurable boon to his business. She brought men in by the hundreds, and when they gave up on her, they went to the gaming tables to ease their rejection. He was getting rich off them.

But that didn't mean he liked to share her with any one of them. He hadn't realized he would feel that way. He wanted her every bit as much as any one of these men standing here at the bar beside him did; he wanted her more.

His temper darkened as he realized she was ignoring him again. It wasn't the first time she had left him to stew in his own juices, damn her. He nodded an order to Oliver, who stepped close to her and took the whiskey bottle from her hand. She glanced back over her shoulder with angry blue eyes. Without enthusiasm, she came toward him. The closer she came, the harder his heart pounded; he remembered the feel of her in his arms and felt himself becoming aroused. How many other men lining this damn bar were standing there with erections?

Damn witch! What was she doing to him?

Tempest arched one eyebrow at him when she stopped at the end of the bar. She bent over, and he looked down the straight line of her back to the gentle curve of her buttocks. Sweat broke out on his skin. She straightened again, put a glass on the bar by his right hand, and poured his red wine without a single word.

She talked to the other men—why in hell couldn't she talk to him? Wasn't he keeping her out of a mud hut, seeing that she ate something more than roots and acorns, making sure she was warm and protected?

She put the bottle back. He looked deeply into her blue eyes, searching for and failing to find an expression from which he could take some hope. He wanted to reach across and shake her violently. He wanted to drag her back into the privacy of his quarters and throw her down on his bed.

"Will that be all, mon?"

"Talk to me," he whispered hoarsely, angry.

"About what?"

"How about starting with what happened between us last week? I'm getting damn tired of your cold-shoulder treatment." He stared at her. He'd never seen eyes as blue as hers: wide, pale, and clear, fringed by thick heavy black lashes. Sometimes they were the only part of her he could see. They pulled him. If they were mirrors to her soul, she didn't have one.

Her gaze flickered and a faint, troubled frown crossed her brow.

She's remembering the other night too, he thought, satisfied. Whether she wants to or not, she's thinking about that kiss. His mouth felt dry.

"What's a Persian curtsand?"

His heavy mood lifted. "You mean a *Parisian courtesan?*"

"Whatever," she bit out.

"A French whore."

Her face cleared in understanding.

He grinned. "What did you think it was?"

"No telling." She shrugged.

"Hey, Stryker! Don't keep Tempest to yourself!" a miner yelled down the bar.

"Privilege of the house." Jared grinned at them, trying not to show how much they grated on him. Ignoring them, he leaned forward and smiled into her wary gaze. "How long have you been wanting to ask me what a Parisian courtesan was?" he teased her gently.

She lifted one shoulder in a defiant gesture. "I wouldna ken such things."

With another accent and better clothing, she'd have passed as a Bostonian schoolmarm, he thought in amusement. "Would you like to know? You've only to ask and I'll tell you whatever you want." He winked.

Her blue eyes flashed. "I learned enough."

"And never had any fun or pleasure from it, if I could hazard a guess," he retorted succinctly.

"She's blushing," some fool miner said loudly enough to draw more unwelcome attention. The men at the bar weren't the only ones amazed by this phenomenon. Tempest glared at Jared fiercely.

"Did I finally strike a nerve?" he asked, studying her face. She looked away. "Don't let them bother you," he murmured roughly.

"Are ye going to drink it or not?" she demanded, glancing at his wine pointedly.

"Don't change the subject."

"Hey, Jared! Ol' Oliver here pours right fair enough, but he ain't much to look at!"

Men laughed, Oliver himself among them. Jared's impatience and irritation grew. This was hardly the time or place to try for an intimate conversation. Tempest was restless, embarrassed, and angry, and he was too tense. Later would be better. He nodded for her to go on back to work. The men cheered, slamming shot glasses on the plank bar for her to refill. She sloshed liquor into them and glared at each man before passing on to the next.

Tempest leaned far forward to stroke one bearded miner's bewhiskered cheek while saying something to him in a low voice. Jared watched as the miner leaned toward her, and she yanked hard on the tip of his beard, drawing a yelp of surprised pain while others laughed uproariously. She straightened and rubbed her fingers together beneath the miner's nose and waited for him to produce his gold pouch before she poured.

Jared noticed the buckskin moccasins she wore when she leaned forward. They were the kind that fitted the calf and laced up to the knee. She should have high-buttoned shoes or pretty leather slippers, he thought in disgust.

A young, dark-haired man took a place next to Jared. "What's up, Missouri?" Jared asked after taking a sip of wine.

"There's a gent at Scotty's table."

"Cheating?" Jared had watched Missouri cheat at his own table for half a dozen hands, then took him aside and confronted him. He could take a job watching over the gaming tables, spotting other skilled cheaters, or he could find himself hurting. Missouri had taken the job. Over the past week, he'd uncovered no less than half a dozen sharkers.

"No, he's no cheat, just a damn fool."

"Then what's the problem?" Jared smiled.

"He's emptied his pockets already and is writing notes on his inventory."

"So?" Jared set his glass down and glanced at Missouri impatiently.

"You don't mind?"

"Merchandise can be sold."

"All right." Missouri smiled, his gray eyes malicious. "It's no skin off my nose if you want to be stuck with a shipment of mosquito netting and Panama hats."

Jared swore. "Why didn't you say so right off?"

By the time Jared reached Scotty's table, Levinson had stacked half a dozen notes in the pot to raise the bet higher and regain his lost poke. Scotty was pulling in the mound of winnings from Levinson and four others across the table. Jared put a hard hand on his shoulder. "What do you think you're doing?" he growled, and reached down to pick up several of the notes Levinson had passed over.

Levinson himself was a thin young man with watery blue eyes, a full mouth, and a dapper figure. His face was pale, lined, and sweating profusely as he eyed Jared.

"I'd like to talk with you in my office, Mr. Levinson," Jared said politely. "If you'll come this way." He gestured. Then, to Scotty, he said, "You take anything but gold dust and I'll have it out of your ass. Got that?"

"Yes, sir," Scotty said.

When Jared and Levinson were in his private office, Jared sat down behind the plank table and leaned back to look at the young merchant. Scotty had told him what the bets were before he'd left, and Jared tapped the notes in the palm of his hand grimly.

"These aren't worth the paper they're written on, let alone

enough to cover a hundred dollars in gold to raise and two more hundred-dollar bets to call."

Levinson cleared his throat nervously. "I beg to differ with you, Mr. Stryker—"

Jared cut him off. "Beg to differ all you want, but you'll make those bets good or take the consequences."

"Consequences?"

Jared just looked at him coldly.

"But that's—that's almost everything, Mr. Stryker. I swear to you."

Jared crumpled the notes and tossed them on the table in disgust. "You take me for a fool, Levinson, and that's something that makes me extremely angry."

Sweat broke out on the young merchant's face.

Jared leaned forward, making a tent of his fingers. "No one loses an entire poke and a shipment of valuable merchandise in less than half an hour unless there's a reason for it." He flicked the crumpled papers. "Mosquito netting and Panama hats," he said in cold derision. "We both know you were unloading this crap on me, don't we, Mr. Levinson?"

Levinson turned a dark, guilty red. He scratched his head, then licked his lips. Jared let him sweat.

"I—I didn't know what else to do, sir," Levinson whined. "I—I admit I brought all the wrong things to sell out here, but that's not entirely my fault. I was told by someone who said he'd been here that California had a tropical climate and that there were women out here wanting the things our eastern ladies have as a matter of course."

"As far as I know, no eastern lady wears Panama hats or uses mosquito netting," Jared retorted angrily.

"But I can't afford to keep storing my shipments at Mr. Brannan's prices, and he doesn't want the shipment in place of payment, so I had to do something with the crates."

"You could have burned the lot," Jared told him frankly.

Levinson looked sick. "But, sir, those crates have the finest watered silks, sateens, cambrics, and percalines. The pearl buttons came from France and I imported the lace from Ireland. Oh, sir, I—I just couldn't burn all those beautiful materials!"

Cloth, pearl buttons, lace? "What in hell are you babbling about, Levinson? You wrote down—"

Levinson picked up the notes, spreading them out with shaking fingers. "See, here is the silk. This one is for the percalines—bolts of red and green and blue and yellow, even purples. They'd fetch a fine price if California were civilized. But there are no ladies in this territory. Just Indians, Mexicans, and whores from Chile! That's not my fault, sir."

Jared had a vision of Tempest in fine gowns made from Levinson's stock. He leaned back slowly in his chair. Levinson rattled on with frantic appeals for mercy and Jared, distracted, didn't stop him. Finally, Jared raised his hand.

"All right. We'll call it square under one condition."

"What?"

"You don't come back unless you have gold dust. Fair enough?"

"Yes, sir." Levinson exhaled audibly, nodding vigorously. Color came back into his face.

Jared saw him out and then poured himself a brandy. A faint smile played on his mouth. Fate had just delivered into his hands a lure that might just turn the head of a half-breed Indian girl who'd never known anything better than pioneer rags and buckskin.

Let each man exercise the art he knows.
                                        —Aristophanes

Jared hired an Indian seamstress who had worked for Sutter's European wife, who had arrived and, with Sutter, was now ensconced at Hock Farm. Given instructions and drawings, the squaw was able to recreate the effect Jared wanted and made several beautiful gowns that would have been fashionable in Charleston when Jared left several years before. One was an exact replica of a gown Geneva Stafford had worn to tea at the White Oaks plantation. The sight had fixed itself firmly in his memory.

However, when Jared proudly presented his generous gifts to Tempest, she thanked him grimly and hung them on the room divider, where they remained for two days. Somehow they became an even thicker barrier between them, rather than the hoped-for entrance to her affections.

Finally Jared confronted her, asking her to wear one. She flatly refused.

"Why won't you try one on?" he demanded hotly, seeing nothing wrong with the gift.

"Ye meant well, mon, and I thank ye, but dunna expect me to wear anything that bares my chest. I've trouble enough already."

Jared was taken aback. So it was her modesty at stake. All she needed was a quick lesson in fashion. "The gowns won't bare anything. Everything that needs to be hidden will be, I guarantee," he said, and grinned.

She raised one derisive eyebrow in disbelief.

"Granted, the necklines are lower than what you're used to," he agreed, running a finger along the line of one dress, "but believe me, the greatest ladies in the land wear dresses exactly like these." Or did two years ago, he thought.

She laughed.

"Tempest, I know what I'm talking about. Fashion merely

emphasizes certain . . . parts of the female form. One year, for instance, it's the shoulders."

"This year, 'tis breasts and arse," she put in with smooth disdain, flicking the folds of the back of the skirt.

"These are an improvement over the rags you've been wearing, don't you think?" He was annoyed with her stubbornness. There was a decided mule-headedness to her that was far from conducive to being a lady, but then she was no lady, after all.

"What I wear covers what I have," she retorted.

"What you have," he snarled, looking at her breasts beneath the buckskin shirt, "will be amply covered by any one of these gowns." He jerked his head toward the rainbow of colors displayed against the drab canvas.

She tilted her head in a gesture he already understood too clearly: her heels were dug in right to the ankles. "Mon, ye're trying to tell me that ladies bare their breasts and make their arses look like the side of a frontier fort, and ye expect me to believe it. I ken the difference between gold dust and horse manure, and ye're trying to give me a sack full."

He sighed. "I swear it's true. Women dress like this in the east."

Her mouth tightened. "Jared, if I wore one of those," she waved her hand at the dresses contemptuously, "and bent to pour whiskey, I'd fall right out the front."

"No you wouldn't," he told her, but the idea was interesting—providing it happened before him and no one else. She said nothing, and he leaned back against the table, dangling one foot as he surveyed her. "What would it take to get you to try one on and find out?"

"Why're ye so determined?"

"Because I know how you'll look in them. Because, right now, you look—well, you could look like a lady."

Her blue eyes darkened with anger. It was what he didn't say that she understood quite clearly.

His own temper rose sharply. "I'll pay you a hundred dollars just to put one on and find out how it looks."

Something flickered in her blue eyes. Surprise? Hurt? He wasn't sure which, but he knew he'd made a grievous mistake. "Tempest, forget it," he began apologetically.

"Put your bloody gold on the table."

"Look, I said—"

"On the table."

Her tone riled him. "All right!" He stood and walked past

her into his side of the quarters and took up a pouch of gold from his trunk. He came back and slammed it on her small table, then sat down beside it, crossing his arms and dangling one leg casually as he called her bluff. For, surely, that's what it was. "It's all I have at the moment. The rest is at the assayer's vault."

A muscle jerked in her cheek as she met his eyes. Her own eyes grew overbright as she unlaced the top of her buckskin shirt and yanked it off, flinging it onto the cot.

Jared was startled. Somehow, he hadn't really expected her to go through with it. She was angry and so was he, but he hadn't meant to degrade her. "That's enough, Tempest," he told her softly, straightening.

"'Tis what ye wanted, isn't it? 'Tis what ye've always wanted." She reached behind her to unbutton the faded brown skirt. "Ye've been just dickering yer price—"

"Tempest, don't." He reached for her shirt, intending to hand it to her.

She dropped the skirt to the floor.

"Jesus," he choked, his breath cut off. The buckskin shirt slipped from his fingers as he stared at her. "Don't you ever wear anything underneath?" he gasped.

She reached for a blue satin gown with puffed sleeves and French lace trim around the neckline and cuffs. He stared at the long, sleek, curved lines of her body, the way her full, perfect breasts rose as she raised her arms. Then the heavy gown shimmied down over her, hiding the treasures he had suspected but never fully realized.

"I canna do the buttons," she told him, and he saw how her mouth trembled. "Ye'll have to do them for me." She turned her back to him, holding the front of the dress up against her.

He had known she would need help dressing when he had had the gowns made, had thought about what it would be like to do this service for her. Now he felt self-conscious. "You don't have to wear them if you don't want to."

Her head jerked up. "Ye paid the price to see me in one."

Why should he feel like such a bastard for wanting to dress her in fine clothes? He stepped close, his fingers grazing the silken, pale-brown skin. She tensed. He looked down her proud back and, unable to stop himself, slipped his hands inside the gown and rested them on her tiny waist. He could feel how taut she was and the faint quiver of her body at his touch.

"You'll see that I'm right, Tempest," he whispered softly.

He hadn't meant to hurt her. It took him a long time to do up the tiny pearl buttons, and by the time he had accomplished the task, the front seam of his own tailored pants was stretched taut.

He rested his hands on her shoulders, lowering his mouth to the gentle curve of her neck. She tasted good, and he could feel her wild pulse as he brushed his lips back and forth. He wanted to bring his hands around in front and fill them with her breasts.

"Turn around and let me see how you look," he murmured huskily.

She turned slowly.

His eyes lowered to the pale, soft mounds of quivering flesh that swelled above the blue satin and delicate lace. "Beautiful," he whispered, and raised his gaze. Her breathing was heightened and he saw the dark, velvety look in her eyes.

"I dinna think ye should look on me that way," she said shakily.

"Why not?"

"It makes me . . . feel strange."

"You want me."

Her chin tipped haughtily.

His smile teased. "I can see, Tempest."

She raised her hand and pressed it against the tantalizing cleavage. "I ken what ye con see."

"Just enough to whet my appetite for more and only what a great lady would dare show." He reached out slowly and stroked her cheek, sliding his hand into her rich, soft, black hair so that he could explore the small, sensitive, shell-shaped ear with his thumb. He felt her trembling. "You're even more beautiful than I expected. You're more beautiful than any woman I've ever known." He meant it. "But what I meant was the way you're breathing, how your eyes look so soft and dark, how you're shaking now when I touch you like this." His fingertips caressed the slender column of her throat, tracing the rapid, pounding pulse downward until his hand covered hers over her breasts.

She gasped softly and moved back. He let her go, watching how her hand dropped and spread over her stomach in a telling gesture.

"Desire, Tempest. That's what you're feeling," he said huskily. "You feel you can't get enough air into your lungs. Your heart pounds. Blood rushes hot in your body until your skin feels flushed with the warmth of it. You feel tense and restless and there's an ache in the pit of your stomach—and lower. It becomes a pain after a while." He spoke softly, everything he was describing happening to him as he came to stand right in front of her again.

"It feels good, doesn't it?" he murmured hoarsely. *"Exciting..."* Taking a bold chance, he took her hand and spread it against the front of his pants. Her lips parted. "I hurt with wanting you," he said frankly. He expected her to pull her hand away, but she didn't.

"Abram used to go to the barn."

He stared at her, and then comprehension jolted him. He let go of her hand and stepped back. "Jesus Christ! You mean every time your husband wanted you, you sent him out to the barn to take care of it for himself? He must have been a fool!"

"He was kind!"

"Kind, hell! He was out of his mind! You belonged to him, for God's sake. You said he bought you from your father— that gave him the right to do anything he wanted."

"He didna see it that way."

"Obviously not." Another thought struck him. "Didn't he ever consummate..."

"Yes. When I was ready."

He laughed harshly. "And how'd the poor guy know when that was?"

"I told him."

He stopped laughing. Looking down at her, a wave of heat shot through him. "You told him? Just like that?"

Her mouth tightened fractionally. "Yes."

"And what then?" he asked. The fact that she was so hesitant and ignorant about sex indicated that the man must have made it very unpleasant.

"He rolled me onto my back and got on top."

Jared let out a shocked breath. "I didn't mean..." He rubbed the back of his neck. "Was he rough? Did he hurt you?"

"A little, the first time. He wanted to be gentle. Usually he was very quick."

"I'll bet. He was probably ready to explode by that time." He leaned against the table again, surveying her grimly. "What'd you both do during the evenings before he took you to bed? Before you ... told him he could make love to you?"

"He read to me from his Bible and we talked," she answered, smiling slightly.

His mouth fell open. Then he let out a sharp breath and stood. "Now I'm beginning to understand," he said grimly. He raked a hand through his hair and stood, arms akimbo, glaring at nothing.

Jared knew the type exactly. Abram Walker had probably been a stiff-necked, churchgoing Protestant farmer who came to California for good bottom land. The fact that the man had bought Tempest from her father indicated a certain lustful tendency, however, Jared thought in cynical disdain. But he was sure Walker had prayed hard to overcome his natural urges. When Tempest had told him to take her, Walker had undoubtedly given in, gotten the deed over with as quickly as possible, then sat in judgment on her for tempting him like a she-devil. Sex had only one purpose to such a man.

"He wanted children from you, didn't he?" he asked flatly.

"Yes." Tempest turned away.

"Ah, yes. 'And ye shall be fruitful and multiply,'" he quoted dryly.

Tempest glanced at him in surprise. "Ye've read the Good Book."

"Some." He laughed harshly. *"Enough."*

"Will ye read to me?" she asked, stepping toward him.

He looked at her sharply. "No!"

"Why not?"

"Because I happen to believe that people were made to *enjoy* each other without guilt or shame."

"God made people."

Jared let out a sharp, derisive laugh. "Your husband really drilled it all into you, didn't he?"

"Dunna say a word against him!" she said fiercely.

Her defense of such a man snapped Jared's tenuous control. "This is what people were meant to do together," he snarled, yanking her into his arms and kissing her with ruthless purpose. One arm looped tightly around her waist, arching her into him, while his other hand held her head still as he plundered her mouth with his tongue. She fought for a few moments, and then he felt how her body melted into the hard angles of his. He went on kissing her, savoring the honeyed sweetness of her mouth, the soft warmth of her lips, because he couldn't stop.

He arched her back over his arm, his mouth leaving hers to course down to the firm mounds that rose and fell heavily before his rapt gaze. He tasted her luscious flesh, pulling at the shoulders of the gown to ease it lower still. His goal was just out of sight; he slid his fingers into the bodice and lifted her breasts free, lowering his open mouth to the dark-rose nub. Her body jerked convulsively as he found his goal and drew on her tender flesh, hearing her soft cry.

He raised his head after a moment. "This is what life's all about," he whispered hoarsely, drawing her back toward him as he moved to brace himself against the table. He wanted to rip her dress off, but it was the only fine thing she had to her name and he couldn't do that to her.

Spreading his legs, he brought her between them, kissing her with an ardor he couldn't dampen. She tasted so good, felt so alive and warm, so . . . female. He filled his hands, his mouth, his senses. He could hear the soft, gasping sounds she made, and each one sent his pulse higher, hardened his body even more.

"This is just the beginning," he said hoarsely, drawing a portion of her voluminous skirt up enough to get his hand underneath. He stroked her bare hip, each time lowering his hand a little and then caressing the smooth, firm skin of the front of her thigh. "Just the beginning," he whispered, sliding his hand up, just brushing his fingers over her before spreading his hand on her abdomen.

Her eyes were half-closed, dazed, her lips parted with soft, quick breaths.

His hand slid down slowly and he could feel her body trembling violently. He stroked tormentingly while kissing her eyes, her temples, the corner of her mouth. She sought his lips then, but he evaded her, forcing her to take some action.

"This is what you're supposed to feel," he murmured against the corner of her mouth while he clasped her close, his hand seeking and finding her womanhood. "Oh, Tempest . . ." He began the gentle stroking that Alicia had taught him, the slow, silken, gliding touches that made a woman's body shudder as Tempest's was shuddering now. She moaned against his neck.

He could feel sweat breaking out hot on his skin, and battened down his own desires in order to show her what he wanted her to know. "It builds inside you," he whispered against her ear, keeping her locked against him. "You feel hot all over and heavy and tense. There's an ache inside you, isn't there? Right here," he said with a groan, and she drew in a slow, agonized breath, her hips coming forward. He watched her eyes close and her head fall back, revealing the pounding vein in her throat.

"It's almost pain now, isn't it? But in a minute, it's going to feel so good," he whispered roughly, drawing the edge of his teeth along her neck. "And it'll feel even better when I'm in you..."

Someone ran up just outside the flap. Jared tensed for an intrusion. "Jared! We've got big trouble!"

Tempest's body stiffened at the sound of Oliver's voice, and Jared uttered a short word beneath his breath.

"Get lost!" Jared ordered.

"There's trouble—"

"Handle it yourself, dammit. I'm busy!" Jared ground out tersely, his hands still full of Tempest. She was trying to free herself but he yanked her closer, his mouth against her ear. "Stay still. He'll go away."

"You don't understand, Jared," Oliver persisted, his agitation clear in his voice.

"Just give me a few minutes, will you?" That's all it would take. One more minute.

"There's fire down the hill and the wind's blowing this way!"

Come, give us a taste of your quality.
—William Shakespeare
Hamlet

Jared cursed and put Tempest away from him. He went to the partition and jerked back the flap.

Tempest sagged heavily against the table, a shaking hand pressed hard against her heaving breasts. Her skirt hem shimmered down around her ankles again, but her body coursed with new, frightening life. Hot quivering sensations flooded her veins and the hard ache in her lower abdomen remained. What was happening to her?

Jared returned, letting the canvas flap slap into place again. Pulling her into his arms, he kissed her fiercely. He dragged his mouth away from hers, nudging her so he had access to the throbbing pulse in her throat. "Get some things together," he said huskily. "Just in case." His hands moved down over her hips, rubbing sinuously. "God, what a time for a fire *outside* when I've got one raging in my belly," he groaned. He raised his head. Cupping her face, he kissed her gently. "We'll finish this later."

When he went out again, she rearranged her dress and tried to think. Men were shouting wildly in the casino, Jared's voice audible above the rest, giving commands. She went to the flap and stepped around it to see what was happening. Men were scrambling for tables and chairs, hauling them out of the casino. Oliver was slamming whiskey bottles on the bar while another man transferred them into wooden crates.

Tempest pressed through the crowd. Outside, chaos reigned. Men were running in every direction, panic-stricken. She saw the ominous flicker of firelight down the hill. Men lunged past her out of Jared's casino, shouting, cursing, yelling at one another. The flames grew even as she watched, devouring tents and shanties and cabins, and the acrid smell of smoke filled her nostrils as the terrifying orange-red glow traveled up the hill. She could hear its roar even above the shouting men as they tried desperately to save whatever they could before the inferno came nearer.

Her throat was parched and her heart pounded in heavy, body-shaking strokes. Her feet seemed rooted in the mucky ground, holding her paralyzed.

"Why in damnation doesn't it rain now when we need it?" someone screamed above the din.

Across the street, several men were yanking up the stakes on a ragged canvas tent, trying to get it down before the fire was upon them. Down the hill a man was screaming "My gold!" wildly as his shanty was engulfed in flames.

Mud splattered the blue satin as Tempest stood in the street. Men bumped her, jostling her from side to side.

"Get clear of the fire!"

"Head for the fort!"

"Head for the river! Run for the river!"

"Get the whiskey!" Jared roared, his voice carrying above them all. He hefted a crate from the bar and headed across toward her. She stared back at him, her mouth agape as she gasped for breath. She couldn't breathe. "Come on, damn it! Move!" Jared railed at his men. "Get what you can out into the street and wet it down! Hurry!"

"We haven't got any more water!"

"Then get it from the bathhouse!"

"They're using that to save the tents up—"

"To hell with the tents! We've got to save the whiskey. Take what we need if you have to kill someone to get it! Just get the water down here fast! Now, *move!*"

Oliver, Missouri, and half a dozen other men ran up the hill.

"Tempest! Help me!" Jared shouted, grabbing up a bucket and sloshing water over the pile of tables, chairs, and crates of whiskey while tents burned on the hillside below.

Someone knocked against her, jarring her from her panic. Jared shouted at her again, and she responded instinctively to the note of authority. She took up a bucket of water and swung it.

A booming voice rose from down the hill. *"Komma ut! Get out! F ge sig i väg! Run for it! Leave it!"*

Tempest saw a giant of a man standing in the middle of the muddy street just below them, gesturing violently for the men down the hill to run, his blond hair whipping about his face. She looked at Jared, frightened, wanting to run like everyone else, but he was intent on saving what was his.

Someone was screaming in pain and Tempest looked around again to see the big man sprinting down toward another whose shirt was on fire. Throwing him to the ground, he rolled him and then dragged him up, pulling him along until he finally paused long enough to sling him up over his broad shoulder.

"Goddamn it! Where's the water?" Jared was roaring. "Hurry up!"

Oliver and Missouri ran toward them shakily, a bucket in each hand. Others were following.

"We need it here!" someone shouted and was ignored as the water cascaded over plank poker tables, crates of rotgut whiskey, and oak chairs.

The towering flames were scarcely a hundred yards away. Tempest saw another half a dozen tents and shanties engulfed, more men running, some of them screaming. She was shoved from side to side as men scrambled and stumbled past her, carrying saddlebags, carpetbags, clanging mining gear, jouncing canvas sacks, whatever they could salvage and carry.

Then she suddenly remembered her own precious few possessions.

Fifty yards away and devouring everything in its path, the hungry fire roared against the star-studded sky. Tempest ran.

"Tempest!" Jared hollered, diving for her. She slipped past him into the casino, racing for the canvas flap into her sleeping quarters. Jared grabbed her from behind, jarring her to an abrupt halt. She fought.

"No!"

"What're you doing? You're crazy!" he shouted, yanking her around and dragging her back. She fought free but he grabbed at her again.

"What're you doing?"

"I've got to get them! I've got to get them!" she screamed, twisting and turning in his arms, but he wouldn't let go this time.

"There's more where they came from! We've got to get out!"

"They're all I have!" she cried. *"Let go!"* Tempest swung her arm in a wide, arcing blow and shifted her weight expertly. Jared lost his balance just as she hit him. She had run scarcely

a few feet before he caught her again, and this time slapped
her once, hard. She sagged, stunned by the blow, and he swung
her up into his arms.

As they reached the sweet night air that was rapidly growing
rancid with smoke, her head cleared. *"No!"* Twisting against
him, she fought his firm hold. He swore.

"What's the matter with you?"

She broke loose, flailing violently when he grabbed her
again. He dug his fingers into her shoulders and shook her
hard. *"Stop it!"* When she still fought him, he caught her by
the hair and yanked her head back. "I don't want to hit you
again, damn it. *Tempest!"*

"Vat iz matter with flicka?" a gravelly, accented voice asked
from behind him. Anger and concern were mingled in the
question. Jared glanced back and saw a tall, muscular man in
seaman's clothing standing with arms akimbo and looking at
him with narrowed eyes. Jared had all he could handle hanging
onto Tempest as she fought wildly against him.

"I just gave her some new gowns—" he started to explain,
seeing that the Swede was getting ready to intercede in Tempest's behalf.

"Bloody hell," she screamed at him. "I dunna care about
them! I want my *saddlebag!"* she cried, sobbing with unrestrained frustration and fury. "My saddlebag and pelt! In the
back. *In the back!"* she screamed at the big blond man, who
was looking at her intently. He turned away.

Jared stared down at her, his face darkening ominously.

"He's going in..." Missouri said. "That dumb Swede's
going in there! Hey, *it's going.* Are you mad?" he shouted.
One side of the canvas casino began to smolder with the intense
heat of the fire in the shanty next door. Within moments, it
was bursting into a circle of spreading flame that hungrily ate
away at the south wall.

"Oh, nooo..." Tempest moaned, staring at the flames as
they went up the side of the huge tent, realizing that the man
was still inside.

Jared's fingers dug into her arms brutally, drawing a sharp
gasp of pain from her parted lips. She looked up at him wide-
eyed. "Your frigging *saddlebag?"* he grated. Furious, he thrust
her violently away from him.

Missouri was intently watching the huge tent. He laughed
exuberantly. "By God, *he's going to make it!"*

Tempest's head swung around and she saw the big blond

man sprinting across the last open space inside the big tent, her burning saddlebag clutched in his hand. She ran toward him in spite of Jared's shouted command to stop. The Swede dove through the entrance into the street, looking straight at her.

"Let me have it!" she cried, but he caught her roughly around the waist and hustled her a safe distance back from the inferno now caving in the top of Jared's casino.

Jared watched it go, his face a grim mask of anger. He looked at Tempest as she straightened from the Swede's strong hold and grasped her saddlebag.

"Let me have it!" she cried, yanking it from the Swede's hand and dropping it to the muddy street. She went down on her hands and knees to pound at the burning portion with her bare hands in her desperation to save it, then slapped mud on the smoldering leather.

When she was sure it was saved, she sat back on her heels, panting. She curled her fingers into the flap and dragged it closer, picking it up, uncaring of the mud. She spread her hands on the leather, feeling the comforting, hard, square edges of the big book inside. Lifting it, she clasped it to her chest and started to stand.

The big blond man bent to help her. She felt his hand, firm and warm, beneath her arm. Looking up at him, she felt a rush of tears, and gave him a watery smile as she gained her feet. "Thank ye. Who be ye, mon?"

"Bjorn Lindahl." His blue eyes gazed into hers intently, his hand still firmly at her elbow. She swayed and his hand tightened without hurting. She held the saddlebag against her breasts as she placed her other hand against his chest to brace herself for a moment. She could feel the hard, fast pounding of his heart and the rise and fall of his chest as he regained his breath from the run.

"Forlát, flicka," he said in a low-pitched, rough voice that was surprisingly gentle. He pressed a calloused hand over hers as it lay against him as though he meant to hold it here. "I am sorry. I did not find pelt. No time—everything was going." Two creases deepened in his bronzed face and his eyes crinkled as he smiled.

Tempest relaxed, feeling an uncharacteristic desire to press herself against him and give him a firm hug of gratitude. She smiled up at him, searching his face.

"Bjorn!"

Bjorn stepped back and turned, his eyes searching. Then he raised a fist into the air and gave a thunderous shout before starting to laugh. A short, well-built man with dark hair shoved his way through the throng of men gathering around them and confronted Lindahl with a few snapped words, at which Bjorn grinned broadly and hit his chest.

"I am alive. No trouble!"

The smaller man looked at Tempest curiously.

Jared shouldered his way through the crowd of men and caught hold of her wrist. "Are you satisfied now?" he snarled, and pulled her to his side. He raised his head and gave the Swede a hard, amused look. "You must be drunk or crazy, mister," Jared challenged. "No man with an ounce of sense would risk his life for a saddlebag."

Bjorn looked down at Tempest and grinned. "It seemed to matter."

She raised her head proudly and smiled back. "It did. Greatly."

Jared didn't like the way the Swede was looking at her, nor the way Tempest was smiling at him, her eyes shining. He drew her away from Lindahl.

The danger had subsided. The fire was passing on, hungrily engulfing the next dwellings up the hill. Down the slope, small patches of orange-red still glowed brightly in the night, revealing the path of destruction the fire had taken. Men mulled around in a dull, disheartened search for whatever they could salvage.

Jared kept a firm hand on Tempest's wrist, pulling her along with him, heedless of her feelings. "Oliver! Gather what we have left and have it moved to the new place on the Sacramento! We open for business tomorrow night!"

"Right, boss!"

"Missouri, when the work's done here, open a couple of bottles of the bourbon. If Sally's still in business, eat there on me. Tell him I'll settle up."

"Ye're hurting me, Jared," Tempest protested, trying to tug loose. He turned on her, eyes glittering darkly.

"I thought you were after the gowns I gave you," he snarled. "What's in that damn saddlebag that you'd risk your life for it?"

"'Tis everything in the world I have."

"The hell it is." What of the things he had given her? He reached for the bag to yank it away, but her arm tightened fiercely around it and the raw, frightened look in her eyes stopped him. "Damn you," he said harshly. "Is it worth your life?"

She bit her lip. "It was worth the chance."

"And that fool over there took it, didn't he?"

Tempest looked back at Bjorn Lindahl. He was standing among the men milling around the rubble, staring across at her with Jared, a grim look on his weathered face.

Jared caught her by the shoulders and gave her a shake. The Swede took a step toward them. "You already thanked him." Delving his hand into her disheveled hair, he tilted her head back. "You almost got yourself killed," he said hoarsely.

"Jared—"

He kissed her, taking full advantage of her parted lips to deepen the kiss and plunder her mouth with his tongue. He hoped the Swede was watching. He wanted him to see. He wanted every man in camp to know that Tempest was his woman and no one else's.

After her first startled struggle of protest, Tempest melted against him. The heavy saddlebag was the only barrier between them as Jared went on kissing her in the middle of the firelit street thronged with men falling silent to stare at the scene.

Jared raised his head, his breath harsh, his eyes glowing. He put a firm arm around her and let her sag against him, feeling how she was shaking. Any man looking at her would know who she belonged to. He raised his eyes and looked directly across at the Swede watching them. He smiled coldly as he let his hand slide slowly down Tempest's back.

Bjorn Lindahl stared at him hard for a long moment, and then turned abruptly away, pushing his way through the crowd and disappearing with his friend into the shadows beyond.

The lady doth protest too much, methinks.
                                    —William Shakespeare
                                    Hamlet

Tempest stood in the middle of a large, bare upstairs bedroom in the new casino downriver from the fire. She looked around at the dark pine walls and smelled sawdust. This one room was half again as large as Abram's cabin had been, and it wasn't constructed of logs, but of expensive milled lumber.

"I want a door put on tonight," Jared ordered someone in the corridor. "And a bed."

A low voice answered.

"I don't care how much. When you find one, tell them they'll be doing a lady a favor."

Tempest's heart thumped heavily as she heard Jared come into the room again. She didn't turn to look at him, but could feel his gaze on her. Did he expect to finish what he had started before Oliver had warned them of the approaching fire? Her stomach tightened and a light shivering sensation coursed through her body.

It was raining again. The pattering against the roof began lightly, then quickly became a heavy pounding.

"The fire will be out soon," she said huskily. It was dark, and the room was shadowed. She turned. "I would have a candle, if ye please." She still held the saddlebag pressed tightly against her breasts.

"In a minute," he said, and came toward her. The closer he came, the harder her heart pounded. He reached out for her saddlebag and her fingers tightened. "You can't hang onto it all night, Tempest," he said grimly. He tugged once, and she let go. He flipped it open and shoved his hand in. Her mouth tightened as she watched him draw out the big, heavy black Bible. A muscle clenched tautly in his square jaw and he gave her a blazing look.

"A two-dollar Bible," he snarled, shoving it at her. She grasped it gladly, clutching it to her, and watched in grim dismay as he plundered her saddlebag yet again.

"What else do you have in here?" he growled, rummaging. "The Queen of England's jewels?" He drew out his hand and opened his palm, staring dumbfounded at his find. Then he swore vilely, glaring at her, his face a distorted mask of rage. "*This* is what you went after?" he demanded in cutting contempt, thrusting his hand into her face.

Her hand shook as she reached out for her treasures, still clutching Abram's Bible tightly. "Give them to me, Jared, please," she pleaded, afraid of what he would do with them.

His hand clenched. "You *bitch,*" he breathed hoarsely, his face pale. "I gave you gowns worth a thousand dollars in gold, and all you care about is a handful of buttons you could buy at any county fair for two bits!"

She clutched wildly at his fingers, but he retracted his hand sharply. "Jared! They're mine. *Give them to me!*"

He flung them wide, slamming them off the bare pine walls so that they ricocheted back across the dark floor. "Look for them, damn you!"

"Oh, Jared," she wailed, going down on her knees to search frantically with one hand while she still clutched the Bible against her with the other.

"Beads are two a penny at Sutter's Fort. I could have had Manhattan Island for twenty-four dollars!"

She didn't understand the reference, but she heard the cold sarcasm, the deep, biting insult of his tone. She picked up one precious enamel button and stood.

He was breathing hard, but already regretting his angry words. His expression was haggard and filled with conflicting emotions. He looked at her and grimaced inwardly at what he saw. "I didn't mean that, Tempest," he said, raking his hand through his hair. He was shaking.

"Didn't ye now, laddie?" she sneered.

"My temper's always been—hell, Tempest, listen," he tried again, taking a step toward her.

She stepped back, her chin tipped. "Aye, ye meant it right enough," she went on, her eyes burning. "It's been in yer head from the beginnin' that I'm naught but a squaw with a white mon's eyes. Ye thought that once ye had me under yer roof, ye'd have me easy enough in yer bed!" Her brogue thickened as her anger grew.

But Jared was no stranger to unrestrained temper. His own

had caused heartache before. His dark eyes flashed and he took three steps and grabbed her roughly by the shoulders, shaking her. "If that were true, I'd have taken you long ago and not spent the last few months with a hard knot in my belly!"

She tried to twist loose, but his fingers dug into her arms with cruel determination, his teeth bared as he shook her again. "If you were still in that mud hut, fifty men would have had you by now. I've kept you safe! I've seen that you had plenty of food when you were damn near starving like a dog. I've given you shelter. And I gave you gowns that would have cost more than that farm your precious Abram owned! What'd you get from him but some rags that belonged to his other wife, a handful of buttons, and his *Bible!*"

Frightened by his rage and unable to free herself from his brutal grip, she brought her knee up sharply. The heavy, mud-stained satin skirts hampered her speed and aim, allowing him time to sense and dodge the blow. He drew in his breath harshly and drove her back against the hard wall, almost knocking all the air from her lungs with the force. He grasped her wrists so tightly she thought they would snap as he pressed them back against the wall, his weight against her. "I've *waited* for you," he hissed. "And if that damn fire hadn't happened when it did, I'd have had you by now!"

She lifted her head to give an angry response and he captured her mouth. The force of his kiss parted her lips. She tried to turn her head away and he brought her wrists down so that his forearms were braced on either side of her head as he continued to ravage her mouth.

Fiery sensations flooded her body at the onslaught and she felt his body rubbing an age-old message against hers. The hard, heavy demand of his mouth gradually gentled, playing seductively as it had done before. His breath came quick and strained as he pressed fevered kisses against her temple.

"I'll bet that bastard read to you from that Bible every night before he took you, didn't he?" he muttered derisively, his body shaking with desire and jealousy.

Her lungs felt as if all the air had been squeezed out at his harsh condemnation of Abram. He had no right, no right at all, she thought, feeling the hot burning in her eyes and throat, the heavy, sick pain in her chest as she thought of Abram. She wanted to tell Jared never to mention him again, but the only sound that came out was broken and strangled.

Jared raised his head and looked down at her. "Are you crying for him?"

She clutched the button in her hand. Jared's fingers tightened on her wrist and he shook her until her fingers were forced to loosen and let it drop to the floor. "You're mine. You don't belong to him anymore. He's *dead.*"

"He *loved* me," she gasped out. "And I loved him."

"The hell you did. You don't know anything about love yet," he said harshly. "You were just getting your first taste of it this afternoon! Maybe you liked him. Maybe you had an *affection* for him. But you didn't love him."

All her strength pitted against him wasn't enough to gain her freedom.

"Don't cry," he whispered harshly against her temple.

"Go away," she murmured brokenly, her body racked as the grief for Abram welled up and washed over her in a torrent of pain. Where were her buttons? Where was Abram? It wasn't fair.

Jared drew back slowly, letting her go. She pushed past him trying to see where the buttons lay. Shadows were everywhere.

"You can't find them in the dark," he told her grimly.

She didn't answer, but went down on her hands and knees again, searching.

Jared left the room without another word.

The silence he left behind rang in her ears. She ran her hands across the floor all around her. She tried not to think of the darkness, the walls, the smell of smoke, the pounding rain, but her heart beat faster and faster in hammer blows of rising terror.

Abram had made things right for her. But Abram was gone.

She found a button and clutched it tightly. She couldn't move.

Light flickered in the corridor. She glanced toward it sharply.

Oliver came in with a kerosene lantern. "Jared said you needed this." He set it just inside the door, looking at her in question as she sat back on her heels in the middle of the floor and made no effort to stand. "Are you all right?"

She moistened her dry lips, but couldn't speak. She nodded once. He didn't look convinced, but he went away.

She found all the buttons and put them back into the saddlebag along with the Bible. She felt for and found the sharp edge of the small tin thimble Jared had missed finding. Closing the flap, she held the leather satchel in her lap.

She sighed shakily and then sat staring at the glow of the lantern a few feet away. All she could hear was the rain beating on the pine shake roof.

She wasn't even aware of the tears that streaked her pale face.

Tempest awakened with a startled cry as someone shook her shoulder. She recoiled as Jared came down beside her on the wood floor. He shoved away the saddlebag she'd been using as a pillow and pulled her onto his lap. She struggled, but he held her fiercely, his lips against her temple.

"I've a vile temper, just like my father," he said raggedly, refusing to allow her freedom. Her fingers spread in protest against the hard warmth of his chest. "I always said I wouldn't be like him, and then I go off like a madman over—" She flinched back again, lifting her head, and he kissed her, his mouth hungry. His hand gripped her head, holding her still, demanding her response.

She began to tremble, her fingers clutching at his shirt, her lips parting as he sought to deepen the kiss. When he drew back finally, their breaths mingled. He stared at her and then kissed her again, fiercely, and she felt all her senses opening to him.

"I can give you more than buttons, Tempest," he said raggedly against her lips, his body trembling. "Don't pull away from me!" He yanked her back. "I can give you pleasure you can't even imagine yet. Do you remember what you were feeling just before the fire?" he murmured hoarsely, his mouth gliding warmly against the arched curve of her neck. "That was just the beginning."

Her breath caught sharply in her throat as she felt his hand slide into the low neckline of her ruined dress.

"Don't . . ." she moaned, struggling.

"No bed, but a locked door," he said, lowering his head. She gasped as she felt his mouth, open and moistly hot on her flesh. He bent her back, one hand in her hair tugging her head far back. She felt his hand unloop the buttons and her bodice sagged. She felt his mouth, hot and open on her breasts, the edge of his teeth, his tongue, and then a gentle pulling that drew a soft cry from her parted lips.

"You're alive with me." He pressed her back farther, one leg across hers holding her down as he kissed her again and again. "Did he ever make you feel like this?" he demanded thickly, kissing her possessively until her back arched toward him. He drew back from her, yanking up the heavy skirts.

She saw the hard look of unrestrained desire in his eyes and tried to sit up. He spread one hand against her breasts, pressing her back, as his other quickly opened the front of his pants.

"No!"

His legs between hers were like iron. He caught her hands, jerking them up above her head. She arched, trying to escape, and he took her with one swift, sure thrust and then used his weight to hold her down.

"You're mine. You've been mine since that day we saw each other at the river. It's time you knew it!"

With every movement of Tempest's to free herself, Jared buried himself deeper inside her.

It wasn't the same as it had been with Abram. Her body was on fire; sharp tingling sensations rushed through her; an ache grew in her loins as Jared moved his hips hard against hers, his mouth playing against hers too. He was filling her everywhere. Her awareness was reduced to the dragging withdrawal of his body and his hard lunge to take her again. She heard soft, moaning sounds, and with a shock realized they were coming from her.

He drew back, bracing himself on his hands above her, staring down at her as his body moved within hers, and his face was a feral snarl of uncontrolled desire.

Tempest felt her body tensing, hardening, throbbing. The pounding grew in her brain as well as in her body. Everything centered on him, on his body locked into hers. He was being rough, but it was a roughness that drove her senses higher and higher until she felt herself trembling on the edge of something shattering.

"Ohhh . . ." she cried softly, her head thrashing.

Jared withdrew abruptly and she let out her breath in appalled protest, hardly aware of doing so until the agonized frustration gripped her.

"How do you like it?" he growled, bending to open his mouth hotly against the burgeoning peak of her breast. She arched sharply. "Hell, isn't it? This is what you've put me through, and you're going to know how it feels."

But Tempest was not made of the gentler stuff that Jared was used to. She pushed at him, trying to roll free, but there was no strength in her arms and her body quivered.

"Bitch," Jared groaned, jerking her back, his hand moving down and closing on her with cruel purpose. "How does it feel? It's driving you mad, isn't it? *Isn't it?*"

She tried to close her legs, but his were there between, and his hand was also. He knew just the touch to use to make her body writhe. He brought her up to the edge again, the pressure inside her making her shake violently, then stopped, his expression satisfied as he heard her groaning sob.

She swore at him.

Pinning her down, he looked into her eyes. "It's all right. Just say you want me. Damn you, *say it!*"

She gritted her teeth.

He moved against her and her lips parted. He kissed her, his body stretching over hers, and she knew she was defeated. "Say it," he groaned, and she knew instinctively that this victory was not all his.

"Aye."

"All of it."

"I want ye," she moaned softly.

But it wasn't enough for him. "Your Abram didn't make you feel like this, did he?" he demanded fiercely.

"Oh, God . . ." Tears came.

"Did he?" His hand shook as he plowed it into her loosened hair, yanking her head back so that she had to look up into his dark, tormented eyes.

"No," she admitted, her mouth trembling.

No gentleness came into his eyes. They seemed to darken even more with hard desire and determination. "Maybe he gave you God," he said harshly, "but I'm going to show you heaven."

He took her then, the hard contours of his body seeming to become even harder. His lips were drawn back in a growl as he moved slowly, each plunge driving her need higher until she hovered once more in agonizing suspense. Then her senses leaped sharply, hung suspended, and then soared upward in a fiery wave. She heard someone scream. She felt Jared's hard hands digging into her hips as he held her back just long enough to catch up with her.

Slowly she descended, dazed and shaking, breathless, her skin damp.

"Tell me now that you don't love me," Jared murmured against her neck, his own breath ragged and his body still heaving against hers. He caught hold of her and rolled her on top of him, his hands delving into her hair, lifting her face.

"Tell me that I don't love you," he said hoarsely.

Her mouth trembled. "I loved *him*."

He shook his head. "No, you didn't. This is love." His hands moved down as he raised his body into hers, holding her down firmly.

She closed her eyes tightly. So this was what Abram had meant, she thought, despairing, her body blooming with heat around Jared.

"Don't cry."

"Ye dunna understand—"

"He's *dead!*" Jared said, angry. His hands tightened. "Is that what you want? To go on caring about a dead man? Bury him, damn you." He cupped her face, his hands hard and strong, pulling her down. He kissed her wildly, then more gently as he gained her response, and drew her closer against him. His hands moved down her body, curved over her buttocks. "Love me, Tempest," he pleaded thickly. "Just love me." Lifting her slightly, he moved slowly beneath her, his own need greater than hers.

She kissed him boldly, opening her mouth over his. She felt the wave of surprise shudder through Jared's body and reached up to bury her hands in his dark, springy, thick hair, her arms and legs tightening. The deep sound in his throat was one of exultation. He rolled her onto her back, a low, unbidden laugh coming from his gasping lips.

"I knew it. I knew how you'd be the first time I saw you. Oh, my love, it's just going to get better...oh..."

But somehow Tempest knew far better than he.

It should've been you, Abram. God, why wasn't it? Oh, why wasn't it?

Love sought is good,
but giv'n unsought is better.
——William Shakespeare
Twelfth Night

Tempest saw Bjorn Lindahl standing at the bar of the California. She smiled at him in warm welcome, drawing speculative glances from other men along the mahogany bar. He smiled back broadly, his blue eyes sparkling. Then his gaze dropped, taking in the daring red-rust satin gown Jared had had made for her and which enhanced her olive skin. Its deep neckline was one of the main attractions in Sacramento.

His shorter friend was with him. Tempest had learned that his name was Claus Janssen. The two men talked together, Bjorn still looking at her. His gaze left her as he cast a contemptuous glance over his shoulder in the direction of Jared's monte table.

Bending, Tempest reached beneath the bar for an unopened bottle of Jared's best imported whiskey. The young man leaning on the bar in front of her stared at her breasts, his mouth agape. Several others nearby leaned forward as far as they could. She straightened and gave them a sweeping, disdainful glance.

Ignoring several urgent requests for more and better whiskey, she paused beside Tick, the new bartender. He was very protective of her and glowered at the men who were laughing and trying to get her attention. No one knew his real name, but when he became angry, he had a tic beside his right eye that showed just before he reached for someone. Twice in the last week, he'd dragged men half across the bar when they'd made lewd remarks to Tempest. It was obvious to every man who came in that the barrel-chested, bearded bartender liked her and would put up with no foul talk in her presence.

Oliver was working the other end of the bar, but he saw Lindahl. He looked across the room at Jared, who was momentarily engrossed in his gaming. He poured several more shots of whiskey, then tucked the bottle back into the shelf

300

underneath and went out the gate at the end of the bar. He had orders to follow whether he liked them or not.

Tempest stopped in front of Bjorn. "Are ye rich yet or just killing time with a few drinks?" she asked, turning slightly to get two glasses off the shelf beneath the mirror. She set one down in front of Bjorn and the other before Claus and poured.

"You take in more dust over this bar in a few minutes than we've panned in the last three weeks," he said in his thickly accented, laborious English. He pushed the full whiskey glass to one side and leaned on the bar. "You look good, flicka, but you show too much."

Some imp of Satan made her lean on the bar and smile provocatively into his warm blue eyes. "Men are flocking to the bar," she told him. "'Tis good for business."

He didn't look at her décolletage, though she knew by the way his eyes darkened that he was very aware of it. "They would flock anyway," he said. He took the bottle from her hand and looked at the label. "How much for this?"

She straightened. "Keep yer gold," she said in a thickened brogue. "I owe ye more than all the whiskey ye con drink from now till doomsday." She glanced at Claus. "Ye're included as long as ye're with him."

Claus laughed. "Then I will stay by his side." He lifted his glass and dispatched the smooth, fine whiskey with one bend of his wrist. "Is good," he said approvingly.

"Best the house has to offer," she told him. "From Jared's private stock." She took the bottle again to pour, but Janssen shook his head.

Leaning toward her with a conspiratorial look, he nodded toward Bjorn. "You must watch out for his quick hands, flicka," he said very seriously.

Bjorn gave him a sharp, fierce look and growled something in Swedish.

Claus laughed. Pushing himself back from the bar, he slapped him on the back. "And then what would you do in the next brawl without me to keep them off your back?"

"Don't believe him," Bjorn said, looking at Tempest with a grim, half-impatient expression.

"I go to lose my pants at the faro table," Claus said, and grinned.

"Your shirt," Bjorn corrected, his good humor restored.

"That too," Claus shrugged and walked away.

"He did not mean it about my hands," Bjorn told her gruffly. "He was . . . not serious."

"No?" Tempest said, smiling slightly at his intentness. His square, ruggedly handsome face was deeply tanned from years of sailing. Goodwill and earthy interest showed boldly in it. She felt drawn to him. Perhaps it was his roughness after Jared's smooth manner. He was very tall and broad, but it wasn't only his size that made him stand out in the crowd of men, nor even his pale, sun-bleached hair that grew in a thick mane past his frayed shirt collar.

He saw her fascination and raked his fingers through it. "Svedish gold."

"Would make a fine scalp," she remarked, grinning broadly.

He leaned toward her and gazed intently into her eyes. "You want to put your hands in it, flicka?"

"I've been warned by yer friend to keep a safe distance," she countered, wondering at the warmth his look caused her to feel. She felt easy with him, but drawn as well.

With great melodrama, Lindahl placed his big, square hands palm-down on the bar. "You are safe now."

She laughed softly.

"Touch," he dared her.

She wanted to, but knew that if she did she would bring trouble on him. Jared was very jealous of this Swede and would no doubt have him dragged outside to be beaten if he saw her running her hands through his golden hair.

"Do not worry about Stryker. I can hold my own against any man," Bjorn told her.

"No doubt," she said, "but I dunna want trouble. He doesna like ye as it is."

"I do not like him much either," Bjorn said frankly.

Men along the bar were calling for her to pour their drinks. "Ignore them," Bjorn said softly, seeing how her face tightened. He turned his head and looked down the line of men, some more than half drunk on rotgut whiskey that they paid dearly for with the labors of their aching backs and their broken dreams. He pitied some of them, but not enough to tolerate their treatment of Tempest. His hard glare deterred most of the attention. He met Tempest's eyes again. "You do not belong in this place."

She lifted one shoulder dismissively. "I make gold aplenty." She wanted to share what she knew with Bjorn Lindahl in order to help him. Leaning on the bar, she lowered her voice. "Go to the Tuolumne. There be gold for ye and yer friend. Ye con make yer big strike there still."

Bjorn could hardly breathe for the heavy hammering of his heart and the sudden rush of pressure in his groin. Her full young breasts were almost revealed to him by her posture and swelled bare inches from his trembling hands. Stryker dressed her like a whore and made money off the men who came to stare at her. Then he took her upstairs . . .

"Are ye listenin', mon?" Tempest said, half-impatiently. She leaned closer. "I was there long ago with my da. Ye con—"

"Tempest," he said roughly, lowering his eyes pointedly, "no closer."

She thought he was jesting and laughed softly, putting her small hands over his. "Stay them a moment longer and I'll tell ye where ye con make yer fortune."

Bjorn raised his eyes to hers and her smile dimmed. She had seen sexual hunger many times before, but Lindahl's blue gaze burned with much more than that. He was powerfully angry. Her eyes widened in confusion and she straightened, taking her hands from his.

"I'm no less a man than all the rest," he told her. "You should not dress like this."

Surprisingly, his words hurt. She lifted her chin. "The Tuolumne, Bjorn Lindahl."

He caught hold of her wrist. *"Var så gud,* Tempest, but gold is not so important. And I would not go so far from here.. From you."

"Ye'd best let me go or there will be trouble for ye," she said softly. "I'm Jared's woman and not up for grabs."

He muttered something in Swedish.

She looked into his eyes. "Don't be like all the rest. Ye set yerself apart that night when the fire came. Ye con be my friend, Bjorn Lindahl. And I dunna say such a thing lightly." She drew her hand away as far as his hold would allow. "But ye canna be anythin' else."

He sighed heavily and let her go.

Oliver came in the gate at the far end of the bar and said something to Tick. Tick approached Tempest. "Jared wants to talk to you," he told her grimly.

"Aye," she said, and looked back at Bjorn. "Enjoy yer whiskey." She moved the bottle closer and then turned away.

Jared was waiting for her at the far end of the bar. He wasn't

looking at her but glaring down the distance at Bjorn. Glancing
back, she saw that Bjorn was behaving no better. Two male
animals wanting to square off and fight for possession of the
female. How many times had she seen it in the wild?

"What's he doing back?" Jared demanded.

"He's having himself a whiskey." She looked back at Bjorn
as he poured himself a glass. He lifted it to her, drained it
slowly, and turned the glass upside down on the bar. Taking
the bottle, he turned to leave.

"That's a bottle of my imported bourbon! Do you know
what it costs?" Jared snarled angrily, glaring after the Swede.

"If it worries ye so much, Jared, take it out of my share of
the bar profits," she told him stiffly.

"Tick will pour for him from now on and he'll get the same
whiskey every other man does," he told her, his face darkening.

She stared up at him defiantly.

"He wants you. I don't want him anywhere near you again."

She laughed sardonically. "He *wants* me? Every mon at this
bar *wants* more than a shot of whiskey." Her head tilted. "You
included."

His eyes raised and moved slowly over her face, taking in
the glittering eyes and the faint flush of anger. He smiled
slightly, leaning forward so that his lips brushed the curve of
her smooth cheek. "Me *especially*," he whispered.

She drew back, angry at her own response to him even when
he was insulting. Even standing a foot away didn't slow her
quickened pulse as she looked into the now familiar invitation
and promise in his dark, amused eyes.

"You've been working the bar for two hours," he drawled.
"Perhaps we both need . . . a respite."

Heat poured into her cheeks and he chuckled. Her mouth
tightened mutinously. His smile became mockingly rueful. "Not
in the mood? I take it you're going to make me wait until later."

"I'll pour for the Swede anytime I choose."

A muscle twitched in Jared's cheek and his eyes glinted.
"Why push the issue?"

"The mon did me a good turn. I'll not shun him."

A cold, thoughtful look came into Jared's face. He shrugged,
standing back from the bar. "Whatever you want, ma'am." He
walked away.

Rain pounded heavily on the roof all that night. Jared didn't
come to her. Two nights passed without him lying next to her
in the big brass bed. He spent his days gaming, not even looking

at her from across the room. She knew he was punishing her for her defiance, and his method of torment made the anger and hurt burn deeply.

Bjorn Lindahl returned on the third night and she poured for him. "I make trouble for you," he said simply, seeing the dull look in her eyes. He didn't stay.

Jared's temper, short by nature, was by now on a hair-trigger balance. Tempest was only one of the problems preying in his mind. The rivers were rising with the continuing, unabated rains.

"We'd better move what we can, while we can," Missouri said, unease chiseling his features into a grim frown. "Two streets are already underwater, and there's only one more before it gets to us."

"First fire, now flood," Tick grumbled.

Jared's eyes flickered to Tempest as she sat eating breakfast in the early dawn hours. She didn't look at him, though she felt him watching her just as intensely as if he had reached out and taken hold of her. She didn't want him to see her hurt, to turn it even more against her.

By mid-morning, water was lapping at the casino door and the place was filled with homeless miners. By noon, men were heading up the hill to higher ground and Jared and his people were moving what they could up to the second story.

"The place is strong enough to stand."

"Jesus Christ. I can't swim," Oliver said.

"Flooding usually brings sickness," Johnny Lightfoot remarked.

"We've got enough trouble without borrowing more," Jared said grimly, standing on the landing and looking down into his flooded casino below.

"How long are we going to wait?" Oliver demanded, clearly afraid. "The water'll be up to the landing by morning if the rains keep up!"

"The water down there is a good two feet deep now," Tick added.

"I'm getting out now," Oliver announced, and headed down the hall to get his gear.

"What do you say, boss?" Lightfoot asked, leaning his shoulder against the wall and waiting for orders.

"I'm staying. The rest of you do what you want."

Tempest knew that the others would stay as well. They all went into one of the upstairs rooms to play cards and talk, while she returned to her own room. She stood at the window looking out on the brown floodwater and the gray weeping skies, overhearing the murmur of voices as Jared talked to Oliver in the hallway.

The door closed quietly behind her. "Wondering where your Swedish sailor is?" Jared asked coldly.

She turned. Her throat closed up at the look in his eyes. Fighting tears, she shook her head.

He sighed heavily. He didn't move, but stood there looking at her with bleak anger in his eyes. "Come here," he ordered softly.

She crossed the room and stood in front of him. Still he didn't move. His expression was veiled, his eyes dark and enigmatic, but she saw the muscle working in his jaw.

"If you want to leave, Oliver will accompany you to high ground. You can come back when the water recedes."

Why had he changed so much toward her? All over the Swede, or was it something more?

Jared's impatience grew. He knew who'd be looking for her if she left, who'd take care of her while he was stuck here watching out for what was his. "What do you want? You've only got a minute to decide."

It didn't matter one way or the other, she thought in misery. Not to him, it seemed. She knew, however, that she had to be close to Jared. "If ye stay, I stay also."

Something came into his eyes that she hadn't seen in days. He turned away and went out. She heard him talking to Oliver in the hallway again. She didn't expect him to return. He'd play cards with the others while they waited out the flood.

The door opened again and she glanced up sharply from where she was sitting on her bed. He looked at her briefly, then walked across and stared out the window. "What a godforsaken place this is," he muttered, his back to her.

Hesitant, but hopeful, she waited. He said nothing more. Standing slowly, she went to him. It took all her courage to put her arms around him and press herself against his back. She felt the tension go out of him, and he sighed deeply.

"I admit I'm a jealous ass," he said roughly.

"Bjorn wilna come back."

He stiffened. "No? How do you know he won't?"

"He said he made trouble for me and left."

"Gallant bastard, isn't he?" She started to withdraw but he caught hold of her wrists. "Something about him grates on me,

Tempest. Don't ask me to explain—I can't. I just don't want him anywhere near you." He let her go and turned. "We've more important things to worry about anyway, I'd say." His hand lightly caressed her arm, drawing her toward him. She tilted her head up as he lowered his.

The kiss lasted a long time, and when Jared finally raised his mouth from hers, both were breathless. He pulled her close. "Floodwater coming up to the window frames, and all I can think about is making love to you," he murmured in self-mockery. He looked down at her dress and grimaced. "When I give you silk and satin, why do you still insist on wearing buckskin and gingham every chance you get?"

Soon she wore nothing at all.

Their coming together was swift and impetuous, all youth and vigor. Heedless of their peril, prurience reigned, all reason forfeit to the consuming drive to feel flesh against flesh. Their bodies worked against one another toward the same transcending purpose, the shuddering earthbound exultation.

The rain pounded. Jared plunged. Tempest arched.

And down the hall three sane men stood at the window watching the floodwater rise and wondering if they would still be alive in the morning.

Oh, tell me about that land of wickedness, gold
    and death. Is there any salvation?
        —Methodist Minister William Roberts

    "We should've gotten out of here two days ago," Tick
grumbled, and drank from a bottle of whiskey before passing
it on to Lightfoot.
    "What the hell. The rain's stopped." Lightfoot passed the
bottle on to Missouri who was swearing under his breath and
shivering.
    "If someone doesn't get us pretty soon, we'll starve up
here."
    Jared, already warm from whiskey, grinned at the three men.
"We're safe enough, and we won't lack for water." He waved
his hand, indicating the swirling brown sea around them as
they perched precariously on top of the California's roof, where
they had been for the past four hours.
    Tempest sat in front of Jared, his legs raised on either side
of her as she leaned back into him. Her body radiated heat as
she slept.
    Thin sunlight fought its way through the gray-shrouded skies.
A bloated body floated by. The four men watched it roll slowly
in the strong current.
    "Wonder if Oliver made it," Missouri said grimly.
    Tick tipped the bottle again. It was almost empty. He wiped
his mouth with the back of his sleeve before passing it to
Lightfoot again. Missouri shot to his feet.
    "A dinghy! Hey! *Over here!*" he shouted, waving wildly.
Tick stood and joined in. Lightfoot sat swilling the rest of the
whiskey, more than a little drunk.
    Tempest stirred against Jared. He knew she would be groggy
when she awakened. He'd made her drink two good measures
of brandy last night before they had begun their climb up the

rope to the roof. By the time they all reached it and she sat for a while in the cold night air, the strong spirits had done their work.

Jared watched the small boat approaching.

Lindahl!

Anger swept through Jared, fueled by his numerous pulls on the whiskey bottle. Why did it have to be that damn Swede to come to the rescue? He swore softly under his breath, his eyes narrowing on the distant figure sculling toward them.

He battened down his temper. Why should he worry? Tempest belonged to him. Her eyes didn't smolder when she looked at Lindahl, while Jared had only to look at her to make her body come alive. She was a one-man woman. He knew that much about her.

Yet, there was a look in her eyes for the Swedish ship's deserter that was never there for him. He didn't like it. He had seen it in her eyes the night of the fire. And now, here Lindahl was again, coming to her rescue.

As the dinghy came closer, Jared lowered his head and lightly tongued Tempest's ear. She made a soft sound and moved sinuously. He kissed the sensitive spot on her shoulder while sliding his hands around her and up to gently knead her full breasts. The men on the roof were unaware of what he was doing, but Jared knew Lindahl was watching. He raised his eyes and stared across the expanse of brown water at him, moving one hand down over Tempest's belly. He grinned mockingly.

"Lindahl!" Missouri laughed. "By God, man, am I glad to see you again!"

Jared bent his head again and nuzzled Tempest's neck seductively. "Wake up, my love. We're about to be rescued by the Swedish fleet," he whispered against her ear. She was coming around slowly, sluggishly. She raised her head. He let her go and stood up.

"Tempest!" Lindahl shouted.

She rubbed her face and then stood up shakily, swaying. Jared steadied her. "Aye, Bjorn."

"Are you well, flicka?"

"Aye." She smiled. "I be glad to see ye. 'Tis a cold loathsome place to spend a night." She gestured at the damp roof.

Jared fought down a hot stab of anger. He knew he should have gotten them well away from the California much earlier.

He had been so sure the waters wouldn't come any higher. He had risked all their lives.

The Swede looked at him and Jared read easily all the contempt that look held, though it lasted but a bare second.

"I have a blanket," Bjorn told her.

"Is there room for all of us?" Missouri grinned. "Or did you just come for her?" He cast a brief glance in Jared's direction.

"There is room."

Jared watched Lindahl scull the boat closer, bumping it hard against the second floor of the casino building. Glass shattered from an upper window. Peering over the edge, Jared watched the Swede securing the dinghy.

Tempest came to stand at his side. He put his arm around her and looked down at her. "I'm sorry," he whispered roughly. "We should have left sooner."

"It's turned out all right," she told him, searching his taut face curiously.

Bjorn Lindahl watched them. The other men were talking to him and he answered, but he had eyes only for her. She looked down at him and smiled. He held his arms up. *"Skutta,* Tempest. Jump to me."

Tempest glanced back at Jared. "Go ahead," he told her grimly, hands on his hips.

She hesitated before stepping to the edge of the roof, pulling her skirt about her ankles, and dropping gracefully. Lindahl caught her easily, five feet below. Jared saw the look on his face, and his mouth tightened. Bjorn didn't put her down, but spoke to her in a low voice. Jared clenched his fists, watching them. She smiled again and put her hand lightly on his shoulder as she answered.

"Hey!" Missouri said. "What about us?"

Lindahl bent to put Tempest on the slat in the dinghy. He picked up a heavy blanket and put it around her as she looked up at him. Lindahl straightened. Turning to look up again, he gestured.

"Komma hit," he told them. "Come ahead. Use the rope." He tossed it up to them so they could tie it securely to the chimney and then lower themselves.

Little was said as the Swede sculled the dinghy to the high, damp ground around a Methodist church. It was overburdened already with wet, weary, grim-faced young men thick in beard and thin in belly. A minister greeted them. "Welcome to God's house."

Tempest clutched Jared's arm in a viselike grip. He glanced down at her. "What is it?"

She was staring at the simple building with wide, blue eyes. "This is God's house?" It was not at all as she expected.

Jared laughed softly. The minister was talking to Lindahl. A few minutes later the Swede left. Jared was glad to see the back of him.

As they went inside, Jared muttered, "I hope we won't be graced with too many sermons on the mount while we're stuck here."

Tempest's presence stirred chivalry among the displaced men. Within a few minutes, she had another blanket, a mug of strong, hot coffee, a hunk of bread, and a small steaming bowl of beans. Jared and the others fared as well, but less quickly and by their wits.

Jared had had enough foresight to pocket a deck of cards and several dice. To the dismay and annoyance of the good reverend, gaming began. Jared laughed at his objections, but agreed to move the poker game outside. Missouri shot craps against the steps. By the afternoon, Jared had a dozen men who owed him debts enlisted to clean up the California as soon as the waters receded.

He came back inside to slouch against the wall in exhaustion. "We're back in business," he told Tempest with a slight, arrogant smile.

Tempest had only to look at the minister's face to know the impropriety of Jared's entire venture. She pulled the blankets around her and drew up her legs. Lowering her head, she avoided meeting the churchman's eyes and was immensely relieved when he went into the back room of the church. Then she looked up at the cross above the altar.

Abram had said when he died that he would come here, to God's house, to live. This was a place of *many mansions?* Its close quarters, fetid smells, human groaning, and misery made a grim scene. Outside, dead, bloated men who'd been dragged out of the floodwater were being laid out for later burial. *This* was God's house?

Closing her eyes tightly, Tempest tried to feel Abram close to her.

I miss you, Abram. Maybe if I'd prayed harder . . . maybe if I hadna cursed God for letting ye suffer so, ye'd be alive still.

"You're shaking," Jared said. "Here. Come closer." He put

his arms around her. "Are you cold?"

"No," she choked. Her throat was squeezed shut and her eyes burned.

Jared nuzzled her. She felt his mouth against the curve of her neck as he brought her back firmly against him, her back to his chest. He kept kissing her.

"Dunna, Jared," she whispered, looking around. No one was looking. It was dark and nearly all the men were sleeping.

"I wish we were in bed behind a closed door," he murmured, his hand groping beneath the blanket.

She stiffened. "Not *here*."

He laughed softly. "Not here?" he mocked. "Why not *here*? I want to touch you." His hand stroked the soft, full swell of her breast beneath the soiled shirtwaist. His fingers teased. "See? Doesn't matter where. Feels just as good, hmm?" He began to unbutton her clothes, questing, the blanket around her hiding what he was doing.

She pushed his hand down. "'Tis God's house, Jared. Have a little respect."

"Respect?" He tipped her chin back. "You've more than enough superstition for both of us, I think." He shifted her. "Move back a little more. I can lift you just enough to manage things. I'll put my hand over your mouth if you get the urge to scream, all right? Everyone's sleeping. We don't want to wake them up, do we?"

She knew he was laughing at her, but she saw the excitement shining in his eyes. She stared back at him, realizing that he would dare God himself for the pleasure of the rush it gave him.

He sighed, his eyes glinting. "That damn farmer of yours again," he said sardonically. "Tempest, whatever he told you or read to you, there's no God."

"Dunna say that," she gasped, terrified.

He'd never seen her so frightened, and he felt sudden anger at her deceased husband. It didn't amuse him anymore, this bent she had for religion. It didn't fit what she was.

"It's all a hoax perpetuated by men of the cloth."

She didn't understand him, but she saw the derision in his eyes. "Ye mustna say that." She put her fingertips to his mouth. He caught her hand and jerked it down.

"If there was a God, do you think He'd let all this misery go on? If He gave a damn about His *children*, that is."

"There is a God, Jared. Dunna dare Him."

He gave a curt laugh.

"I prayed to Him once and He answered me," she told him, frightened for him.

"Prayed *what?*" he drawled.

"For something to happen, and it did," she said, unwilling to open herself to his mockery.

"Coincidence." He leaned toward her. "You know why the Jesuits came here to this territory? To get the land, not to spread the gospel. There are churches in Europe that could house a thousand people, Tempest. If the priests melted down their gold crucifixes, they could feed their starving parishioners. The Vatican itself has more gold and jewels in it than any other place in the world! So much for vows of poverty," he sneered.

Little of what he said made any sense to Tempest, who knew nothing of Europe, crucifixes, or the Vatican. She only heard the utter contempt in Jared's voice, a contempt for God Himself, and shuddered.

"Ye're a bloody fool, Jared, to dare the Almighty Himself," she told him. "He'll punish you. He *will*."

"You sound as mad as that preacher who came into the casino two weeks ago and said that God would rain hell on us for living in sin."

"And He did, didna He?"

Jared looked at her pale, strained face. "This is the first time I've seen you really scared, Tempest. And of what? *Mist.*" He tipped up her chin. "Why're you so sure of this God of yours?"

"Because He's there. He punishes ye if ye do wrong. He killed my baby after—" She stopped, seeing the sharp change in Jared's expression. Realizing what she had been about to blurt out, she closed her eyes and put her forehead against her raised knees, feeling sick. She wrapped her arms around her legs tightly.

"You made a baby with that farmer?" he said softly.

"Almost," she whispered, raising her head slightly.

"What does that mean?" He felt sick.

She looked up at the cross. "God killed him when he came out of me. The bairn never drew one breath."

Jared sat in silence for a long moment. "What'd your farmer tell you about God then?" he asked with cold mockery.

"Abram was dead. He died just before the baby was born."

He thought he understood then. "That's probably why it died."

"Aye," she said, certain.

"Shock."

"It was God who took the bairn from me," she said, looking back at him, her eyes glistening with tears.

"There is no God, Tempest. You want me to prove it?" He looked up at the cross. "If You're there, God, strike me dead."

"No," she gasped. "Dunna say that!"

He clapped a hand over her mouth, yanking her back against him. "Strike me dead," he challenged again. Tempest closed her eyes tightly, tears squeezing out.

Please, God, no. I canna bear to lose anyone else. Please. Please!

"See? Nothing happened." His hold on her eased. "Because there's nothing there."

She shook her head, confused.

Jared shifted her body and pulled her back between his legs again, her back to him.

"No," she whispered frantically.

Gripping her hard about the waist, he pulled her even closer. She caught hold of his hands desperately. "Dunna do this," she whispered tearfully.

"I'm going to show you once and for all that there's no God," he whispered hoarsely against her hair. "I need you," he added, holding her tightly. He caught hold of her hand, drawing it back around her to press it against his manhood.

Her heart raced.

"Just relax," he ordered huskily against her ear, rubbing her hand up and down on him. "No one's going to know what we're doing, least of all a God who isn't there."

Tempest's eyes searched the darkness. "He will. He sees everything."

Jared laughed low, disdainfully. "Let him watch then. We'll go to hell together. It wouldn't be all bad, would it?" His breathing had heightened. He made a low sound in his throat and she felt him open his clothing.

Men were snoring and occasionally shifting where they lay. Jared's hands moved surely, and she knew she was lost. He lifted her and lowered her again. She drew in her breath.

"Hmmmmmm," he moaned very softly against her neck. She could feel his chest rise and fall heavily against her back. She shook her head. "Too late to save me," he groaned raggedly, and she knew that what he said was more than right for her, too. Her soul was already doomed for what she'd done, even before she'd taken Abram's life.

Jared moved slowly. Her lips parted as the heat spiraled and grew heavy and hard. He put his hand snugly over her mouth, his other hand moving down the front of her. "Shhh . . . oh, there . . . heaven coming . . ." His hand tightened convulsively and she felt his body trembling violently as he opened his mouth against her neck. She heard his sharp, hot exhalation as his crisis came.

He went very still. His breathing gradually slowed, and he nuzzled her tenderly. "He didn't strike us dead, did He?" he whispered mockingly, and bit her earlobe. "Right here in His parlor and He let us live, depraved as we are. Proof enough that He isn't there."

Tears streamed down Tempest's face as she stared into the darkness at the roiling shapes and shadows. One candle still burned on the altar.

She looked at it, her mouth trembling. "Perhaps we're just no longer worth it."

Without hope we live in desire.
—Dante
The Inferno

As soon as the weather cleared, men evacuated the rainswept, flood-ravaged valley in droves and headed for the streams again. The hard winter had washed down more treasure from Mother Nature's hoard.

Gold! This indeed was manna from heaven, Jared declared to Tempest as the California was opened again. It alone could bring you all you desired. Anything—name it!

Tempest wondered how much gold was enough for him, what he really wanted. When she asked, he said, incomprehensibly, "White pillars and tobacco fields." His expression was distant.

Glowing kerosene lanterns, shining brass, crystal chandeliers, whiskey, and loud laughter: these were paradise to men living in a land of mud, hunger, despair, and loneliness. Tempest heard one man singing "bringing in the sheaves" as he raked in a pot of winnings at a poker table.

But outside, serpents gathered, with fangs bared. Cholera struck. Not once, but three times.

Jared stood outside their bedroom. "What in hell is this?" he demanded of her, nodding toward the red mark on their door.

"Lamb's blood."

"I know it's blood. What heathen ritual is this?"

"One from Moses. I did it so that death would pass us over."

Jared stared at her as though she had lost her mind, but he said nothing more. She marked all the other doors of the California, and word of it spread like wildfire throughout Sacramento.

Some people laughed. One was Levinson—bitterly, just before he died.

Few whites succumbed to the disease, but the California Indians were decimated. Tempest began to wonder whether there could be a just God after all, that it should be the innocent who suffered most. No one who worked in the California was struck down. Jared insisted it was luck, but still she wondered.

Spring came and with her came thousands of argonauts by way of the Isthmus of Panama, by windjammers and barkentines around Cape Horn, by overland wagon trains. A hundred, a thousand, twenty thousand, where there had been but a few four years before. The Californios' ranchos were overrun by gold seekers and squatters. The land was filling up, overflowing, mostly with Americans determined to keep all foreigners out of the rich gold fields—Indians, Mexicans, and blacks included.

The provisional government ran the territory like a ratified state. It was only a matter of time, after all. The constitution was submitted to Congress, and California was declared a free territory. Most men had been outraged at the mere imputation that gold mining might be work deemed appropriate for Negro slaves!

But slaves there were, anyhow. Laws were made, bent, and broken. Some were simply ignored.

Tempest stood by staring in fascination at the big Negro standing behind Thomas Jefferson Green. The Texan threw in his cards and leaned back in his chair, smiling ruefully at Jared. "You've got yourself a nigger, Stryker."

"I'm much obliged," Jared drawled in return, looking over his acquisition assessingly. "What can he do?"

Green laughed as he stood up, pushing his chair back. "I imagine he could do just about anything you ordered. He came from Savannah—belonged to one of those gentlemen who purchased land in Africa so the niggers could all be sent home. But he died. This darky was sold at auction to cover back taxes. Now he's all yours. He goes by the name of Procopius, and he's best at making trouble."

Jared leaned back, his hands resting lightly on his hard thighs. "Perhaps he just needs a master he can respect." He laughed softly at the Texan's expression. "Have a drink on the house before you leave, Mr. Green."

Jared stood as the man stalked away. Tempest put her hand on his arm, gazing curiously at the black man. She had never seen anything like him, with his skin so dark that there was an almost blue sheen to it. His eyes were glowing pitch, his expression emotionless and secretive. He was thin to emaciation and weary, though he held himself erect, his head high.

"Jared, what will ye do with him?" she asked, nodding toward the Negro. He had been standing silently where he was for the past three hours of gaming, and when he had been relinquished to Jared's ownership, not a muscle had moved.

"Keep him, of course. He's a valuable asset," Jared said, looking him over like a horse he had just bought. "Besides, I won him fair and square."

"Ye canna keep him. He's a mon!"

"He's a nigger. There's a difference." Jared glanced at her coolly, his expression clearly warning her not to interfere in his business.

"What difference?" she challenged.

"Some races are meant for servitude. The Negroes are one."

Her eyes flashed. "And what others, Jared?"

His eyes flickered. Then his expression grew indulgent. "Don't worry, darling. You're only *half* Indian." He leaned down to kiss her teasingly, but she stepped back sharply. He looked into her blue eyes and knew he had made a mistake, possibly an irretrievable one. "Don't try to understand something you're not capable of understanding, Tempest."

"I understand well enough."

Jared's eyes darkened. "All right. I'll give you a taste of being a master. He's yours."

Appalled, she glanced at the black man. "I dunna—"

"He's your responsibility," Jared ordered.

A pair of pitch-black eyes, as well as a hundred others around the casino, stared at her.

Jared addressed his next words to the slave. "Procopius, Miss Tempest here is your new owner. Do you understand?"

The Negro said nothing.

"Do you understand?" Jared repeated in a low, coldly authoritative tone.

"Yassuh."

"You will do exactly as she commands you. And if you dare to disobey her, I will flog you myself. A second defiance and I'll have you shot."

Tempest gasped. She looked from one to the other, Jared arrogant and assured, Procopius silently placid, accepting; no, acquiescing.

Jared turned to her, cocking his head mockingly to one side. He caught her chin, lifting it. "We'll see how you manage as a mistress," he drawled. Releasing her, he smiled sardonically, then walked away.

Everyone in the casino was watching to see what she would do. She looked at Procopius, and felt uneasy. He was not all he seemed, she sensed. His eyes were veiled and his stance respectful, but something smoldered just beneath that enigmatic calm.

Treat people the way you would like to be treated, Abram had told her more than once.

"Come with me," she said, turning toward the stairs.

Jared intercepted her. "Where do you think you're taking him?"

"Even a slave needs food, drink, and a warm place to sleep," she told him coldly.

"Then take him out back to the stable."

Her eyes glinted. "Ye said *I* was his master."

Jared's face whitened in anger. "I said take him out back."

"Shall I stay there, too?"

"If you see yourself as a slave, yes."

She said nothing more, but stepped past him and headed toward the corridor to the back of the building. Procopius followed. Jared watched them go, a heavy frown darkening his countenance. He'd talk to Tempest later, sort things out between them. For now, he had a casino to run and didn't have time for a woman's tantrum.

Tempest led Procopius into the kitchen and indicated for him to sit down at the long table. She glanced across at the surprised young miner-turned-cook who was looking at them.

"Where'd he come from, Tempest?"

"Jared won him."

"What're you going to do with him? California's a free territory 'cording to the new constitution."

"Right now we're going to feed him," Tempest said, her hands on her hips as she surveyed the silent black man. "Johnnie, cook the mon a rare steak, plenty of potatoes, and some greens. Do we have any milk?"

"Not much. Costs more than whiskey. It's over there under that wet canvas in the crate, what we do have."

"I'll get it, while ye see to that steak." She got the jug of milk and set it down before Procopius. She took down a big pewter mug and put it in front of him as well. He didn't touch either. "Go ahead, mon. Drink."

He did then, his black eyes meeting hers.

She stood back away from him, watching. What was she supposed to do with him once he was fed?

Johnnie set a plate of food down on the table. "Eat," she ordered, and Procopius wolfed the meal down in a matter of minutes. She wondered if he thought she might take it away from him. She would rather have approached a puma eating its fresh kill than reach out for the plate that was before the black man.

Johnnie watched him as well. "Ain't got any manners, that's fer sure. Eats like a pig, don't he? We should've put his food in a trough for him."

Tempest remembered another people, another time. "Any mon eats like a pig when he's been starved. Go out and buy a good cot and several blankets. Jared will settle up for the bill."

Johnnie left to do her bidding.

Procopius had finished his meal and was watching her again. She stayed where she was, studying him solemnly. He was ill-dressed for a cold, wet winter. He must be hardy to have lasted at all, she thought, realizing that his previous owner had probably hoped he wouldn't.

His belly now full, the warmth of the wood stove at his back worked on him. Tempest saw how he fought against sleep, but the deep lines in his face softened and his head bobbed. She remembered how many hours he had stood straight-backed and silent behind that bloody Texan's chair while the gambling went on, his own life and future at stake.

Moving to the table, she swept the platter, jug, and mug to one side. "Sleep easy, mon." She left the kitchen, almost hoping that he would flee the premises by morning and relieve her of all responsibility in dealing with him.

Upstairs, she undressed for bed. Jared came in without knocking, closed the door and locked it behind him, then leaned back against it, crossing his arms over his chest. He smiled wryly. "How does it feel to be master of a man's soul?"

She didn't answer.

He laughed softly. "Still mad?" He walked across the room to pour himself a brandy from one of the decanters he had had shipped up from San Francisco. He sat down in a chair near the bed and stretched out his long legs. Sipping, he studied her face as she sat cross-legged on the big four-poster bed, brushing her hair.

"What did you do with him?"

"Saw to it that he had a decent meal. He's sleeping in the kitchen."

Jared swirled his brandy. "I understand from Johnnie that I'm to settle up for a cot and two heavy blankets. That comes to three hundred and seventy dollars."

When she remained silent, he sat watching her, drinking his brandy and frowning. He set the glass down and stood. He approached the bed, and Tempest tried to still her automatic response to his closeness.

Sitting down, he took the brush from her hand. "If you don't want him, just say the word. I have plenty to keep him busy."

"As simple as that?"

His eyes darkened. "You'd free him without a thought."

"As he should be. As any mon or woman should be."

Jared tossed the brush aside. "Perhaps, but that's not the way it is in the real world."

"This be a *free* territory. I've heard talk at the bar: there's to be no slavery in California!"

Jared laughed softly, derisively. "The only reason they came to that conclusion is because no man at the constitutional convention wanted to admit that working the streams and mines is labor fit for niggahs," he drawled. "They have no qualms about using Indians."

"Procopius is mine. If I wish to free him, 'tis for me to say."

"Go right ahead. He'll be dead before the day's out. There are men in this country who would sooner kill him than look at him."

"Ye mean the way they're already killing the Indians? Shooting them down like rabbits for the mere sport of it?"

"Exactly."

"Or beating them half to death, like that Mexican who came in here two nights ago?"

Jared stood abruptly. "I had nothing to do with that, damn it!" he said hotly.

"Aye, ye be right, mon, but then ye did naught to put a stop to it, either."

"It was none of my business."

"What is yer business, then, mon? Aside from selling men too much overpriced rotgut whiskey, then cleaning them out at cards of what's left in their hard-earned pokes!"

She had gone too far. Jared's eyes grew dangerous, his smile glacial. "Look to yourself, darling," he drawled. "You pour that whiskey, collect your share of the gold, and then warm my bed. What does that make you?"

The truth stabbed at her like a fiery poker. Her stomach churned with sick pain as she saw the open contempt in Jared's dark eyes. How was she any better than him? Perhaps she was worse, for she knew better, while this way of life seemed utterly natural to him.

She saw everything glowing in his eyes. _He doesna like me, but he wants me_. But was it any different for her? How could she have fallen in love with this man, _knowing_ what he was? Why was it _his_ touch, _his_ possession, that drove her mad with passion?

Jared watched her face and knew that his thrust had hit squarely. Satisfaction and regret battled within him. His anger burned hotly: no half-breed girl of sixteen or seventeen was going to condemn him. Yet there was another part of his nature that made him want badly to reach out and pull her close, to apologize, to tell her how much he loved her. For love her he did, even while he fought hard against it.

The first time he had looked into her eyes, he had sensed that his destiny lay with her. The first time he had gone into her, it had felt as if his soul, what there was of it, had torn free to pour into her. He almost hated her for it.

"We con change things easily enough."

Her thickened brogue told him everything. Swift pain gripped him as he acknowledged that she was indeed strong enough to change things; but she didn't know that yet, and he had to weaken her before she did.

"How?" he sneered. "By going back to grubbing in the muck for tule roots, wearing stinking buckskins and rags, and living in that stick-and-mud hut?"

Tempest swung her legs slowly from the bed and stood squarely in front of him, her pride severely wounded but her head still high. "There be worse things than a wickiup." She stepped past him.

Jared grabbed her and whirled her around. "You arrogant little half-breed bitch," he snarled, shaking her violently, his temper out of control. "Who're you to put your nose in the air?" Dragging her against him, he said into her face, "This is all you're good for!" Then he took her mouth in a savage kiss, grinding her soft lips hard against her teeth. She wouldn't open her mouth, and he dug his fingers into her thick, soft hair, yanking her head back as he went on kissing her. She fought for breath but he wouldn't relent. Her body began to loosen and he plundered her mouth, his hands moving down over her buttocks, pressing her into him, rubbing against her to further his insult.

Then he let her go abruptly, pushing her away from him, his own breath hard and fast with rage and desire.

She slapped him.

Sucking in his breath sharply, he slapped her back. Her head whipped to one side, and when she looked at him again, her teeth were bared and her eyes wild. This time she clenched her fist and went for him as a man would. He blocked her attack and slapped her again, harder, sending her reeling back against the bed.

"You deserved that! Don't expect to hit me across the face and get away with it!"

She tried to straighten, but her legs were shaking too badly. She sank down onto the bed. Lowering her head, she fought back tears.

Jared stared down at her, shocked by the whole episode. He was shaking as badly as she was, and he stared down at his burning hand as if it couldn't possibly be a part of himself. He had hit a woman. He had hit *her*.

She hit me first, he thought in angry self-defense, but his chest squeezed tight and he felt sick. "Let me see," he said in a rough whisper, stepping close and brushing her cascading hair back, tipping up her face.

He had never seen her so pale. Her blue eyes stared up at him dully, filled with tears. He felt his own eyes burning and swallowed hard. One side of her face was darkening already. "Look what you made me do," he murmured raggedly. He sat down beside her and put his arm around her shoulders, pulling her close. She came willingly, leaning heavily into him, pressing her bruised cheek against his chest. He stroked her wild hair, closing his eyes tightly. "I'm sorry," he whispered, his voice breaking.

He knew she was crying. She uttered not a sound, but he felt the dampness soaking into his shirt, silent tears of devastation. He wanted to go back, but how? Jared didn't even know that he was crying, too.

Leaning back, he dragged her with him, stretching out across the bed, pressing her down, his head against her breasts. He could hear her heart, the steady beat picking up speed. He raised himself up.

When he kissed her this time, she opened her mouth to him. Heat expanded in his chest and the ache in his groin matched the one in his heart. Want, endless want.

"We're no good for each other," he whispered hoarsely. "But I couldn't let you go now. I couldn't."

She reached up to touch his face, seeing her own mark there. "I'd die without ye, Jared," she murmured brokenly, and believed it.

"It's the same for me."

At that moment, they both spoke truth. But there were other unspoken truths between them.

Tempest didn't want to think. Neither did Jared. They both wanted only to *feel*. They wanted sensation. They shed their clothes like trees shed autumn leaves.

Their bodies lay tangled across the big bed, writhing against one another in an agony of knowledge. A line had been reached and crossed, and both wanted desperately to go back, to deny it. They *would* deny it! They both had to if they were to go on together.

"I love you," she moaned, tears streaking her face.

"I love *you*," he groaned, his mouth opening wide over hers, kissing her as though he wanted to draw the very soul from her body.

It wasn't enough.

She reached down and he gasped. She stroked lightly up and down, tormenting him. He lay still, allowing it, and when her touch became too much to stand, he caught her wrist tightly and held it against the bed while he lay full on top of her, his legs hard against hers. He rubbed slowly against her. He could feel her body shaking with the tension building inside her. Her head moved back and forth and her lips parted.

Gliding down against her, he opened his mouth over one full breast. She cried out as he used tongue and teeth to drive her higher. Then his mouth coursed lower across her belly, along her hip, down farther. He pressed her legs open, gently nibbling her inner thighs, moving higher. Her flesh burned. He moved higher still.

He raised himself enough to rub his face against the firm warm flesh of her belly. Then he moved down again, unerringly finding his goal.

Tempest cried out. Jared didn't stop. His hands held her, his mouth demanding and hot. She clutched at the blanket, twisting it. Her body shook violently and she made a sound of anticipation. He stopped when she reached the edge, sliding his body up beside hers. He kissed her deeply, his hand working where his mouth had been, maintaining the excruciating need, but pausing just short of answering it.

Rolling onto his back, he turned his head and looked at her. She raised herself slowly, searching his eyes. He put his hand up, touching her cheek for a moment, then stroked her hair, his hand coming to rest on her back. She obeyed the slight pressure and let him guide her down.

"Slow . . . oh, yes . . ."

She knew what she was doing to him and exulted in it, feeling her power over him. She knelt beside him, her hair cascading over his belly and hardened thighs. It was his turn to feel the aching torment. He groaned harshly in his throat and caught her by the hair to stop her. "Let me," she pleaded.

"Yes." He raised up, his face flushed and sweating. "But this way." He pushed her flat, sliding her up so that her hip lay warm against his shoulder. He rolled to one side and buried his head between her legs, reaching down at the same time to guide her back.

They wanted to fill themselves with one another, and did; but each wondered why, even in the sated aftermath of ecstasy, they should still feel so empty.

Later Jared held Tempest on top of him, her body stretched warm, smooth, and velvet-soft over his as he moved his hands down over her, wishing he could press her right into him through his skin. "I didn't mean any of it, Tempest, none of what I said. That's not the way I really feel about you."

"Nor I," she murmured, her head against his bare chest.

But they had meant it. And they both knew it.

Every man is as heaven made him, and
sometimes a great deal worse.
——Miguel de Cervantes Saavedra

As Tempest worked the bar, she fought against the
nausea. It wasn't summer heat bothering her, nor stale beer,
sweating male bodies and heavy smoke. She was with child
again. God would probably take this one, too. In retribution.
Jared wouldn't believe her or care that she believed it. Besides,
he didn't know yet.

Why was she afraid to face him with it? Her mouth curved
sardonically. She knew why.

Fear.

How much of her life was governed by fear? Yet her greatest
fear was of losing this baby. She hoped desperately that God
heard her prayers. Could he when she was pacing a bar, getting
men drunk on cheap whiskey? *Please, God, don't kill this baby.*
She'd tip the bottle and refill a glass. Laughable. Terrifying.
How could God listen to her when she nightly let Jared do
anything he wanted with her. Worse, would God forgive where
and how this bairn had been conceived?

There is no God, Jared had insisted.

Please, God, bring Abram back to me, she'd prayed. And
God had.

So she could lay his throat open in the name of mercy.

Forgive me!

No! He wouldn't. He couldn't because she'd do it again.
If she had it to do again, she'd do it sooner and spare him
more.

A curse trembled on her lips. Someone shouted from down
the bar. She did her job, collected coin, put a finger in the air
before a man's face when he said any woman could be had at
some price, and hated herself.

God rewards His people, Abram had told her.

Abram had died in agony.

Now, here was Jared getting filthy rich off whiskey and

gambling. How many times had she seen him grinning and raking in gold while humming one of Abram's hymns, "Bringing in the Sheaves."

Where are you, God?

Men grumbled up and down the bar over the latest strike made up on the Tuolumne river near an area heavily populated by Sonorans, many of whom were experienced miners from Mexico with peons working for them.

"The Mexicans are crawling all over the country, stealing all the gold that rightfully belongs to us," one grizzled New Englander muttered into his glass.

"If they're paying Green's foreign miner's license tax, there's not a goddamn thing we can do to stop them."

"The hell there isn't," put in another down the bar. "Ought to run the bastards back over the border the way we did in Texas."

"Christ," another young man said. "I came out here to get rich, not to get in a war."

"Twenty bucks a month tax ain't enough to send 'em packing," one miner declared. "Should raise it to two hundred. Then the gold fields would be cleared for the rest of us."

"You think they're going to pay? Hell. Would you?" another snorted.

The man's jaw jutted. "You calling me a dirty, mackerel-snappin' Mexican?"

"Aw, shut up down there!"

"Hit 'er up agin, Tempest. Ahh, thank ya kindly, honey chile."

"Keeeerist," muttered a now-familiar voice. "This stuff tastes like horse piss with the foam farted off."

"Drink up," Tempest told him. "It might just make a man out of ye, though I doubt it." She patted his cheek mockingly and walked on.

"Give me the chance, and I'll show you how much man I am already," he called after her, grinning broadly.

"It ain't just the Mexicans overrunning us," the conversation buzzed on. "There's Frenchies and Chileans and those damn Ducks from Australia."

"Don't forget the Chinks. They're coming in like a yellow tide lately."

"We gotta do somethin' ta stop 'em from takin' all our gold!" someone cried loudly and then belched.

"Whadya say, Professor?"

Heads turned to look at the slender young man at the middle of the bar. He was Tempest's worst and steadiest customer. He came every Friday and Saturday night and sat there dressed in a well-worn but clearly well-made suit. The elbows were patched, and his white shirt had the yellow tinge of age. He could make one shot of whiskey last half an hour, and he never went to the gaming tables.

"Gentlemen," he said slowly, his expression pensive and his eyes gleaming enigmatically, "it is our duty as Americans to abide by the law or we will all be out here in the wilderness stahving togethah."

"So if they don't pay their twenty bucks a month, we run the bastards out or hang 'em from the nearest tree! I agree with you, brother. I agree!"

"Aw, shut up down there," the same voice as before shouted. "Hit 'er up agin, Tempest, ma'am. Ahh, thank ya kindly, honey chile."

Tempest poured and ignored.

"Hear you got Lola Montez coming to do her spider dance for us," one man said as Tempest replenished his glass.

"That be so. Twenty dollars to get a seat to watch."

He swore. "Nothin' free in this world anymore."

"Never was. At least we're getting *culture.*"

Someone laughed. "We've had culture all along. There's a veritable art gallery just down the street a piece. Haven't you seen it?"

Tempest knew he referred to the erotica lining the inside canvas walls of a new establishment that was in competition with the California. She could always tell a man who had just come from there by the glazed look in his eyes as he stepped up to the bar and asked her for a drink.

"Magnificent murals, indeed," another sighed, watching Tempest.

She moved back in the other direction, pouring whiskey from a new bottle and stowing the other in a crate of empties under the bar.

"They strung up two Mexicans by the fort two days ago."

"They werena Mexicans," Tempest said with a sharp glance. "They were Californios."

"What's the difference?" a drunk slurred from down the bar. "They *came* from Mexico, didn't they? Should've gone back where they belonged when they had a chance."

"And where did ye come from, mon?" she retorted hotly.

"I beg your pardon, ma'am," the customer mocked. "I forgot you were a red-high Indian yourself."

Several men shouted and swore. There was a crash and then a thud as the man was knocked back off his stool. He stood up, paused, swayed, and keeled over backward, sprawling unconscious beside a monte table. No one even glanced up. One of Jared's minions came over and dragged him out by the heels.

"You all right, ma'am?" several men asked as Tempest braced her hand on the bar, a wave of faintness bringing spots before her eyes. It passed after a moment.

Tick flipped up the gate to come behind the bar and take over. He glanced at her, then put his hand beneath her elbow in support. "You look like hell, Tempest."

"Thanks." She looked toward the corridor. "Have ye seen Jared?"

"Haven't seen him since this afternoon. A rider came in with a parcel of letters from the East. He went into his office with them." He shrugged. His gaze ran the length of the bar, then returned to her. "Any trouble?"

She shook her head. No more than the usual arguments, scuffles, and evictions by Lightfoot. Her head ached; the noise seemed unbearable tonight. She longed for the quiet of high mountains or the sound of corn rustling and birds in song. What was wrong with her? Why this feeling of impending doom? Surely God wouldn't take this child. Hadn't he taken enough already? He was done with her.

She left the bar and went into the back of the building to the kitchen. Procopius was toting wood. He nodded to her, pausing to await any instructions she might have. She smiled faintly at him and sat down at the table. Johnnie, the young miner turned cook, had left, and another had taken his place, another young man with sunken cheeks, dull eyes, and lines of disillusionment in his face.

"What can I fix you, Tempest?"

She shook her head. She didn't think she could hold anything down.

Procopius dumped the wood into the bin. Jared had been right after all. She had freed him; and the Negro had chosen to stay. He seldom said a word and did whatever was asked. She paid him a share of her own gold at the end of each week and often wondered what he did with it, for he wore the same clothes she had bought for him when he arrived. Glancing up at him, she wondered what went on inside him, if anything did.

She was tired, so tired. She couldn't sleep at night for thinking of the child she carried. She kept remembering the other babe, lying dead on the dirt floor of Abram's cabin.

A mug of milk and some bread was set down in front of her. She looked up through blurred eyes at Procopius's pitch-colored eyes. "I will heat your bathwater for you, Miss Tempest."

She nodded. Maybe that was what she needed—to sit in a big tub and let the warm water soak her body, let the heat ease her. She felt so cold all the time, a permanent chill inside her that even the fiery heat of Jared's possession couldn't assuage.

The milk and bread seemed to settle her stomach. She finished them, then went to Jared's office and found his door closed. She tapped softly. No response came from within. "Jared?" She tapped again, needing to see him, talk to him.

Inside, Jared sat at his big desk with the lantern burning and three letters from Charleston lying open in front of him. One was from his mother, newsy and with a brief, amusing mention of Alicia Hampton's remarks about "the scarcity of good young men." His father's was more enlightening and had made his heart pound. But it was the last and shortest missive that had excited him almost to exultation.

Geneva!

She was a widow, her husband killed in a carriage accident as he returned home from a neighboring plantation. Her letter was brief, but he drank in what she didn't say, what he sensed she was trying to get across to him.

Then his father's letter informing him that Duprés had been heavily in debt, the plantation mortgaged to the second-story rafters. "If I had the money, I could buy it, but I have put all my available capital into another venture. Had I but known . . ."

Jared had never in his wildest dreams hoped for this to happen. Geneva was free, needing him, wanting him still if her letter was any indication; and he was *rich*. There would be no barriers between them this time.

But what about Tempest?

He heard her tap again. "Jared?" He gritted his teeth and closed his eyes, trying to shut her out completely. He didn't want to see her or talk to her. He wanted time to think, time to decide what to do.

Yet he already *knew* what he would do, what he had always

been destined to do. Geneva was the woman he wanted, not this ignorant, half-breed girl. Geneva was his fate.

He had given Tempest everything. Gowns, jewels, luxurious quarters, a slave to wait on her, anything she wanted. They had shared ecstatic moments of physical passion such as she had never experienced before. So why this niggling guilt when everything he had ever wanted lay within his reach?

"Jared?"

He still wanted her. Damn, but he still wanted her. He had only to touch her and his body grew hot and hard. Sometimes just looking at her did it to him. But she was what she was. And he was what he was. He could never marry her—he didn't *want* to marry her. She wouldn't be a fit wife for him. Imagine the reactions of his family and friends back home if he were to take such a one as Tempest McClaren Walker to wife, to give her his children!

While Geneva...

His father would be so proud. Strykers on a plantation at last.

He thought of Geneva the first time he had seen her. He had been eighteen, she sixteen—Tempest's age. But hardly dressed in filthy rags. Geneva had been all in white, her golden hair like a halo about her perfect oval face, her eyes dreamy. Tempest was dark, her blue eyes filled with earthy knowledge. The contrast was so unbearably great that Jared expelled it from his mind.

Geneva came from an old family, old money, so far above him that she was unreachable. He had coerced invitations in order to be close to her, just to see her and exchange a few precious words. They had met once secretly and he had taken one chaste kiss. Then her betrothal had been announced. She had sent him the note that he still carried.

And now Geneva could be his. Everything he had ever dreamed of could be his if he just reached out and took it. Why did he hesitate? He laid his hand on Geneva's letter, his heart racing.

"Jared, con I speak with ye?"

"Goddamn it, leave me alone, will you?" he shouted, incensed.

"So be it."

He heard Tempest walk away and let out a shaky breath, resting his head back against the chair. If only it could be that easy. She was the last thing that stood in his way.

Why was he worrying? Tempest would be all right without him. She was a survivor; she had never really needed him in the first place. He had practically forced her to come to him.

Damn, he didn't want to think of that.

He'd see that she had plenty to live on. Hell, he'd *give* her the California. It was half hers by right anyway, and he didn't want the stain of it on him when he went back to claim Geneva. All he needed was the gold it had brought him. He'd take that, and if Tempest wanted to carry on here, she could do so on her own.

She doesn't even know the power she has.

She would hate him.

Reaching out, Jared drew a bottle of brandy toward him and uncorked it. He spent the rest of the night rationalizing and getting drunk.

Tempest lay awake waiting for him, her hands spread solemnly on her belly. Why this feeling of unease? Surely Abram had spoken truth when he said God was merciful. *If ye be there, hear me. Forgive me. Dunna take this babe. Not this time—please.*

Silence answered.

Where was Jared? She needed him.

She finally slept in the small hours of the morning, alone.

Jared was red-eyed and foul-tempered the next day. He shouted orders at his men and told Tempest tersely that he had business to attend to and didn't want to be distracted by anyone. His message was cold and clear. Tempest stayed away from him, confused and frightened by his sudden disaffection. What had she done?

Jared's banker came to call, and he and Jared remained locked in the office all day. The man looked pale and distraught when he left. "You're sure you want to do this, sir? California is a growing—"

"I know what I'm doing." Jared cut him off, seeing Lightfoot standing silently nearby, listening.

"We'll have things taken care of, then, and I wish you luck, Mr. Stryker."

Lightfoot looked pointedly at Jared when the man left. Jared met his eyes in challenge.

"You're pulling out, ain't you?" The answer didn't need to be voiced. "Does Tempest know?"

"I'll handle her," Jared told him. "You hold your tongue.

One word of this before it comes from me, and you'll be out of a job."

Lightfoot's mouth curved faintly. "Seems I will anyway, doesn't it?" he murmured under his breath as Jared passed him.

While Tempest worked the bar, Jared had Procopius pack all of his things into several trunks. Everything was taken care of now. He'd be leaving on the morning ship going downriver to San Francisco. There he would take one of the new steamers down the coast to the Isthmus of Panama. He'd be home within three months, possibly less. *Home!* He'd sent letters ahead to notify everyone of his coming.

Geneva would be waiting for him. He *felt* it.

He had only to tell Tempest he was leaving.

Tempest.

He sat in the wing chair by the bedroom window, drinking brandy and waiting for her. He had sent Procopius down to fetch her. When he heard her voice in the hallway as she said something to the Negro, his mouth tightened slightly. She always talked to that nigger like he was free and white. When she asked something of him, it was a request, not an order. She would never learn, would never understand, he told himself, trying to widen the gap between them. Jared held onto that conviction as he watched the door open. He felt pain suddenly, like a hand gripping his throat, choking him. He stood up slowly and set the snifter down, hardening himself to the glowing, familiar look in her eyes. She thought he had called her to the bedroom for another reason, and cursed his body's answering response. He still wanted her. Distance would kill that, though; tomorrow she'd be out of sight and out of mind, past history. He could think of Geneva, waiting.

Her smile faded as she saw the trunks stacked in the middle of the room. She stared at them blankly, then lifted her eyes questioningly. "We be leavin'?"

"Not we. Me."

"You?"

It still hadn't hit her. He straightened, taking a deep breath. "I'm leaving for North Carolina tomorrow morning. I've received word from home. I'm needed there."

"When will ye be comin' back?"

He could lie. He could tell her he would be returning in a few months. It would make his leaving tomorrow morning easier, avert a storm.

"I won't be."

Her eyes flickered, raw, questioning, confused, frightened. "Just like that, Jared?"

"I've only taken the gold," he went on doggedly, determined not to acknowledge the look in her eyes. He had never seen it before, and it lashed at his conscience. But the worse she made him feel, the angrier he became. What right did she have to stand there looking at him like that? He had been good to her; he had made her happy. She might still be down in that wickiup by the river, starving, or even be dead by now.

"Tick and the others will look after things for you. They'll know how to keep the place running, and I've left enough gold to operate the tables. All you have to do is sit back and rake it in. Hell, Tempest, you could be the richest woman in California. You'll be able to marry any man you want." Pain shot through him even as he said it. He swore softly. "We don't belong together," he told her fiercely. "We come from two different worlds, you and I. And I'm going back where I belong, going back to take my rightful place."

"And what be yer rightful place, mon?"

"I'm going to own a plantation on a river. I'm going to have tobacco fields. I'm going to marry Gen—" He stopped.

"Marry who?" Her eyes changed. The pain was deeper and more intense, but there was something more.

"Geneva Stafford," he told her. Suddenly he wanted Tempest to understand. "She had a prior claim on my heart, Tempest. I thought she was unreachable. I've loved her for years."

"Why did ye come here at all?"

He had never seen her so pale. "Because she married someone else—someone rich."

"Then she dinna really want ye."

"You don't understand. Things are different in the East. She *wanted* me, but Duprés had *money*. The family plantation was in difficulty. He's dead now, and he lost almost everything anyway. And I'm rich. There's nothing to stand in our way."

"Except me."

He said nothing for a moment. "You can't do a thing to stop me, Tempest."

She spread her hands over her chest, her eyes filling. "What of the promises ye made me?"

He steeled himself. "What promises?"

"That ye would take care of me—"

"I have."

"Ye're leaving me!"

"You've got the California."

"Ye said ye loved me."

"I did. I still do, but not in the way that counts for anything. I love Geneva in that way."

"Were ye thinking of her every time ye bedded me?"

"No," he said harshly, almost hating her.

"Then ye dunna love her. Ye love me."

"Don't do this to me, Tempest. We've had some good times together. We enjoyed each other for a while. Let's leave it at that." Damn her, why did she have to look at him like that?

"I need ye, Jared."

"Jesus. Don't beg."

She came close, reaching up to touch him. He shoved her hand away. She clutched his coat strongly. "Ye canna just leave—"

"Let go."

"No!"

He tore her hands loose from him and held her wrists in a viselike gripe. "Where's your damn pride?"

"Where be yers?" she retorted. "Ye would cast me off for no better reason than to run back to a woman who married someone else simply because he had more gold than ye did?"

"You're not fit to even speak of her!"

"Geneva Stafford. Bitch whore," she spat, tears blinding her.

Jared wanted badly to hit her, so badly that he thrust her away roughly, his fists clenching at his sides. "You're the whore, Tempest," he said, going for her life's blood this time. "Just an ignorant, half-breed slut." He knew she would come at him then, and stood ready for her. "See?" he snarled, catching hold of her and yanking her close so that he could spit the words into her face. "Just a red-high little savage with claws and teeth bared like a beast. You're not fit to walk down the same street as Geneva Stafford."

Hot blood rushed through his veins at the feel of her body against his and he shoved her away abruptly, wanting to get away from her as fast as he could.

She uttered a cry of fury and pain and came at him again. He blocked her blows, his anger rising. Finally, enraged, he grabbed hold of her and dragged her roughly across the room. "All right, you bitch!" He threw open the closet door and flung her in, slammed it. "Act like an animal and you get treated like one." He dragged a chair across and propped it firmly under the doorknob.

"Nooooo!!!" she screamed, pounding on the door.

He crossed the room and pulled the door open. *"Procopius!"*

The Negro came on the run. Jared gritted his teeth against Tempest's screaming; she did sound like an animal, clawing wildly at the door, making that hair-raising noise. "Take those trunks downstairs. Now!" Wide-eyed, the Negro looked toward the closet door. "Goddamn it, did you hear me?!" Jared demanded dangerously.

"Yassuh," Procopius said quickly, coming in and shouldering one trunk while dragging out another.

Tempest was quiet when Procopius returned for the last two trunks. Jared stood by the window, drinking brandy, wanting desperately to be quit of the place. It was nearing dawn. His ship would be leaving in a few hours.

"All ready, suh," Procopius told him, straight-backed.

"I'll be right down." He jerked his head in cold dismissal. When Procopius had left, Jared crossed to the closet door. "Tempest?"

She didn't answer.

"If you promise to behave yourself, I'll let you out."

Still she didn't answer.

"All right. Have it your way."

Jared turned and walked out, slamming the bedroom door behind him.

PART III

With Sling and Stone

A faithful friend is the medicine of life.

—Ecclesiasticus 6:16

Bjorn Lindahl sat leaning comfortably against a granite boulder and watched Claus finish his third trout and toss the naked fish skeleton into the fire. He had already polished off a plate of beans with half a loaf of sourdough bread.

Bjorn grinned. "Still hungry."

Claus let out a dignified, complimentary belch and sighed contentedly. He patted his taut belly. "You know I have a small stomach, *komrat*."

"Any smaller and we would be in *big* trouble." Bjorn laughed. Tilting his head back, he looked up at the star-studded sky. The alders just down the hill reminded him of home. He no longer had the yearning to go back: too much had changed since he had left. He had learned how much on his last return, three years ago.

He thought of Tempest again. He could not get the girl out of his mind, though he knew it was hopeless to have this passion for her. She was Stryker's and he kept a possessive eye on her. Bjorn wanted to go to the California again, but he knew that his presence there, and her deference to him because of his foolhardy act of saving that saddlebag, would only cause her trouble.

Why do women always love such men, he wondered, by no means for the first time. Men like Stryker seemed to cause a fever in a woman's blood. He'd seen the way Tempest looked at him, like a small creature mesmerized by a deadly snake.

"We had a good day," Claus said, leaning forward to pour himself a mug of strong coffee.

"Ja."

"I would give half of the gold for one deep breath of salt air." He sipped the strong brew and watched Bjorn's pensive face over the rim. He could tell by his grim expression that he was thinking of the half-breed girl again. Since the night of the great fire, Bjorn had been able to concentrate on little else

338

but his hopeless fascination with her.

"Perhaps we will find enough gold to buy a ship?" Claus tried again.

"Maybe."

"I would be happy to have a berth on a windjammer and be sailing for Sverige again," Claus said.

Bjorn's eyes cleared. "Would you give up going 'round the Horn? The straits have always gotten your blood up."

"Ja," Claus grinned. "To go up the mast in a storm again—that makes a man feel alive!"

"Remember you and me untangling the ropes while those cowards hid below decks?"

"Two Swedes are worth a dozen others," Claus said, raising his mug. "Let's leave this place and go back where we belong."

"To hardtack with weevils in it and getting the lash when we do not obey?" Bjorn demanded. "No. If I ever go back to the sea, it will be at the helm of my own ship."

"We will have to buy a fleet of dinghies," Claus told him wryly. "We will be old men before we smell the ocean again or feel the wind in our faces."

Bjorn stared grimly into the fire, thinking again of Tempest. He couldn't purge himself of her.

Claus watched him for a long moment, and then sighed heavily. "You want to go back to the California, ja? And see the flicka again."

Bjorn glanced across at him bleakly.

"Why are you such a fool over this girl, Bjorn?"

Bjorn rested his head against the boulder and closed his eyes.

"You know what you will find," Claus reasoned. "She will be at that bar. You will want to kill every man there because they all stare at her breasts. She will smile for you and get your blood up, but it's Stryker's whiskey she gives you and when he bends his little finger, she will—"

"Stop!" Bjorn snarled, lunging forward in a surge of anger. "Not another word, Claus." He stood and moved away into the darkness. A fit of black temper seized him, and he broke off a thick, low-hanging branch of a tree, smashing it against the trunk before flinging it violently into the darkness beyond. He swore through gritted teeth.

"We could have used that on our fire," Claus said drolly.

Claus was right. Bjorn knew he was being a fool, but the

knowledge didn't stop the gut-ache he felt for the girl. What exactly was it about her that gripped him so strongly that he couldn't seem to break the bond? For it was certain that she felt no such bond to him.

She was beautiful, but other women were beautiful. Her body was perfect, her breasts full and ripe and heavy enough to fill his hands. But he'd lost himself between the thighs of other perfect female bodies before in seaport whorehouses around the world.

He raked his fingers into his hair and closed his eyes.

The night of the great fire, he'd looked into Tempest's wild blue eyes and something had moved inside him. It hadn't moved back again, and he felt himself forever altered because of whatever he'd seen. All he'd known was that he had to get that saddlebag for her, and when he had, he had stood helplessly, watching the agony shining darkly in her eyes as she fought to save it, uncaring of the manure and mud in which she knelt, ruining the expensive satin gown. When she'd looked up at him then, he had wanted to lift her and hold her close and never let her go.

And he was a fool.

He came back into the circle of firelight and hunkered down to pour himself a mug of coffee.

"You're going back," Claus said simply.

Bjorn raised his eyes.

"I've never seen you this way about a woman," Claus said sadly. "Why don't we go to Placerville? There is a whorehouse there. You can burn this fever out and have a cure bought with your hard-earned money."

"Ja, and crabs or the pox."

"You have always chosen your women carefully."

Bjorn's blue eyes narrowed. "Tempest is not a whore," he said gruffly.

Claus leaned forward intently. "She is *Stryker's mistress*, like it or not. Get it into your head, Bjorn, and have done with this before it destroys you. You have heard from a dozen others that she has only been with him a year. Where was she before that? How many others—"

Bjorn swore and flung his tin mug aside. "I will not listen—"

"Her eyes are a hundred years old. How did someone so young come to look so—*wise? Kamrat*, a fox can take care of itself. It survives by cunning. But it has no soul to touch."

"It's Stryker who has no soul!"

"And the girl chose to be with him."

Neither spoke for a long time. The fire burned low. Claus got up and prodded it with his booted foot before laying on another log to last the night. He looked at his friend, who was staring at nothing, his expression tormented, and pitied him.

"I must go back, Claus," Bjorn said hoarsely. He raked his hands through his hair. "I must go back and see her again."

Claus sat down. He knew what to expect. They would go to the California and Bjorn would sit at the bar. Stryker would glower at his back and order Tempest away, and she would obey his will. Bjorn would leave the casino and get drunk. Before the night was over, he'd be in the middle of another brawl in some tavern on the Embarcadero, and it would be left to Claus to see that no man put a knife in Bjorn's back.

"Ja," he said with a heavy sigh. "We go back." He couldn't let Bjorn go alone.

There was no accounting for why a man fell in love with a woman. Certainly reason had little to do with it, for if it did, men would pick their mates more wisely.

Claus stretched out and pulled a blanket over himself. Bjorn was still silently staring at nothing, but the look in his eyes told Claus that his thoughts were far from pleasant. Bjorn knew also what they would find at the California, and worse, he knew what it would do to his friend. But he couldn't change it.

Claus looked away. If ever he loved a woman, he prayed she would be innocent. He hoped she would be a hardworking farm girl from his homeland, a woman he'd make children with and cherish until the day he died.

A churning throng of shouting men jammed the street in front of the California. A barker was standing on the second-story veranda shouting down at them: "Five hundred dollars and you can have a chance at being half-owner of this money-making enterprise! Step on up, gentlemen, and lay that gold dust down. You're never going to get a chance like this again!"

Bjorn stared. "Something has happened!" He swore.

"Fight starts in fifteen minutes!" the barker shouted. Men laughed and shouted ribald remarks. Some raised pouches of gold dust and shoved through the pack to reach the barricaded entrance of the casino.

"If you've got the dust, all you need is guts!" the barker

challenged. "Chance of your lifetime! Come on! *Come on!* Last man standing when it's over will be half-owner of the California!"

"What happened to Tempest?" Bjorn shouted.

"She goes with the place," someone answered, and there was lewd laughter.

"If I had the gold dust, *nobody* could keep me outta there," another man shouted.

Bjorn looked back at Claus wildly. "I've got to get inside."

Claus, looking resigned, made a gesture to proceed. "You first. I'll follow in your wake."

Bjorn lowered his head like a bull and began shoving his way through the crowd, ignoring insults and curses, blocking half a dozen blows and returning several, before he made it to the swinging doors of the casino.

Tick and Missouri stood behind a sturdy barrier, two more men with rifles flanking them. Inside, the casino was jammed with men, some already fighting, others standing around with whiskey bottles in their hands.

"Lindahl," Tick said, recognizing him immediately. He grinned broadly. "Jared gave orders once to keep you out of the California."

"Raise the gate or I'll smash your face in," Bjorn growled, leaning forward.

"Five hundred dollars in gold dust and you can step right on over it and join the others in the ring."

"Where's Stryker?"

Tick's face hardened. "Bastard left a week ago. Took all the assets with him, except Tempest. She's upstairs."

"Was this your idea?" Bjorn demanded, jerking his head toward the throng inside waiting for the fight to start.

"No, sir," Tick answered grimly. "Tempest's orders." He nodded toward a trunk filled with pouches. "Enough gold to make this place a palace and we'll find a man to—have at the helm," he said, gauging Bjorn's height and breadth and the look in his eyes. "Pay up, Lindahl, or stand aside. Others are waiting."

Bjorn yanked his poke of gold dust out of his pocket and slammed it on the plank. Claus choked softly behind him, and muttered, "There are two hundred men in there, Bjorn. Are you trying to get us killed?"

"I'm going in."

Claus muttered something in Swedish about two months of

back-breaking work in water cold enough to freeze the balls off a brass monkey and stubborn, stupid Swedes who didn't know any better, but he took out his gold dust and laid his pouch on the counter beside Bjorn's.

Lightfoot weighed the pouches on a scale and nodded. "Just made it."

"Come on in," Tick told them, grinning. "Check your weapons at the bar, if you have any. This is going to be a fair fight. May the best man win."

Bjorn put his hand on the plank barrier and swung himself over. Claus followed. They strode to the bar, checked their two revolvers and hunting knives, and turned around to survey the considerable competition.

"You've done it this time," Claus groaned.

"Old shipmate, you just keep them off my back," Bjorn grinned, rubbing his hands together.

No one else came in, everyone who had the requisite amount of dust being already inside. At a signal from Tick, Missouri jumped up on the bar. "Pick your partners, gentlemen! The Sacramento Waltz is about to begin!"

Men laughed and milled around, facing off, their fists raised.

Claus leaned back against the bar. "Why don't we just sit the first part of this one out," he suggested blandly.

Missouri raised a small derringer and fired. Deafening noise filled the casino as men began scrapping with fists, bootheels, and heads.

"Eeeeya!" cried a man close to the bar, and struck Bjorn squarely in the jaw before he could duck, slamming him back against the long bar.

Men pressed against the windows outside, peering in and shouting encouragement, making bets, swearing vehemently when their standard-bearers dropped.

One man in the center of the casino was swinging a chair, clearing a wide circle around him. The prostrate body count was mounting, the number of remaining competitors diminishing.

Bjorn braced himself against the bar and used his feet to propel two attackers back, then took one of them down with a hard right and came at the other like a battling ram, head to chest. The man uttered a great whooff and sailed backward like a barkentine before a good wind, downing three men behind him before he fell, skidded, and thudded hard against a wall. He sat there peacefully, out of the running.

Claus laughed and ducked, laughed and ducked again, wagged his finger in an opponent's reddened face, ducked again, and then delivered a hard, expert blow to the man's jaw. Bjorn let out a bellow of pure joy and dove into the melee. His golden mane danced about his face as he swung to the left, to the right, to the left again, leaving a trail of the fallen behind him as he made his way to the center of the room. He swiped the chair from the sweating whirling dervish who was wielding it and sent it hurtling through the air toward the grand mirror behind the bar. The man had one second to open his mouth like a beached fish before he was caught by shirt and crotch, heaved up, spun once, and sent flying after the chair.

"Aaaahhhh!" *Crash!*

Bjorn dusted off his hands, grinning from ear to ear. He turned in a slow circle, Claus at his back, and beckoned to the surrounding men.

It was readily apparent to every man in the casino where the greatest threat came from. The two men standing in the center fought as a team, well-honed and infinitely practiced from years of barroom brawling in every major port around the world. Bjorn's bright blue eyes glowed.

"Komma!" he challenged, his teeth bared, and laughed low. *"Tilltrada!"*

The surrounding men growled. The circle closed.

From outside the California, men tried to peer in, seeking a better vantage point. "Who's winning?"

"Hell if I know!"

"Who's that bellowing?"

"That damn Swede."

"Keeerist! *Look out!*" The crowd at the window ducked as a man came flying through with an explosion of glass.

Men were being catapulted back from the tight knot of men in the center of the California amid the noise of shouting, swearing, and laughter cut short. In less than thirty minutes, two hundred fighters had been narrowed down to fifty. In another thirty minutes, the count had narrowed to six: Bjorn, Claus, a burly Texan with black hair and a handlebar mustache, a wiry Georgian, a dapper Frenchman who was better at duck and parry than at hitting, and a Pennsylvania farm boy who rarely connected a punch but whose head was harder than granite.

Bjorn worked on the Texan with his punishing right and left while Claus, at his back, grappled with the Georgian. The farm boy was chasing the Frenchman around the room. Outside there was ribald laughter and hooted insults.

With a quick lunge, Bjorn shoved the Texan back, stuck his foot out to trip the Frenchman, and used interlocked hands to connect a blow front and center to the farm boy's head.

"Five," he said smugly.

"You talk too soon," Claus laughed, and Bjorn glanced back to see the farm boy stagger, sway back and forth like a tree in a hard wind, then turn slowly, but hold his feet.

"Jacklar!"

The Texan's fist split Bjorn's lip and sent him jolting backward. He kept his feet. "No quarter," Bjorn grinned, wiping the blood from his mouth and taking up a fighting stance. The Texan crouched at the ready, and Bjorn let out a lusty roar and came at him, all sails set. Stunned, the Georgian glanced back as Bjorn thundered past, and Claus landed a blow with a jaw-splitting crack.

"Fem!"

"Fyra!" Bjorn counted down, putting everything he had into a blow to the Texan's stomach and another upward thrust to the jaw. The big man sagged slowly to the plank floor.

The Frenchman hotfooted it around the floor, smiling nervously at first Bjorn and then Claus as they worked him toward a corner. When he was trapped, they turned to one another to consult briefly. Claus tapped his chest. Bjorn shook his head and tapped his own chest. Claus gave him an indignant look. Bjorn bowed and gestured dramatically toward the Frenchman, who said, *"Sacre bleu!"* as Claus stepped forward with lightning speed and sent the poor man reeling back against the wall. He slid slowly down until he sat like an idler dozing against the wall.

Bjorn turned and watched the farm boy staggering around the barroom, tripping here and there over unconscious or groaning forms.

Claus brushed off his hands and tucked them into his pockets, leaning back against a wall. Bjorn rolled his eyes and trod carefully toward the boy.

"Har, komrat," Bjorn directed the boy's attention. The farmer swung, missed, swung, missed, and swung again. Bjorn shook his head, brought his fist back, and connected. The boy staggered back but didn't go down. Two more blows still didn't flatten him.

Claus walked casually across the room, picking his way

carefully so that he wouldn't step on anyone. He reached Bjorn, who was grunting Swedish curses and nursing his bruised hands. Claus, sweeping his leg wide, hit the farmer squarely behind the knees. The boy toppled with a thud. When he started to push himself up on his elbows, Claus sat heavily on his chest, put his hand firmly on the boy's face, and pushed his head down again. *"Somna,"* he commanded softly. "Sleep." He patted the boy's battered face, then crossed his arms over his chest and nodded at Bjorn.

Upstairs, Tempest heard a booming roar of wild, jubilant laughter that reminded her piercingly of McClaren.

In much wisdom is much grief.
—Ecclesiastes 1:18

"Congratulations, Mr. Lindahl," Oliver said from the stairs and stood to one side ceremoniously, lowering his rifle and raising one hand toward the landing above. His smile became lascivious as Bjorn slowly came up the stairs. "She's all yours, if you can man her."

Bjorn's blood still rushed hot with the fighting, and with the excitement of seeing Tempest again. His heart pounded, and he forced his breathing to evenness. He stopped on the step below Oliver so that their eyes were level. "One thing we get clear from start," he said coldly. "You speak of Tempest in that tone again and I will put you under six feet of dirt. *Förstå?*"

Oliver's eyes grew wide and his skin went sallow. "I meant no disrespect."

"That is good." Bjorn looked up the stairs pensively. Running an exploratory hand over his bruised chin and glancing down at his clothes, he grimaced. "I will need to clean up before I see her."

"Yes, sir," Oliver said quickly. "Just tell the darky you want water and he'll fetch it for you right away."

Bjorn smiled at him coldly and went up the stairs.

A big Negro with the blackest eyes Bjorn had ever encountered stood in the upstairs hallway. He was on guard before a door, his body rigidly at attention, his arms crossed over his broad chest. He looked at Bjorn enigmatically, then started to turn to knock. Bjorn held up a restraining hand and shook his head.

"What's your name?"

"Procopius, suh."

"Well, Procopius, I need to wash up. Oliver said you'd show me where."

"Yassuh." The voice was deep and slurred with an ignorance

347

that somehow didn't match the intelligence in those pitch eyes. Bjorn studied him as he walked down the hall to open another door. "I'll fetch clean water for you, suh."

"Var sä gud." He entered the room as the Negro left. Stripping off his shirt, he ruefully eyed the torn seams and the bloodstained front. A mirror over the empty washbasin showed him his very battered face. His right eye was almost swollen shut, and his lower lip was split. Wincing, he drew his lips back in a painful smile and saw that one of his front teeth was chipped. His nose looked out of line again. Placing his fingers on either side, he shifted the cartilage with a groan, straightening it. His eyes watered.

The Negro came in with a steaming bucket of water. Bjorn stood back as Procopius poured some into the porcelain basin. Bjorn nodded with a smile, then bent to splash water on his face. He sucked in air through gritted teeth as needles of hot pain shot through him. He lathered his hands and washed, rinsing again, then he groped for his shirt to dry his face and felt a towel placed in his hand instead.

Straightening, he dried his face and shoulders while studying Procopius. The black man's pose was deferential, but his eyes were anything but. "Free man or slave, Procopius?"

"Ah don't rightly know, suh. That'll be up to you now as you seem to be the new mastah around heah."

"You're free, then," Bjorn said, tossing the towel aside.

A faint, humorless smile touched the black man's mouth. "Yassur," he said dryly.

Bjorn looked him over. "We look about the same size. Can I borrow your shirt?" He held his own up with a grimace of distaste.

Procopius covered his surprise quickly. He'd never met a white man who would willingly don the cast-off shirt of a slave, let alone request one.

"Ja?" Bjorn pressed, impatient.

"I will get you a clean shirt, sir," Procopius said, and left.

Bjorn turned back to the mirror to study his face again. "You're one hell of a mess, Bjorn Lindahl," he said grimly and shook his head.

Jared Stryker had been a remarkably handsome man, he had to admit. Lean and hard, self-confident, aristocratic, and possessed of one of those lopsided smiles that ooze virility. Bjorn had seen Stryker turn that sexual smile on Tempest more than once, and he had also seen Tempest's response.

glowed with fire. Her chin tilted up. *"You,"* she repeated again, and he sensed an accusation in the defiant pride in those chilly eyes.

He didn't know what to say. He couldn't have spoken had he known the words.

She raised one eyebrow. "So be it." And began to undress.

His lips parted as she reached behind and loosened the gaudy dress. The front dipped. He lost his breath. She pushed the gown down, letting it drop to the floor in a fiery heap, then straightened and unlaced the bone and lace corset, allowing it to fall slowly, dramatically open. She held the hard edges out and then dropped the garment with a cold casualness that shook Bjorn to the core.

Cupping her breasts, she raised them and then rubbed them licentiously. She ran her hands slowly down and smoothed off the silken underwear, all the way down until she stepped out of them.

Her eyes never once left his. Bjorn had seen that same expression in the eyes of an old prostitute who'd blocked his way just outside an alleyway in Hong Kong. He felt sick.

With a softly muttered imprecation, Bjorn strode across to the big bed, grabbed hold of the spread, and yanked it off, striding back to drag it around Tempest's body.

For one second, Tempest's face twisted. Then she drew in a choking breath and shoved the covering off again. "Ye were the last mon standing, Bjorn Lindahl," she said thickly, her eyes wide and blurred. She stepped forward with determination, her mouth trembling slightly, then pinching tightly as she rubbed her svelte body against his.

"Don't," he said hoarsely, grasping her shoulders and putting her away from him.

"Why not? Ye *won*. A bargain is a bargain," she sneered, her eyes far too bright. "Am I too thin?" She ran her hands over her slender hips. "Or too fat?" She raised her breasts again. "Dunna ye like me anymore?" she pouted like a practiced whore.

She had the most beautiful body Bjorn had ever seen, but there was no desire in him, only an agonized despair at what he saw in her face. A man who found himself used by a woman invariably became a woman-hater, but a woman who found she had been used by a man turned her hatred inward against herself.

"Do I have to show ye what to do?" she purred, and put her hand boldly against the front of his pants. He made a harsh, growling sound in his throat and grabbed her wrist, jerking her hand away from him.

"*Stanna, flicka,*" he ordered raggedly. "Stop it!"

Tempest winced at the pain of Bjorn's bruising hold, but was inwardly satisfied by it. Wasn't it exactly what she deserved, what she wanted? Push him far enough, and perhaps she could bring him to use his fists on her as well. She forced a bland expression to her face and raised her chin insultingly. "What be the matter, mon? Isna a half-breed slut good enough for ye?"

"*Varfor gora du sä till dig själv?*" Bjorn rasped hoarsely. "Why do you do this to yourself? It's him you should hate, not yourself!"

Her eyes fell away before the pained expression in his. He let her go and she stepped back slowly, unable to look up at all. Finally, she managed to look at him. Spreading her hands, she said, "This is what I am good for."

"Is that what the bastard told you when he left?"

She drew in a breath and closed her eyes tightly. Bjorn stepped forward, bending his head so that their faces were close. "Look at me, flicka," he pleaded softly. "Did you sell your body to him or give yourself, all of yourself, because you loved him?" he demanded very quietly, catching hold of her shoulders and forcing her to face him. He knew the answer already, and wished it were not so.

"What does it matter, mon? It all comes down to the same thing."

It wasn't what he had expected. His hand cupped her smooth, cold cheek. "No."

She lifted her head, her eyes brimming. "Why did it have to be you, Bjorn Lindahl?"

"Thank God it was no one else," he murmured huskily, smiling grimly down at her.

She moved back from what she saw in his eyes. She nodded toward the bed coldly. "Ye dunna want me?"

"I didn't say that. I just do not want you *this* way." He bent and retrieved the colorful blanket lying on the floor and wrapped it around her again. He bent and snatched up the red satin and black lace gown. "And never in something like this!" He ripped it violently from bodice to hem so that it was irreparable, then wadded it up into a crushed lump, heaving it into a corner.

She watched him dispassionately. The coldness had gone from her pale blue eyes, but now there was nothing at all to fill them again.

"Where are your clothes?" he asked, crossing quickly to the highboy. There was satin and lace everywhere—the wardrobe of an expensive prostitute. He finally found a halfway decent robe and dragged it out, bringing it to her. She stood all wrapped up in the bedspread, her face calm, her eyes turned bleakly inward. She didn't even seem to see the robe he held out for her.

Dropping it, he took her in his arms gently. Her body was rigid and cold, but he felt an inward trembling. Silent grief, contained fury not even yet acknowledged; it would eat her alive.

"Why did this have to happen to you?" he murmured. *Oh, min kara, how do I change it now?*

He felt her hands against his chest, pushing back. He let his arms loosen, let her go. She reached for one of his mangled hands and lifted it. She looked at it for a moment and then pressed her cheek against it. "It should never have been you," she whispered.

His eyes burned and he raised his hand to lightly smooth the dark, soft hair. She moved back, raising her head, her eyes meeting his as she let go of his hand.

"Once, a very long time ago, I told another man that he couldna change what I be," she said very solemnly. "I will warn ye the same now, Bjorn Lindahl. For yer own good, mon."

And what are you, California Tempest, but the woman I've looked for all my life and never thought to find? I knew the night I saw you who you were.

"I don't want to change you, *min älskling.* I want to make you mine."

So had they all said—Abram, Jared, and hundreds of young men at the California's bar. Each in his own way had wanted to consume her just as completely as the wolves who had clawed frantically, hungrily, at the stones before a burned-out fireplace. The wolves had only begun; Abram had continued; Jared had finished.

And now this mon has come to pick at the last remaining pieces of me, until there is naught left but darkness and shadow.

Or was that all there ever was?

Aye. *'Tis true.* It was only the infrequent glimmer of light that had blinded her.

Tempest looked up at Bjorn's solemn, battered face and raised one eyebrow. Her smile curved faint and bitter. "I am already yers, mon. All ye need do is claim the prize." She turned her head slowly, her gaze pointedly grazing the bed before remeeting his eyes. Hers showed no emotion. "Any time ye want. Any way ye want."

But Bjorn left the room instead, after softly murmuring, "Another time, *min kara,* when you have the heart for it."

Let each become all that he was created capable
of becoming.
—Thomas Carlyle

Bjorn went back downstairs and assumed command
of the California. Those who still remained from the brawl he
hired to clear away the rubble. By daybreak, the broken chairs
and tables had been toted away to be junked or repaired, the
window frames had been cleared of jagged glass, and the casino
had been swept and swabbed clean of whiskey, shards of glass,
and blood.

In the kitchen, big pots of mulligan stew were put on to
simmer. By midday most of the losers had gone, each with
some gold dust in his pouch from honest labor and his stomach
full of good, hot food.

Bjorn sat at the long bar drinking whiskey. He flexed his
hands.

"You are very grim for a man who has won the way to all
his dreams," Claus observed quietly, leaning sideways against
the polished bar and studying Bjorn's heavily lined countenance.

Bjorn sloshed more whiskey into a glass and shoved it down
the bar toward his friend. "Nothing is wrong. *Har. Skoal!*" He
raised his own replenished glass.

"How is Tempest?" Claus asked over the rim of the glass.

Bjorn clenched and unclenched one hand. "Not good. But
I am going to make her better."

"How are you going to do that?"

"I don't know," he admitted glumly.

Claus glanced back and cleared his throat. "Why don't you
ask her?"

"Bjorn," Tempest said from behind him. Bjorn's head came
up and he glanced to one side, seeing how Claus's eyes widened
and took her in from top to bottom and back to top again.
Grimly, Bjorn set his glass down, turned and stood.

She was wearing a flowing green satin gown trimmed in cream-colored lace and black ribbons. The bodice was low, but not so appallingly revealing as the red and black gown of the night before. Yet he liked this one no more than the other. It had the same cut and line of disrepute; it was a gown a woman would wear to sell herself. The lace dragged a man's eyes down to the tan mounds of soft flesh, down to the slender waist he could easily span with his hands and have room to spare, down to the trim hips emphasized by scalloped folds of shimmering satin.

Worse than the dress was the worldly look in her eyes.

Claus glanced at Bjorn's face and excused himself.

"Why be the door closed at this time of day?" she demanded, tilting her head back to look up at Bjorn. She was tall for a woman, but still scarcely reached his chin.

"The California is closed until things are cleaned and repaired. A day, two. Maybe more."

"We are losing money."

"What's a little gold dust?" He shrugged. "Have you eaten, flicka?"

"I'm not hungry. We can open now. We have plenty of whiskey and there are tables for gaming."

"Why are you in so great a hurry?"

"We are losing money," she repeated, her eyes glittering.

"I am no gambler. I know nothing of running a place like this. Don't even know if I want to." His gaze swept, derisively about the huge, garish room.

"Then why did ye bother to fight for it?"

"I fought for *you*," he told her frankly, his eyes holding hers again.

Hers flickered at his intensity. She studied him uncertainly and said, "Ye gambled in the fight and won. Now ye have me *and* this. One doesna come without the other."

"Why did you do it?" he demanded softly. "To make yourself cheap because of what that bastard did to you?"

She stiffened. "Jared has nought to do with this anymore."

"No?"

"The California is all I have, and I will hang onto it. I will make it pay."

"Why?"

She would not answer the angry demand in his eyes. Some things she could keep for herself as long as she was able. "I couldna control what was happening," she admitted darkly.

"We have dealers who take gold, men who steal bottles from the bar, men who beg in the kitchen for food. I needed a mon strong enough to keep the peace, to make sure what is mine *stays* mine. Ye're that mon, Bjorn."

His mouth curved in self-mockery. "Because I can hold more whiskey than most men and be the last one standing in a barroom brawl? That's why you need me?"

"Why else would I need ye?" she asked, and only felt worse for the look that flickered across his face.

"You make men pay to fight for you."

Inwardly she winced. "For the California," she said, tipping up her chin.

"No, flicka, for you. No man here fought only for the California, and if it was only this," he jerked his head angrily, "that the brawl was for, why did you throw yourself into the pot?"

"To sweeten it," she said bitterly, her eyes burning.

"No. To debase yourself for what he did to you, for what you let him do."

She drew in a sharp breath. He caught hold of her arm before she could turn away. *"Han är inte så gott för det,"* he said harshly. *"Min kara,* he is not worth this."

She shook his hand off and faced him fiercely. "Dunna pretend to want anything different from me," she hissed. "This is what I be. This is what ye get."

Looking into her face, he decided then and there that if it took all his life, he would crack wide that hard shell and get to the softness inside her. For he had seen it once, when she sank to her knees in the mud to save an old saddlebag, uncaring about the rich satin she wore. Somehow, some way, he had to give her back her self-respect.

Bjorn smiled. "We talk business now, flicka. Ja?"

She came closer, facing him like a proud warrior instead of a vulnerable young woman who had been cruelly betrayed. He wanted to pull her close and protect her; he wanted to love her. None of that was possible. Not now—not yet.

"We need to clear things up," he said. "Last night, when I won, I gained half-ownership of the California and all of you along with it. Do I understand correctly, flicka?"

She blinked slowly and a pained expression dimmed the glittering defiance that had been in her eyes a moment before. Laid out plainly, it was a blow to her pride, and one she had given herself. She nodded once, solemnly.

"I have your word?"

"Aye." Her mouth tightened at his doubt.

"We shake on it." He held out his big hand, the knuckles cut and swollen from the fight. She put her hand into his. She shook hands like a man, firm, decisive, without restraint. He liked that in her. She would keep her word, he knew. Whatever he demanded of her, she would give—not because she wanted to do so, but because she had sworn it.

"I give you back to yourself, Tempest," he told her, his hand tightening. "I here and now relinquish all rights to your person—on one condition."

Her eyes had widened at his first words, then narrowed on the last. "What condition?"

"That you will give yourself to no man unless you love him," he said, still not letting go of her hand.

Her eyes went wide again, her lips parting slightly. Then her eyes cleared slowly and she looked at him, really looked at him. "Aye, mon. Ye have my word on it."

"Good." He let her go, wondering briefly if there ever would be a day when he could touch her for himself. "*Se så,* what do you want from all this?" He indicated the casino and bar. He struggled with his English, seeing that she didn't understand what he was asking. "What do you want to *accomplish* with owning the California?"

Her chin tipped arrogantly, a grim, cynical smile touching her lips. "I want to be the richest woman in California." Only then could she hope to command respect.

"So. That is our only goal, ja? To make you rich. And me along with you." He gave a decided nod of agreement. "If it will make you happy, we will do it." His smile was warm and challenging, and his blue eyes glowed down at her. "You will be my captain and I will be your first mate." His smile broadened into a teasing grin.

Alarm raced through Tempest. "Ye must run the place."

"Me? No. The California is yours, not mine. You have first claim, you get first honors. You tell me what you want and I will see that it gets done."

"But ye dunna understand, mon. I dunna ken what to do!"

"Did you think an ignorant sailor would?"

She swore softly, not at him in particular but at her situation in general. "What do I do now?" she muttered in angry despair.

Bjorn decided to offer a few hints. "Who handles the gold?"

NOT SO WILD A DREAM

"Jared did."

"When he left?"

"Oliver, but we made very little."

Oliver. He would be a man to watch.

"Who orders your supplies?"

"No one."

"How do you pay the men who work for you?"

Exasperation lit her blue eyes. "I have done naught for the past week. I dunna ken what is going on, other than that everything is falling apart around us!"

"So, we put it back together. Simple. Tell me what you want to do first. Put out word you are wanting to hire a bookkeeper and clerk?"

"Canna ye do what needs be done?" she asked hopefully. "Con ye read and write?"

"Ja, a little. In Svedish. Not much good here." He grinned.

She let out her breath and chewed indecisively on her lower lip. After a long, grim silence, she gave a curt nod. "Aye. Find us a bookkeeper and cleric."

"A clerk, flicka." He smiled, then trailed one finger gently down her smooth cheek, his eyes growing serious. "Someday, we will find a cleric, ja?" He raised his whiskey glass to her. "We'll make 1851 a better year."

Word was put out, and dozens of men showed up at the California ready to apply for the positions. Tempest sat at Jared's big desk, with Bjorn perched on one corner, and listened to what they had to say. Some told of impressive backgrounds, expensive eastern schools, family businesses. Some even gave her printed résumés listing their qualifications and experience. Tempest pretended to read them, wondering vaguely if they mocked her. Bjorn told each one when he finished that a decision would be made as soon as all the others had had an opportunity to present their credentials.

By nightfall, Tempest's head was throbbing. She felt sick and faint. "Tell the rest to go away." Bjorn went to dismiss the rest of the applicants.

Procopius came in with a large tray on which were two covered plates, a pot of fresh coffee, and a pitcher of milk. "You must eat," he said softly. She shook her head.

Bjorn came back and closed the door. "So, who do you decide?"

She stood up and slammed her fist on top of the pile of papers. "I canna read a bloody word on these. I canna even remember the name of the first man who talked to us this morn." She swore, her eyes brimming with tears of abject frustration and self-contempt.

Bjorn picked up the papers grimly, helpless in his own lack of knowledge of written English. He spread them across the desk with a dramatic gesture and nodded down at them. "Pick two. We'll post them and sit back to see who shows up first. Simple." He grinned.

Tempest snorted. "Aye. And what if 'tis that beady-eyed polecat Sam something from whatever-it-was, New Jersey?"

"Taylor from Princeton," Bjorn remembered. "Attorney-at-law, he said." He sifted through the papers, painstakingly deciphering names, then picked up three and crumpled them. "So much for the Sams."

Tempest laughed. She sat down again. "I dinna like that one from Ohio."

"Revell?" Bjorn remembered how the man had looked down his thin nose at Tempest, obviously put out at having to apply for a position working for a half-breed Indian girl. He peered over the sheets, plucked one out, and crumpled it as well.

"What about all those who dinna give us one of these?" she asked, thinking of several men who had seemed more to her taste.

"They eliminated themselves. If they cannot write a summation for us, how good a bookkeeper or clerk would they be?"

Tempest's mouth curled. "And if I canna even read letters from them, how good an owner am I?"

Procopius set a plate in front of her that held a rare steak, string beans, and a roll. He put a mug of milk beside it. "I can read them for you."

She stared up at him. "You? But ye were a slave."

"Master Robert taught all his slaves to read. We were to be shipped back to Africa where he and others had purchased a land they called Libya. Unfortunately, he overinvested and put his plantation in trouble. He was shot," he said darkly. "His slaves were confiscated and sold off at auction."

"Ye con read," she repeated.

"The question is, can you cipher?" Bjorn said, grinning.

Procopius stiffened. "I would not presume to take over,"

he said with immense dignity. "I can read these letters for you so that you can make a well-informed decision about whom to employ."

Bjorn threw back his head and laughed heartily.

Tempest's mouth tightened. "Why? All this time ye've played the bloody fool. Why would ye not shout it from the highest mountains that ye con read?"

"A simple matter of survival, Miss Tempest."

"Miz Tempest, yassuh," Bjorn chortled, imitating Procopius's original manner. Procopius said nothing, nor did he grace him with a look. "We done got a solushun to this heah problum." He grinned broadly at the black man's look of consternation.

"No, sir!" he said firmly.

Bjorn's humor died. "What do you mean, *no sir?*"

"If you put me in the position of accountant and purchasing agent after two hundred white men have applied, I will be dead by noon. No, sir! No, ma'am!"

"I canna believe ye be a yellow-bellied coward."

"I am yellow all the way through, ma'am."

"Ye be black as the ace of spades and I trust ye better than any mon-jack who crossed the threshold today."

"Be that as it may, Miss Tempest, I will not do it!"

"Aye, ye will!"

"I thought you *freed* me," Procopius said with the majesty of an insulted senator.

"Free ye be, but ye'll do it, by God!"

"Perhaps we'd better consider why he won't," Bjorn temporized, his good humor restored as he watched them argue.

"I had my back laid bare to the bone with a bullwhip once because I read the Bill of Rights aloud to half a dozen slaves. These men here won't stop with whipping. They'd hang me from the nearest lamp-post for taking a white's man's job."

"He speaks the truth, Tempest."

"Aye," she agreed, and swore eloquently. She glared at the papers and swore again. "Read the bloody things."

Procopius read through the résumés, which included those of teachers, bank tellers, merchants, farmers, draftsmen, ship's captains, lawyers, and one self-proclaimed master of all trades.

When Procopius had finished, Tempest looked at Bjorn, waiting. He smiled down at her placidly. "Well, what say ye, mon? Who will it be?"

"The decision is yours."

Her hand balled into a tight fist in her lap and her breathing seemed constricted.

Bjorn's eyes softened. "Lawyers are more slippery than whale blubber, and I'd be careful of any sailor who's become a landlubber."

She arched one imperious dark eyebrow. "Aye, he might just end up owning half of the *California*."

Bjorn laughed appreciatively. He grinned across at Procopius. Tempest looked at the black man as well. He cleared his throat.

"A merchant deals with figures as well as purchasing," Procopius said as he leafed through the pile of papers.

"Farmers are honest," Tempest said, her expression guarded.

"Farmers are good at bartering, but they seldom see any gold," Bjorn remarked.

Her eyes misted and there was a distracted look on her face that disturbed Bjorn. "Flicka, don't let this become a great burden." She blinked and looked up at him. He reached out and touched her cheek gently. Her skin was cold and she started slightly at his touch. He frowned, wondering if he was giving her too much say when she wasn't ready. "The merchant from Sandusky, ja?"

"Sandusky?"

"Michael Schaeffer," Procopius supplied.

Tempest's eyes cleared. "Aye, then, on one condition."

The two men glanced at one another and then waited.

She looked squarely at Procopius. "That ye will read all work done by this Schaeffer and tell me if he is cheating me of what's mine. If ye find him doing so, ye will tell me what he has done and how's he done it so I con confront the bleeding son of a bitch. And just to make it worth yer while, I'll pay ye twice what ye be getting now, plus part of whatever ye save me from thieves." She stood up. "Is it a bargain, Procopius?"

Procopius's mouth was ajar as he stared across the desk at her. She came around to stand in front of him and held out her hand. "Is it a bargain?" she repeated.

He straightened, his black eyes glowing. "Yes, ma'am," he said strongly, and shook hands on it.

Certainty fled Tempest's face as she looked up at him almost shyly. She placed her other hand over their still clasped ones. "I be asking ye another big favor, mon," she said, and swallowed before going on. "Con ye please teach me to read?"

For one moment, Procopius's hesitation made Bjorn certain he was going to have to break the man's neck for disappointing her. Then Procopius grinned broadly. "If a dumb niggah slave can do it, so can a *mere woman*."

Tempest gave him McClaren's grin.

He that maketh haste to be rich shall not be
innocent.
—Proverbs 28:20

Tempest felt she had gone back to being less than she
had been before Abram. She was again sitting in the shadows
of the edge of light, not knowing how to get into the circle of
warmth. As a child, it had been her Indian blood that had set
her apart, that and her mad Scots father who went into drunken
rages for no reason. As she neared womanhood, it had been
her own fierce, defiant, heathen nature, her lack of social understanding, her ill grace with people after so many years of
living in the wild with a wild man.

And here she was again, alone, deserted. She had been
flung away like offal. She was a cast-off whore in spite of all
her sworn resolve, her *pride*. She had fed at Jared's mahogany
table on beef rather than at a trough on slops, but where was
the real difference between her and those squaws she had so
disdained for selling themselves so cheaply? She had not sold
herself cheaply; she had *given* herself away.

Jared was gone and he would not be back. He had taken
his million in gold and returned whence he had come to take
his *rightful, honorable* place among other masters of slaves
and owners of great lands. He would smoke his fine cheroots,
drink his French brandies, and bed his blue-blooded white wife.
Would it matter to anyone there that he had smashed the dreams
of hundreds of men and cheated them of their hard-earned gold,
that he had gained his wealth through gambling? Hadn't she
known from the beginning, sensed it in her very vitals, that he
was a liar and a blackguard? And still she had given in and
given all to him, had spread herself open to him in wanton
passion and known in her heart what would happen.

She hated herself more than him. She had known what she
was long before Jared had thrown the truth at her the night he
left. His ignorant, half-breed whore. Yet before him she had
had her pride and her self-respect. Now she had nothing.

But she could buy it back again with enough gold.

Jared had once told her that enough gold could buy anything in this world. His would buy him a place in the upper class of landowners and the aristocratic woman he wanted.

Hers would buy respect.

The way to get enough gold was so simple, so obvious. It had stared her in the face across the long bar for months, in the eyes of a thousand men.

Women.

To this purpose, Tempest sent Missouri to San Francisco to seek out and bring back the comeliest soiled doves he could find. "Offer them what ye must to get them here."

Bjorn went into the first fit of rage Tempest had ever seen him in when he heard of her plans. *"I am no whoremaster!"* he roared, slamming his fist on her desk.

She stared at him, amazed. "I've not asked it of ye," she told him, not showing her fear. "Ye own the casino. What happens upstairs will be my business, not yers."

He leaned across the desk, his blue eyes flashing. "You gave me your word you would be no whore to any man!"

The McClaren temper rose and she stood abruptly. "Aye, I gave my word, and I will keep it! Dunna doubt that!" She gave a contemptuous, unladylike snort. "I'll lay for ye as ye wish, for that was part of the bargain," she said bitterly, and then leaned forward on the desk, face to face with him. "But beyond that, mon, ye dunna own me. Ye canna be tellin' me how to run my business, how to make my fortune. And gold I'll make aplenty with this enterprise, by God!"

Bjorn was breathing hard. "What's the difference between you selling your own flesh and selling the flesh of another? *Gudskelov*, Tempest! What you do!"

"I dinna make these women whores," she said, straightening, her head high. "I canna be blamed for their means of living. I'll only bargain a wee bit with them so I con share in the profits—and increase them."

He struck the desk again. "You cannot do this!"

"Aye, I con. The one thing I want and con buy is *respect.*"

Bjorn straightened and studied her face. "You won't get it this way."

"The hell I wilna," she said through gritted teeth. "See the world for what it is, Bjorn Lindahl," she said, gesturing. "I've seen it all my life, and I ken. If a mon be a big enough scoundrel, but *successful* at it, he is *exalted* by his peers."

"No."

"Open yer bloody eyes, mon, and look around ye!" she railed. "Sutter built his fort on lies and promises! He cajoled property and favors from the Mexican government, from the Californios, from the Russians! He couldna repay; he *knew* that. And yet he is *respected*," she spat. She marched around the desk and stood before Bjorn, her hands on her hips, glaring up at him. "Does it matter to a damn soul now that Sam Brannan robbed the coffers of his own mother church to finance his enterprises? By God, no! He is rich now. He has power. He is *respected!* 'Tis the true way of the bloody world and I will *make the best of it!* By damn, by heaven, I will!"

Bjorn wondered if she even knew she was crying. She was shaking violently and the look in her eyes was so wild he was afraid for her.

"People are what they make of themselves—"

She uttered a short, foul expletive. "Ye dunna ken anythin', Bjorn."

"I understand that this way you'll be selling your very soul!" he said desperately.

She turned away from him and walked around the desk again. "Mon, my soul was spewed up on a mountainside years ago," she said in a dull tone. "I had one small chance to regain it when my da sold me for five dollars in gold and a bottle of whiskey." Her expression became vague and distant. "And we ken where that ended," she said, almost as though she were speaking to someone else.

Bjorn stared at her, transfixed. "Is that how Jared got you?"

"Jared?" She blinked, her expression clearing as she looked at him questioningly. Then she understood. "No." She sat down heavily and closed her eyes for a second. "No," she repeated.

"Who bought you for five dollars in gold and a bottle of whiskey?" Bjorn felt sick.

She looked up at him. In some ways, he reminded her piercingly of Abram—he cared too much; he believed too deeply. She couldn't hold his gaze, and lowered her eyes to stare at the buttons on his cambric shirt. "Leave it be," she said quietly.

"I can't, Tempest."

"You had better," she told him sadly.

Leaning down, he put his palms on the desk again. "Don't

do this," he pleaded roughly. "Send word to Missouri, now, before this deed's done."

She shook her head. "Downstairs men pour gold onto a faro or monte table. They bet on cards. They watch a wheel spin and lose their last ounce of gold and get a drink on the house and naught else for all their days of back-breaking work. Upstairs, mon, they'll have paradise for a short time." She gave him a cynical, humorless smile. "Now, who's to say if that be wrong or right, Bjorn? Have ye not in yer own experience of seaports around the world bought a little *solace?* Be honest. Which vice, gaming or women, gave ye the grandest pleasure?"

Bjorn thought of how many times in the past he had bought just what Tempest planned now to sell to the scores of miners. She *knew* the answer.

"It does not have to be *you* who procures bawds for the men. What of your dignity, Tempest?"

"I'll have all I ever had." She shrugged, not willing to look him in the eyes.

"You *have* seen too much of the world," he conceded angrily, "and all the worst of it, flicka. Maybe your ship was wandering lost in a storm because of your father or a hundred other reasons, but when Stryker took command, he took you out into deep water and scuttled you! Now all you can see around you is *rock bottom.*" He straightened abruptly.

"People always find a reason for what they do," he went on, "an excuse for the mistakes they make. The truth is that we do it to ourselves most of the time, just as you're choosing to do this to yourself now." He stalked out of the office, slamming the door thunderously behind him.

Tempest flinched, her eyes flooding. She looked at the closed door for a long time, her mouth trembling. After several moments, she regained control and willed herself not to cry over Bjorn's words, refusing to acknowledge just how very much she admired him and respected him.

She couldn't let him come to matter to her. Someday he'd be gone, too.

Everyone left—Da because he thought it best for her, Abram because he had no choice, the child because God had exercised his justice on her, and Jared because she wasn't good enough for him and he had loved someone else.

All she had was his baby and half of the California to make her way in the world. She couldn't pray. If she let God know

how much the child mattered, He would take it from her as
punishment for conceiving it in sin. *"In His own parlor and
we're still alive . . ."* She shuddered at the very thought of what
she and Jared had done in God's house.

But how could she keep a secret from God who knew everything? Had He really turned His back on her, or was He watching, waiting for the right moment to take His justice?

Once she had overheard a man at the bar claim that one
could buy God's forgiveness. "Enough gold in the palm of a
priest, enough candles lit on an altar, and the blackest soul will
rise to heaven." Was that true?

Abram had said differently. He had told her that God was
always there for her, that God was merciful and loving. Yet
that merciful, loving God hadn't heard his last prayers screamed
from his deathbed. Only she had heard.

Tempest pressed her hands to her face. So what was the
answer? She scrubbed the tears away fiercely. The course she
was taking.

Gold. *Manna.* With enough of it, perhaps she could buy
the miracle of her child's life and then enough respect that no
one would dare to do to her child what had been done to her.

Until she found a better answer, she saw no other way.

"Try again, Tempest," Procopius said at her shoulder,
pointing to the words in Abram's great book.

"I canna get it," she said in frustration.

"You've done well. Now concentrate. One letter at a time."
She looked at the word again.

Out in the casino, someone let out a high-pitched hoot. It
sometimes happened when someone won big, but this time the
noise rose and others took up the shouting and joyous cheering.
Shrill whistles pierced the air as well.

"You expect too much, too soon," Procopius said. "Take
one letter at a time, and then work the sounds together until
you can figure the word out."

She tried again, but a loud knock sounded at the door. She
swore, slamming the book closed and standing abruptly. "What!"
she shouted at the door.

Missouri opened it and peered in tentatively. "I have some
ladies for you to meet," he said, smiling smugly.

"Ye had a short trip."

"Aren't many women around, Tempest. I brought back the
best I found."

She could hear two of them squabbling in the hallway. She sat down and nodded. Missouri opened the door wide and bowed, sweeping his arm out in a gesture telling them to enter the brightly lit office.

The first to enter was a dark-haired, dark-eyed, haughty-looking young woman. She was wearing a beautifully cut mauve velvet traveling suit, a boa and a flower, and a plumed hat perched neatly on her head. She didn't smile as Missouri introduced her as Delight from Paree.

A second girl closer to Tempest's age entered. Her simple rust-colored frock and thick knitted shawl had seen better days, but she was beautiful, with curly red hair and solemn green eyes. "Meg from Ireland." She gave a small nod and stood next to Delight, though her shoulder was hunched slightly as though she didn't want to get any closer to the French girl than she had to.

"Angelita is from Chile," Missouri said as a third girl came in, and grinned. "She don't speak English, Miss Tempest, but the men won't mind much." Angelita was a buxom brunette with dark, shining brown eyes and a mouth that wore a secretive smile. *"Buenos días, California Tempest. He oído mucho de tí."*

Tempest asked her what she had heard. The girl's eyes widened in surprised pleasure. *"Hablas Español!"* Tempest answered that she did speak a little Spanish, and then asked the girl where she came from, to which the girl answered Nicaragua, not Chile. She went on to inform Tempest that the men in her home country were always too busy fighting among themselves to be interested in love, so she had come north with a shipful of men but had run out of money by the time Missouri had found her. She would have continued talking, but Tempest nodded once and looked back at Missouri.

"Jade," he introduced the next girl. "I won't have to tell you where she comes from."

The tiniest woman Tempest had ever seen shuffled gracefully into the room, wearing an outfit that looked elegantly coolie. Her hands were clasped in front of her as she bowed deeply before Tempest. Everything about the girl was exquisite, from the glistening thick black braid that hung past her waist, dark almond-shaped eyes, and thin, almost boyish body to the sing-song words she murmured softly in reverential greeting.

Tempest glanced at Missouri with raised eyebrows. "Does this one speak English?"

"Yes, ma'am," the girl answered, and proceeded with her careful, heavily accented vocabulary to list the positions and services she could render while Missouri listened, gaping, at the door.

Procopius rattled some cups and saucers together onto a tray and almost ran from the room. There was a crash in the hallway, muttered apologies, and a soft, husky laugh, and then a tall girl in a dove-gray tailored dress with black piping stepped through the doorway. Her golden hair was covered modestly by a black cap, her skin pale and devoid of makeup, contrasting her with the others immediately. She had a full mouth, a patrician nose, and wide-set brown eyes.

She entered the room with a sedate grace that didn't match her profession. Stopping before Tempest, she smiled, her brown eyes lighting with amusement. "Since Missouri seems to have lost his tongue, I will take it upon myself to make my own introduction. I'm Charity." She glanced at the Chinese girl. "Since Jade has proclaimed her many specialties, I will warn you that I have only one. But as Horace once said, 'The fox has many tricks, the hedgehog only one. But it's a good one.'"

"And what be yer specialty?" Tempest asked carefully.

The young woman's eyes shone with mischief. "I am a virgin." She put her index finger to her chin and gazed upward in dreamy pensiveness before meeting Tempest's stunned eyes again. "I've been a virgin for . . . let me see, now, five years and more times than I can count. I guess you could say I'm the most experienced virgin in all the California Territory."

Tempest said nothing to that. She looked at each of the women again, judging them all to be at least a few years her senior. They were far different from the naive squaws who gave their bodies for tin looking glasses and beads. Now what? She bought time to think by addressing Missouri, who was still standing in the doorway. "This is all ye brought back?"

He had to clear his throat before he could speak. "Yes, ma'am."

Not as many as she had counted upon, but probably more than she could handle, she thought grimly, glancing briefly at Charity again.

"Thank ye, Missouri. I'll settle with ye later. Close the door on yer way out."

"Yes, ma'am."

Tempest let out her breath slowly, her heart pounding nervously as she looked from one to the other of the women again, hoping that her expression didn't give away her uncertainty. Delight was surveying her long fingernails with a bored air. Meg stared straight ahead without any expression at all. Jade stood with her hands tucked into her flowing white silk sleeves, her head bowed. Angelita was gazing around the large room with interest, mumbling softly to herself in Spanish. Only Charity was looking at Tempest with as much interest as she looked at them.

"When con ye start working?" Tempest demanded.

Charity laughed. "From the reception we received when we came through the saloon, I would say we could start immediately and work for the next month without rest."

"I'm *tired*," Delight sighed in her throaty, petulant way. "I've a headache and every inch of my body aches from zat horrible carriage ride."

"All you have to do is lie on your back, Delight. The men will do all the work," Charity remarked.

The French girl drew in an indignant breath and snarled, "Perhaps zat is ze way *you* work, but I put a leetle finesse into what I do."

"I don't think these men will mind if you rest while they release," Charity said, chuckling. "Didn't you see those poor randy souls out there, starving for a little love? How can you even think of refusing? We're harlots, ladies, not heartless."

"*Sacré bleu*," Delight sighed, her eyes turned heavenward, her attitude one of long-suffering.

"We don't all enjoy the work, Charity," Meg said softly.

Charity looked at the sad-eyed Irish girl. "I suppose that because it's my calling in life does not necessarily mean it's yours," she conceded. Then she glanced at Tempest again and cocked her head in inquiry. "What is our cut?"

Tempest assumed she was talking gold, so she plunged ahead, trying to appear knowledgeable and confident when she was groping desperately to find out what would be an equitable agreement.

"Ye will charge fifty dollars in gold per mon for yer— services."

Delight jerked the feathery boa tighter and gave a disgruntled sigh. "A shovel costs three hundred. *Certainement* I am worth more zan a shovel."

"A shovel lasts a man longer than we do," Charity chortled.

"You mean a shovel lasts longer than *they* do," Delight corrected haughtily.

"Aren't you lucky you don't have to?" Charity retorted. "You think you're tired now—"

"What is a fair price?" Tempest demanded, looking from one to the other. "Three hundred is too much," she said, giving the French girl a level, cold stare.

"Zat should depend on ze services, *n'est çe pas?*"

"Fifty for plain fare," Charity suggested, "and one hundred for those specialties Jade listed earlier."

"Anything else is above and beyond the call of duty," Meg sighed softly.

"And should be charged for accordingly," Charity added irrepressibly. "We will need protection, of course. Missouri is very handsome and sweet, but I don't think he could manage to throw out anyone who wasn't willing to go."

Tempest nodded, thinking of Tick, the burly blacksmith-turned-bartender. "Ye customers will pay my mon before they come up to ye. Ye will receive one part of gold to my four parts."

"Isn't that rather—unfair?" Meg dared.

"I dunna think so," Tempest said firmly. "Each of ye will have yer own private quarters with the best furnishings available, good food, servants to see to yer personal needs, a doctor if ye need one, protection, and a sum for clothing."

"You're very generous," Charity said sincerely.

"I expect ye to work very hard." She turned her head slowly and looked directly at the arrogant French girl, whose stance was indolent. "If ye're too tired too often, ye'll be plying yer trade elsewhere and for less profit than what I be offering ye."

Delight's eyes grew wide and frightened. *"Oui, madame."*

A rap at the door announced Bjorn. He strode in, paused briefly as his interested gaze swept over the women, and then gave a laugh as he muttered something, obviously approving, in Swedish.

"Hmm, *magnifique,*" Delight cooed, coming to life. She loosened her boa so the décolletage of her traveling suit showed boldly. "And who are you, *cheri?*"

"This is Bjorn Lindahl," Tempest told them coolly. "He is half-owner of the California."

Charity offered him a fluttering, downcast look and an innocently provocative smile that made him laugh. Jade bowed low as he moved slowly forward toward Tempest. Angelita sashayed into his way and said something in Spanish that he didn't comprehend, but which brought vivid color into Tempest's face. An unpleasant curling sensation tightened inside her as she watched Bjorn tease back, his grin becoming rakish. He tweaked Charity's cheek and slapped Angelita on the bottom to move her out of his way. Then his expression changed as he placed his hands on Tempest's desk and leaned toward her, all business. "If these ladies are willing, I suggest you have them begin work now. Otherwise we will soon have a riot on our hands."

"Je suis willing," Delight said, moving closer. "You first."

"Give the gentleman a choice," Charity smiled, winking at him.

Angelita ran the tip of her finger around her low neckline, giving him a bold look that dropped slowly to the button fly of his dungarees.

Tempest's hand curled into a fist as she stifled the urge to run them all out. Instead she said, "What do you say, ladies?"

They agreed, only Meg remaining silent. Bjorn went out to get Tick and two new men, Hitch and Darbey, to escort the women up the back stairs to the rooms on the top floor. He came back and remained after they had all departed.

Avoiding his watchful eyes, Tempest stood up. "I will have to tell the men out there . . . what is what."

"Things are plain enough." He closed the door firmly and leaned back against it, his hard arms crossed over his massive chest. It was the first time they had been alone together since their argument two weeks before. The silence between them was uncomfortable.

"How does it feel to be the first madam in Sacramento?"

She looked away with a shrug, but he saw how her hands clenched at her sides for a moment. He walked slowly across the room and sat on the edge of her desk. She glanced at him, the briefest brush of her eyes with his. Hers were overbright. He watched her. She kept her face down as she shuffled papers with trembling hands.

Bjorn reached out and turned the lantern wick down slightly so that the harsh brilliance was softened. "Why do you always burn them so high?" he asked softly. "You could start a fire."

Her chin came up and she looked at him, her eyes fathomless. She was shutting him out again. "What did ye think of my women?" she asked imperiously.

"They are all very beautiful, each in a different way."

"Yes," she said simply after a hesitation. Her expression softened, became pensive and faintly anxious. "Did ye like one better than the rest?"

His blue eyes flashed. "Are you giving me my *choice?*" he said harshly.

Her chin rose slightly, but her eyes dulled. "If ye wish."

He said nothing, searching her face. She couldn't sustain his look and lowered her head again.

He wanted badly to come around the desk and take hold of her, to stroke away all the pain of her life, learn all the secrets behind her despair and fear, protect her from ever being hurt again. He wanted to tell her how much he loved her, for love her he did and knew he would never be able to stop.

He didn't agree with Tempest's means of making her fortune, but he admired her determination, her willingness to fight for her own in this man's world. He felt pity for her ignorance, but pride in her efforts to gain knowledge. He was amazed by the strange friendship she had established with a black slave, but encouraged it, for Procopius of all people could teach her what she so longed to know: how to read, how to write, how to act like a well-bred lady.

She was hungry for so many things, and Bjorn wanted to fill her up, to sate her. Right now, the best way he could help was simply to stand back and to be there if she needed or wanted him. She wasn't ready for the safe harbor of his love, but needed now the freedom to become everything she could be. He wanted to see her flying along, all sails unfurled; he wanted to give her a strong headwind.

But sometimes he feared that she would turn her course into the jagged rocks for some final destruction. To punish herself because men had used her? Or was it more? Sometimes he was certain it was more.

Tempest McClaren Walker was the hardest, most ruthless and unyielding female Bjorn had ever known; but so, too, was she the most vulnerable.

"*Min kara,* the only one I want is you," he told her softly.

She raised her head and looked at him then, a bruised, raw look in her eyes that he couldn't understand. Wanting to comfort her, he reached out, but she drew back from his touch. She had invited him to her bed to rut and use her body, but not once would she let him lay one finger on her because he *cared*.

Why?

He wanted to know so much about her. He wanted to know why she burned down several candles every night, keeping her bedroom lit until dawn's light. He wanted to know why she didn't hate the father who had sold her. He wanted to know whom she had belonged to before Stryker. He wanted to know what she was thinking when she put on that opaque, distant look that shut him out and herself in.

"Prata, min älskling," he said huskily. "Talk to me."

"About what, mon? Business be fine."

"I want to talk about *you.*"

"Ye ken all there is."

"I know *nothing.*" Except that whether she knew it or not, she needed what he had to offer, and that he couldn't stop loving her even if he wanted to.

"Ye ken enough," she said quietly, and looked into his eyes. He wondered at the way she looked at him.

She saw so much in his face, a lifetime. A hardened seaman, he had seen the world several times over. He drank. He fought. He swore. Procopius had once told her that with a horned helmet, Bjorn Lindahl, a head taller than most men and built solidly and well, would look exactly like his Viking ancestors. At times he sounded like one.

She had witnessed one of Bjorn's infamous fights in the California. Trouble had brewed between two men at the bar. Words had escalated into a fistfight. Bjorn had stepped in, and one man had fallen back quickly, but the other, a man with the depth and breadth of Bjorn himself and a violent temper to boot, had gone at him. It had taken some time, but Bjorn had finally sent him to the floor. The men watching had roared with cheers.

Jared never would have dirtied his hands on the ruffian. He would have quietly ordered a couple of his men to drag the man outside, give him a sound beating if he tried to come back in, and leave him in the muddy street, preferably face-down.

Bjorn had helped his downed opponent up, slapped him on the back, and given him a bottle of whiskey. The man had been back a dozen times since and never once caused another ruckus.

Bjorn Lindahl was an admirable man. She had held him in high esteem since the night of the fire when she had seen him helping men out of burning shanties, while Jared stood by watering down his poker tables and crates of rotgut whiskey.

Bjorn Lindahl was a *good* man. Like Abram Walker.

"Ye dunna belong here."

He had seen the softening of her eyes and the warmth that had glowed there for a spare moment. It made him hope. He leaned forward with a roguish smile. "You are starting to like me, ja? I am going to stay around until you more than like me, flicka. I will grow on you like barnacles on the hull of a ship."

As persistent as Abram, too.

"Aye," she said very softly. "Then ye will leave." Like all the rest before him, when she needed them most. She couldn't take that betrayal again.

He held her gaze firmly. "I will stay."

"No. Ye will leave. 'Tis the way of men."

"Because Stryker left you does not mean *I* will," he said stiffly.

"Bjorn, I mean no disrespect to ye. Believe me when I say that. But I ken things ye dunna, for all ye've seen more of the world than I."

"Min kara," he said, touching her cheek. This time she didn't flinch away from him. "I will stay. *Always.*"

But she knew too well that he wouldn't. He couldn't. She had watched him closely and seen the longing that lay in his eyes. How many times before had she seen it in others?

"'Tis like the salmon going upriver, Bjorn, like the swallows coming home, and the bear returning to its old den. Da went back to his mountains, Abram to his God, and Jared to his high-bred woman. And you, Bjorn Lindahl . . . ye'll go back to the sea."

I do not understand, I pause, I examine.
—Michel Eyqueum de Montaigne

Tempest's lantern burned high and her excitement blossomed. She realized she had reached the story of Noah in the big black book. She had just worked out the familiar words, "The Lord saw that the wickedness of man was great in the earth."

She drew in her breath with a joyous "Oh!" and reread the words again triumphantly.

Someone tapped softly on her door and she stood quickly, gazing down at the book once more before crossing to answer.

Charity stood in the hallway, her usually merry brown eyes solemn. "Can we talk, Tempest?"

"Aye." She moved back, opening the door wider. She guessed that the woman probably wanted more money for clothes. She closed the door again and walked over to her chair near the fireplace, unaware that Charity was watching her, her lips parted in stunned surprise.

"*Lord in heaven!*" she gasped, and Tempest glanced back sharply in question. "You have a bun in the oven!" The solemnity gone and a delighted smile spread across Charity's face.

Tempest looked down, her hands immediately going protectively to the slight swelling of her abdomen at which Charity stared. She glanced at the girl again and squared her shoulders. "What did ye come to talk about?" she demanded, letting her hands fall to her sides.

Charity's expression fell at Tempest's abrupt manner. She answered hesitantly, "It's about Meg. I'm worried about her."

"Has she been drinking again?"

"Not while she works," Charity assured her quickly.

Tempest indicated the chairs near the fire. She took up a big fur rug from the foot of her bed before sitting opposite Charity.

Charity glanced about the room, taking in the big brass bed,

377

the expensive mahogany side tables on which were matching candelabra holding half-burned candles, the lantern burning brightly on the table, and a huge book lying open.

Looking at Tempest with interest, she saw the veiled coolness of those blue eyes watching her. The girl never ceased to awe Charity. She couldn't be more than nineteen or twenty, and here she was a madam of six women senior to her and half-owner of an enormous business enterprise. She had a remarkable beauty as well, with those pale eyes in the middle of her olive-skinned face and a thick, glistening mane of raven-black hair. And if Charity was correct, the book lying open on that table was a Bible, of all things! Contrasts and inconsistencies.

Tempest would be far more interesting as a friend than Delight, who was only interested in perpetuating the ridiculous story of having been mistress to Napoleon III, or Angelita, who made no effort to learn English, or Jade, who when not rendering her impressive talents on her gasping patrons sat in opiated dullness before her mirror, brushing her long hair.

Charity watched the way Tempest covered herself carefully with the heavy fur. The room was comfortably warm. Was it shame or modesty that made her cover herself before another woman? Her mind never far from the pleasures of the flesh, Charity found herself wondering how Tempest and Bjorn were together. He would be delicious, she suspected, but she had difficulty imagining this self-contained, silent girl in the throes of wanton passion. Besides, she had never heard any noises through the wall, and her own room was right next door.

It had to be Bjorn Lindahl who had fathered the child, for she had never known Tempest to be closeted in private with anyone other than him or that big Negro Procopius, who had a Miwuk squaw living with him in a little house out back.

"What about Meg?" Tempest asked with an arched eyebrow.

Charity wanted to ask about the baby, but Tempest's cool blue eyes didn't encourage her to speak of more than that which had brought her. "She's getting thinner every day," she answered, trying hard to curb her natural curiosity.

"Aye, I've noticed. Is she ill?"

Charity heard the note of concern in Tempest's tone and was inwardly gratified. She could not be as hard as she looked. "Heartsick," she sighed. Tempest said nothing and Charity went on. "We all do it for different reasons. Delight, for example; well, she does it because it makes her feel she has power over her men. Jade was trained for it. They do things differently in China, you see. Sex is—well, considered necessary to a man's well-being, and the women who provide it are respected. Now, Angelita, she's just plain greedy. She makes a chalk mark on a slat every time a man comes to her room, just to make sure you're not cheating her. But Meg," she shook her head sadly, "she doesn't like to be with a man. She became a whore because she would have starved otherwise."

Tempest looked at her steadily. "She can leave any time she wants."

"Tempest, if you turn that girl out, she'll go right down to that muddy river and drown herself."

Tempest frowned. "I wilna turn Meg out. But if she wants to go, I wilna be trying to stop her either. She's free to choose."

"Free," Charity sniffed. "Are any of us free? Lord, she should have been married off to some potato farmer or coal miner so she could have been a proper wife and had a dozen children. Her mother died of consumption and her father was a dreamer who brought her with him to look for gold. Unfortunately, he died on the voyage. Apparently there were only two other women on the ship, both prostitutes, and the men grew tired of them and decided to take turns on Meggie. Once she reached San Francisco... well, she didn't think she was worth anything." Charity looked at Tempest. "She would have been far happier back in Ireland in the middle of a potato famine."

"What about that Aussie who always spends his poke on her?" Tempest asked thoughtfully, referring to a man who returned to the California every time his pouch was full and proceeded to use it all for Meg's time.

Charity grinned. "I thought Tick was the only one who knew who went in and out of our rooms."

Tempest grinned. "Angelita isna the only one who has a slat she marks to be sure she dunna get cheated."

Charity laughed. "All that, and tending bar, too." Her laughter became mischievous. "Or are you just keeping tabs on that big, handsome Swedish sailor of yours?"

Tempest's face went cold. "Bjorn is free to be with anyone he wants."

Touchy, touchy, Charity thought, and cocked her head. "The

only one he wants is you." She smiled openly as she looked to Tempest's fur-covered lap.

"We were discussin' Meg."

Charity accepted the stern reprimand with a patient sigh. "Yes, ma'am. Have you any suggestions? I've tried every way I can think of to cheer her up and make her enjoy her lot a little more."

Tempest smiled slightly. "We'll give her to the Aussie next time he comes."

Charity's eyes widened at Tempest's quick solution. "Just like that?"

"Why not? I think he'll want her," Tempest defended her idea. "And it'll be cheaper this way than the way he's been having her."

Charity suppressed a grin. *So she's a romantic after all.* "But what about Meg," she countered. "She doesn't think she's fit for any man's wife now that she's been a whore."

"Then we'll sell her to him so she doesna have a word to say about it."

Shocked, Charity sputtered, "That's little better than slavery!"

"Aye, but where's the difference between doing it that way or having dowries? I hear there be dowries in her homeland." She shrugged. "And she'll be better off with a miner than being here."

Charity grinned wickedly. "Oh, I don't know. Personally, I think sleeping with the same man all the time could be downright tedious."

Tempest laughed.

Charity rested her graceful hands lightly on her dove-gray dress that seemed to be her uniform of the trade. "Now that Meg's problem seems to be solved, I'll leave you in peace if you like." She met Tempest's eyes levelly and waited, a small hope clear in her eyes.

Tempest relaxed. "Is yer name really Charity?"

Charity grinned, embracing Tempest's invitation with enthusiasm. "Yes, christened so at birth. My father was a minister in Connecticut. He was truly a man of God, but I became very disenchanted with his ways."

"Why?"

"All the parishioners seemed solely intent on outdoing one another, whether in bonnets and gowns, carriages and horses, or even the tithes. I've never seen such backbiting. And there was my poor father at the pulpit each Sunday trying to make Christians of them. Love one another, he would tell them. They would nod and smile in agreement during services, fill the brass hat, and then stand in the narthex gossiping about *her* dress and *her* child's behavior, and *his* worn harness and the fact that *he* got a little tipsy at the local saloon on Friday night."

"Were they all that way?" Tempest frowned.

"Oh, no. There were some who were very sincere and had that special glow about them." She smiled, her eyes sparkling with amusement. "Usually the very young ones who were being confirmed or the old ones nearing the grave." Her eyes lost their amusement as she went on in a less effervescent tone, "The worst offenders were the most *obvious* about their Christianity. They did good works and then expected constant praise for it, and they made it so difficult for those others who were more sincere to be a part of things by making them feel—well, just not good enough."

"Is that what they did to you?"

Charity's eyes cleared. She laughed, never able to stay serious for long. "Lord in heaven, no. I just found another way of spreading a little love around. As a matter of fact, I started with the son of the most pious member of our church." She laughed, resting her head against the wing chair. "In the hayloft while his mother was conducting a meeting to plan a church social."

Tempest was amazed. "But are ye not afraid ye'll go to hell?"

Charity gave her a thoughtful look. "Does it worry you?"

Tempest looked into the glowing fire and didn't answer. Charity debated continuing the conversation. She watched Tempest's fingers rub lightly on the arm of her chair in a nervous, distracted gesture and read some deep, hidden pain in Tempest's troubled silence.

"I'm certainly not one to speak of God," Charity said softly, "but my father always said that the distance between heaven and hell is a mere eighteen inches."

Tempest looked at her. "Eighteen inches?" she repeated incredulously.

Charity smiled. "Yes. The distance between your heart and your head."

* * *

Procopius was going over the books Schaeffer had prepared, pointing out several small errors. Tempest put an ink dot next to each figure and memorized the numbers so that she could discuss them properly with the young accountant from Sandusky.

The door slammed back against the wall and Bjorn stormed in, his face white and drawn. He stopped before her desk and jerked his head toward the door. "Leave us, Procopius."

"Yes, sir." The black man gave Tempest a worried look and left, closing the door behind him.

Tempest stared up at Bjorn, bewildered and frightened by the wild look in his eyes, a mingling of pain and fury so reminiscent of her da. Leaning down slowly, he planted his huge hands on her desk and said in heavily accented English through gritted teeth, "A bun in the oven?"

Her eyes went wide, her face dark red. She shrank back against her chair. "Charity wasted no time," she choked out.

Bjorn straightened with a violent movement. Tempest closed her eyes tightly. "She thought I knew!" he shouted. "She congratulates me for *good work!*" He said more in Swedish, and slammed his white fist twice on the desk, making the kerosene lantern jump.

Trembling, Tempest watched him. He leaned down again, his eyes raw. *"Jacklar!"* he swore. "Why did you not tell me this?"

"It dunna concern ye."

More vehement, violent Swedish followed. "Did that bastard know before he left you stranded?"

She bit down on her lip, worrying it.

"Did he?"

She shook her head.

He swore again.

Hearing condemnation in his voice, she said, "If he dinna want me, a bairn wouldna have made a difference."

Bjorn looked down at her pale, strained face. Why this with all she already had to take? When Charity had laughed and nudged him with her hip while congratulating him on his virility, Bjorn had gone cold with shock. The men around him had cheered wildly and made ribald jokes. Someone thrust a glass of whiskey into his hand and he'd tossed it down as rage swept up inside him.

He had known immediately it was Stryker's, for Tempest

would have died before breaking her word. He wished with all his heart that he had that bastard in the same room with him so he could beat him to death with his bare hands.

He clenched and unclenched his fists at his sides. "It's his child, too."

Tempest watched those hands, her heart thundering. "He wouldna see it that way, and the fault is my own. I dinna say no."

He shut his eyes and made a deep, growling noise in his throat. "Do you want me to bring him back?" he demanded raggedly. It would tear at his very guts, but he was ready to sail off on the mission if it was what she wanted.

She blinked, confused. "Bring him back?"

"Ja, to do what's right." And if not, to break his neck.

"No," she said softly.

Bjorn stilled. "No?"

"He left me and that be the end of it."

And what was ahead of her now? he wondered. A man should be at his woman's side to see what his pleasure brought, just as his own father had been at his mother's side through the birth of each child. Bjorn remembered her with piercing clarity, remembered the nausea she had suffered for months, her pallor as each child became a heavy burden in her womb, the long, painful hours of birthing, and the weeks of recuperation and the fight to gradually regain her strength.

Tempest would suffer all this, too, because of that damn rogue, that son of a bitch.

Love sometimes brought a burdensome bounty, Bjorn thought, painfully recalling his childhood. His father and mother's passion for one another had brought another mouth to feed every other year. "Chew slowly so it will last a long time," his father had told them at suppertime, but it hadn't stopped the aching in Bjorn's belly when he went to bed at night.

Times had been grievous for everyone, and his father had been more kind than practical. When friends in need came, he signed notes for them, and piece by piece the Lindahl lands were taken until only a small parcel remained. Bjorn's father went to work in a mill to hold what was left, and by lantern light worked his remaining fields.

From boyhood, Bjorn had dreamed of the sea, but his mother resisted, reminding him, "Uncle Carl never came back. He drowned." But as Bjorn grew, so too did his determination as he saw what was happening to his family. He could send money, and there would be one less to feed.

"You're only eleven," his mother cried. "Wait until I'm gone."

The maternal love smothered him, tears a gelding weapon.

Bjorn's sister Kerstin left to work at a dairy. His brother Roland, only a year older, was apprenticed to a printer in Stockholm. Albert was going away, too. But his mother held him still, urging, "You're strong, Bjorn. You can work with your father at the mill and help with the farm."

Bjorn hated the mill, and he began to loathe his father, too, as his mother grew full-bellied again.

"Claus is leaving with his family's blessing," he had told his parents. "It is time, Mama. I am a man."

She was ill, she said; just wait a few years more! It was the cough that wouldn't go away. "You're a boy! You're only twelve!" she cried. "Please. You don't even know how to swim!"

Bjorn's pride rose. He was no longer a boy; he did a man's work beside his father, whatever his age. But his mother's hold on him was unyielding. Claus left. Bjorn argued long and hard, and was finally ordered to silence by his father. "Look what you do to your mother!" he shouted.

Bjorn left that night, leaving a letter on the mantel asking their forgiveness and promising to write and to send money. He had kept his promises in the years that followed.

It took him two days to catch up with Claus on the road. It was four years before he and his friend returned to Sweden. When they did, Bjorn's mother was dead and his father had remarried.

"The children needed a mother," Lars told him solemnly. "Ida is a good woman, Bjorn. She is kind and practical."

Indeed. Ida was a widow without children, and Bjorn saw that she treated his siblings as her own. The money she had inherited from her husband had brought prosperity back to the family. Some of the lost lands had been restored to his father, and no longer did Lars Lindahl slave in the mill; now he toiled his own fields again. Bjorn couldn't fault his father's decision, or his new wife.

But neither could he stay. It hurt too deeply to see another woman in his mother's place, and he couldn't purge himself of his sense of guilt. Her words haunted him. "Wait a little longer . . ." It had only been eighteen months more.

Walking through the birch wood with his father, he had broken down, and admitted his deepest feelings.

"No, Bjorn, you had to go. Jenny knew that. There was nothing to forgive." His hand had rested comfortingly on Bjorn's bent back. "She grieved for you, yes, but she understood. What was there for you here but the mill and watching her die slowly of consumption? Better that you left when you did."

With all the hardship, his mother had lived a life filled with love. What had Tempest Walker ever had in her life? A father who had sold her, a man who'd used her and cast her away, and her with his child coming. What did she have? This riotous establishment that brought her riches and a ruined reputation, a stain on her soul?

He remembered his mother piercingly. Even with illness, pain, and the eventual departure of the children she loved, she had told him once that every child born, even in the worst of times, was a blessing. "A baby is a miracle, Bjorn. It is God's blessing on the joining of a man and woman."

How could God have so blessed the relationship between Tempest Walker and Jared Stryker?

He imagined Tempest and Stryker together, creating this child; the thought ate at his very guts. How could she put the bastard out of her life and forget him now? He had left a part of himself behind, firmly planted in her womb, her very body nurturing that part of him with her own life's blood. How could she not think of him forever?

Tempest saw the stark violence and pain in Bjorn's eyes as he stared at her in silence. She stood up, frightened by his scrutiny, and moved away from the desk. Da had looked like that sometimes when he stared into the campfire, his mind filled with black, demon thoughts. Glancing back, she saw Bjorn's gaze following her fixedly. "Why do ye stare?" she cried out.

His expression altered. "How many months?"

"Five moons have passed since I bled," she said bluntly.

He raked a shaking hand through his gold hair. "Four months more, then," he muttered. She had hidden her secret well. Perhaps he had seen and just refused to acknowledge it to himself.

She watched the expressions chasing each other across his face. "Do ye need a whiskey?" she demanded, taking refuge in mockery and gesturing toward the tray of decanters.

His face whitened. "I need my hands around that bastard's throat!" He moved restlessly, the blood pounding in his head. When he came toward her, she backed away, her eyes wide. He frowned. *"Min älskling,"* he said softly.

She continued to back away from him as he advanced and he saw she feared him. That hurt him deeply, for he would fight anything to protect her. She bumped against the cabinet by the wall, and her eyes grew huge as his shadow fell across her.

"Min älskling," he whispered again, and gently touched her cheek. She was trembling. "You know I would not hurt you," he said huskily and put his hands lightly on her shoulders, damning himself for having frightened her with his fury. "It will be all right. We will get married with great ceremony. Everyone will think the baby is mine."

"Are ye bloody mad?" she whispered, staring up at him as though he were. Such an act would be mocking God.

"The child is there. You cannot ignore it. Charity told me at the bar; everyone in Sacramento will know within an hour that you're pregnant!"

"I'll not marry any mon, least of all you!" she said fiercely.

He let go of her, appalled to discover that words could hurt so much worse than any physical beating he'd taken.

She saw what was in his heart and grieved. "The bairn isna yers, Bjorn. Why would ye be askin' to claim another mon's discarded seed?"

He winced. "I'm not," he said harshly. "I want to lay claim to you. Don't you understand that yet?"

Her throat constricted. "Ye'd be a bloody arse to do that," she told him hoarsely, her eyes filling. He deserved a proper wife, not her.

"Would you rather the child was born a bastard rather than marry me?" he demanded gruffly.

"The child *is* a bastard," she said simply. "I canna change what is, and I wilna stand before God Almighty and claim a lie." She fought against the wish to reach out and press herself against this man and accept the comfort he offered.

"It could've been mine. If I had jumped ship the first time I came to Yerba Buena, I would have gotten to you first," he said.

"But ye dinna, mon, and it isna yers."

"People will—" he began, taking another tack to wear her down, but she interrupted.

"It matters not what people think, but what is the truth. We live with that, and with ourselves."

"You take the hard way always," he said, half in anger.

Tears welled in her eyes. "I go the only trail I have left, Bjorn. I want this child," she admitted, her mouth trembling. "I want the bairn with every part of me. 'Tis not to do with the father, but the child itself. And me." She pressed her hand against her breasts. *"Me!"*

Bjorn tilted her chin up firmly. "What do you fear? The pain?"

"Retribution."

He frowned heavily, seeing that she was serious. "Has some preacher been after you?"

Abram had read to her once that the sins of the fathers were visited on the sons. So, too, would it be with a woman and her misbegotten child. Sins she had in plenty, unforgivable sins.

Bjorn searched her pale, distraught face. "No one will punish you, *min kara*," he promised. He drew her close, putting his firm arms around her. She stiffened for an instant and then clung to him, pressing her face into the hard curve of his arm, hiding herself. Bjorn felt her shoulders shaking violently and the dampness soaking into his sleeve, but she remained silent. "No one," he repeated, bending his head to brush his lips against her dark hair.

She held on tighter. She could hear the steady, hard pounding of Bjorn's heart, feel his warmth and strength. She *needed* him, needed his caring, loving nature. But God knew, he didn't need her. He stroked her and murmured Swedish in a voice so tender that her throat squeezed even tighter, choking her.

Jared had held and stroked her, too, his hands caressing and exploring her for the sole purpose of cracking her will and opening her wide to his possession. *Possession.* He had wanted everything, and had been granted his wish. And in the end, he had wanted nothing of her after all.

She clutched at Bjorn's shirt, bunching it in her fists, pressing herself even closer to him. He was so like Abram.

Abram.

The blackness in her own soul had made her fall in love with Jared instead, thus ruining her for this man.

She felt the tightening of Bjorn's powerful back muscles beneath her palms. How long since she had become aware of him as a man? She heard his heart quicken and his breathing halt. His hands tightened on her back, pressing her breasts more firmly against him. Her own heart began to pound harder, faster, her senses sharpening to the musky scent of virility.

She remembered desire. It grew inside her, a hot coal in her belly.

Whore she was to want so much.

Bjorn stood still, feeling how close she was, so close that he could feel every womanly curve of her body. He felt hard desire taking hold of him and fought to suppress it. He wanted to lift her chin and take her mouth with his. He wanted to rub his hips against hers. He wanted to open her clothing and touch every part of her body. He wanted to lie with her and feel their bodies join and lock together.

His breathing grew shallow and strained at his thoughts. He closed his eyes tightly and swallowed hard, reminding himself that she needed tenderness now, not passion. She would let him take her, he knew, and his passion was such that he would hurt her or the baby.

The baby. Stryker's baby.

It cooled his ardor slightly to remember that. He gently disengaged her. Tempest looked up at him, and there was a world of hard-won knowledge in her eyes. She knew a man's lustful nature, and he wished she didn't.

His desire for her was fierce and strong. But so, too, was his patience. Passion gripped his vitals; yet his passion wasn't only of his body, but intensified by his love. Before he went into Tempest, she had to understand it.

And, pray God, return it.

He had to see her through this, had to put aside his own fears and help her face hers. But he couldn't help wondering what she would remember most about Stryker: his betrayal, or the passion that had flamed between them to create the child she bore. For all that she said it was ended, it wasn't. It never would be.

But none of that changed anything. Not for him.

"I will stay by you always," he told her. "I will take good care of you, flicka. You will have a strong baby." Gold she had. All she required was love, and that he had in abundance. All that she might want, he had to give, and more.

Looking into his clear blue eyes, Tempest sensed that. Something softened and warmed inside her body, like spring just touching a wintry land, like life returning. This man would fight anyone, anything, she knew, and for her, he would dare all the more.

But no one can fight God Himself.

If this child in her was to live, somehow she had to find her own path to the Almighty's forgiveness. And the only way to do that was one page at a time in Abram's big, black book.

Mea culpa, mea culpa, mea maxima culpa
           —The Confiteor

    If Tempest had drawn attention before, she did so even more with the coming child. The greater she grew, the higher the anticipation ran among the men. No one seemed interested in news of the Taiping rebellion against the Manchu Dynasty; so what if it was bringing a new flood of Chinese to the "Golden Mountains"? Who cared that vigilantes were stringing up men on lamp-posts in San Francisco? So what if there was a Society of California Pioneers, or a new, though infant, State Library? What in hell was all the fuss about a place called Yosemite that had been discovered by the Mariposa Battalion? Who gave a damn about a rock pile if it didn't have a vein of gold in it?

    But gold, for once, gave way to another topic at the California. A child was to be born! Conversation at the bar and the faro tables dwelt on it.

"On Christmas, I'll bet!"

"How much?"

"A hundred dollars."

"You can't do better than that?"

"Make it two hundred then."

"You've got yourself a deal!"

"You shouldn't be on your feet so much," Bjorn told her, and thereafter refused to allow her to work the bar. She spent more time closeted with Procopius working on her reading, writing, and ciphering. When she wasn't studying, she was in her room. Charity was the only one who was ever invited in, and she seemed more worried about Tempest than anyone.

"She's not well, Bjorn. She seems so distracted. I don't think she sleeps very much, but that could be due to the child. She looks like she's ready to have it any minute."

Bjorn winced. Every time he looked at Tempest in her swollen condition, he thought about Jared Stryker creating that child inside her.

"Can you make her see that doctor Delight services?" Charity asked. "I mentioned him once, but she said that if God was going to take a life, he would, and no doctor could stop him. Where did she ever get these ideas of hers?"

"Does she think she's going to die?"

"She doesn't say what she thinks. But I think every woman must fear that at this time."

"We'll bring the doctor when the time comes, whatever she says," Bjorn decided.

Charity laid her hand gently on Bjorn's arm. "This ought to draw you two closer, and yet I never see the two of you together anymore."

"By her choice. Not mine."

"I wonder," Charity murmured, looking up at him. "It's a little late for remorse, wouldn't you say? But, then, perhaps a sailor doesn't know that when you put good seed in fertile soil, you get a bumper crop." She smiled. "For someone who's seen as much of this old world as you have, I would think you'd know how to be more careful."

He gave a humorless laugh.

Procopius told him the next morning that Tempest had ordered all her profits to be done up in sacks. "She told me she's going to give it all to God's house. I asked her what she meant and she wouldn't say. Then I asked her which God's house, and she just sat there at the desk and started to cry." He shook his head. "I didn't know what to do, Bjorn. I asked her what she wanted done, and she said to divide the gold equally and have it loaded in a wagon so she could deliver it herself."

"The hell she will!"

Bjorn found her lying on her bed, her face ghastly white. She looked up at him and crumpled. "He's going to take it. I *know* it."

Bjorn didn't know what she was talking about, but he saw the fear and despair in her eyes. He stretched out beside her, drawing her close. "I don't care if you give away all your gold, but you're not going to load down a wagon with it and drive around a city full of cutthroats giving it away."

"Ye dunna ken, mon. I have to do it! Gold is the only way I know to strike a bargain, and the only bargain good enough for Him is everything I have!"

Bjorn tipped her chin up, searching her bleak face. "With God? You can't strike bargains with God."

"I con try."

"You're not going to die, Tempest," Bjorn told her firmly.

"If this child is taken, it wouldna matter to me if I did."

"Don't say that," he said roughly. His hands shook as he cradled her face between them. *"Som du prata.* How you talk! Do you know how much I love you? Do not tell me the child is all that matters to you, even if it is the truth!"

She had never meant to hurt him. But neither did she have the time to make him understand.

Bjorn and several armed guards took Tempest around the city to deliver the sacks of gold. Bjorn helped her down from the carriage at each church, but she insisted upon carrying the gold in herself. He followed to watch from the door, expecting her to give her offering to a minister or priest and then receive absolution for her sins and a blessing. Instead, she spoke to no one. In each church, she walked straight to the altar and put the gold there herself. Then she walked out again, silent, her eyes haunted.

Bjorn knew that things were not right with her by the time they returned to the California. It was dusk and she was near complete collapse. Her face was white, her mouth pinched. Once during the ride back in the carriage, he had seen her clutch tightly at the brace, her chin lowering as she clenched her teeth and closed her eyes.

He carried her swiftly upstairs, ignoring the questions shouted from the crowd of men at his back. "Charity!" he roared when he reached the landing. He paused at her door to kick it.

"Sorry, dear," she said from inside. "Just hold on for a moment. I'll be right back." She opened the door. "Bjorn, are you mad? I've got—" She looked at Tempest. "Oh! I'll be there as soon as I can." Turning away, she said, "A fast one for the road, darling, and you can come back tomorrow for a full course."

Bjorn shouldered his way into Tempest's room, carrying her across to the bed and laying her down gently. Charity's bed banged against the wall as Bjorn gently stroked the dark tendrils back from Tempest's strained face. "She'll be here as quick as she can."

Tempest rolled her eyes and laughed softly. "She's going to—" She stopped and gritted her teeth, staring up at Bjorn with suddenly immense eyes.

He kept stroking her because he didn't know what else he could do. "There is nothing to be afraid of, *min älskling,*" he soothed, but his own heart was pumping like one of the new hydraulic systems on the river. Was she strong enough to endure this after her grueling day? Why had he let her carry all those sacks herself? Damn him for a fool! "As soon as Charity's here with you, I'll get the doctor," he told her.

The bed still banged and he stifled the urge to pound on the wall and yell to Charity to hurry it up, knowing that it would only slow things down. A moment later, the man gave a loud cry, and all the noise stopped.

The door opened and Charity bustled in, buttoning up her simple gray dress. She glared at Bjorn. "I doubt *he'll* come back," she told him. "I think I broke it."

Tempest laughed huskily. "Ye canna blame Bjorn for yer lack of care. Did he pay first?"

"Do be quiet, dear," Charity said sweetly, bending over the bed and smiling slightly. "You've got other things to worry about besides your pockets." In spite of Tempest's remark, Charity saw a heart-wrenching desperation in the blue eyes.

Bjorn left to get the doctor. When he reached the shanty up on the hill, he learned that the physician had gone back to the diggings. Someone suggested another man who had taken up medicine, but one look at him and Bjorn knew he wouldn't trust the man to doctor a dying horse, let alone touch Tempest. His hands were filthy and he was so drunk he couldn't even stay on his feet.

Bjorn ran all the way back to the California and bounded up the stairs three at a time. Charity jumped at his entrance, then relief flooded her worried face. She got up hurriedly and came to him.

"Is the doctor following in your wake?"

He looked across at Tempest. *"Han hargott,"* he muttered darkly.

"Lord in heaven, Bjorn Lindahl, will you speak English?"

"He is gone . . . back to the diggings."

Charity stared up at him, appalled, as he stood still panting heavily from his run and not knowing what to do next. "Gone?" she repeated dumbly.

"How is she?"

Panic set in. "What do you think, you great oaf? She *hurts!*" She immediately regretted her words at the look that came into

Bjorn's eyes. She sighed and patted his arm. "Never mind. It goes along with the job." She glanced over at Tempest, who was watching them. "Everything's fine," she said, and smiled brightly. She turned back to Bjorn. "What now? I don't know anything about birthing babies, only how to prevent getting quick with one."

He muttered hoarsely in Swedish and raked his hand through his hair.

A soft sound from the bed made them both turn. Tempest's eyes were tightly closed, her hands clutching the bedclothes at her sides. She turned her head away from them, but they could hear her gasping as she tried to ride out the pain.

"This one's longer," Charity said, and returned to the bed. She bent down and touched Tempest's sweat-beaded brow. "It'll pass in a moment, dear." She glanced up at Bjorn. "We could use some cool water."

Bjorn strode to the door, opened it, and bellowed an order. Then he strode back across the room and stood at the foot of the bed. Charity gave him a droll look.

Tempest let out a long breath as the pain eased. "He's going to take it," she murmured.

"Who's going to take what, sweetheart?" Charity asked gently.

"'Tis another punishment from God."

Charity frowned, seeing the wildness and despair in Tempest's glistening blue eyes. "You think God's angry with you? Why ever would you think that?"

Tempest's body arched and she closed her eyes again.

There was a rap at the door and Bjorn answered it. He took the pitcher and basin and the cloths that someone had had the foresight to bring as well. As he came around the bed, he saw how Tempest fared. Charity took the things and brushed him aside. She dipped a cloth in the water and squeezed it, then gently dabbed Tempest's pale forehead.

The pain eased again and she breathed more evenly, though her eyes were frightened.

"God's not angry with you, honey," Charity told her. "You're just having a baby, that's all." She turned and Bjorn took the cloth from her hand to freshen it. "But I hope He's listening right now, because I'm going to need a little help getting through this," she said sotto voce.

"Aye, he's angry. He—" Tempest moaned deeply as another contraction began and strengthened.

"Tempest—" Charity said softly, leaning down.

"Abram prayed," Tempest whimpered. "He prayed and prayed for it . . ."

Charity cast a worried look at Bjorn, wondering how he was taking Tempest's talk of another man while she was having his child.

"'Twasna Abram's fault," Tempest cried. "I dinna ken what Da was about, what was in that pot . . ." She shook her head, her eyes wild. She closed them tightly again as the pain mounted. She ground her teeth. It peaked and eased off. "Abram had naught to do with it," she panted.

Bjorn walked slowly around the bed to stand closer to her on the other side. Charity looked up at him and saw that he wasn't angry at all, but listening intently. "Do you know what she's talking about?" she asked softly. He shook his head, but there was torment in his eyes. She put her hand over Tempest's tightly. "Just forget whatever it was—"

"All he asked of God was a wee bairn. All he asked of me, too," she said brokenly. Another contraction began and took her breath away.

"It won't be long now," Charity tried to encourage her.

"Hurt so . . ." Tempest moaned.

"I know, sweetheart. I wish I could make it stop."

"He hurt . . . he was all swollen up . . . and . . ." She gritted her teeth, breathing fast as the pain intensified. Charity glanced up at Bjorn. He was leaning down slightly, his hand white as he gripped the brass rail at the head of the ornate bed.

". . . and I ken he was dying," Tempest gasped. "God wouldna listen! Abram screamed and screamed!"

"This isn't good for you, Tempest. Now stop—" Charity pleaded.

"I couldna stand it . . . I had to do something . . . I—" Her fingers dug into the bedcovers and twisted them.

"You forget all that hogwash about silent Indians," Charity told her firmly. "Scream like hell if you want."

But Tempest didn't. Her knuckles whitened and she shook violently. "I made it fast," she gasped out. "Da taught me how to kill swiftly. One cut and life runs out. I sharpened my knife. He dinna even feel it—I made sure of that. God let him suffer enough. I couldna let him . . ."

Charity put her hand up to her throat. "Lord in heaven," she whispered.

"'An eye for an eye,' his book said," Tempest cried softly.

Charity leaned close. "All right. Listen now. That does not
mean God is going to take your baby," she said forcefully.

"Aye, it does!"

"You showed mercy to a suffering man—"

"I killed him when he was helpless, and God took the child."

"The baby hasn't even been born yet," Charity reasoned.

"Aye, the other was," Tempest sobbed. "He took the bairn
as Abram drew his last breath. God dinna even give it a chance.
He—" Her eyes rolled back as another wave of pain took hold.

"Tempest," Charity tried to shush her. "You've got other
things to concentrate on right now. We'll talk about the other
later."

"Let her talk now if she wants," Bjorn said gruffly.

"She needs her strength—"

"Abram said God knew everything," Tempest gasped. "He
knew all that had happened, all that would happen. He . . ."

"Bjorn, tell her to stop."

"No."

"If God knew, why did He answer my prayer and send
Abram back to me? Why did He do that if he knew I would
be the one to kill him? Why take the child's life and not mine?"
she sobbed.

Now Bjorn understood what she meant by retribution.

He bent over her. *"Min älskling."*

She looked up at him despairingly. "Ye con do naught,
mon."

"'An eye for an eye,'" he murmured gently and stroked her
cheek, looking into her eyes. "Your debt is paid, ja?"

Her mouth crumpled and she shook her head.

He cupped her chin firmly. "You gave your Abram release
from pain, and God took your child."

"Bjorn," Charity protested, but fell silent at his sharp, quelling look.

"The slate is even, Tempest," he said softly.

She shook her head again. Looking up at him, her eyes
streaming, she whispered through trembling lips, "On nicht of
flood, begotten in God's own parlor." She bit down on her lip.

Bjorn's eyes cleared as he comprehended, then darkened.
"His sin, not yours," he told her. He braced one hand on either
side of the bed so that he was above her, staring down into
her face. *"His,* Tempest."

"My child—" Her jaw stiffened and her head came up slightly
as her body bore down. Bjorn shifted back. He pried her hand

from the bedcovers and held it. She had plenty of strength left.

"Oh, dear," Charity muttered. "Ready or not, here it comes."

Bjorn glanced back at her sharply. "Wait. I'll see if there is someone downstairs who knows—"

"Tell that to the baby."

Tempest's face was dark red, and her hand tightened again on Bjorn's. Her knees came up.

Charity drew down the light covers. "Just stay out of the way, Bjorn." She repositioned herself. "Sweet Jesus, guide me, please. I promise to listen this time!"

"Do you know what to do?" Bjorn asked worriedly, watching as she rolled the blankets down to the foot of the bed.

"Never lost a baby yet," she told him, and knelt at the foot of the bed.

"You said—"

"Let's not discuss that now, hmm?" she said, and hitched up Tempest's thin gown. Bjorn's face went red and averted his eyes.

"Mother Nature is supposed to take care of this," Charity murmured with a nervous sigh. "*Oh!*" Bjorn turned his head back to look at her. Her face was pale. She gave him a frantic look and muttered, "How did I ever get involved in this?!"

Tempest's body curled forward. She opened her lips and murmured something.

"So help me Hannah," Charity gasped in exasperation as she knelt, waiting. "If she starts to talk about God punishing her again, you gag her. This is not the time for a theological discussion!"

The baby's head emerged, and Tempest expelled a deep breath before bearing down again.

Charity was shaking with a surge of adrenaline. "Squalling from the hatch," she said, and grinned at Bjorn, whose face was the color of ashes. "Thar she blows!" she cried as the baby slid free of Tempest's body and lay wailing on the bloody sheets between her shaking legs. "I need some warm water, Bjorn," Charity instructed.

"I need a whiskey," he muttered. "Where am I supposed to get warm water?"

"Where do you think? Downstairs." She laughed. "Tempest, you can let go of his hand now. He was here for the launching."

Bjorn looked down and saw that Tempest's eyes were open, but she was focusing on sound rather than sight. He straightened carefully, not wanting to jar the bed and hurt her more. He

crossed the room quickly, threw open the door, and bellowed
down the stairs for warm water.

Charity laughed. "That should bring things on the run." She
shook her head. "Ho, long-legged little bugger, aren't you?
Three legs! It's a boy! Praise God, you've got yourself a son!"
She lifted her head slightly to look at Tempest. "I hope this
means I'm going to be godmother," she quipped with her usual
irreverence.

Tempest smiled for the first time in hours.

Another contraction brought the afterbirth. Warm water arrived and Bjorn toted two steaming buckets across the room,
not letting anyone else in. He set the buckets down by the bed
and looked at Tempest's pale face. She was watching Charity
tend the baby in a daze of confused, joyous wonder. Bjorn
looked at the wailing baby still covered with its thick, white
womb coat. Charity was cutting the cord.

"Don't you dare pass out on me," Charity warned him,
seeing what little color remained in his taut face drain away
completely. "Here. You wash the baby while I see to Tempest."
She shifted the infant to the end of the bed and nodded toward
the bucket and cloths. "Well, don't just stand there."

He didn't want to touch Stryker's son, let alone wash him.
The infant flailed on the tumble of blankets Charity had pushed
to the end of the bed, wailing pathetically. Charity gave him
an odd look when he still didn't move, but it was the way
Tempest looked at him with complete understanding that made
him pick up the cloth and dip it into the warm water and squeeze
it out.

Gazing at the thatch of black hair, Bjorn began to wash the
child. The quivering mouth ceased its wailing long enough for
the baby's eyes to open. They were blue; he wondered if they
would later turn brown like his father's. With a grim frown,
he cleansed the baby's face, hair, ears, and neck. As he worked
downward, he saw the strong, rapid heartbeat that showed
through the translucent skin of the child's chest. The baby's
bones were as fragile as a bird's. Its bowed legs kicked upward
as the babe began to wail again. Its arms flailed, its tiny fingers
flowering out.

"Listen to him roar," Charity chuckled as she washed Tempest's thighs gently, and looked up to wink at Bjorn. "Lungs
like a Baptist preacher or a drunken sailor."

Bjorn winced and, hard-faced, went on washing the child's
body, legs, and feet. He lifted one small, pale arm. The child's

tiny fingers closed around the pad of his thumb. They couldn't even completely encircle it, but they clung, warm and surprisingly strong. Bjorn drew his hand back slowly, trying to gently break the hold. The baby's arm straightened out and its pale shoulder lifted from the blankets as its clutching fingers whitened with effort.

Bjorn stared down at the child for a long moment. His face softened. *"Jacklar,"* he swore softly, and gave in to the gentleness in him. What difference who had sown the seed? The crop was in.

Bjorn wrapped the clean baby snugly in a fire-warmed linen cloth and lay the baby in the curve of Tempest's arm. He bent over her and brushed his lips against her forehead, aware that she had been watching him closely for some time. He smiled into her eyes. "I think you both could use some sleep." He bent and brushed the baby's forehead with a kiss also. Tempest's eyes filled with tears.

"What about me?" Charity teased. "Don't I deserve a kiss, too?"

He whacked her on the bottom. "Pretty proud of yourself, aren't you?" he said, grinning.

"Considerably," she agreed, and grinned impishly. "I'm starving, too. Would you have something brought up for us, please? And don't you dare stand in the doorway hollering for it! Besides, Bjorn, you've an announcement to make downstairs, don't you? Gold is riding on this, I'm sure."

He looked down at Tempest again, not really wanting to leave her yet. She smiled, her eyes hazed with weariness. She should sleep. He looked at Charity. "Will you stay with her?"

She patted his arm and walked him to the door. "You know I will. Now, go on. I think you do need that whiskey." She closed the door behind him.

Coming back to the bed, she removed the soiled linens and left them in a heap by the door. She put fresh ones on the bed, gently rolling Tempest onto her side and then back again, as she had learned to do when she had once nursed her grandmother for a few months before she died. Finishing the chore, she stood back and brushed sweat-dampened tendrils of hair back from her flushed cheeks. She smiled warmly down at Tempest. "What a lot of work for such a little bundle," she murmured, and bent to caress the velvety cheek of the sleeping child.

"Thank ye, Charity," Tempest whispered huskily.

Charity nodded simply, her own eyes overly bright.

"God dinna take him this time."

"No, God didn't. And I don't think He will." Charity sat gently on the bed and took Tempest's free hand. She patted it. "You said your Abram wanted that other baby."

Tempest swallowed hard. "Aye," she whispered. "He'd prayed for a child for years. Even with his first wife . . ."

"No more crying, Tempest," Charity told her. "You let yourself fill up with joy. You have a healthy son in your arms and a man who loves you more than life itself." She squeezed her hand gently. "I want you to think about something."

Tempest waited.

Charity hesitated, not sure if what she was about to say would help at all. "Did you ever once stop to think that God was answering Abram's prayer and not rejecting yours?"

"What do ye mean?" Tempest frowned.

"The God my father knew wouldn't punish someone for an act of mercy."

"It says in Abram's book, 'Thou shalt not kill,'" Tempest said solemnly. "I killed Abram. So—"

"You listen to me, Tempest," Charity said with gentle but firm determination. She leaned closer, her eyes holding her friend's. "Maybe God wasn't taking your baby away from you. Maybe He was *giving* it into Abram's keeping."

Tempest's lips parted.

"An act of love, not of vengeance," Charity said, and nodded once. She smiled. "With God, you must use more of this," she murmured, tapping Tempest lightly on the chest, "while you use this," and she brushed Tempest's damp temple with tender fingers and smiled down at her.

She stood slowly, still holding Tempest's hand. "When you're up and around again, and not completely occupied with nursing this baby, you are going to start reading that big Bible over there again. But this time, you start with the Book of Matthew and go from there. When you know the end of the story, you can go back to the beginning and read it all with a little clearer understanding—and far less fear."

She stretched and rubbed the aching small of her back. Smiling, she asked, "What are you going to call your son, by the way?"

"Abram," Tempest said without hesitation. "Abram Mc-Claren Walker."

A woman's place is in the home.
—Anonymous

Two weeks after little Abram was born, Bjorn bundled
Tempest and the baby and took them out for a carriage ride.
Her first real sight of the city in some time was a shock to her.
She felt she had come out of a dark cave after a long hiber-
nation.

A year with Jared. Six months with Bjorn. Her focus had
been too limited. Casino walls, a bedroom, her own soul.

Sacramento had changed. No longer was this a tent town.
There were streets lined with wooden homes. Buildings bigger
than the California were under construction, some being made
of brick. The lower streets were well protected now by the
levee constructed after the flood in 1850. Plans were being put
into effect to reroute the great river itself so miners could see
how much gold the bottom might yield.

"I've been away from the bar too long," she murmured,
interested in everything she saw. She had kept abreast of hap-
penings by listening to the men talk, yell, debate and fight.

"You're never going to work behind that bar again," Bjorn
said in an unyielding tone.

She looked at him slowly. "When I did, I knew everything
that was going on in Sacramento and California itself. Now I
know naught."

"Some things you've no need to know."

She raised her eyebrows. "Ye be changing yer tune. Ye
shoved me off a cliff to see if I could fly, and now that ye
know I can, ye be wanting to cut my wings."

"Trim them a little," he said, grinning. "There's something
I want to show you."

"The *Sverige?*"

He let out a sharp laugh and looked at her. "How long have
you known about her?"

"It's hard to hide a steamship," she said wryly. "I knew

401

when she came upriver, but I suspected something before that. Ye were taking yer gold out of the California and putting it someplace else."

"Importing whores and adding on to the building isn't what I want to do with my money." He turned the carriage up a side street. "I've done well with the ship. Men pay more to come up the river to the diggings than they did for passage around the Horn or by way of the Isthmus. I've another ship coming and two windjammers are going to be towed up here. They were fallowing in San Francisco harbor, so they came cheap. A little work and some good rigging will set them on good course again."

"And you with them?"

He looked down at her, unsmiling. "Depends on a few things: but for now, I'm staying on land."

"What about Claus?"

Bjorn smiled slightly. "He's ready to sail. He hasn't been too happy running a steamship," he said. "He wants to run a ship before the wind again."

Tempest saw women other than prostitutes walking along the streets, pioneer women. Not many, but more than there had been a few months before. And more were coming.

"Big business is taking over the diggings, Tempest," Bjorn was saying. "Things are going to change fast now. Hundreds of men are being pushed out of the fields already, and they are going to need a place to settle, jobs to work, food to eat."

She glanced at him curiously. He was building up to something.

"It's time you got out of what you're doing," he said without looking at her.

"I ken naught else, Bjorn," she told him seriously.

"Then you'd better learn!" He let out an angry breath. "The California is no place to raise your son, unless you want him to grow up a whoremaster or a gambler." He almost said "like his father," but caught himself in time.

Anger coursed through her, but she said nothing, staring instead along the shop-lined street and at the people. Hadn't she been thinking the same thing from the moment she had held little Abram in her arms? Wasn't it up to her to see that he grew up to be like the man for whom he was named, rather than like the one who had accidentally fathered him?

Or like this man sitting beside her in the carriage, she thought, glancing at Bjorn again.

"Aye," she agreed softly. "Ye be right. But what do ye suggest?"

The last thing he had expected was capitulation. All the arguments were set in his head ready to be trotted out, and he stammered for a moment, trying to change his course. Then he knew. "Sell the California."

"That I canna and wilna do."

"Why not?"

"Because it makes us a fortune."

"Other enterprises make money."

"Not as much."

"How do you know? You haven't tried anything else."

She sat stony-faced and silent, as stubborn as he.

"All right. *Jacklar*. Keep the California. But do what I've done and take the profits out, put them into legitimate businesses. Mercantiles, for example."

"I ken naught about mercantiles." Her, a merchant!

"How much did you know about gambling houses and whorehouses before you started?" he demanded roughly, not looking at her. "But you've managed."

She gave him a wry look. "Ye have great faith in me."

"More than you have in yourself," he said, serious.

He had reached the outskirts of the sprawling town and urged the horses on. His heart pounded in slow, dull thumps. What was she going to say when she saw where he was taking her?

"I'll think on it," Tempest said, still dwelling on the old subject. She looked out at the countryside spreading out before her.

How long since she had sat astride her horse and ridden across an open field, or walked among the marsh reeds, or heard birdsong, or breathed in that sense of freedom? How long since she had listened to silence?

"Oh," she said softly, and it was a muted sound of infinite relief.

Bjorn glanced down at her. She looked right with the baby in her arms and that relaxed curve to her lips. She was changing like everything else around him. The haunting sadness had softened out of her cold blue eyes, at least when she looked at the child—and sometimes when she looked at him. A calmness had settled over her, though he sensed she was still relentless in her ambition. Sometimes he felt her enigmatic gaze on him and wondered what she was thinking.

"Where are ye taking me, Bjorn?" She looked up at him,

and the clearness of that blue gaze set his pulse hammering.

"Over there," he said, nodding toward a grass-covered knoll on which sat a two-story white house. It was a simple structure, solidly built, and probably the only whitewashed one in Sacramento.

Tempest looked at it and then up at Bjorn. He was frowning heavily, and she wondered at the grimness of his expression and the way he avoided looking at her.

He drew up at the rail a few minutes later and jumped down, tethering the lead horse and then coming around the carriage to help her down. "Whose house is this?" she asked as he lifted her, the baby nestled against her just as she was against him. He didn't put her down, but carried her up the path. "Bjorn?"

"Yours."

The door opened and Wind Reed, the Indian girl who had made clothes for her over the past two years, was standing at the threshold, smiling.

Bjorn felt Tempest staring up at him. He carried her into the parlor, but still didn't put her down. It was the first time he had held her like this, and he wasn't going to relinquish the moment, or her, too quickly.

Tempest looked around vaguely, seeing the fine furnishings that must have come from the East: a settee, a highboy, two wing chairs, a long, low, curved-legged table on which rested a silver tray with a shining tea service. The floor was polished wood, better than anything in the California, and there were real windows and brocade drapes and soft, lacy curtains.

"Put me down," she said quietly.

With a grim sigh, Bjorn did.

She walked slowly around the neat, elegantly furnished room.

"Besides this parlor, there's a den across the foyer and a kitchen—it's part of the house, not separate. There are two big bedrooms upstairs. It's not a big house, Tempest, but I had it built so that it could be expanded if—" His voice dropped off as she stopped near the wooden rocker in front of the glowing fire.

She touched it lightly to set it in motion. Old memories flooded her. Her mouth quivered.

"So you can rock the baby while you nurse him. There's another in your bedroom upstairs," Bjorn said gruffly.

She looked up at the mantel, almost expecting to see a big black Bible lying there just underneath a mounted long-rifle. It was bare.

"Ye take so much for granted, Bjorn," she murmured huskily.

"I don't take anything for granted," he said sharply. "But it's time you lived somewhere other than above a saloon in a room beside that of a prostitute, kind as Charity is." His Swedish accent was heavy and it was a few seconds before she realized exactly what he had said.

She studied him as he stood with his feet planted, his jaw hard, his eyes fierce. "Look around," he told her. "If you don't like this, I'll build another. Or we'll change what is here."

Little Abram stirred and she pressed him closer. He nuzzled, making soft sucking sounds against her neck, searching.

"Say something," Bjorn pleaded hoarsely, his eyes bleak.

She shook her head, knowing that she couldn't. If she did, she would cry. Lowering her eyes, she walked out the room and out the front door.

"Tempest!" Groaning, Bjorn followed her.

She stood outside, a soft breeze stroking her warm temples and cooling her burning eyes. A big sycamore grew beyond the house. Down the hill were several scrub oaks.

Bjorn looked down at her pale, distraught face and the way she held onto Jared's son, and felt a deep, inconsolable despair. Perhaps, if he had just left things as they were . . .

"Tempest . . ." he said, wondering if he could go back again. He stepped closer, but she turned her back to him and shook her head. He had to clench his hands tightly at his sides to keep from touching her. He cursed himself for a fool and reminded himself strongly that a man didn't cry.

Abram cried for him.

Tempest stroked the child, but he wouldn't be quietened. His mouth opened against her neck, sucking, and when he didn't get what he wanted, he cried louder, his little legs making froglike jerks within the warm blanket as Tempest held him against her.

She walked toward the sycamore. Bjorn followed grimly. She sat down, the soft folds of her blue dress swirling around her, and laid the wailing baby in the cradle of her crossed legs while she unbuttoned the front of her dress.

"We must talk, Bjorn," she said.

"I'll come back when you've finished," he answered, gazing down at her. He had never watched her nurse the baby before; it was a private moment between mother and son, a time on which he had never tried to intrude.

"Sit down, mon," she told him softly, looking up at him with soft eyes.

He looked at her questioningly, then sat down slowly.

She lifted little Abram and cradled him against her. The puckered mouth caught hold and worked frantically for a few seconds before slowing in satisfaction. Tempest looked out at the land, her face relaxed.

Bjorn gazed at her. Did she know so little about how he felt that she could think nothing of letting him watch? The baby's hand pressed against her breast, and his stomach felt like a hard knot.

"Do ye long for the sea, Bjorn?" she asked quietly, still not looking at him.

He studied her face. She was so incredibly beautiful. "Ja. Sometimes," he admitted, knowing that he longed for her far more than that other cruel mistress.

A pulse beat visibly in her throat. He stared at it for a long moment before his eyes dropped slowly to little Abram again. The child still nursed, but his eyelids had grown heavy. Tempest's hand supported the baby's shoulder, his head in the crook of her arm. She had fine hands, long fingers, and short, clean fingernails.

Bjorn looked at all of her and remembered against his will the night, months before, when she had taken off her clothes and stood naked before him, her eyes dull.

"Aye," she murmured. "As I have longed for this."

He had lost track of what she had said before, and looked at her blankly.

She smiled slightly. "Da and I rode over the mountains with our horses loaded down with beaver pelts, and there it was. California. Stretching out before us in a misty haze, all purple and gold, yellow and red with flowers, it was. I'd never seen anything so beautiful."

He thought he understood. "And now hillsides lie torn open like gutted whales, rivers are diverted, and the land is crawling with greedy men."

"'Tis the way I felt," she agreed slowly. "All I could see and hear was the men downstairs or along that bar and that piano mon playing that bloody song 'Oh, Susanna' over and over again." She sighed. "They were all prodding their pain, keeping it alive." She gave Bjorn a faint, humorless smile. "As I've been prodding my own."

She gazed down at the baby and shifted him, covering her

breast and laying open the other side of her bodice to offer him the other.

"Tempest," Bjorn whispered hoarsely.

She looked up at him. "I lie awake in the night sometimes and try to remember how the earth smelled, how the air tasted, how the birds sounded. All I could ever hear was the men shoutin' and laughin' and swearin' at their bad luck." She held his eyes and added very softly, "Or Charity's bed hitting against my wall and making me remember Jared."

Bjorn swore.

"No," she said, and put her hand out in supplication as he started to get up. "Hear me out, Bjorn."

"You're never going to forget him." He said something more in Swedish, then let out his breath, glad she couldn't understand. But his tone had been enough.

"No. I wilna forget," she told him truthfully. "It was a lesson hard learned, and one I canna forget."

"You would forget fast enough if he ever came back and wanted you again," he said flatly, standing in spite of the look of entreaty on her face. He had faith in her in everything, save this.

She watched him walk away and stand gazing away down the knoll from her, the gentle breeze playing softly with his blond hair. She let the baby finish nursing and lifted him against her shoulder, lightly patting him until he burped. Then she put him down on the grassy earth and opened the muffling blanket and removed all his clothes. He gurgled and kicked his legs, his arms flailing.

"Feel the earth and the sun and the wind," she whispered. She left him there as she went down to Bjorn.

This time it was he who had his back to her. She touched his shoulder, and his muscles stiffened. His head came up, but he said nothing. She came around in front of him and saw his face. Reaching up, she touched his cheek very gently. "'Tis a fine house, Bjorn Lindahl."

He stared down at her, his eyes searching hers.

She cupped his face in both her hands and drew him down. "Better than anything I've ever had before," she murmured, and kissed him softly on the mouth.

He drew a swift, harsh breath and caught hold of her.

She had often wondered what it would be like, but had never suspected it would be like this. She gasped beneath the hungry onslaught of Bjorn's mouth and felt the strength and warmth of him all down her length. Long moments passed and she felt no desire to press for her freedom, though he scarcely allowed her a chance to draw a breath. Nor did she try to stop his hands from moving freely over her.

Finally he drew back, breathing raggedly, and looked down at her bright, glowing blue eyes. He said something in deep, thickened Swedish as he held her tenderly.

She hadn't understood that he was saying he could wait a little longer. All she knew with certainty was that no one, ever, had wanted or loved her as much as this man did.

And no one would again.

> A great flame follows a little spark.
> —Dante
> *Paradiso*

Tempest took Bjorn's advice and threw herself into other business ventures, using the California's profits for funding. She opened a mercantile and put it under the management of an Ohio merchant who was sick of standing in icy water, shoulder to shoulder with hundreds of other men. Seeing the success of Levi Strauss, she undertook a similar venture, having Indian women construct canvas coats lined with fur and waterproofed with blended oils. She unloaded the warehouse down by the river where Jared had stored the consignment of fabrics he'd won from Levinson, and opened a women's dress shop with the bolts of cloth, putting Delight in charge and another half a dozen Indian seamstresses under her command. Then she hired a crew of carpenters to renovate the empty warehouse, adding walls, bunks, a bar, and an eatery. Tempest planned to open it as a hotel by the river.

Charity went on running the upstairs of the California for Tempest, while Bjorn turned over the casino to Missouri so that he was free to put his time into fortifying his infant shipping line. Without his knowledge, Tempest opened another whorehouse up near the now deserted fort that had once been the hub of California's pioneers. Angelita became madam over ten Chilean prostitutes.

"Naught is comin' in. It's all goin' out," Tempest complained to Bjorn one evening.

"You're just getting things started. You have to make capital investments before you can expect profit."

"If you spread yourself too thin, though, your financial empire could come down like a house of cards," Procopius said, sitting with ledgers spread out across the big oak table Tempest had had moved into the parlor.

"Con ye not handle more?" She was afraid she was expecting too much of him already.

"No more than what you've gotten into already, Miss Tempest," he admitted grimly, "and I need some help to keep up with that."

She glanced at Bjorn, who was stretched out on the settee, his hands behind his head and his eyes closed. He wasn't asleep. She could tell by the faint smile on his lips. She knew what he was doing, and her mouth tightened angrily. He had never yet made a decision for her and she knew he wouldn't do so now, even though it was by his suggestion she had gotten herself into all this confusion.

"So be it," she told Procopius. "Get yerself the help ye need."

He suggested several men about whom he had heard good reports, while she paced before the parlor windows cooing softly to Abram. He seemed to favor one man, a Jew who already worked for another big business concern, but who might consider working for her if the offer were good enough.

She nodded. "Offer him the least ye think he will take, then go from there." She glanced over her shoulder. "Then we con start on that banking venture," she said, her eyes mischievous.

Procopius sputtered. "It takes *capital*—"

She laughed. "Canna ye be taking a joke, mon?"

"Sometimes I wonder if you *are* joking," he grumbled, and cast Bjorn a fulminating look. "Life would have been easier if I'd never read those letters and had kept to the 'yassuhs.'"

Bjorn grinned broadly. "You'd be a lot poorer, too." As soon as Procopius had gathered up the ledgers, reports, and his coat and hat, Bjorn saw him out. Tempest heard the two men talking outside and Bjorn's laugh rang out again. She liked the sound of his laughter.

The Indian girl, Wind Reed, peered in after she had taken Abram up to say that the baby was sleeping soundly in his cradle, and was there anything else Tempest required? Tempest answered no and thanked her, and Wind Reed retired for the night.

Alone again, Tempest rocked slowly in her chair near the fire, thinking about Bjorn Lindahl. She remembered how he had held her the first day he had brought her to this house six weeks ago. Yet he hadn't touched her since. Charity said it was probably because he knew her body couldn't take him yet.

"He's probably got his sails hanging limp waiting for you

to give him a good, warm wind to fill them," Charity had said, grinning. "I imagine it wouldn't take more than a light puff to get him going."

Bjorn came back into the parlor, poured himself a glass of brandy, and stood with his back to the fireplace, his legs splayed. He grinned at her as he raised his glass. "I think we can safely say you are now the richest woman in California."

"Aye."

"What do you want to do now?" he teased after downing half the draught.

She studied him but saw no hint of his own hopes and expectations. "Go on as I am," she told him.

He looked back at her pensively. "What is it? Are you worried about what Procopius said about it all being a house of cards that could come falling down?"

Charity had told her she would have to make the first move, that Bjorn was waiting for her. It was a new situation for Tempest to be in, after having always been the one pursued. "Just tell him you want him again," Charity had said, still believing him to be the father of Abram.

But was it that simple?

"If it did fall, what would ye do, Bjorn?"

"We'd scrape it back together and start with a new deck," he said carelessly. "But you will do fine, *min kara.*"

He was so sure of her abilities. She rested her head against the back of the chair and looked at him steadily, a faint smile on her lips. "Why do ye never ask anythin' for yerself?"

"Such as?"

Her heart beat heavily as she met his eyes. She stood up slowly. "Do ye want things to stand as they be, or would ye have them different?" she asked quietly.

Bjorn went very still, his smile dying. His stomach tightened. "What are you saying to me, flicka?"

"I think ye ken, mon, if ye but think a moment," she said faintly, and smiled.

He stared back at her. His pulse mounted steadily until he didn't think he could draw a single breath without making a loud sound in the stillness of the room. "Ja, I want things different," he admitted hoarsely, but added, "Are you ready for that?"

"It's been a long enough time since the bairn was born. I con take you."

Worldly sailor though he was, she realized with surprise

that she had deeply embarrassed him.

"I did not mean . . . in that way," he said gruffly.

"How then?"

"Can you think only of me when—" He stopped, made a distressed gesture with his head, and then tossed back the rest of the brandy before setting the glass firmly on the mantel.

She couldn't promise that she wouldn't make some comparisons; she couldn't say that she never thought of Jared Stryker. Those were the things she knew Bjorn longed to hear, but if she gave him the words now, he would know she lied.

"I dinna think of Jared when ye kissed me the first day ye brought me here," she said carefully.

He said nothing for a long moment, then gave her a small, bleak smile. "But did you feel anything yourself?"

"I felt it was right," she said without hesitation. "And that be something that I never felt with Jared in all the times he touched me."

Bjorn's blue eyes glowed. "I will ask for something then. I will ask for you to marry me."

Her throat tightened.

"You said I never ask anything for myself. Well, that's what I want. You and me, married."

"Ye must think on what ye want more then, mon," she told him painfully. She came close and put her hands on his chest, just to feel the hard warmth of him as a man. His heart was pounding hard and fast. "What was I when ye first saw me, Bjorn? How have I changed since then—in any way that matters?"

His eyes darkened. "You can read and write. You dress like a lady and not like a whore on display. You manage half a dozen businesses," he said harshly. "You stand on your own now. You'll never be forced to be with anyone unless you want to."

Was that how he had seen it?

"I have always had choices," she said, wishing she didn't have to admit it. "I could have remained in a hut by the river and not gone to Jared. He dinna force me to do anything. I ken what he wanted from me from the beginning."

She knew he didn't like what she was saying. Truth always came hard.

"Did you?" he said intently. "You thought he loved you."

"He did, in his way."

Bjorn took his hands away from her, his face pale. She

caught hold of one, sorrowing at what she saw in his eyes. "Bjorn," she whispered brokenly, "part of what I am today is due as much to Jared as it is due to you." She saw that he didn't understand and she clutched tighter at his hand. "What I am is not only what is inside—the blood Da and my mother gave me—but the sum of everything that has happened to me, everyone I've known. 'Tis the same for you, for anyone. Ye canna forget anything or anyone, because they be a part of what ye become—good or bad, right or wrong. Do ye ken what I say?"

"Ja," he said, and added grimly, "but Jared is one thing in your life I could wish had never happened to you."

She smiled slightly, understanding, and her eyes filled. She reached up and stroked his cheek. "Just remember that ye are the best of it all, Bjorn Lindahl," she told him warmly, holding his gaze steadily.

The look in Tempest's eyes for him was not the same one he had seen there for Stryker.

Upstairs, the baby cried. Bjorn felt niggling resentment that things would have to stop here and be saved for another evening, but quelled it. "I will go. We talk again tomorrow."

She held his hand as they walked together to the foyer. He paused in the doorway and looked down at her. Then slowly, still with trepidation, he lowered his head and kissed her. Her hand glided up around the back of his neck, and he felt desire beat through him. He didn't draw her any closer because he didn't want her to feel the effect a simple kiss had on him.

He raised his head and smiled. She held tight to his hand and took a step toward the stairs. He looked at her, frowning.

She smiled slightly. "I ken what I am about, Bjorn."

He went with her up the stairs.

Standing inside the door of her bedroom, he watched her cross the room and pick up the baby, nuzzling him. Then she walked toward the bed and began unlooping the buttons of her bodice. Bjorn felt as though his shirt collar were too tight. She stretched out on her side and laid the baby snuggly against her so that he could nurse, then looked up at him and smiled.

"Ye con come in, Bjorn."

He ran a shaky hand around the back of his neck and crossed the room to restoke the fire in the hearth, but his gaze kept drifting back to her lying on the bed with the baby at her breast. He'd made love to many women, but he had never known one who was a mother, or likely to become one.

When the baby was finished, she rose and held little Abram against her shoulder, gently rubbing his back as she murmured to him lovingly. She walked very slowly to the cradle and settled him there again, readjusting the soft blanket around him as he slept.

Bjorn waited.

She had left the buttons unlooped.

The room was stifling him, but he quelled the urge to go open a window, knowing that the heat of his skin had nothing to do with the fire burning in the grate, but with the one burning even hotter inside himself.

What if he couldn't bring her to satisfaction? What if she didn't like his body when he removed his clothes and she got her first good look? He was scarred from a flogging when he was fifteen—what would she think of the marks he bore? What if she was already changing her mind anyway?

She met his eyes solemnly. "Is there a way to make this any easier for both of us?" she whispered.

He gave a soft, husky laugh. "I don't know." He wished he did.

She smiled. "'Tis a comfort knowing ye are as scared as I am, Bjorn."

He grinned sheepishly. They stood across the room from one another, their nerves raw. If she had been a whore, she would have known exactly how to make this part easy. He was glad she didn't.

He approached and stood in front of her. Taking her hand, he drew her a few feet away from the cradle and the sleeping baby. Then he turned her gently so that they were facing one another. He lightly caressed her cheek with his knuckles. "Let's start by just touching each other."

"Aye," she breathed, and her eyes closed slowly as his hand moved down the curve of her neck and across her shoulder.

He unbuttoned his shirt with his other hand and then took her hand, placing it against his bared chest. Her fingers spread. He held his breath at her touch, burning hotter than a tropical sun against his flesh.

He shrugged off his shirt and let it drop. He had been bare to the waist thousands of times before men and women and never once had felt self-conscious until now, with this woman he loved so much looking upon his naked chest for the first time.

She had no fear at all of touching him. His skin was smooth, warm, and gilded with hair. The muscles beneath were hard from years of physical labor. He drew in his breath sharply as her hands moved over his rib cage and across his taut belly.

His fingers shook as he edged them beneath the open bodice and felt her velvety skin. "Can we take this off?" he whispered huskily.

She helped him with the dress, then the camisole. She wore no corset. Everything else slipped to the floor easily.

Bjorn stepped back to look down at her.

She listened to his murmured words of Swedish. His gaze was only for her body now, but she felt no shame. She took his hands and placed them against her breasts. He moved forward again, bending so that he could slide his rough palms down along her waist, hips, and thighs, then back up again as his mouth caressed the arching curve of her neck.

She closed her eyes in ecstasy and arched her spine. His hands kneaded the firm flesh of her buttocks. She gently rubbed her face against his chest. She could hear his breathing, feel the racing beat of his heart. She let her hands explore his back, feeling along the ridges of scars and wanting to stroke away all the pain he had ever felt. Her hands moved down, her fingertips dipping into his dungarees, moving slowly around the rigid muscles of his spine to his abdomen.

He said something throatily and stepped back. He tugged off one boot and set it down quietly so he wouldn't disturb little Abram, then removed the other. His hands went to his belt as he gazed at Tempest's slender, perfect body, at the full, dark-tipped breasts, gently curving hips, long slender legs, and the soft, noticeable protrusion of her belly, still lax from the child.

Always before, Bjorn had shucked his pants with cocky male pride. He had never worried over frightening the robust women he had always chosen, knowing full well they would appreciate all he had. But Tempest...

How was he going to keep from hurting her? Already he could feel the urgency and immediacy of his desire knotting in his belly. He had never had to proceed with care before.

How long was it before a woman was properly healed from the birth of a baby? Could she take him? Worse, could he manage to hold back any part of himself once he began?

"Do ye need the lantern turned down?" she offered quietly, waiting.

She thought he was modest. He was, afraid of what she

would think when she saw him. He sighed heavily. It was her turn after all to get a look at all of him, he thought. Then she could always change her mind.

His expression grim, he finished what he had started, straightening and watching her face closely, frowning.

One dark eyebrow rose slightly. She took her sweet time.

Sweat began beading along the back of Bjorn's neck. "Have you seen enough?" he asked roughly, sure that in another moment he would humiliate himself.

She laughed and held out her hand. He took it firmly, tugging her forward. "I will try to be careful," he said thickly. She tilted back her head and he kissed her hungrily. When her arms encircled his neck and her mouth slanted beneath his, he entwined his fingers in her hair and gave himself over to the way he really wanted to kiss her.

After several moments, he lifted her. When he laid her upon the bed and stretched beside her, she quite matter-of-factly parted her legs to welcome him. He made a hoarse sound in his throat, levering himself up to stare down at her. Did she just want him to get it over with quickly? But her pale blue eyes were soft as he had never seen them. He was warmed by them, reassured. When he felt her hands on him, his breath stopped.

"Ye need wait no longer," she murmured. His giving nature made her want to give in return, to love him as he should be loved. Yet she could only give what she had left and hope it would be enough until time took care of the rest.

He spoke Swedish against her skin, trembling as he tried to keep his considerable weight off her. She wanted his weight on her; she wanted to feel the hard, warm blanket of his body covering her. He was searching, tentative. She shifted and made it easy. He drew in a ragged breath, then exhaled slowly.

Bracing himself on his forearms, he stroked her cheek gently as he eased very slowly into her. "Am I hurting you?" he said hoarsely.

Tenderness flooded Tempest and she wanted to cry. He was, but she wouldn't tell him so. How much had she hurt him, and still would, that she could claim a physical pain? Heartache was infinitely worse, profoundly incapacitating. Hadn't Jared struck her heart a mortal blow?

And Bjorn had set about her resurrection.

"Dunna worry so," she whispered, combing her fingers

through Bjorn's blond hair and feeling its thick, fine texture like sunshine in her hands.

Why not the wild, tremulous, heart-shaking passion with this fine man that she had felt with Jared? Life was not fair.

But what she felt was so good. It wasn't quicksilver, fiery heat racing through her veins; this was warm, full, wonderful surges of life.

She spread her hands across his hard back, closing her eyes, sensing him through her fingertips. She lifted her legs up so that she felt his hard buttocks beneath her calves.

He made a deep sound and moved. He must have heard her faint gasp, a telling noise that she tried to mute, for he said something in a choked tone and started to propel himself off of her, rolling to one side. She went with him.

When she looked down at him, she saw the stunned look on his face, the beads of perspiration on his pale brow. She stroked his cheek as he had hers. Shifting her own weight, she took him into her.

He caught hold of her about the waist, his knees raising slightly off the bed as he planted his feet, helping her. He muttered thickly in Swedish and rolled her beneath him again, his hands like callused iron.

He was too male, all the softness in him gone, and she felt a moment of womanly fear. Then everything was right again. More than right.

There was a sameness to this act of human joining; it was still the ebb and flow of flesh on flesh, flesh in flesh. Yet it was more.

Tempest felt the difference through her skin, deep inside her, in the blooming warmth that glowed like a lighthouse inside her soul, guiding him steadily. With darkness all around them, the light was there with them, closer than it had ever been before.

"*Oh,*" she said, and it was the simple yet complex word of a psalm.

There were no ashes in the aftermath—not this time. With this man, there never would be again.

> Endure, my heart: you once endured something
> even more dreadful.
>
> —Homer
> *The Odyssey*

When he asked again, she still wouldn't marry him. Even she was not sure of all the reasons.

"*Jag alskar dig,*" Bjorn had murmured his love as they lay together, the fire crackling low, another man's child in the cradle nearby.

But she didn't respond in kind. It wasn't memories of Jared that held her back, or even lack of need and want for all Bjorn offered of himself. It was not lack of love.

She owed him. After all, gratitude did count for something in this hellish world. Perhaps humble gratitude was the only thing that mattered at all. Ever.

Civilization was upon them. Her father had fled it for his own private reasons, reasons she would never fully know, yet instinctively understood. Civilization could be devastating to an innocent people. She had seen what it had done at other times in other places, and knew what it would do here.

She had changed. She was better than she had been. Yet she was the same, too. She was a half-breed, a mongrel, a girl who had killed a helpless, dying man, the cast-off whore of one man and mistress of another, a woman who ran casinos and whorehouses.

And she would never, could never, forget the yellow-haired woman in the trading post.

California was changing. Men who two years ago had cared nothing about what they had to do to gain their fortunes were suddenly turning moral again. The home rules. Old laws in a new land. Wasn't Sam Brannan himself organizing vigilantes in San Francisco?

Bjorn saw her now only through clouded eyes. Someday, he would come to see her more clearly. Time was all he needed. Just a little more time. And common sense.

"Why are you crying, flicka?"

She shook her head, silent.

"Marry me on Saturday. That Methodist minister you like said he—"

"No."

"Why not?" he demanded roughly, seeing that she was dead set against it.

Her unspoken answer was because she held Bjorn Lindahl in the highest esteem. But he thought Jared Stryker still stood firmly planted between them.

Tempest finally regained all her strength when Abram began sleeping through the night, allowing her to rest deeply. With Bjorn gone all day, the child occupied much of her time. She talked to him, played with him on the hearth rug like a child herself, and often simply gazed at him in wonder. He was so perfect—so beautiful, this small part of herself.

He loved the sunshine and lying on his back, arms and legs waving, as he made delightful, throaty noises. She tickled him with a blade of grass and laughed at his expressions. She told him about the land and the treasures he could find, gold the very least of them.

In the evenings, Bjorn came to the house. Often Procopius came as well. They both kept her well informed of what was happening with her various business enterprises. It seemed she had only to be comfortable, protected, cosseted, and still the gold flowed in a steady stream into her open purse. It seemed somehow obscene.

She hadn't seen Charity in weeks. Her letters came and Tempest worked to decipher the clear handwriting, learning what was going on at the casino, upstairs, in the town. She learned some things the men did not tell her. Procopius no longer had time for lessons, but Tempest still read the big black book, page by laborious page.

It was not enough. She was beginning to feel the separateness of the white house. Everything was done for her now, when once all had been done by herself.

"It's a rough town, *min älskling*. You are best off here," Bjorn told her when she said she wanted to go out again and see what had changed.

"The vigilantes have taken care of much of the trouble."

"Ja, but not all," he told her, not adding that he was very

much involved. He suspected that she knew, although he didn't know how. She knew many things that she shouldn't. "You have much to keep you busy here," he added, setting Abram on his knee and jogging him. *"Rida, rida, ranka, hasten hetir bhan alka..."* he chanted, and was rewarded by a wide, gummy grin. He laughed, picking Abram up and kissing him. "You like that, *ja, pueka?* My mama did so to me."

Tempest propped her head up on her hand as she lay stretched out on the bed watching them. She wondered at this man's capacity for love. It didn't seem to matter to him at all that he held another man's child. Every evening he seemed to have another toy made by a wood-carver in the town; tonight it was a small horse.

Bjorn put Abram on the rug again and handed the toy to him. Grasping it, Abram gummed the head. Bjorn came across and sat on the bed, bending down to kiss her.

"Ye love him, dunna ye?" she said, teasing his ear.

"I love his mother even more." His hand moved down her body in a lingering caress. He looked back over his shoulder at Abram, who was squealing in delight, laughed softly, and said something. He always spoke Swedish to the baby.

"What do ye say to him?" she asked, running her hands over his forearms, sitting up just to be closer to him.

He turned back and kissed her boldly. A moment later, when they were both breathless, he said against her ear, "I am telling him to get sleepy because I need his mama."

She laughed softly. "Hmm, do ye?"

The look he gave her left her little doubt. He unbuttoned her shirtwaist and slipped his fingers in to stroke gently. Her breath caught. He raised his eyes and looked straight into hers. "I am a very good man, Tempest."

She smiled at his serious expression. "Aye, the very best."

"Why won't you marry me?"

Her smile became fixed. "I have heard 'tis wise never to marry a sailor. His first and most beloved mistress is the sea." Inside, she wept.

"I am a man first, a sailor second," he said sternly.

"Aye. Always a man." She touched him intimately.

He caught her wrist so tightly that she winced. "I want you in *all* ways, *min kara,* not just that way!"

She felt shame at the angry pain in his glittering eyes. She put her hand gently over his, holding back tears. "Bjorn, I will be here for ye always, in any way ye want or need. But dunna ask me to become yer anchor."

His eyes softened. "Ja, I will ask it. A man needs an anchor to keep him off the rocks."

She lowered her head.

He tilted up her chin. "I want to moor my whole life in you, Tempest," he said roughly.

She looked up at him, everything in her yearning toward him, but hard wisdom held her back. "I must see to the child," she said after a long moment, and moved away from him.

Bjorn caught hold of her with an angry utterance. His hands hurt her, but she didn't protest. A look of desperation came into his eyes and then was gone. He let her go slowly. "Ja," he said simply, and got up. He left her alone.

She thought perhaps he had gone downstairs for a glass of brandy. But she heard the front door slam. She got up quickly and raced down the stairs. By the time she threw open the front door, he was down the hill, striding in among the encroaching line of houses.

She went back upstairs and sat on the rug with Jared's son and cried.

Bjorn didn't come back the next day. Or the next.

"Last I heard of him, he was roaring drunk in a saloon on the Embarcadero," Procopius told her three days later.

Tempest stood staring out the window, her hand trembling as she held back the Nottingham lace curtains. Her throat felt thick. "Was he all right?"

"I was told he could still manage his feet when it was finished. There was a lot of damage. It would have been worse if Claus Janssen hadn't been standing at his back."

She said nothing for a long time. "What do I do, Procopius?"

"What do you want to do?"

She closed her burning eyes tightly. "What's right."

He made a derisive sound from behind her. "In a world gone wrong, you want to do what's right," he muttered.

She turned, defensive. "'Tis all fine and dandy for a mon to have a *California Tempest* as his mistress. But to marry her?"

"You're a fool."

Her mouth trembled. "I see what's coming. A *civilized* world—"

"Let it come! Do you think anything will make a difference to Bjorn? He *loves* you."

"Love," she said, closing her eyes.

"This is not Jared Stryker we're talking about," Procopius said, his black face set into hard, angry lines, the onyx eyes sharp. "He'll let you drain him dry."

"I dunna want to do that to him!"

"Then marry the poor bastard or cut him loose," he said simply, then added grimly, "But do something."

She put her hand over her eyes and sank down onto the couch. She hunched forward, rocking herself as she cried.

"When are you going to forgive yourself for being human?" Procopius asked sadly, his hand on her bowed back.

Later that day, she went down the hill to Tick and asked for some leather. She spent the evening sewing. Her fingers were raw when she finished. She lay in bed, weary but awake, waiting for sunrise.

"Time ye saw the world, laddie," she murmured into Abram's warm neck while she rubbed his back after he had nursed. She laid him down on the buckskin and began lacing it up. Abram protested vehemently at being so confined until she hoisted him onto her back and secured the straps over her shoulders and across her breasts.

She wore a fine leather riding skirt Jared had given her, moccasins she had made herself, and a brightly colored shirt-waist Bjorn had given her. She tucked the thimble and the enamel buttons into her pocket, but left the Bible on the table. Before she went out, she rolled up two thick blankets and tucked them into her pack.

"He's grown fat," she told Tick as he brought the Indian pony out.

"Doesn't get enough exercise," he said, frowning slightly as he looked her over. She had braided her fine, black hair like an Indian. "Where are you going, if you don't mind my asking?"

"How far do ye have to go to get away from all this?"

"Ma'am?"

She swung up onto her horse after tying the pack on. Abram gave a squeal of delight. Somehow Tick thought she looked more right there than she ever had behind the plank bar at the California where he had first seen her. She had an odd glow in her blue eyes.

Worry creased Tick's brow. "You all right?" He stepped

forward. She held her hand out for the reins he still held, and he handed them over to her unthinkingly. "Where you going?" he asked more firmly, wondering what he could do to stop her short of pulling her down off the horse.

"For a ride."

There was hardly a movement of her hands or body, but the horse turned. She walked the animal out the yard, Tick following. She went out along the white picket fence Bjorn Lindahl had put up.

"Procopius comes by in the mornings, don't he, Tempest?" Tick called after her. "What do I tell him if you aren't back soon enough?"

She kept walking the horse. He heard her give a strange laugh as she glanced back over her shoulder. "Tell him none of it means a bloody damn."

Tick frowned. He hadn't heard her swear in months. She had reached the end of the fence. A few houses were beyond, then open fields, oaks, hills. Where was she going? Tick started to run after her. "Hey! Wait a minute! Hold up! *What do I tell Lindahl!*"

Tempest dug her heels into the big pony and he surged forward impatiently.

"Wait!" Tick ran harder.

Tempest rode on without looking back. Just as her father had, six years before.

> Why are ye fearful, O ye of little faith?
> —Matthew 8:26

Tempest didn't know where she was going. She had acted instinctively, propelled out of the white house, out of the crowded, sprawling city, and by the pain.

She only stopped twice the first day, both times to nurse Abram and to allow him time to play on the blanket, the spring sun warm on his naked skin. He made her smile in spite of everything.

Late in the afternoon, she felt her own gnawing hunger. Scanning the landscape, she headed toward a grove of cottonwoods and a stream she knew would be hidden there. It had been so long since she gathered her own food that she was momentarily afraid she had forgotten how. As soon as she saw the reeds she knew she hadn't. It all came back, a part of herself tucked away for safekeeping—how to survive.

As the fire burned low, she lay curled warmly into the blankets, her hunger sated, with Abram nursing himself to sleep. The old fear stirred as she gazed out into the darkness. She had expected it, waited for it. And it was there, familiar and strong—an old enemy.

"Be thou near me," she whispered, repeating the words she had read.

She could see things out there. Strange, terrifying shapes, odd movements, noises. She drew in her breath, her heart thundering, her body sweating coldly.

Abram sensed her distress and fretted. His fretting turned to loud squalls, mirroring her own silent screaming.

Tempest forgot herself.

"Shhh, laddie," she murmured, stroking him. "Nothing there but the rocks and trees and an old hoot owl. Hear the crickets rubbing? There. A bullfrog, all puffed up and calling for his love."

Old words, long since forgotten, from another time in another mountain range before the nightmare came to pass and

Da changed. She remembered them now for her own child.

After a while, it came to her that she wasn't afraid anymore.

Startled, she looked around again and realized that she knew what every shadow was, what caused every sound. She lay back slowly, Abram sleeping contentedly in the curve of her warm body, and looked up at the blue-black sky. Starlight. Moonlight. Light everywhere. Why had she never really seen it before?

She closed her eyes and listened to the earth speak to her, each sound distinct, unthreatening. "No wolves," she sighed softly. "Not a single one, Abram."

She slept soundly for the first time in days, dreamless for the first time in years.

Sunlight and little Abram awakened her. She nursed him, played with him awhile, ate a tuber that she warmed in the coals, and rolled the blankets. She secured Abram in his carrier, made sure the fire was completely out, and mounted the pony again.

"Where am I going?" she asked aloud. Just riding somewhere? She didn't know, and received no answer. Why then did she have this sense of well-being?

At the end of the second day she camped on a hillside. It was a warm, windless night and she could see far. She almost imagined she could still see Sacramento. She closed her eyes, remembering the piano-man playing 'O, Susanna' over and over again while a hundred sad-eyed, laughing men called for a bottle and her attention.

"Act like an animal and you get treated like one." The last words Jared had spoken to her before he locked her in the closet so that he could leave and go back where he thought he belonged.

"I did love him," she said, holding Abram on her thighs, looking down at him. "Too much perhaps, or not enough. I dunna ken." She sighed softly. "I have you, and for that I'm grateful."

That night she dreamed of Abram Walker putting a canteen in her lap when her thirst was so great she thought she would die of it.

"Min älskling . . ." she murmured.

In the morning, she knew exactly where she was going, but wasn't sure she could bear it.

Ask, and it shall be given you; seek, and ye shall find; knock, and it shall be opened unto you.
—Matthew 7:7

Tempest closed her eyes tightly as the horse walked slowly to the top of the knoll. He stopped and she felt him tug the reins from her numb fingers so that he could graze. Abram slept at her back.

Slowly, preparing herself to see the burned cabin, weeds high in Abram's fields, the barn falling down, she opened her eyes again.

She gasped, her heart stopping. Her eyes went wide.

It lay below her as she had seen it so many times before: plowed field, corn growing, the same barn, painted now; the paddock with a milk cow, chickens pecking in the yard, a vegetable garden, crows and sparrows flirting with the scarecrow, the smokehouse and corncrib, the cabin with smoke coming from the fieldstone chimney, and a tall, broad-shouldered man hard at work.

She closed her eyes again, tightly, disbelieving, but when she opened them again, it was all still there. She felt faint.

He is dead. I killed him.

"Hello there," the man called out, one hand raised in a friendly greeting. Sunlight touched his burnished hair.

I've gone mad like Da.

"Hello," he called again. She took up the reins and urged the horse down the hill at a slow walk. She had to know. As she reached the boundary of the corn field, the man was walking toward her. Her heart thundered. She felt her body shaking and couldn't do anything to stop it.

Then everything went still and slow again.

It wasn't Abram Walker after all. It was another man, younger, not as good-looking, but with warm brown eyes and a handsome smile.

"We don't get much company here," he said, "so we're right pleased when someone chances by. Name's Daniel, ma'am,

Daniel Rawlings." He stepped forward and extended his hand.

Leaning down, she shook it firmly. "Tempest McClaren Walker."

He frowned slightly. "Walker," he repeated. "Heard tell a man named Walker once owned this place." He let go of her hand.

"If ye've been here two years, I'd say it belongs to ye now, whoever lived here before," she told him simply, making no claim.

He nodded solemnly and pushed his hands into his pockets. "Where you heading?"

"Home," she said without thinking, and gave a soft laugh, her eyes filling.

"You look all tuckered out, ma'am. Why don't you stay awhile? Martha, my missus, would be glad of a little woman talk. We've food to spare and a warm place by the fire."

Tempest smiled. "Aye. I would like that. Thank ye." She slid slowly from the pony and shrugged off the carrier, balancing Abram on her hip so that she could see his angelic sleeping face.

"My son, Abram."

"A right proper name."

Tempest glanced toward the cabin and saw a woman in the doorway. She was young and pregnant. She came out into the sunshine and walked toward them, smiling. As she came closer, Tempest saw that she had a plain prettiness, her face framed by brown hair combed back into a neat bun beneath a dust cap. Her eyes were gray-green and soft.

"A baby!" she said and clasped her hands together, giving a delighted laugh. She nodded to Tempest as her husband introduced them. "He's beautiful." She leaned forward slightly and one wash-roughened hand rested tellingly on her own unborn child.

"I'll see that your horse has oats and water," Daniel said, taking the reins. Tempest thanked him.

"Does he like being all trussed up like that?" Martha asked.

"He likes it well enough if he has his time to play freely on a blanket."

"Come into the house," Martha said, smiling. "I'll put the kettle on."

Tempest wasn't ready to go into the cabin. She was still adjusting to the shock of seeing everything as it had been,

seeing people living here where once she and Abram had lived.
And loved . . . If she stepped over that threshold, she'd feel the
grief again. Abram's blood had soaked into that earthen floor
along with their son's.

And her own.

"I—I should wash my baby down at the creek," she said.

"Oh, but I have a pan inside you can use."

"The creek will be fine."

"All right," Martha agreed easily, and walked beside her.
She laughed. "Why, you're heading right for my washing place.
Oh! You'll need something for little Abram to lie on."

Tempest had forgotten to take a blanket from her pack.
Martha went back to the cabin and brought out a bright quilt
with yellow and green fabrics stitched into stars on a cream-
colored background. " 'Tis a fine thing," Tempest said, running
her hand over it.

Martha blushed. "I made it myself."

"Be ye sure I can put Abram on it? I canna promise he
won't do something on it."

Martha laughed. "It'll wash."

Tempest laughed as well, liking the young woman immensely. She unlaced Abram and lifted him free. He made a
smacking noise and began kicking his legs and waving his arms
as she untied the diaper. Martha sat watching him in hungry
fascination while Tempest washed the cloth in the stream and
draped it over a bush to dry.

"What do you do about another?"

"I usually let him play as he is until that one is dry."

Martha grinned. "He seems to like it well enough, doesn't
he? He's gotten brown. Look at his little legs go like double
windmills!" Her eyes were moist. "Did you have an easy time
when he came?"

"Aye. Like a cork from a whiskey bottle." Instantly, she
could have cut her tongue out for not saying it in a nicer way.

Martha Rawlings didn't seem to mind. She was watching
Abram raptly as he rolled over and pushed himself up. He
fingered one of the blanket's bright star designs and tried to
eat it. "Is he hungry?"

"Soon." Tempest chuckled.

"Sometimes I worry about being this far from other people,"
Martha admitted, glancing at Tempest and then watching Abram
again. "But I suppose when a baby starts coming, it's all in
God's hands anyway, whoever's there to help."

Tempest nodded, unable to offer any banal comment to dismiss the young woman's worries. She remembered her own fear and respected Martha's.

"Where have you come from, Mrs. Walker?"

"Sacramento."

"Where you headed?"

"West." She looked around the farm.

"I didn't mean to pry. It's only, well, I hope you'll stay the night at least." Her gray-green eyes turned on Tempest with unconcealed appeal.

"Aye," Tempest said, unable to refuse. She looked at the cabin again and then around. "Ye've done much work here."

"Oh, yes. Daniel built the cabin himself. There was another one there at one time, but it burned down. We found human bones in the debris." She pointed to an oak on a western hillside. "We buried them over there."

Tempest's throat felt hot and dry.

"Daniel used the same stones for our fireplace. I think he did a grand job."

Tempest still gazed at the far hillside. She could see a cross. Martha dropped into silence, watching her curiously. "You look so sad. I hope I haven't said something—"

"No," Tempest assured her quickly and shook her head. She sighed and gave Martha a faint smile. "'Tis a fine place. Good land."

"That's what Daniel said. He's sure anything will grow here. Most especially children." She laughed, looking toward him as he went back to his work. "He wants a dozen, he says— eight boys and four girls." A certain beauty lit the woman's plain face as she watched her man toiling in the field.

"He sounds a mon who knows what he wants."

"And sets about getting it." She blushed crimson. "I mean with the land, of course."

"Aye," Tempest said gently. And other important things, she thought to herself.

Abram began fussing. Tempest picked him up and his mouth worked against her neck, making it clear what he wanted. When she didn't give it to him at once, he wailed pathetically.

Martha paled visibly. "Is he all right? Do you suppose he's getting sunburned?"

"He's hungry."

"Oh, then, bring him into the house. Daniel made me a rocking chair. It's right in front of our fireplace. You can nurse him in comfort there while I make us some coffee and a meal."

"Oh, I canna—"

"Please don't say no, Mrs. Walker."

"All right," Tempest said slowly, and stood. "But my name is Tempest."

Martha's face was radiant. She gathered up the quilt and her step was light as she led Tempest to the cabin.

Abram protested his mother's tight hold. She stood on the threshold of the Rawlings cabin, her heart pounding, her stomach churning. It was almost the same inside as before.

"Come in, please."

Tempest stepped in slowly. There was a big book on the mantel and a gun mounted above.

"Sit down, please," Martha insisted, moving quickly about the place, straightening things here and there. Tempest scarcely noticed. She felt as if she had lived it all before, and the odd sensation left her shaky and confused. She went across and put her hand on the big leather book.

"That Bible was a gift from Daniel's parents before we came across. Our marriage was the first entry. Our baby will be the second."

Tempest sat down and unbuttoned her blouse so that Abram would stop crying, nursing him as she looked around.

"We were married just before leaving Pennsylvania. We didn't have much to bring with us, except plenty of linens." She smiled. "Anyway, it was a good thing we didn't have much, because the Conestoga barely made it at all. It broke down so many times in those Sierras we thought we'd have to walk to California. Oh, what a hellish place, and so beautiful."

She nodded toward the big bed. "That's what's left of the wagon. Actually, it's very comfortable. I stitched up the canvas and stuffed it with dried moss. Makes for a soft bed. Daniel kept the wagon wheels so that he could build a new wagon for transporting the harvest to market." Her eyes brightened. "We've been all the way to Vallejo."

Tempest listened to Martha's light talk, sensing the deep loneliness that drove the young woman to pour out so much to a stranger. She watched her move about the cabin, tidying things.

Yellow and white flowered curtains hung in the four windows. A wedding quilt much like the one Kathy Walker had once had lay across the foot of the bed, and a quilt with another pattern stretched to the head. On the hand-hewn oak dinner table was a mason jar filled with wild roses. Everything was clear, polished, much better kept than she herself had ever managed for Abram—even when she had been willing.

Finally she looked down slowly at the earthen floor. The blood would have been there near the big bed.

Only hard-packed earth.

"Daniel wants to make a proper house someday, with a foundation and all. My father and mother's house has a basement."

"A basement?"

Martha looked at her. "It's a big room dug in the ground under a house, best way I can tell you. Don't they have anything like that here?"

"Not that I've seen. The adobes are built on hard-packed earth like this. The buildings in Sacramento have wood floors, some of them, but no holes underneath that I con say."

She talked to ward off the memory of a cave in the side of the mountain. She could almost see the heavy plank door her father had slammed and barred. It had been cold and damp in that dark, silent place. Fire had warmed it, but she'd had to stay near the cracks in the great door just to breathe. With the wood gone and the fire out, the fetid air had almost choked the life from her before Da had come back.

And with him, brought death.

God, forgive me. I didna ken what I was doing.

"What did you say, Tempest?"

Her eyes cleared and she saw Martha looking at her worriedly. The strong, wonderful smell of fresh-ground coffee beans filled the small cabin.

"I was thinking of another time," Tempest said huskily, and shoved the piercing memory far back into her mind, vowing not to follow it there. She concentrated on Martha's questions about Sacramento, telling her about the rough mining camp that had turned into a city.

Daniel came in late in the afternoon. He'd washed already, his sleeves rolled up and his forearms and hair still damp. Tempest remembered Abram coming in the same way. Martha blushed when he brushed her cheek with a kiss. Then Tempest had to go through it all again about Sacramento for Daniel.

"Seems strange they don't make it the capital instead of Vallejo," Daniel commented, lifting the lid on the pot that was suspended over the fire. He glanced back at Tempest and Martha as they sat at the table, sharing the last of a second pot of coffee. "Seems everything is happening in Sacramento." He put the lid back on. "Smells right good, sweetheart."

Martha stood quickly. "Sit down, Daniel, and I'll serve you."

Embarrassed, Tempest stood as well and crossed over to the bed where they had placed Abram when he slept, spent from playing on the quilt before the warm hearth.

"Where do you think you're going, Tempest?" Martha said. "You sit yourself right back down this minute. There's food aplenty and we mean to have you share it with us."

"Besides," Daniel said, grinning and taking Abram from her, "Martha has had the better part of the day with this young 'un while I haven't even gotten to hold him till now."

Abram chuckled merrily as he was hefted high and jostled over the farmer's head. Martha laughed. Tempest looked on with a shaky smile.

They prayed together before breaking bread. Abram Walker was everywhere in this place; Tempest could almost feel his presence across the table from her. She remembered exactly how he used to smile at her.

She wasn't afraid.

Martha, Daniel, and Tempest talked more of Sacramento while sitting before the fire. "You must have been here long before the rush," Daniel remarked.

"Aye, long before. My father was a trapper. Worked for the Russians on the coast for a while, and even for Sutter."

When Abram fussed to be fed, Daniel tactfully went out to have a last look about the farm. When he returned, they talked more of Vallejo, San Francisco, Sacramento, vigilantes, booming businesses, changing times.

"Thought of having a go at panning myself," Daniel admitted. The familiar gleam was there in the young man's eyes.

"You never told me that," Martha said, surprised.

"I talked to some men about it in Vallejo, but they told me things about the diggings that made me change my mind. I didn't want to leave Martha on her own, and I sure didn't want to take her up there and let her see what men can be like when they're at their worst."

"It was different in the beginning," Tempest said. "Most were honorable men then. But most of them have gone back to their land now."

"The gold is giving out?"

"I doubt there was ever as much as some people thought.

Certainly it was not lying about, nuggets the size of a man's fist as I heard it was claimed in the East," she went on. "And more men have died panning gold than plowing the land."

"Is that how you lost your husband?" Martha asked.

Tempest shook her head slowly and looked away into the firelight.

Martha reached out and touched her hand. "I'm sorry," she whispered. "It must be terrible hard to be a woman all alone. Especially with a child."

They were all quiet. Abram slept in Daniel's arms. Tempest thought to herself that she had never in her life felt less alone than she did at that moment.

"Daniel, why don't you give Abram to me and read to us for a while?" Martha suggested softly.

"You just want to hold him again," he teased. She smiled back and held out her arms. Winking at Tempest, he put Abram into his wife's embrace.

Tempest wasn't surprised at all when he turned and took down the book from the mantel. "We've read it through three times," he said, smiling proudly. He opened it at a place marked by a white tatted cross and began to read: "St. John, Chapter 8..."

Tempest listened raptly to the story of the adulteress. She had never heard it before, and her own reading had not carried her so far. She was still going from the beginning, even against Charity's advice.

"He that is without sin among you, let him cast the first stone at her," Daniel read with feeling, and Tempest waited to hear that all had taken up a rock to kill the woman.

But none did.

" *'Neither do I condemn thee,'* Christ said, *'Go and sin no more.'* "

He read on to the end and Tempest heard that the stones were taken up against Jesus instead. But one part kept turning over and over in her hungry mind. *"I am the light of the world: he that followeth me shall not walk in darkness..."*

Daniel stood and stretched. "Morning light is going to come too soon."

Martha gave the baby back to Tempest and went to open a trunk.

Tempest stood up, holding Abram close. "Thank ye. For everything," she said, her brogue thick.

Martha straightened, a bundle of quilts in her arms. Her

eyes widened. "You can't leave *now*," she said, watching Tempest open the door. "It's night."

"I'm not afraid of it."

"Well, you're here now."

"The barn would be more than fine."

"You might not mind the barn for sleeping, Tempest, but we mind you two being out there in the cold," Daniel said. "Especially when there's room before a warm fire." He held out his arms for the baby. "Give me that boy again, and you and Martha set about making up a bed."

Tempest knew their offer was heartfelt. Unable to speak, she did as she was told.

The Rawlings both asked her to stay on awhile, and Tempest acquiesced. She left little Abram in Martha's care the second day and went out gathering. That night, she prepared for them a feast the like of which they had never seen before.

"You must teach me," Martha said, and Tempest took her out the next day and showed her what to look for right on their own farm.

Each evening Daniel read, as Abram had done before him.

On the morning of the fourth day, she laced Abram into the carrier.

"Won't you please stay a little longer?" Martha pleaded, her eyes overly bright.

Leaving Abram on the bed, Tempest turned to her. Without thought or hesitation, she hugged Martha and whispered, "Ye'll be all right. I know. I just know."

Martha hugged her back. "I think so, too."

They both let go at the same instant and avoided one another's eyes in embarrassment. Tempest lifted Abram to her back. Martha's eyes met hers as she turned, and they both laughed softly.

"Come back."

"I might. Someday."

Martha said nothing more, walking with her out to where Daniel had the pony waiting. Tempest mounted.

"If ye could have anything, what would ye want?" Tempest asked them.

They exchanged a curious look. Martha smiled slightly. "A healthy baby." She glanced up with a teasing look at her husband. "I suppose *you'd* ask for a new plow."

His gaze was serious as he curled his broad, callused hand about his wife's waist and drew her close against his side. He kissed her lightly on the forehead. "No, I wouldn't," he said softly.

Tempest didn't say good-bye as she walked the horse toward the edge of the cornfield.

"I thought you were going west!" Daniel called after her.

She glanced back over her shoulder, and smiled. "This place is called *Fairfield!*"

He stared. "Then you are *that* Walker, aren't you?"

She smiled and waved without answering.

"Go with God, Tempest," Martha called, waving back and smiling.

And Tempest did.

Lead us not into temptation.
— from The Lord's Prayer

Tempest reached the outskirts of Sacramento as dusk
came on the second day of her homeward journey. She rode
to Tick's to leave the pony with him, and he swore at her for
a full minute without stopping to take a breath. Then he snatched
the reins and sent the pony into the stable with a loud smack
on the rump.

"Where in Hades you been? Lindahl damn near skinned me
alive when he learned you'd ridden off to parts unknown!"

"'Twas none of it yer fault, Tick. I'll explain."

"Hell, that don't make no damn difference! You're back
and safe, and you'll leave again over my dead body. Stupid
woman! You know he's sent men out in all directions looking
for you? He went himself! You ever seen a sailor try to ride
a horse?"

"He didn't get hurt, did he?"

"It's no horse that'll put him under," Tick said, and looked
at her directly.

"It won't be me, either." She smiled.

He frowned. "There's something different about you, lady.
What happened out there anyway? Where *did* you go?"

"A ways." She saw the lines about the blacksmith's eyes,
and knew she was the cause. "I'm sorry to have worried ye."

"Should have thought of that before," he grunted.

"Aye, but I dinna think of anything but cuttin' Bjorn loose."

"If it was like that, why in hell did you come back?"

"I changed my mind."

"Just like a woman." But he smiled slightly.

Everything was going to have to wait. Abram was hungry
and he needed to be bathed. Tick walked up to the house with
her. Wind Reed was at the door, her broad, handsome face
beaming, no questions asked. Tempest shrugged off the carrier
and handed Abram over. "I'll be with ye shortly." She turned

to Tick again. "Con ye take a message to Bjorn for me? And another to Procopius?"

"Yes, ma'am. I was going to anyway, whatever you said about it."

To Bjorn, she wrote: "I be to see you in the morn. T." And to Procopius she wrote: "Come, plez. Have to spek with you tonit. T."

Tick tucked the two notes in his pocket and left. Tempest nursed Abram, washed him in a big pan with warm water, and rocked him to sleep before the fire.

Waiting was the hardest activity in the world.

Procopius came quickly. He was no less angry than Tick, but he didn't swear at her. He had a deeper, more succinct way of pointing out her many faults and the misery she had caused with her disappearance.

"There are better ways of handling things, Tempest."

"Aye, but I dinna know of one, and this way set me on the right trail after all." She shook her head when he started in again. "Not now. We have important things to discuss. I want ye to sell everything."

His eyes grew round. *"Everything?"*

"Aye, and offer it first to those who have been carrying the greatest burden of work. Give them a good, fair price. If need be, let them pay over a period of time. We con work it out."

"You might just be giving your gold away if you do that."

"I dunna think so. Ye give a mon a gift and ye take away his pride. If he works for it, it belongs to him."

Procopius nodded, a faint smile playing on his lips. "Anything else, ma'am?"

"A good plow and the best workhorse ye can find," she said without hesitation. She had her own debts to repay, even knowing that it was the last thing expected. A plow and a horse were cheap when set against all she had, cheaper still when set against her very life. But more would be unacceptable.

When she'd explained about the Rawlings, Procopius said he'd take care of it. "You've got more trouble since you left than you know, Tempest," he said cryptically.

"Tell me."

"You'll find out soon enough."

She thought he meant Bjorn. "I've a lot to answer for, I ken. And I will, whatever it takes."

"Too bad everything comes all at once," Procopius said, getting his hat and coat. She walked him to the door.

"Ye've been a fine friend, Procopius. I hope ye'll always remain so." She held out her hand.

"Count on it." He gave her a considering look. "You're cleaning house, aren't you, Miz Tempest?" he said in the old way.

She gave him McClaren's grin. "Aye. 'Tis what a woman does best."

With a hug and a few words, Tempest sent Wind Reed off to bed. Then she heated and toted her own water upstairs so that she could bathe and wash her hair. She sat cross-legged before the fire with Abram sleeping in the cradle nearby, and brushed her hip-length black hair until it was dry. She couldn't sleep for thinking.

In the morning, she dressed very carefully after seeing to the baby. She went through all her things and chose a simple high-necked, deep-blue gown trimmed in cream-colored lace and with the hem decorated with passementerie. Bjorn liked it best of all her dresses, telling her it made her eyes look bluer than the sea he'd once seen surrounding a Pacific atoll. She left her hair flowing free in glistening black waves down her back to her hips.

She planned to have Tick prepare the carriage for her. She had never driven it, but there was always a first time, and reins were reins, a horse a horse.

As she came down the stairs, Wind Reed following with Abram, whom she would care for in Tempest's absence, Tempest heard someone at the front door. She smiled, lifting her skirts and running down the last few steps and across the foyer to open it quickly.

Jared Stryker stood on the front stoop, dressed in a fine dark suit, hat in hand.

"You!" she gasped, her heart beating wildly right up into her throat as she looked up into that devastatingly handsome face. His brown eyes took her all in in one hungry, sweeping look from her face and free-flying hair down to her flowing blue skirt. The solemn eyes glowed as they devoured her in the way they had before, only even more hungrily.

"God, you're even more beautiful than I remembered," he murmured, and took a step toward her.

She jerked back, her hand tightening defensively on the doorknob, her breath catching. "Why be ye here?" she choked.

"I've come back," he said simply.

"Why?"

"You should know."

Her lip curled.

"We need to talk."

She stiffened. "Talk? Dinna ye say it all before ye left?"

Lines deepened in his face, lines that hadn't been there a year before. "I was a fool," he said softly, taking another step toward her and putting his hand against the door so that she couldn't close it. "Please, just listen to what I have to say to you, Tempest. If you want me to leave after that, I will. I swear."

As he had sworn other things before.

"Ask me in."

She'd never seen quite that look in Jared's eyes before, and she hesitated. He applied just enough pressure and stepped inside. He started to put his hand over hers and she flinched back again. He closed the door slowly, letting out his breath softly in relief. "Where can we talk?"

Tempest looked up at him narrowly and then nodded toward the parlor. Wind Reed had already taken Abram back upstairs.

"Can I pour myself a drink?" he asked, glancing back at her as he tossed his hat onto the settee and crossed over to the decanters. When she said nothing, he went ahead, and then promptly downed the entire amount he had poured in one swallow.

"In need of a little courage?"

He faced her. "Frankly, yes." He unbuttoned his coat and pushed one hand into his pocket, assuming that indolent stance she remembered so well. The old physical attraction stirred in the pit of her belly.

Jared looked at her from across the room as she watched him so dispassionately. His own heart was pounding so hard he thought he'd choke on it. He wanted to take hold of her and kiss her, wanted to know she was back in his arms again as he had dreamed she would be night after night on the arduous trip back by way of the Isthmus. He'd damn near died getting here; his body was still slightly weak from a bout of fever. He would have crawled on his knees that last stretch to get to the steamer that had brought him up the coast to San Francisco.

It had been Lindahl's friend who'd captained the ship that brought him upriver to Sacramento.

Lindahl!

He held down the surge of jealousy, knowing well enough

that he had no right to ask whether that damn Swede was still around. No one would tell him anything, but he guessed he couldn't blame them after the way he'd walked out.

But she'd done all right for herself. The California was still going strong under her ownership; in fact, it looked classier than it had before. He had learned there that she now lived in a white house at the southwest end of town. Whoever had built it had obviously spent time in New Bedford.

He had to get Tempest back! There had to be something left of the love they had shared. Nothing that strong could die completely.

"Ye said ye wanted to talk. So talk, and then get out."

"I made a hell of a mistake."

She raised one eyebrow in the old defiant gesture he remembered. "Coming back?" Her eyes were colder than he had ever seen them before.

"Leaving you at all."

"Did yer lady turn ye down?"

He winced. "No. She was waiting for me."

At first the sight of Geneva had dimmed the pain he'd carried with him over Tempest. She was just as he had remembered: blond, perfect, all those things a merchant's son dreams of in a wife. She had begged his forgiveness for marrying another man, saying that there had been severe family pressures on her. She said that Duprés was never the man Jared was, that she had never stopped loving him and wondering where he was after he left Charleston.

Her kisses had been chaste, but it hadn't taken long for Jared to realize that there was a practiced coquette working behind the demure facade and the veiled looks through lowered lashes.

Tempest had intruded on his thoughts from the beginning. He remembered how she had fought against submitting to her physical desire, how he'd tried every way there was to buy her love and then she had given it to him as a gift.

Geneva had offered him everything without a single qualm. He'd had her in her own bed within the first few days of his arrival home. He tried desperately not to see her for what she was: a shallow, selfish young woman used to the best of everything and not willing to go without it, whatever she had to sell. He'd carried Geneva in his heart too long as his Belle Fleur leading him to the Holy Grail to see what was really there.

He'd touched her soft skin, gone into her body, and known like a blow that she was dross and he a fool. She did everything right, and left him empty. Flat champagne to Tempest's strong, fine brandy.

For a few days he had hated Tempest for haunting him, for ruining what he longed to grasp. This was what he had wanted all his life: Geneva, a river plantation, status in Charleston—not some nameless half-breed girl who didn't even know when she was born, or where.

God, how could this ever have happened to him?

Even Charleston seemed stale and lifeless after California. He slowly realized that even the bitter disillusionment of broke, half-starving miners was better than the staid complacency he saw everywhere about him.

Now he stood before Tempest, determined not to lose this dream as well.

"I thought I knew what I wanted, what was best until I got back home. All the way back, I thought of you. I couldn't get you out of my mind," he said grimly. "I relived every minute we ever spent together—"

"But tried ever so valiantly to forget it," she said, her eyes clear and knowing.

"Yes, I did," he admitted, knowing that she would accept nothing but the truth.

"And didna yer Geneva live up to yer expectations?" she asked in a sarcastic tone that riled him. "Poor Jared. So ye left her, too."

"You've every right to hate me, Tempest," he said. "God knows, after the way I treated you." He'd never been able to purge his mind of the look in her eyes as he had slammed that closet door.

She said nothing. She just looked at him with cold passivity.

"I love you."

"Did ye tell yer lady that I had first claim on yer heart?"

He had forgotten just how biting her tongue could be. "I told Geneva I was going back where I belonged. Here with you."

"Ye took too much for granted."

He came toward her entreatingly. "You hate me now—you've reason to. But you can't have forgotten how it was between us! Do you think it'll ever be that way for you with anyone else? We belong together!" He came closer and saw her hands clench at her sides. His heart pounded even harder. He held out his hands and saw her step back.

"You feel it," he said with certainty. "You did the moment

you saw me standing at your door. Don't even try to deny it."

"Like too much whiskey, some things aren't good for ye."

He smiled slightly, seeing the familiar darkness in her eyes. Everything wasn't lost after all. He still had a chance. "Nothing has really changed."

"Least of all you."

His smile dimmed slightly. "I want to marry you this time. No more living together without benefit of clergy. You'll be my wife."

"I suppose I should thank ye for yer generous offer to make me an honest woman, but dunna ye think it comes a wee bit too late?"

"Granted, but better late than never, they say."

"Who says?"

She was baiting him as she used to do. He reached for her and she flinched back, slapping at his hands. He laughed softly, advancing. "God, how I've missed your fire." He caught hold of her. Just touching her again made him want her fiercely, and everything Jared had ever wanted he had taken.

"Let go!"

He pulled her to him and kissed her. He felt her body stiffen against his own, but she was warm. She clenched her teeth against him, but he caught her hair, drawing her head back, tasting the warm, soft skin of her throat, feeling her pounding pulse. He took her mouth again, impatient after all the long months of being without her. She wouldn't deny him now, she couldn't! After that first time he had made love to her in the upstairs bedroom of the California, there on a hard, cold, wood floor, she had never denied her love or need for him again.

Life filled his body. Oh, how he had longed for this surging feeling inside himself, and Tempest in his arms again, the only thing that did it for him. It was the only thing that mattered at all. He hadn't realized how necessary she was to him. Now he knew that if he didn't have her back, he had nothing.

"Oh, my love, I'll make it up to you. I'll make you happy—"

"Have ye finished yet?"

He held her tighter. "No!" he rasped, angry. "I'll never be finished with you." He kissed her again. For just an instant, he felt her response and he fought to hang onto it. But she went passive again and didn't fight him at all.

He let her go. "All right," he said huskily. "Be stubborn for a while. I didn't expect you to be easy." But when he looked into her blue eyes, he had an aching gut feeling that nothing would ever be good for him again.

"I'll build you a better house than this," he said desperately. "I'll give you anything in the world you want—gowns, dresses. We'll go to Europe. Let me love you—" He froze.

Somewhere in the house a baby was crying.

He stared at her, his stomach churning uneasily. The sound came closer, and an Indian girl came in carrying a fretting baby. He remembered the girl vaguely, but not her name. She said something to Tempest in her own language. Tempest held out her arms, and as soon as she took the baby, it quietened.

Jared's eyes narrowed. "What's *that?*"

"My son, Abram," she said without hesitation. Her heart raced. Should she tell him now that he had fathered a child before he had deserted her for another woman? Maybe then he would know—

"Whose baby?" he said through clenched teeth, and she saw then very clearly that it would never even have occurred to him that it might be his own.

"Well, now, laddie, that's an interesting question, considering all things."

His face went fiery red. He stared at the baby, black hatred in his face.

Abram cried. Tempest saw the danger glinting in Jared's eyes and turned back to Wind Reed. "Give him ground wild rice and apple, and then the sugar teat for a while," she instructed in the girl's native tongue. Glancing from her to Jared and back, the girl nodded quickly and left.

"Who built this house for you?" Jared choked out the words thickly.

"Bjorn Lindahl."

His hand balled into a hard fist. "You mean that dumb sailor who ran into the fire for your two-dollar Bible and a handful of buttons?"

"Aye, the same."

He could hardly breathe. She had a faint smile on her lips and a look in her eyes that made him want to strangle her. "How long was it after I left before you turned to him for *consolation?*" he demanded in a low, shaking voice.

"The first week. He was the best mon around."

"You goddamn bitch-whore," he said, stunned.

His words still had the power to hurt her. She felt brittle inside, looking up at his enraged face and furious eyes. God help her, there was still a part of her that yearned for him. When she had seen him standing there in her doorway, some of the old passion had risen.

Yet now she knew for certain that nothing had changed. Nothing would. He had always seen her as an ignorant half-breed girl. Bjorn had seen her always as a special woman.

"Never a whore, Jared," she said calmly. "An entrepreneur." She lifted her head proudly. "In case ye be not aware, I am the richest woman in California. I con thank ye for that much, since ye left me the means, the California."

He raked shaking fingers through his hair and swore vilely. "You took him just to get back at me, didn't you? You did it all to get back at me! That should tell you something! Hatred is very close to love. *Isn't it?*"

She saw his pain, as real and deep as her own had been.

"All right," he said hoarsely. "I'll forget what happened. I'll forget all of it. We're even. I'll try to forgive you."

She uttered a soft, disbelieving laugh.

"You're mine, Tempest," he said, catching hold of her. "You were mine from the moment we looked at one another. You always will be, and you know it! That damn little bastard of yours upstairs won't make any difference!"

If she had felt even the slightest desire to tell him Abram was of his own seed, he had killed the inclination in that instant. He didn't deserve to know. She glared up at him with all the contempt she had ever felt in her life.

"I belong to no one! That was something ye never ken or bothered to try to understand. Ye dunna *buy* people. And ye dunna *win* them. 'Tis something ye'll never ken, laddie-boy, but Bjorn Lindahl was man enough to know it from the beginning."

She snatched up his hat from the settee and held it out to him.

A muscle worked in his hard jaw. His brown eyes burned in his pale face. "It's not finished between us. It never will be."

"'Tis finished, all right, and it was long before ye ever left. We both ken that."

"You're wrong." He took his hat, and leaned toward her threateningly. "Someday you'll admit it to me. You'll have to because it's the God-given truth!"

"God forgive me, but if it's truth ye want, Jared, then I'll give ye a little to take on yer way. Ye're one bleeding selfish son of a bitch, and I've had all of ye I ever want. Now, get out."

He slammed out of the house, stalked down the hill, and then stopped at the gate to glance back. The curtain was pulled back. She was standing there in the window watching him. She tilted her chin up and turned away.

If it was the last thing he ever did, and if it took the rest of his life, he swore to himself then, he was going to get her back.

Whatever he had to do.

Until the day break, and the shadows flee away.
—Song of Solomon 2:17

       Tempest had to delay setting out to see Bjorn. She wanted to wash and change after Jared's manhandling, and then Abram required tending. Finally, as an afterthought and to reassure herself that Jared would not darken her life again, she painstakingly drafted a brief note to him. "This iz the onlee thin u left behin that u wil be getin bak." She took it down the hill to Tick and asked him to have the black stallion, Alexander, returned to Jared.

"With pleasure!"

"But before ye tackle that, I will need the carriage."

At the harbor, she searched excitedly for Bjorn. It had been nearly two weeks since she had seen him, and the longing to see him again and set things right was so strong it was a physical ache. Both steamers were tied up at the dock, but she couldn't find him anywhere. She finally asked a worker, but he refused to tell her anything. He took her along to the Lindahl Shipping Line offices and a man named Albert Larson who was in charge of operations.

Larson stood when he saw a woman being escorted in. He surveyed her with pleased surprise and frank admiration. He had seen many beautiful women around the world during his sailing days, but this one was something special indeed, something extraordinary. It was her eyes that struck him most of all.

Then he realized that he was looking at the infamous California Tempest, the young woman who had led his friend and associate such a miserable dance. He took his seat again, leaving her standing.

"Where is Bjorn Lindahl?" she asked before she said anything else or gave him a chance to speak.

Arrogant hussy. She was far younger than he had thought she would be, considering what she had done, not more than twenty at a guess. But sometimes it was the very young woman who played the worst havoc on a grown man and blinded him to everything but the feel of soft, yielding woman's flesh.

"Gone, madam," he answered with satisfaction. Maybe a year or two of sailing would clear Bjorn's brain. At his first port of call, he would probably burn out his fever on top of a willing and far more warmhearted whore than this one.

"Gone?" Tempest repeated blankly. "The steamers are in dock. How did he go?"

Larson wondered at those eyes. "He sailed the windjammer. He won't be back for a year," he said coldly.

Her lips parted.

Larson studied her standing there, silent, her face white, staring at nothing with those beautiful blue eyes that a moment before had been almost burning with intense life. He felt almost as if he had beaten a helpless animal. He stood. "Perhaps you should sit down," he suggested uneasily.

She made a visible effort to control and hide her emotions. She failed.

"He waited for you. You did not come. He sent a messenger and then learned that you were with someone else."

She glanced at him sharply. "And thought I'd—*oh!*" She shook her head and put a trembling hand to her face. Then she lowered it, clenching it tightly at her side. "I said I would come. I never break my word. Did he think I would change my mind?" She could almost feel Bjorn's pain as if it had been her own.

She does love him, Larson thought, stunned. *"Yag ar ledsen,"* he apologized. "He sailed at noon."

"Noon." Her hands unclenched and clenched again. He would sail for a year thinking she was back in Jared Stryker's arms, back in his bed. What would that do to him? "Noon," she said again, and swung on her heel.

She didn't care how people stared at her as she ran back to the carriage, her skirts held up. She raced the carriage through the streets of Sacramento until she reached Tick's house, all the while burningly aware of the position of the sun.

Tick was gone, and she left the carriage and horse untended in the yard as she ran up the hill. She gave quick orders to Wind Reed about Abram as she raced up the stairs, unbuttoning her dress and ripping it back off her shoulders as she went. She dressed hurriedly in her old buckskins and braided her hair in one long plait. Then she ran back down the hill, realizing she had forgotten her moccasins in her haste, but not willing to go back for them.

Noon! She glanced again at the sun, knowing that she had little if any time. So much depended on the wind, the river current, her horse, on her. Oh, God!

Tick still hadn't returned from the errand and she threw on the bosal herself, swinging up onto her barebacked Indian pony. She rode him hard out across the southwestern hills until she reached the river beyond the edge of the sprawling, rough town. Men panning along the banks straightened to watch her as she thundered by. When her horse began to show signs of tiring, she slowed him, controlling the impatience that burned inside her. If she rode him to death, she would never reach Bjorn, never have the chance to tell him what he needed to know in order to go back to his first mistress in peace.

When she knew the pony had rested enough, she kicked him again into a breakneck pace. Crouching down against him, she moved with the lunging strides of the powerful animal, feeling the coarse mane whipping against her already raw face. Mile after mile she rode, slowing when the horse needed it. When she caught sight of a tall ship in the distance, she didn't let him slacken again. Finally the animal stumbled, almost pitching her over his head, and she swung off in one fluid motion and began to run, leaving the exhausted horse behind.

"Please," she said through gritted teeth as she ran with everything she had.

The few sails deployed were full, a strong wind coming across the land and sending the ship downriver toward the Pacific.

Tempest ran until her lungs burned hotly and pain sliced along her sides. She couldn't catch up. It was the old nightmare all over again. She tripped and her momentum sent her flying forward; she hit the ground with a force that knocked all the remaining air from her abused lungs. She lay there dazed for a long moment, her body heaving for oxygen.

A year.

She began to cry, deep, wrenching, audible sobs. She pressed her face into the grass, not wanting to look up and see Bjorn's ship going downriver. If only she had had the chance to talk to him, how much it might have meant to them both!

"Oh, God," she choked. "Tell him." She wiped her nose on the sleeve of her buckskins and raised her tear-streaked face, unable to stop herself from looking again. It would be her last sight of him. He might never return; why should he, thinking what he must? He could always send word to sell.

The ship was still there in sight, moving steadily.

Tempest stood shakily and pressed her fists against her mouth. It would be just like before, she knew. Like Da, always out of reach, and her running on and on, never catching up; someone she loved, gone forever.

But she began to run again anyway, knowing that it was the only thing left that she could do.

Bjorn stood at the helm, gripping the wheel so hard that his fingers were white and numb. He didn't look back upriver once, but his mind lashed him with memories of Tempest. He closed his eyes tightly, grinding his teeth, and even then couldn't stop the thought of Stryker touching her, kissing the mouth he had kissed, playing with her long, soft hair, falling asleep with her in his arms. He thought he was going mad, the sweat of jealousy and pain breaking out on his forehead and down his back.

Stryker would know exactly how to make her love him again. Men like him always did. They knew everything there was to know about a woman's vulnerability and had no scruples about using their knowledge to take what they wanted.

Bjorn opened his eyes again and glanced up at the sails, wishing that the wind were stronger. Putting the ship under full sail would bring disaster, but he was almost tempted to order it anyway and take the chance.

He had to stop thinking of Tempest. The reality of being without her squeezed his insides until he thought he'd die anyway and be done with it. Then reason intervened, however weakly. He had to control himself; he had to find some way to banish this hopeless desire for her, the sickness of his spirit that made him miss her so much he felt entirely desolated.

She hadn't abandoned him. She had never been his in the first place. He had known that. He had always known.

But it didn't help. It never had and it never would.

Somehow he had to forget the look in her eyes when she had let him make love to her that first time, the way her accent had thickened when she murmured to him, her soft, husky laugh, the smoothness of her body, almost virginal in its softness and perfection, even after the child.

He had thought she finally loved him. Apparently he had wanted that so badly, that above all things, that he had deluded himself.

Truth will out.

"What did you say?" Claus asked from beside him.

Bjorn was rocked on his feet as the ship shuddered violently.

"We're struck hard, sir!" a sailor shouted.

Almost at the same instant, the wind died completely. The stillness was so profound, that Bjorn felt a primeval fear. No one moved. Bjorn stared up at the limp sails.

Another sailor shouted, pointing toward the left bank of the great river.

All thought of anything left Bjorn as he saw a small figure racing along the bank—a small figure with buckskin fringe and a black braid.

Tempest came even with the becalmed ship. She stood for a moment heaving for air, wanting to call out to Bjorn. She could see clearly the name written across the bow: *Tempest.* She searched among the men's faces and found the one she sought.

Without thought, she waded out frantically into the river.

Fear hit Bjorn. "No! Go back! I'll come for you!" he shouted, not even realizing he was speaking Swedish. He left the helm untended and shouted wildly for the dinghy to be lowered, but his American crew didn't understand. Claus quickly repeated the orders in English.

Tempest had only swum halfway out when she knew she had made a mortal mistake. The weight of the buckskins and her own exhaustion were sucking her down into the muddy river. She fought to go on. Raising her head, she could hear Bjorn bellowing. She got a watery glimpse of a boat being lowered, but knew that it would never reach her in time.

Claus Janssen yanked off his boots and climbed onto the main rail. He dove cleanly into the river and struck out toward her with a strong stroke.

Sluggishly, Tempest fought to stay on the surface. In a last, half-coordinated effort, she tried to shed the buckskins, but couldn't. She lurched once more to the surface and gasped in air.

Claus reached her, pulling her up and back, holding her tightly with a hard arm across her chest. She fought in dull, mindless pain and got another lungful of air.

The dinghy approached swiftly and Tempest was grabbed

from above and pushed from below. She rolled over the edge and landed heavily on the solid bottom of the small boat. Blue sky was above her, and then Claus Janssen's concerned face.

She gave him a weak smile. *"Tak så mycke,"* she whispered, knowing just enough Swedish from Bjorn to thank him.

"Var så god, flicka," he replied. He helped her sit up and nodded toward the *Tempest.* "Bjorn would have come himself, but he does not know how to swim." His eyes were kind.

As they came alongside the ship, Tempest looked up at the figurehead—a woman with flowing black hair and blue eyes. She could hear Bjorn's booming voice above her.

Claus laughed softly. "Sometimes he forgets to speak English." He winked at her.

"Is he all right?"

"He will be now, I think." He gave her a direct look. "Ja?"

She was shaking with exhaustion and brimming with impatience as the boat was hauled upward. When it was just beneath the rail, she stood. Claus caught hold of her wrist as the boat swayed violently with her movement. She shook her head.

Bjorn was directly above her, and she reached up to him. His hands were hard as he caught hold of her and lifted her easily over the rail. She almost collapsed when he set her on her feet again. He steadied her.

"Din dumbom!" he railed, his eyes wild. *"Fanighet!"*

She knew he was being far less than polite. She looked up at him, so grateful to see him again, that she had to bite down hard on her lower lip to hold back an audible cry. He railed down at her in harsh Swedish. She heard the love behind every angry word.

"What do you do to yourself?" he demanded finally in English, his voice ragged, his accent thick with emotion. He didn't understand anything except that she had almost drowned while he had been helpless to save her.

She just stood there looking up at him with immense, tear-soaked blue eyes, dripping like a half-drowned rat, the weight of the ancient drenched buckskins almost too much for her.

"Ye're leaving," she said softly.

"Ja! I am leaving! God knows!" What did she expect of him? He almost shouted the words down into her face, pain and fury and jealousy all digging hot claws into his vitals.

"Aye," she said simply, accepting it. She saw the haggard lines in his ashen face, the eyes blurry from too much drinking and not enough sleep. His face bore bruises as well from brawling in Embarcadero saloons.

She wasn't going to try to make him stay—she had no right too. She only wanted to send him away with better thoughts than the ones that had brought such torment to him.

Stepping forward, weary in body and heartsick at losing him, she raised her hand shakily to his cheek. "When ye go, Bjorn Lindahl, know that all I am, all I ever shall be is yers. No one else alive counts for a damn in that way, mon. Before Almighty God, I swear to ye." She dropped her hand to her side, clenching it. "If ye come back, I will be waiting. If ye dunna, go with God always."

He stared at her.

She looked up at him, clear-eyed, loving him with every part of herself, and remained silent.

Claus was leaning back against the rail, watching them. He had been close enough to hear. So had others. No one moved.

Claus grinned wryly. *"Jag skall bara stå där, Bjorn?"*

No, Bjorn wasn't just going to stand there. He caught hold of Tempest and kissed her before his entire crew. They raised a shout that reverberated across the Sacramento River. He didn't release her until the entire front of his body was soaked from her wet buckskins, and she was breathless and flushed, just as she had been the first time on the hill below the white house he had given her.

A sailor shouted. Neither Bjorn nor Tempest felt the shudder of the windjammer as she came free of the obstacle and eased into the river current again. "Wind's up," another called. Seeing that Bjorn was oblivious, Claus bounded to the helm and gave quick directions to the crew.

Bjorn cupped Tempest's face firmly between his hands, his face coming down close to hers. "You are going to marry me, Tempest."

"Aye," she said, feeling the telltale tremor in his hands. "If need be for yer peace of mind. And before God, 'tis right." She smiled.

He kissed her again in relief, his heart racing. Several men called down remarks and suggestions, but he ignored them. "What of the boy?" he asked, dark concern deepening the lines around his tired eyes.

"Abram is safe at the house with Wind Reed." He started to ask other questions, but she put her fingertips to his lips. "Not here. Not now. Some things are best left for private. Ye had best cool down, mon, or ye'll be flying yer own ship's colors yerself."

He laughed softly, her words jolting him as he realized what he was doing and where. He grinned down at her sheepishly. Glancing around swiftly, he saw that things were well in hand. He looked at Claus and his friend made a movement with his head and grinned. Bjorn touched his forelock in a silent, grateful salute.

Turning back to Tempest, he lifted her in his arms. Men shouted after them and there was ribald laughter. Bjorn's mouth tightened, but she smiled up at him. Carefully he negotiated the narrow stairway down to his captain's quarters and nudged the doors closed behind them with his shoulder. He set her gently on her feet. "You must get out of these wet clothes," he said, flicking the sodden fringe at her hips.

She did, wordlessly.

He watched and then yanked a blanket from his bunk and began rubbing her roughly to get some warmth back into her.

He need not have worried. She watched the top of his blond head as he worked his way down the length of her body, stimulating every inch of her skin. She felt an overwhelming tenderness for this big, strong, deep-feeling man. She put her hand gently on his blond hair and he raised his head to look at her. He stood slowly, gazing at her as she unbuttoned his shirt and put her hand against his chest to feel the heavy, fast pounding, the building heat.

"Ye must get out of yer wet clothes as well." She took the blanket from him. She watched him until he was standing as God made him, then began the same ministrations he had performed for her, only she paused here and there to give loving worship.

He drew a harsh breath. "Oh, *min älskling,*" he groaned. Her hands gently and slowly stroked up and down the backs of his thighs. He said something huskily and pulled her up.

It was a quick, fierce coupling, and she welcomed it. She welcomed him with every part of herself. When it was finished, they lay in each other's arms. Overhead the men were singing loudly, and Bjorn suspected that Claus had tactfully put them to it so that they wouldn't be listening for other sounds that might have been audible.

"I'm sorry," he murmured huskily, kissing Tempest's swollen mouth, pulling her even closer. "I make love to you like a battling ram. Did I hurt you?"

She twined her fingers into his golden hair and pulled him down to kiss him openmouthed. He shifted, his hard leg going across her slender hips. Bracing himself above her, he kissed her as she wanted, prolonging it endlessly, alternating between deep, hard passion and gentle tenderness.

Finally, he raised his head and softly caressed the hair back from her temples. "I waited. I had great hope when I received your note. Then . . ."

She kept touching him, solace and joy blending in the knowledge that he was real and there with her. " 'Tis my own fault and none of yers," she said, remorseful at the pain she had caused him. "I should have sent ye word that I was delayed."

"Delayed by Jared Stryker." Jealousy burned darkly in his blue eyes, and he rolled away from her, sitting up.

"Aye. He came and I sent him on his way. He doesna matter one single bloody damn to me."

"You loved him once, Tempest," Bjorn countered. "I saw how you used to look at him." He let out his breath. She had never looked at him in that way.

She couldn't dismiss what he said, for she knew how she must have looked. But now she knew it all for what it was. She had been at the mercy of her body and Jared's considerable experience. Simple, gut-wrenching, wanton lust had brought them together, a shallow thing that was in no way related to the deep complexity of her feelings for Bjorn Lindahl.

"He awakened my body, but he never touched more of me than that," she said, sitting up. "He dinna make me a woman. It took ye to do that, Bjorn. Con ye ken what I be trying to say? With Jared, I only _wanted_. I never _loved_."

"You're cold," Bjorn said, and took up the blanket from the floor, shaking it out before handing it to her.

With Bjorn she felt revered, but speaking of Jared made her want to cover herself. She took the blanket to wrap about herself and sighed heavily as she sat up on the bed, with Bjorn standing above her. She reached out and laid her hand against the solidness of his body. "I want ye, too, Bjorn, but I yearn with more of me than my body. Con ye not see? I want to be part of ye and have ye be part of me. There's a difference between what Jared did to me and I did to him, and what ye and I be together. Oh, mon, 'tis a grand difference! Lust empties ye. Love fills ye up."

He sat on the wide bunk again just to be close to her and to see what was clearly in her eyes, warming him through.

"Did you have to go away to discover this?"

"When I rode away, I was cutting ye loose," she said. She smiled apologetically. "But I am a selfish woman."

He chuckled, tucking a stray tendril of hair back. "That is why you spent yourself coming to tell me you love me, ja? Even knowing that I was going back to the sea, just as you said I would."

The thought of him leaving hurt unbearably, but she didn't let him see it. She put her hand on his thigh. "I couldna let ye go not knowing that I love ye."

He watched her. "You won't ask me to stay?"

"Ye set me free. 'Tis enough to know ye will come back again."

"Ja. I will come back. Always." He kissed her soundly. "What about Abram?" he murmured huskily against the curve of her neck, afraid of the answer that must come. "Jared is his father and connected to you still through your son. You can't deny him his own flesh and blood."

"Aye. I con and did."

Bjorn drew back, staring down at her. "You didn't tell him he had fathered your child?"

"He saw him and called him yer bastard. He said other things that showed him for what he is. Had he thought but a moment, he would have known the truth for himself, but he chose to deny it. So be it."

"You can't, Tempest."

"Aye," she said, the old fierceness in her eyes. "Hear me. Ye saw him born and knew him not to be yer own, yet ye loved him anyway. Another grand difference between ye and Jared Stryker. It takes more than blood to be a father, and ye're Abram's in all ways that count. 'Tis the way I want it. 'Tis the way it will be."

"He'll find out for himself," he warned her.

She shook her head, certain. "Everyone believed the child to be yers from that first night when ye were the last man standing and came to my bedroom. No one knows ye didna take what was yers by right, or that ye waited until I was over Jared and ready to give my love freely to ye. We will leave it that way."

"Tempest," he reasoned carefully, seeing disaster hovering like a dark cloud over them.

"No! Ye know him, too!" she said angrily, leaning toward him tensely. "If he knew Abram for his own blood, he'd not love him. He'd use him. Abram'd become a possession to him, just as I did. Dunna ye see what I be saying?" She put her hand on his shoulder.

"Bjorn, I lived in the wild with me da. I ken there be some father-animals even in God's kingdom that'd devour their own wee ones to feed themselves. By God, there are some that do it just for their own bleedin' pleasure." She tipped her chin knowingly. "Jared is one of these."

She straightened back, withdrawing her hand, withdrawing everything so that he felt chilled by the blue eyes blazing in the set face. "I wilna put my son at his mercy," she said simply.

He'd never known her brogue so thick. Once he had wanted only to break away the hard shell about the soft vulnerable core of Tempest McClaren Walker. Now, he saw that at the core there was steel as well as softness. Such resolve in a woman was terrifying.

Neither spoke. They looked at one another and saw and understood.

Bjorn nodded slowly. He sighed heavily and nodded again. "Ja. Whatever I wish, the boy is not mine." He saw her hand clench and put his comfortingly over it. "I love him just as well, but it is your choice what you do." His hand tightened. "You may regret this someday, flicka. If Stryker ever finds out you denied him his son..."

Tempest made a soft, sharp sound of purest contempt. "The bairn was well set in my womb when Jared denied me. A plan that went awry. No, sometimes the best luck comes disguised as disaster. God was looking out for me when Jared left."

"Things may have changed with him."

"So he said."

Bjorn's eyes narrowed faintly, searching. He sensed something and feared pursuing it. "Be sure," was all he could manage, heart in his throat.

She reached out and touched his cheek. "Just like Abram Walker, ye'd plead kindness for a son of a bitch."

Odd how such words could sound so tender.

She came forward and kissed him, tears in her eyes. "I love *you*," she whispered after a long moment, looking straight into him. He couldn't doubt it.

He held her close and drew her down, leaning over her and letting everything inside him melt as he looked at her smiling. How long had he waited to see just this look in her eyes? "I wish I could protect you from everything," he said solemnly.

Old words, another time, another place, another man.

She laughed huskily. "Oh, I con protect myself. I've always been right good with a knife and better with ma tongue." She gave him one of Charity's bawdy looks, making him laugh. Then she added seriously, "It's love that's hardest. That's what you need to teach me, what I need most to learn. It'll be a long time coming natural." Her smile wavered. "'Tis far easier to spit in a man's eye than it is to tell him you love him. Aye, by God, the hardest thing of all is loving without fear."

He had always known. "You got it out," he told her.

Cupping his face, she said ruefully, "Today I'm brave, but tomorrow I may be a bloody coward again."

"Then say it one more time."

Her eyes glowed soft. "I love you, and though I can do well enough without you, I don't want to."

Bjorn tugged her hair hard. "Three words, not a speech." But he was smiling.

Her hands began to move and his husky laughter stopped. She shifted her body slightly. One brow raised slightly as she surveyed him knowingly, a faint smile touching her lips.

He held off.

She let him.

"Three words," he managed thickly, battening down instinct.

Her arms and legs slid smoothly around his body. Her mouth was sweet against his throat before she gazed up at him, eyes clear. "Truth will out."

Rubied dusk light streamed through the small porthole over the cabin bed. Bjorn was sleeping sprawled naked on his back, his face turned toward Tempest as she contemplated him.

All the deep lines about his eyes and mouth had eased. Sleep made people vulnerable, but he was safe with her. She would look at him, recognize his weakness and safeguard him.

"I am going back to Sacramento with you," he had told her, declaring war. She had not argued or asked any questions though she had felt a deep sadness. A man sometimes put down one life to take up another, but it shouldn't happen, not to a man like Bjorn Lindahl. The sea was too much a part of him. In time he would return to it, renew himself, and come back to her secure in his knowledge that she would wait.

She was learning the things she needed to know. Once she

thought it was the ability to read that would bring about a change in her. Now she knew better. Other things mattered more. She had thought she was trained to see and hear what was really there, but her eyes had been tightly closed and her ears had been sealed.

Da knew.

He had taught her to know the earth, what to eat from the land, how to hunt, how to build a fire for warmth, how to make clothing from tanned animal skins, how to stay alive when the enemy came hunting her. Men had been the enemy. Not just red, but white, not just white but *any* man. Da's world had been fraught with enemies, himself the worst.

Oh, how he had known.

To feed and clothe and warm a body was not enough. It was not life. So he had cut her loose, freed her from hell. She had fought him, clinging to what she knew with fierce determination until he had had to hit and kick her like a man to set her on her way. Fear was a tight claw-grip in the vitals, a boil needing to be lanced. *Grow or die. To stay the same is death.*

Da had taught her well to keep her body alive, but what other knowledge she needed to survive he had lacked. He thought Abram Walker had it, and in part he had been right.

Abram had a soul and God was in him. He had loved. When she had looked at him, he had not turned his face away from her in fear of being seen. He had looked back, openly. *I am here, Tempest. Reach out to me. I am here.*

When she finally had, it had been the barest brush with what was real, what was lasting. It remained, alive, but not tangible. At least he was not lost to her as she had once believed.

Even Jared had given her knowledge of herself. He had taught her flesh, schooled her body. Touch was more than the rubbing of bodies together, the joining of genitals. But Jared hadn't known that. He still didn't know.

She looked down at Bjorn stretched out on the cabin bed. He was all in one. Da in his primitive nature, seeing enemies where there were none; Abram with a soul and love; Jared with his gift of giving her the pleasures of the flesh. And he was himself, different from all the rest, separate from her, yet joined. *Mated.*

She heard seagulls on the wind. Leaning her head back, Tempest closed her eyes.

Birds and animals and fish and even the lowly insects all can take care of themselves. They know, they trust, they abide by the natural order of life. It is only man that questions it, then tries to alter it. And it is only man that fails. He crushes the knowledge he had in the womb, refusing to open his eyes and heart to it.

Man is the lowest form of life on earth. Perhaps that is why he is blessed. His vulnerability is deepest, his need greatest.

But there was a lifetime to contemplate that. For now she had promises to make, a wedding to attend.

She stood, legs splayed, arms wide, palms up, head flung back. Communion.

God, I will raise my son to seek the truth in himself. I will love this man freely, openly, so that he understands I love him. Whatever ventures I take on, whatever gold I make, and I will make much, I will seek to use for worthy purpose.

Beyond that, my God, I am lost. Not in the wilderness of the world, but in the far vaster, far more terrifying wilderness of myself.

I am open.
Come into me.
Show me the way.

Author's Note

Not So Wild a Dream is a novel of California history, telling the stories of people who could very well have lived in that area during the mid-1800s.

This is not a work of history, but is an historical novel based on sound research conducted at the California State Library in Sacramento, at the University of California, Berkeley, at the California Collections of the Burbank and Rosemead Libraries, and through exhaustive personal reading. All medical information was provided or verified by physicians.

Certain mores and social practices prevalent in mid-1800 California, such as the taking of child brides, are distasteful to us in the 1980s. However, at that time, the frequent loss of first wives, the scarcity of women, combined with physiological differences prevalent among young women, made the "child bride" a common occurrence. The taking of a young wife was a necessity of frontier life.

It was a tough time, survived only by those who could adapt to harsh conditions. This is what Tempest McClaren did, aided always by the strong faith in God to which Abram Walker led her.

—Francine Rivers
April 1985